About the Authors

Jennie Lucas's parents owned a bookstore and she grew up surrounded by books, dreaming about faraway lands. At twenty-two she met her future husband and after their marriage, she graduated from university with a degree in English. She started writing books a year later. Jennie won the Romance Writers of America's Golden Heart contest in 2005 and hasn't looked back since. Visit Jennie's website at: www.jennielucas.com

Barbara Wallace can't remember when she wasn't dreaming up love stories in her head, so writing romances for Mills & Boon is a dream come true. Happily married to her own Prince Charming, she lives in New England with a house full of empty-nest animals. Readers can catch up with Barbara through her newsletter. Sign up at www.barbarawallace.com

Chantelle Shaw enjoyed a happy childhood making up stories in her head. Always an avid reader, Chantelle discovered Mills & Boon as a teenager and during the times when her children refused to sleep, she would pace the floor with a baby in one hand and a book in the other! Twenty years later she decided to write one of her own. Writing takes up most of Chantelle's spare time, but she also enjoys gardening and walking. She doesn't find domestic chores so pleasurable!

Italian Playboys

Italian Playboys:
Seduction

JENNIE LUCAS

BARBARA WALLACE

CHANTELLE SHAW

MILLS & BOON

First Published in Great Britain 2021
by Mills & Boon, an imprint of HarperCollins*Publishers* Ltd,
1 London Bridge Street, London, SE1 9GF

www.harpercollins.co.uk

HarperCollins*Publishers*
1st Floor, Watermarque Building,
Ringsend Road, Dublin 4, Ireland

ISBN: 978-0-263-30282-0

MIX
Paper from
responsible sources
FSC™ C007454

This book is produced from independently certified FSC™ paper
to ensure responsible forest management.

For more information visit: www.harpercollins.co.uk/green

Printed and Bound in Spain using 100% Renewable electricity at
CPI Black Print, Barcelona

THE SHEIKH'S LAST
SEDUCTION

JENNIE LUCAS

To Pete,

who said, 'OF COURSE you should go to Dubai!'

Thanks, honey, for giving me the world,
every single day.

CHAPTER ONE

HE KNEW HE wanted her from the moment he saw her.

Sharif bin Nazih al-Aktoum, the Emir of Makhtar, had been laughing at the joke of a friend when he turned and saw a woman, standing alone in the Italian moonlight, on the shores of Lake Como.

She stood past a thicket of trees farther down the hill. Her white dress was translucent in the silvery glow of light, and the bare trees of November left latticed shadows like dark lace against her skin. Her black hair cascaded down her shoulders, tumbling, lustrous as onyx. Her eyes were closed in her heart-stoppingly lovely face as her sensual lips whispered unheard words.

Sharif's laughter fled. Was she a ghost? A dream?

Just some wedding guest, he told himself harshly. Nothing special. A trick of moonlight.

And yet…

He stared at her.

Moments before, he'd been chuckling at the poor bridegroom, who'd recently been a famous playboy but had made the mistake of getting his housekeeper pregnant. The new bride was very beautiful, yes, he conceded, and seemed loyal and kind. But still, Sharif would never get caught that way. Not until the bitter end.

Not until—

Sharif pushed the thought away, jerking his chin in the direction of the lakeshore. "Who is that?"

"Who?"

"The woman. By the lake."

His friend, the Duque de Alzacar, craned his head right and left. "I don't see anyone."

Between them and the unknown woman well-dressed wedding guests were milling about the terraces, drinking champagne and enjoying the coolness of the late-autumn night. The intimate evening wedding, held in a medieval chapel on an Italian tycoon's estate, had just ended, and they were waiting for the dinner reception to begin. But surely his friend could see the angel by the lake. "Are you blind?" Sharif said impatiently.

"Describe her to me."

Sharif parted his lips to do just that, then thought better of it. The Spanish duke was the most reckless, irredeemable womanizer he knew—which reminded him of the old saying about the pot and the kettle. But looking back at the soft moonlight on the *houri* by the lake, Sharif felt the sudden strange need to protect her, even from another man's glance. She seemed from another world. Sensual, magical—pure...

"Never mind," he said abruptly. "Excuse me." He started walking down the path toward the shore. He heard a low snort of laughter behind him.

"Take care you don't get bewitched by the moonlight, my friend," the Duque de Alzacar called. "I'd hate to be soon attending one of these events for *you*..."

Sharif ignored him. Holding up a hand to tell his bodyguards to remain behind, in the shadows of the villa, he went down to the thicket of trees. Where was she? Had he lost her?

Had he dreamed her?

He saw a flash of movement and exhaled. She had moved

farther down the shore. He followed silently in his white robes, stalking her like one of the lions that had existed in his Makhtari homeland centuries before.

She moved so sensually. He heard her softly whispered voice. Sharif's eyes narrowed to see whom she was speaking with, but there was no one. Half expecting her to disappear, he came out into the clearing beside her, feeling suddenly clumsy as he stepped on a branch.

At the sound, the woman whirled to face him. They stared at each other.

She wasn't dressed in white, as he'd first thought, but in a pale pink dress, the color of spring's first blush. Her skin was creamy and smooth, plump cheeks the colour of faint roses, standing out starkly against her long black hair. She was barely over twenty, he guessed, and of middle height. Her features were too strong to be conventionally beautiful, with her sharp nose, slash of dark eyebrows and the determined set to her chin; but her full mouth was tender, and her eyes were deep brown, big and wistful and wise. And they were full of tears.

Looking directly into her face, Sharif caught his breath.

"Who are you?" she whispered.

Sharif blinked. Then frowned. "You don't know who I am?"

She shook her head. "Should I?"

Now Sharif *knew* the woman had to be from another place or time. Everyone knew the playboy sheikh who'd swathed his way through continents of the world's most glamorous women, the Emir of Makhtar who often spent millions of euros on a single evening out with his entourage, who always had six bodyguards close at hand and who was rumored to have a bedroom in his royal palace made entirely out of diamonds—false—and that he'd once offered to buy Manchester United on a drunken whim—true.

Did she truly not know who he was? Or was it a pretense, a way for her to play hard to get? He shrugged but watched her closely as he said, "I'm a wedding guest."

"Oh." She exhaled. "Me, too."

"Why are you crying?"

"I'm not."

He watched as a single tear escaped her lashes to trail down her cheek in the moonlight. "No?"

She wiped her cheek fiercely. "No."

He tilted his head, frowning. "Are you in love with the bridegroom? Is that why you're crying?"

"No!"

"Many women were. Half of the women of London, it is said, wept when they heard Cesare Falconeri was to wed his housekeeper…"

"I'm Emma's friend!"

He tilted his head. "So you're crying because you're planning to betray her, and seduce him after the honeymoon is done?"

She stared at him as if he was crazy. "What kind of women do you hang out with? I would never—I could never—" She shook her head, and wiped her eyes again. "I'm happy for them! They're meant for each other!"

"Ah," Sharif said, bored by such trite, polite statements. "So it is not him. You weep over some other man."

She grit her teeth. "No…"

"Then what is it?"

"What it is—is none of your business!"

Sharif stepped toward her, just two of them hidden behind a copse of trees on the shore of the lake. They were almost close enough to touch. He heard her intake of breath as she took an involuntary step back. Good. So she was aware of him then, as he was of her, no matter her feisty words.

Her eyes held infinite depths, he thought, like a night

filled with stars and shadows. He felt strangely dazzled. He'd never seen eyes so full of warmth and buried secrets. Secrets he wanted to learn. Warmth he wanted to feel against his skin.

It was also possible he was just desperate to be distracted from his own thoughts. If so, this woman offered a very pleasurable distraction indeed.

Lifting his eyebrow, Sharif gave her the smile no woman could resist—at least, none ever had—deliberately unleashing the full power of his attention on her. "Tell me why you're crying, *signorina*," he said softly. "Tell me why you left the wedding party and came down to the shore alone."

Her lips parted, then closed. She looked away. "I told you. I'm not crying."

"Just as you also told me you have no idea who I am."

"Correct."

If she was lying about the one, Sharif decided, she was likely lying about the other. Good to know where he stood. He slowly looked up and down her body. The pale pink dress fit her like a glove. She was so curvaceous. So... different.

She blushed beneath his gaze, becoming more impossibly desirable than ever. Sharif suddenly realized it wasn't just his desire to forgot about weddings and marriage that made him want her. He'd been bored for a long, long time. He craved different. He craved this woman.

And so, he would have her.

Why not?

Whether she knew who he was or not, whether she was truly ignorant of his identity or merely putting on an act in an attempt to gain his attention, this woman was nothing truly magical or rare, no matter what his body was telling him. She was different from his usual type, yes. But beyond that, she was nothing more than a beautiful stranger. And he knew exactly how to deal with a beautiful stranger.

"The night is growing cold." Sharif's voice was a low purr as he held out his arm. "Come back to the villa. We will continue this conversation over champagne. Over dinner."

"W-with you?" she stammered, looking startled. She didn't move.

He cast a quick glance to her left hand. "You are not married. Are you engaged?"

She shook her head.

"I didn't think so," he said.

She lifted her head sharply. "You can tell?"

He bared his teeth in a sensual smile. "You are just not the married type."

To his surprise, she looked furious. More than furious. She looked as if he'd just served her a mortal insult.

"And why is that?" she said coldly.

Because of what he was planning to do to her tonight. Because of the delectable images that had started forming in his mind from the instant he'd seen her, of her curvaceous body naked against his, as her plump lips softly moaned against his skin. It had been impossible—absolutely impossible—that fate would be so cruel to have her already bound to another.

But Sharif didn't think it strategically advisable to explain. Not when her dark eyes were glinting sparks of rage.

He frowned, observing the flush on her cheeks. "Why are you angry? What could I possibly have said to—ah." His eyes crinkled in sudden understanding. "I see."

"See what?"

"The reason you came down to the shore, in this quiet, hidden place." He lifted a dark eyebrow knowingly. "I forget how women are affected by weddings. You no doubt wept through the candlelit ceremony, in romantic dreams at the beauty of *love*." His lip curled at the word. "There is some boy back home that you wish would propose. You feel alone. That is why you were crying. That is why you are angry. You are tired of waiting for your lover."

She pulled back, looking as if she'd been slapped.

"You are so wrong," she choked out. "About everything."

"I am pleased to hear it," Sharif murmured, and he was. If there was no other man in the picture, his path to her bed would be a foregone conclusion. "In that case...whatever your reason for sadness, there will be no more tears tonight. Only enjoyment and pleasure. You are spending the evening with me." His eyes met hers. "Not just the evening, but the night."

He continued to hold out his arm in complete assurance. But the woman just stared at him. Her lips parted as she said faintly, "That's your idea of small talk?"

He gave her a sensual smile. "I believe in cutting through unnecessary words to get to the heart of things."

"Then you believe in being rude." Still not touching him, she lifted her chin. "Excuse me."

And without another word, she walked around him, as if the billionaire Emir of Makhtar were no better than a churlish boy. She walked fleet-footed up the path, heading toward the eighteenth-century villa on the hillside, where music and laughter wafted through the cool November night.

Twisting his head, Sharif stared up after her in shock.

Waiting for your lover.

Waiting for your lover.

The rhythm of the darkly handsome sheikh's words seemed to taunt Irene Taylor's footsteps as she went back up the path.

Waiting for your lover.

Irene blinked back tears. With unthinking cruelty he'd spoken the exact fear that had haunted her heart throughout her friend's beautiful wedding. The words that had driven her to leave the other guests to stand alone on the lakeshore in quiet, silent heartbreak. She was twenty-three years old, and she'd been waiting for her lover all her life. She was starting to think he wasn't coming.

She'd dreamed of the life she wanted, the home she wanted, since she was five years old and she'd come home crying from her first day of kindergarten. Her own house was silent, but their closest neighbor had seen Irene walk by, crying and snuffling with a broken lunch box in her hand. Dorothy Abbott had taken her in, wiped the blood off her forehead, given her a big homemade cookie and a glass of milk. Irene had been comforted—and dazzled. How wonderful it would be to live in a little cottage with a white picket fence, baking cookies, tending a garden, with an honest, loyal, loving man as her husband. Ever since that day, Irene had wanted what Dorothy and Bill Abbott had had, married for fifty-four years, caring for each other until the day they'd died, one day apart.

Irene had also known what she *didn't* want. A rickety house on the desolate edge of a small town. Her mother, drunk most of the time, and her much older sister, entertaining "gentlemen" at all hours, believing their lying words, taking their money afterward. Irene had vowed her life would be different, but still, after high school, she'd worked at minimum-wage jobs, trying to save money for college, falling short when her mother and sister inevitably needed her meager earnings.

When Dorothy and Bill died, she'd felt so alone and sad that when the mayor's son smiled at her, she'd fallen for him. Hard. Even when she should have known better.

Funny how it was Carter who'd finally managed to drive her out of town.

I just wanted to have some fun with you, Irene. That's all. You're not the type I'd marry. He'd given an incredulous laugh. *Did you actually think a man like me, with my background...and a woman like you, with yours...could ever...?*

Yes, she had. She wiped her nose, which was starting to snuffle. Thank heaven she hadn't slept with Carter two years ago. Just the humiliation of loving him had been enough to make her flee Colorado, first for a job in New York, then Paris.

She'd told herself she wanted a fresh start, in a place no one knew about her family's sordid history. But some secret part of her had dreamed, if she went away, she might return self-assured and stylish and thin, like in an Audrey Hepburn movie. She'd dreamed she'd return to her small Colorado town in a sleek little suit with a sophisticated red smile, and Carter would take one look at the New Her and want to give her his love. Not just his love, but his name.

Stupid. It made Irene's cheeks burn to think about it now. She wiped the tears away fiercely. As if living in New York or Paris, as if mere *geography*, could achieve such a miracle—turning *her* into the type of woman Carter would want to marry! As if designer clothes and a new hairstyle would make him take her away from the shabby house on the wrong side of the tracks, the one that had men sneaking in so often at night on paid "dates" with her mother and older sister, to the enormous hundred-year-old Linsey Mansion on the hill!

Well, she'd never know now. Instead, she'd be going home even worse off than she'd left—unemployed, broke and with all the baguettes and croissants she'd eaten in Paris, not exactly thinner, either.

She'd thought she could make a better life for herself.

Even after the unfortunate incident that had gotten her fired six months ago, she'd still held out hope she'd find a new job in Paris. She'd gone through her savings, even the precious thousand-dollar bequest that the Abbotts had left her when they died.

Irene stopped. She pressed her fingers against her eyes, trying not to feel the jagged pain in her throat.

There will be no more tears tonight. Only enjoyment and pleasure. She could still hear his low, husky voice. *You are spending the evening with me. Not just the evening, but the night.*

Why her?

She'd always tried to believe it was just her family's reputation that made people in her home town so cruel. That it wasn't personal. But if that was true, why had the dark sheikh immediately assumed the worst of her, asking if she intended to seduce Emma's husband—as if she would want to! As if she could! Why had he assumed she would immediately fall into bed with him, just for the asking?

Irene closed her eyes, brushing her forehead with a trembling hand. Her cheeks were hot. All right, so she'd been attracted to him. How could any woman not be?

How could any woman not be attracted to a man like that, dressed so exotically in full white robes, with his black eyes and cruel, sensual lips? Anyone would be attracted to that darkly handsome face. To his strong, broad-shouldered body. To the aura of power and limitless wealth that followed him like his entourage of bodyguards.

If Carter was out of her league, then this sheikh was so far out of her league that she couldn't even see his league. It was somewhere out in space. Possibly by Jupiter.

Why would a man like that be interested in her?

It was true that for Emma's sake, Irene had done her best to look nice today, brushing out her black hair, putting on makeup. She'd even worn contact lenses instead of her usual soda-bottle glasses, and had on a beautiful, borrowed designer dress. But that didn't explain it.

Had she just seemed like easy pickings, crying by the lake? Or was there something wrong with her, some black mark on her soul that only men like Carter and the sheikh could see?

She remembered how the man's piercing black eyes had looked right through her soul, seeing far too much.

You feel alone. That is why you were crying. That is why you are angry. You are tired of waiting for your lover.

Pushing the memory of his low, sardonic voice away, she took a deep breath.

She couldn't go back to Colorado. She *couldn't.* But all she had left was twenty euros, a studio apartment in Paris paid for till the end of the week and the return flight home.

Hearing the clanging of a bell, Irene looked up the hill to the highest terrace. Beneath the wisteria-covered trellis with hanging fairy lights, she saw Emma, now Mrs. Falconeri, summoning her guests to the outdoor dinner reception. Emma's new husband, Cesare Falconeri, smiled down at his new bride as their baby son, dressed in a tiny tuxedo, yawned in his arms.

Emma had found her true love, married him, had a baby with him. They were blissfully happy. And kind-hearted. Also, Cesare was a billionaire hotel tycoon, which couldn't hurt anything. Without asking her, they'd simply tucked a first-class airline ticket from Paris to Lake Como in their wedding invitation. *First-class.* She smiled wistfully. Now, *that* had been an experience. The flight attendant had waited on her hand and foot, as if she were someone important. Crazy.

The truth was, she didn't need first-class. She just needed to believe that someday she might have what Emma had, and what Dorothy Abbott had once had: a husband she could love, respect and trust. A happy, respectable life, raising children in a snug, warm home.

She slowly walked up the hill with the other guests. The shadowy terrace was long, filled with three large communal tables placed end to end down the middle, decked out with flowers and glowing candles and colored lights dangling from above. Irene shivered in the November air, in spite of four heat lamps at the corners of the terrace, all going full blast.

She looked at the happy couple holding their fat, adorable baby, trying to ignore how her heart was aching. She was happy for Emma, she truly was. But she wondered at times if she would ever have the same.

Swallowing hard, Irene turned away. And walked right into a hard wall of muscle.

She gasped, her high-heeled shoes sliding beneath her. She started to fall to the stone floor, but a strong hand reached out to grab her wrist.

"Thank you..." Then she saw the face of the wall that had caught her: the handsome, arrogant sheikh, in the white robes with that darkly handsome face and piercing eyes.

"Oh," she scowled. "It's you."

He said nothing in reply, just lifted her to her feet. She felt the warmth and heat of his palm against her skin. It did strange things to her. He looked down at her in the moonlight on the villa's veranda as wedding guests laughed and ambled beneath the fairy lights dangling from the trellis beneath the deep violet Italian sky.

She ripped her arm away. *"Thank you,"* she repeated, in a hostile tone directly at odds with the courtesy of the words.

But he did not immediately turn and leave as she'd

hoped. Instead, he stared down at her, his eyes as black as the cord wrapped around his white headdress.

"You accused me of being rude, *signorina*," he said in a low voice. "I was not."

Unconsciously, Irene rubbed her wrist, as if he had burned it with his touch. "You insulted me."

"When I invited you to spend the night with me?" He sounded almost bewildered. "How was that an insult?"

"Are you kidding? What else could it be?"

He looked bemused. "Women generally take it as a compliment…"

Irene flinched. *Women.* Of course he'd used the line a million times, on a million interchangeable women!

"How lovely for you," she said coldly, "that ten words can usually make any woman fall into bed with you. Sorry I'm not following your agenda."

His lips had parted slightly. His brow was furrowed as he stared down at her. "Have we met before?" he said faintly. "Do you have some reason to despise me?"

"We've never met before, if that's what you're asking. But yes," she said grimly, "I have a reason."

"Which is?"

"Look, I have no idea who you are or why you decided to make me your target, but I know your type."

"My—type?"

"Do you really want me to spell it out? It might hurt your feelings. But then—" she tilted her head "—fortunately I don't think you have any."

"Try me," he said flatly.

"I could say that you're a heartless playboy who accused me, within five seconds of meeting me, of planning to seduce my friend's new husband. Saying I was waiting for a lover and oh, lucky me, you're the very man for the job! How dare you pretend you can see into my soul, and poke at my heart in a rude and selfish way? Those are the things I could say, but I won't, because it's Emma's wedding and she deserves a perfect day. I don't want to cause a scene. Because I was taught that if you can't say something nice to someone, to say nothing at all." Dorothy Abbott had taught her that over oatmeal cookies and peppermint tea. She glared at him. "Some people," she said sweetly, "have good manners. If you'll excuse me."

She started to turn, but he held on to her wrist. She glared at his hand, then at his face. He abruptly let her go.

"Of course, *signorina*," the handsome sheikh said, holding up both his hands. "You are right. I was rude. Please allow me to apologize." His lips twisted. "The better I know you, the more I realize the great mistake I made. Of course you do not want a lover. No sane man would ever want to be *your* lover. It would be like seducing a cactus." He gave her a short half bow with a sweep of his robes. "Please forgive me, *signorina*. And do not allow me to keep you from your eternally desirable solitude."

In a single smooth movement, he turned away from her. Irene stared after him, open-mouthed, as he disappeared into the crowd.

She closed her mouth with a snap.

Ooh! Helplessly, she stomped her foot. *Eternally desirable solitude!* The big jerk!

But at least now he was no longer looking at her—near her—touching her, it was easier to think straight. She was relieved to no longer be under the intense scrutiny of his black eyes, his gaze that seemed to see straight through her soul.

She'd wanted to get rid of him, and she'd succeeded. She did know his type. Well—not *exactly*. A wealthy sheikh in full robes, with bodyguards hovering, was rare in Colorado. Even her mother and older sister had never managed to bring home someone *that* exotic. But she knew the playboy type. She hadn't judged him unfairly. She *hadn't*.

But still—she thought of those dark eyes. Of the way her heart had pounded in the moonlight when she'd first seen him standing in front of her on the lake, the very instant after she'd wished with such reckless, passionate yearning that someone would love her. Of the sizzle that had coursed through her body when he'd touched her—just from the touch of his hand on her wrist!

It was good she'd managed to scare him off. *No sane man would ever want to be* your *lover*. Yup. She'd scared him off thoroughly.

Good, she told herself. Better to be alone, better to be a virgin forever, than have her heart trampled into nothing.

She wanted more.

After her first day of kindergarten, when Dorothy had comforted her and Bill had gone to the school to set the bullies straight, Irene had started spending her afternoons with the retired couple. She'd tried to pretend the Abbotts' tiny, warm house was her real home. When she was older, trying to ignore the cruel taunts of the girls and blatant come-ons of the boys in high school, Irene had once asked Dorothy how she and Bill had found each other. Dorothy had smiled.

"We got married at eighteen, both virgins, nervous and broke. Everyone thought we were too young." She'd laughed, and taken another sip of peppermint tea. "But we knew what we wanted. Waiting made it special, a commitment between us. I know these days, people think sex is no big deal, a moment of cheap pleasure, easily forgotten. But to us, it was sacred. A promise without words. And we never regretted the choice."

Hearing the story when she was eighteen herself, Irene had vowed to wait for true love, too. She'd watched her sister and mother have so many cheap, forgettable affairs until there was no promise left in it, very little pleasure and certainly no joy. She wanted a different life. Her love would last.

She'd nearly gone astray with Carter, but never again. No way. No how. And if there was one thing she knew down to her bones, it was that a man like the sheikh—exotically handsome and rich and full of himself—would never truly love her, not even for an hour, much less a lifetime. She'd been right to scare him off.

But still, as Irene looked for her assigned place at the long wooden table, she was relieved to see it was on the opposite end from the sheikh's place. As the twenty or so wedding guests had a hearty dinner on the terrace, surrounded by heat lamps to make the November night feel like summer, he kept his distance. Irene tried not to look in his direction, but she felt his dark eyes on her. Taking her heart in her hands, she dared to look down the long table—only to discover that he was laughing, as two gorgeous young supermodel types fawned over him. Irene looked away grumpily. Silly her, to imagine he'd been staring at her. She couldn't imagine why on earth she'd thought that....

The fairy lights hung above, swaying in the breeze. The moon was bright like a big pearl in the velvety sky. After the champagne toast and the delicious dinner served by the villa's staff, the long tables were pushed aside to turn the veranda into an impromptu dance floor. A dark-haired man with soulful eyes brought a guitar from the music room and started to play.

She saw a flash of white in the corner of her eye, and her body went on high alert. But, turning, she saw it was only Emma, holding out her baby. "Will you hold him so we can have our first dance?"

"I'd love to," Irene said, smiling, happy to cuddle the

warm, sleeping baby. But after she had Sam in her arms, she had a sudden thought and touched Emma's arm. "There's a sheikh here—one of your guests. Who is he?"

Emma blinked, then frowned in a very "*un*happiest day of my life" kind of way. Looking to the right and left, she lowered her head until her white translucent veil dripped to the floor. "*That* is Sheikh Sharif al-Aktoum, the Emir of Makhtar."

"Emir?" Irene said, amazed. "You mean, the king? Of a whole country?"

"Yes." Straightening, Emma gave her a hard stare full of meaning. "He's very rich, very powerful and *very* famous for breaking many, many, *many* women's hearts."

"I was just curious."

"Don't be too curious about him." She shook her head and said severely, "Just because Cesare reformed from being a playboy, you mustn't expect that any other man…"

"I forgot about that," Irene said. "Cesare used to be a playboy, too…"

Emma sighed. "He was. It used to be my job to buy designer watches as parting gifts for his one-night stands. I actually bought them in bulk. But the point is, Irene, most playboys never change. You know that, don't you?"

Her friend looked so anxious that Irene gave her a reassuring nod. "Definitely."

"Good."

As Irene sat back into her chair with the baby, the new Mr. and Mrs. Falconeri went out alone on the dance floor, hand in hand. Swaying to the music, they looked at each other tenderly and passionately, as if no one else were there. Watching them, wistfulness filled Irene's heart.

Someday…

Someday, a man would look at her like that. And she'd have a baby like this. She looked at the warm, slumber-

ing little boy in her arms, with his dark lashes fluttering
against his plump cheeks. When the time was right, when
fate meant it to be so, she would meet the One. They'd fall
in love and get married. They'd work hard, buy a home,
have children of their own. They would do things properly.

But what if it never happened? What if she spent her
whole life waiting, working hard, following all the rules,
and still ended up broke and alone?

Believe. She squeezed her eyes shut. *Have faith.*

"You are not dancing, *fräulein*?"

She looked up with an intake of breath, but instead of
the Emir of Makhtar, she saw a dignified blond man with
blue eyes. She shook her head, feeling awkward. "No, thank
you." Then, remembering how the sheikh had so *unfairly*
and *wrongly* compared her to a cactus, she forced herself
to smile until her cheeks hurt as she indicated the sleeping
baby in her arms. "It's kind of you, but I can't, I'm holding
Sam while they dance."

"Ah." The man sighed and said with a German accent,
"Such a pity."

"Yes. Indeed," she said, relieved beyond all measure
when he moved on. She didn't know how to react. Two
men hitting on her in one night? This had never happened
during her year in Paris. But then—she looked down at
the sleek-fitting designer gown—she didn't usually dress
like this, either. But still, she wasn't half as glamorous or
beautiful or thin as the other female guests. Not even close!

Irene knew her flaws. Her thick black hair was her one
vanity, but other than that… Her body was too plump. Her
nose turned up at the end, and her eyesight was truly bad.
She blinked hard. Her new contact lenses still felt strange
against her eyeballs. She was used to wearing glasses. She
was also used to being invisible. She was used to avoiding
attention, staying at home reading books, quietly unnoticed

in the corner. She thought longingly of the new Susan Mallery novel waiting on her bedside table.

"Good evening, *señorita*."

Irene looked up at the deep, purring voice. It was the Spanish man who'd been playing the guitar so beautifully.

"You're amazing," she blurted out.

The Spaniard gave a wicked grin. "Who told?"

She blushed. "Your music, I mean. But if you're here, then who…" She turned and saw there was now a four-person band playing the music. She hadn't even noticed the change. She finished lamely, "You are very good on the guitar."

"The least of my skills, I assure you. Would you care to dance?"

"Oh." Her blush deepened. Another handsome playboy, way out of her league, flirting with her? Weird. Had Emma slipped a ten-dollar bill to the most handsome guests in an attempt to boost Irene's confidence? Although these didn't seem like the type of men to be swayed by a ten-dollar bill. Ten million dollars, maybe. Maybe not even then.

Biting her lip, she again indicated the sleeping baby. "Sorry. Emma left me in charge. I'd have only stepped on your feet anyway." She added hastily, "Thanks, though!"

"Another time, perhaps," the Spaniard murmured, and moved on without any apparent heartbreak to one of the wealthy-supermodel types she'd seen the sheikh talking to earlier. Irene looked down at the warm, sleeping baby in her lap. At least she didn't need to worry that anyone had paid little Sam to pretend to like her.

"It must be exhausting," a man's sardonic voice observed behind her, "that the ruder you become, the more you have to beat potential lovers off with a stick."

Irene felt a shock of electricity through her body. She turned her head to see the sheikh standing behind her, his black eyes gleaming. She hid the uncontrollable leap of her heart.

"You would know," she murmured, looking at him sideways beneath her lashes. "Isn't that how it usually works for you? You tell women that they mean nothing to you, that they're just the next mark on your bedpost, and they are so enamored of this thought that they fall at your feet and beg you, *Take me, take me now*?"

His dark eyes held a bright gleam as he took another step toward her.

"Say those five words to me, Miss Taylor," he said softly, "and see what happens."

A tremble electrified her body, from her earlobes down her spine to the hollows of her feet. She licked her lips and tossed her head.

"That's one thing I'll never say to you. Not in a million years."

"I could make you say it, I think," he said softly. "If I really tried."

He looked down at her with eyes black and hot as smoldering coals, and her throat went dry. She felt her body turning into putty, her brain into mush.

"Don't bother trying," she managed to croak. "You'll fail."

He tilted his head. "I don't fail."

"Never?"

"No."

As they stared at each other, the air thickened between them. Something sizzled, something primal. The people around them became blurs of color, mere noise. Held in his dark gaze, Irene felt time stand still.

Then her heart started to beat again. "You used my name. How did you know? Did you ask about me?"

He lifted a dark eyebrow. "I was curious."

"I know about you now, too. The famous playboy emir."

He tilted his head toward her, as if confiding a secret. "I know something about you, too, Miss Taylor."

"What's that?"

With a slow, sensual smile, the billionaire emir held out his hand.

"The reason you refused to dance with those other men," he said huskily, "is because you want to dance with me."

CHAPTER TWO

THE INTENSITY AND focus of his gaze held her down like a butterfly with a pin, leaving her helpless and trembling. Irene's heart pounded in her chest.

"I want to dance with you, Miss Taylor." The sheikh looked down at her. "I want it very much."

Her throat was dry, her mind scrambling. She exhaled when she remembered Sam sleeping in her arms. "Sorry, but I couldn't possibly. I promised to hold the baby and…"

Unfortunately at that moment Sam's mother brushed past them to scoop her sleeping baby up in her arms. "It's time to put this sleepy boy to bed," Emma said, holding him snug against her beaded white gown. She threw the sheikh a troubled glance and said in a low voice to Irene, "Be careful."

"You don't need to worry," Irene said. Really, couldn't her friend see that she could look out for herself? She wasn't *totally* naive.

"Good," Emma murmured, then turned and said brightly to the sheikh, "Excuse me."

Irene looked at him, wondering how much of the whispered conversation he'd heard. One glance told her he'd heard everything. He gave her an amused smile, then lifted a dark eyebrow.

"It's just a dance," he drawled. He tilted his head. "Surely you're not afraid of me."

"Not even slightly," she lied.

"In that case…" Holding out his hand with the courtly formality of an eighteenth-century prince waiting for his lady, he waited.

Irene stared at his outstretched hand. She hesitated, remembering how her body had reacted the last time they'd touched, the way he'd made her tremble with just a touch on her wrist. But as he'd said, this time he was just asking for a dance, not a hot, torrid affair. They were surrounded by chaperones here.

One dance, and she'd show them both that she wasn't afraid. She could control her body's response to him. One dance, and he'd stop being so intrigued by her refusals and leave her safely alone for the rest of the weekend. He'd move on to some other, more responsive woman.

Slowly, Irene placed her hand in his. She gave an involuntary shudder when she felt the electricity as their fingers intertwined, and she felt the heat of his skin pressing against her own.

His handsome face was inscrutable as he led her out onto the terrace's impromptu dance floor. Above them, dappled moonlight turned wisteria vines into braided threads of silver, like magic.

He held her against his body, leading her, swaying her against him as they moved to the music. He looked at her, and Irene felt her body break out in a sweat even as a cool breeze trailed off the moonlit lake against her overheated skin.

"So, Miss Taylor," he murmured, "tell me the real reason you were pushing me away—along with every other man here."

She swallowed, then looked at him. "I will tell you. If you tell me something first."

"Yes?"

"Why you have continued to pursue me anyway." She looked at the women watching them enviously from the edge of the dance floor. "Those other women are far more beautiful than I. They clearly want to be in your arms. Why ask me to dance, instead of them? Especially when it seemed likely I would say no?"

He swirled her around to the music, then stopped. "I knew you wouldn't say no."

"How?"

"I told you. I never fail to get what I want. I wanted to dance with you. And I knew you wanted the same."

"So arrogant," she breathed.

"It's not arrogant if it's true."

Irene's heart was pounding. "I only agreed to dance with you so you'd see that there's nothing special about me, and leave me in peace."

His lips lifted at the corners. "If that was your intention, then I am afraid you have failed."

"I'm boring," she whispered. "Invisible and dull."

His hands brushed against her back as they danced.

"You're wrong. You are the most intriguing woman here. From the moment I saw you on the edge of the lake, I felt drawn to your strange combination of experience—and innocence." Leaning down, he bent his lips to her ear. She felt the roughness of his cheek brush against hers, inhaled the musky scent of his cologne, felt the warmth of his breath against her skin. "I want to discover all your secrets, Miss Taylor."

He pulled back. She stared up at him, her eyes wide. She tried to speak, found she couldn't. His dark eyes crinkled in smug masculine amusement.

He twirled her to the music, and when she was again in his arms, he said, "I answered your question. Now answer mine. Why have you been pushing every man away who talks to you at this wedding? Do you have something against them personally, or just dislike billionaires on principle?"

"Billionaires?"

"The German automobile tycoon has been married three times, but still considered very eligible by all the gold diggers in Europe. Then, of course, my Spanish friend, the Duque de Alzacar, the second-richest man in Spain."

"Duke? Are you kidding? I thought he was a musician!"

"Would it have changed your answer to him if you'd known?"

"No. I'm just surprised. He's a good guitar player. Rich men usually don't try so hard. They expect other people to entertain *them*. They don't care who else gets their heart bruised trying to win their attention, their love—"

She broke off her words, but it was too late. Aghast, Irene met his darkly knowing glance.

"Go on," he purred. "Tell me more about what rich men do."

She looked away. "You're just not my sort, that's all," she muttered. "None of you."

The sheikh looked around the beautiful moonlit terrace. His voice was incredulous. "A German billionaire, a Spanish duke, a Makhtari emir? We are none of us your type?"

"No."

He gave a low, disbelieving laugh. "You must have a very specific type. The three of us are so different."

She shook her head. "You're exactly the same."

His eyes narrowed. "What do you mean?"

"Your eminence... I'm sorry, what am I supposed to call you?"

"Normally the term 'Your Highness' is the correct form. But since I suspect you are about to insult me, please call me Sharif."

She snorted a laugh. "Sharif."

"And I will call you Irene."

It was musical the way he said it, with his husky low voice and slight inflection of an accent. She had never heard her name pronounced quite that way before. He made it sound—*sensual*. Controlling a shiver, she took a deep breath. As he moved her across the stone floor, they were surrounded by eight other couples dancing. The bride and groom were no longer to be seen, the wine was flowing and the lights in the wisteria above them sparkled in the dark night, swaying in the soft breeze off the lake.

"Explain," he said darkly, "how I am exactly like every other man."

She got the feeling he wasn't used to being compared to anyone, even tycoons or dukes. "Not *every* man. Just, well—" she looked around them "—just all the men here."

Sharif set his jaw, looking annoyed. "Because I asked you to dance?"

"No—well, yes. The thing is," she said awkwardly, "you're all arrogant playboys. You expect women to fall instantly into bed with you. And you're full of yourselves because you're usually right."

"So I am conceited."

"It's not your fault. Well, not *entirely* your fault," she amended, since she wanted to be truthful. "You're just selfish and coldhearted about getting what you want. But when you throw out these lines, these false promises of love, women are naive enough to fall for them."

"*False promises*. So now I am a liar, as well as conceited."

"I am trying to say this gently. But you did ask me."

"Yes. I did." He pulled her closer against his body. She felt his warmth and strength beneath his white robes, saw the black intensity of his gaze. "We were introduced five minutes ago, but you think you know me."

"Annoying, isn't it? Just like you did with me."

Sharif stopped on the dance floor, looking at her. "I have never given any woman a false promise of love. Never."

Irene suddenly felt how much taller he was, how broad-shouldered and powerful. He towered over her in every way, and he had a dangerous glint to his eye that might have frightened a lesser woman. But not her. "Perhaps you haven't actually spoken the promise in words, but I bet you *insinuate*. With your attention. With your gaze. With your touch. You're doing it now."

His hands tightened on her as he pulled her snugly against his body. His hot, dark eyes searched hers as he said huskily, "And what do I insinuate?"

She lifted her troubled gaze.

"That you could love me," she whispered. "Not just tonight, but forever."

For an instant, neither of them moved.

Then she moved her body two inches away from him, a safe distance any high school chaperone would approve of, with their arms barely touching.

"That's why I wouldn't dance with the others," she said. "Why I'm not interested in you or any man like you. Because I know all your sexy charm—it's just a lie."

Sharif stared at her. Then his eyebrow lifted as he gave her a sudden wicked smile.

"So you think I'm sexy and charming."

She looked up at him. "You know I do."

Their eyes locked. Desire shot in waves down her body, filling her with heat. Making her tremble. She felt the electricity between them, felt the warmth and power of his body. Her knees were weak.

Most playboys never change. You know that, don't you?

She hadn't needed Emma's warning. She'd learned it well. From the wretched lessons of her childhood. From Carter. She'd learned it up close and personal.

She abruptly let Sharif go.

"But you're wasting your time with me." She glanced back at the beautiful women watching him with longing eyes, as if they could hardly wait to throw themselves body and soul onto the fire. Irene's lip curled as she nodded in their direction. "Go try your luck with one of them."

Turning on her heel, she left without a backward glance. Praying he wouldn't see how her body shook as she walked away.

He'd underestimated her.

Sharif's jaw was tight as he stalked off the dance floor alone. He walked through the crowd of watching women, some of whom tried to talk to him as he passed.

"Your Highness, what a surprise…"

"Hello, we met once at a party, if you remember…"

"I'd be happy to dance with you, Your Highness, even if she won't…"

Grimly, he kept walking, without bothering to reply. Perhaps he was rude, after all, just as Irene had accused. But these skinny women, with their glossy red lips and hollow cheekbones, were suddenly invisible to him. It wasn't their fault. All other women were invisible to him now because he was interested in only one.

The one who wasn't afraid to tell him the truth. Who wasn't afraid to insult him. And who found it so easy to walk away.

Miss Irene Taylor. Of Colorado, the wild, mountainous center of the United States he knew only from skiing once in Aspen.

There's nothing special about me.

He shook his head incredulously. How could she honestly believe that?

He wanted her.

He would have her.

But how?

"Having a good time?"

Sharif stopped. It took him a moment to focus on Cesare Falconeri, the bridegroom, standing in front of him in a tux. "Your wedding has been most exciting," he replied. "In fact, the most interesting I've ever attended."

"*Grazie.* Emma will be pleased to hear it." The man gave him a sudden grin. "And this is just the start. Tomorrow, we have the civil ceremony in town, followed by all kinds of fun for the rest of the day, including the ball at night." He clapped him heartily on the shoulder. "So save some energy, Your Highness."

The rest of the weekend. As Cesare walked away, Sharif relaxed, took a deep breath. He still had two days. He felt rebounding confidence. Yes. What was he worried about? He had the rest of the weekend to seduce her. She'd already given so much of her true emotion away—too much. He knew she wanted him. She was fighting her own desire. That never worked for long. Willpower always gave out eventually.

Sharif would win. As long as he had the stamina for a long, drawn-out siege. He thought of her.

He definitely had the stamina.

But how to go about it?

All day tomorrow. A ball lasting far into the night. By the end of it, she would be in his bed. Simple as that.

He would seduce her, bed her, satiate himself with her,

and they would part on mutually respectful terms the following morning, after the final breakfast. He dismissed Irene's concern about his playboy nature out of hand. Perhaps she'd be right to fear some kind of emotional fallout if they had some kind of continuing connection. But they did not move in the same circles, so it was highly unlikely. This Italian villa—he looked up at the Falconeri mansion— was a weekend party out of place and time. It would be a pleasant memory for both of them, nothing more. One night together would hardly be enough to inspire love, even in a woman as romantic as Irene Taylor. She might be young, but she had an old soul. He'd seen it in her eyes. Heard it in the tremble of her voice as she spoke about the selfishness of playboys. One must have hurt her, once.

Sharif would distract her from the pain of that memory, as she would distract him from his own pain that lay ahead. He would fill her with pleasure. It would be a night they'd never forget.

She'd won the battle tonight, but he would win the war.

Sharif felt oddly exhilarated as he returned to the villa. One by one, his six bodyguards fell wordlessly into step behind him, then peeled off to their assigned rooms as he returned to his suite, two of them standing guard in the hallway outside his door.

Alone in the lavish bedroom, he smiled to himself as he removed his white *keffiyeh* and black rope of the *agal*. He ran his hands through his short dark hair. His head felt sweaty—and no wonder, since every inch of his body had felt overheated since he'd met the delectable Miss Taylor. He started toward the en suite bathroom for a shower, when he heard the ring of his cell phone.

He glanced at who was calling, and his jaw went tense with irritation. He had no choice but to answer.

"Has something happened with Aziza?" he demanded by way of greeting.

"Well…" Gilly Lanvin, the twentysomething socialite he'd hired as his young sister's companion, drew out the word as long as she could, clearly scrambling to think of a way to keep him on the phone.

"Is she hurt?" he said tersely. "Does she need me?"

"Nooo…" the woman admitted with clear reluctance. "I was just wondering…when you'll be back to the palace."

"Miss Lanvin," he snapped. "These calls have to stop. You are companion to my sister. Nothing more. It would be inconvenient for me to replace you so soon before her wedding. Do not make me do so."

"Oh, no, Your Highness. I'm sorry if I interrupted you. I just thought you might be lonely. I just thought—"

He clicked off the phone before he was forced to endure hearing what she'd thought. He needed to replace her. He'd known it since she'd first started making eyes at him two months ago. But Aziza liked her. So he'd hoped to just ignore it until Aziza's wedding, when a companion would no longer be required and he could send the woman back to Beverly Hills on the next flight.

Three months. Just three months and his sister would be married, and it would no longer be his problem. He stalked into the gleaming white marble bathroom and removed the rest of his clothes, then stepped into a steaming hot shower. He turned his mind back to the delicious Miss Taylor. He let his imagination run wild, picturing her in this shower with him, naked, as he soaped up those full lush curves of her body, hearing her gasp as he pressed her against the shower wall and took her deep and hard, as her wide-spread hands pressed against the steamed glass…

Oh, yes. Tomorrow night. Sooner, if he was at the top of his skill.

Climbing naked into his large bed, he slept very well that night, dreaming of everything he intended to do to Irene Taylor, in this very suite, before the next day was through.

He woke to see the sun shining gold through the tall windows. Yawning, he stretched in the huge bed, feeling the Egyptian-cotton sheets beneath his skin. Smiling to himself, he brushed his teeth, shaved, dressed with care. Not the traditional Makhtari dress today. Instead, he reached into the closet for a crisp white shirt and suit tailored for him in London. Unlike many men of his position, he preferred having no valet, something that had caused a minor scandal in his palace. But there were some things a man just liked to do for himself. He ran his hands impatiently through his black hair and smiled at himself in the mirror.

He would have her tonight.

Sharif went downstairs to join the other guests in the breakfast room. Soon, they were joined by the blushing bride and groom, who looked very happy and not a little tired. But there was no sign of Irene. He waited. Even when the other guests piled into the arranged limos, to take them all into town for the civil ceremony, he waited, waving off Falconeri.

"I'm not quite done with my coffee," he'd said by way of explanation. The man gave him a strange look, as if he thought it wasn't an entirely satisfying reason for a guest to miss a wedding. But they all left.

The villa became quiet, except for the low hum of servants preparing the next meal, and his own bodyguards conversing quietly on the edges of the cavernous, brightly painted breakfast room. Five minutes later, he heard high heels clicking rapidly across the marble foyer and sighed in anticipation.

He looked up from his Arabic-language newspaper with a ready smile as Irene burst into the doorway.

"Am I too late?" she cried.

"You just missed them," he replied. "They left five minutes ago."

Irene looked even more beautiful than last night, he thought. She was dressed in black pumps and a 1950s-style day dress that accented her hourglass figure—Valentino? Oscar de la Renta?—topped with a soft pink cardigan and pearls. A smudge of deep pink lipstick was her only makeup, accenting the slight bruise of violet beneath her huge dark eyes that suggested a sleepless night. Perhaps she hadn't found the sensual dreams of them making love quite so comforting and pleasant as he had.

"Dang it!" She hung her shoulders. "I can't believe I overslept. On Emma's special day. I am the worst friend ever!"

"She has *three* special days," he said sharply. "Don't be so hard on yourself. It doesn't matter."

"I can't believe I was so careless." She rubbed her eyes with the back of her hand. "I must have turned off my alarm. I was just so tired, I didn't fall asleep until dawn…"

"Oh?" He tilted his head suggestively. "I'm sorry to hear that. Something keep you awake?"

She opened her mouth, then snapped it closed. "Never mind." She reached for the silver coffeepot and a china cup edged with a pattern of twenty-four-carat gold. As she poured the steaming hot coffee, followed by tons of cream and sugar, she glanced at his paper.

"What are you reading?"

"Today's newspaper from my home country."

"Today's? How did you get it?"

"It was delivered to me by plane."

"Can't you get it online?"

"I like paper."

"So you had a whole plane fly all the way here just because you—"

"Yes," he said. "Just because."

"Ridiculous," she grumbled. Sitting on the very edge of the farthest chair, she sipped her coffee, glaring at him over the rim of her cup. "You expecting some kind of war today?"

"War?" Finishing the last of his espresso, Sharif calmly set the cup back in the saucer.

She looked pointedly at the four bodyguards, all now still as statues in the four corners of the room. "You brought your army along for breakfast?"

"I am Emir of Makhtar," he said, as if it explained everything.

She snorted. "Are you afraid you'll be attacked?" She looked at the cheerful yellow walls, the tall windows overlooking Lake Como, the high ceilings with their early-nineteenth-century frescoes. Her lips lifted. "Clearly this could be dangerous."

He shrugged. "Standard procedure."

"Having four hulking babysitters always hovering around sounds like my idea of hell. Although at least it's easy to get rid of your lovers the morning after."

"Are you looking to start a fight with me, Miss Taylor?"

"You said you were going to call me Irene. And yes, I'm looking to start a fight. It's your fault I overslept. You're the one who kept me up all night."

He hadn't expected her to admit it so easily. "Dreaming of me?"

"Dreaming?" She looked at him as if he was crazy. "It wasn't a dream I heard all night, banging and moaning in the room next door. It was really quite...athletic, the length and stamina of it all. I'm glad you so eagerly took my advice and found another woman more willing to service you."

"Length?" He looked at her with wickedly glinting eyes. He rubbed his jaw. "Stamina?"

Her cheeks flamed a delectable red. "Forget it."

"I'm flattered you immediately assumed it was me."

"Of course it was you," she snapped. "I don't appreciate how you kept me up all night. Now I've missed Emma's civil ceremony because of you. Next time tell your bed partner to keep her opinion of your acrobatics to herself."

"I appreciate the compliment, but it wasn't me."

"Sure," she said scornfully.

Sharif looked at her.

"It. Wasn't. Me."

She stared at him for a long moment, then her expression changed. "Oh." If anything, she seemed to get even more embarrassed. "Sorry." She wiped her eyes fiercely, tried to laugh. "I really seem to be messing everything up today."

"You are really so upset about missing the civil ceremony?"

She blinked back tears. "I don't miss things like this. I don't. I'm the one that people count on. What if she needs me to take care of the baby during the ceremony? What if she's upset because I'm not there? What if…"

"With all those guests around them, she probably didn't even notice your absence."

"I let her down."

"You slept in. It happens."

"Not to me." She rubbed her hand over her eyes. "I'll never forgive myself for this."

"Why?" he asked gently. "Why are you the only one who has to be perfect?"

"Because if I'm not, then…"

"Then?"

"Then I'm no better than…"

"Who?"

Her china cup clattered against the saucer. Snapping her mouth closed, she shook her head. "It doesn't matter. I failed." She looked away. "It's getting to be a habit."

The last thing Sharif wanted was to endure another wedding, especially one in some dreary Italian registry office. But looking at the misery on her beautiful, plump-cheeked face, he rose from the table. Tossing down his napkin, he went to her. "My car is parked in the barn. My driver is here…"

Irene looked up with an intake of breath. "You'd take me?"

"I'm willing to take you anywhere. Anytime." He lifted an eyebrow wickedly. "I thought that was clear."

She blushed but said stubbornly, "Their wedding…"

"Personally, I think attending one wedding is enough. I have no particular need to see it all replayed out, this time in a civil office. But if it truly matters so much to you…"

"It does!"

"Then I will take you. When you're ready." He hid a private smile.

Chugging down the rest of her sweet creamy coffee, she stood up. "I'm ready now." Warmth and gratitude shone in her brown eyes as she clapped her hands happily, like a child. "I take back every awful thing I said about you!"

Impulsively, she threw her arms around him. He felt her against him, right through the fabric of his suit, to his skin, all the way to blood and bone. His body stirred.

Stiffening, Irene pulled back, her eyes wide. He looked down at her.

"Feel free to kiss me," he said lazily, "if you feel you truly must."

Her expression sharpened, and she pushed away. "On second thought, everything I said about you still stands."

She looked with self-consciousness to the right and left at the bodyguards. "When can we leave?"

"Now." Lifting his hand in the smallest signal, he caused the four unsmiling bodyguards to fall in behind them, and they left the villa.

"This feels ridiculous," Irene whispered, holding his arm as she walked close to him. "Don't you feel like...like a prisoner getting escorted to your cell?"

At her words, the trapped feeling rose inside him, the one he'd been trying so hard to avoid, for a reason that had nothing to do with the bodyguards. The thing that had trapped him for twenty years, that was soon to lock him down forever, the thing he'd come to this wedding to try to come to terms with.

"I'm accustomed to it," he said tightly.

She shook her head. "I understand that as a powerful man you need bodyguards, but it just seems like it would be impossible to have any private life, any life at all really, when you have such a thick wall between you and the rest of the..."

Her voice trailed off. Sharif smiled at the dumbfounded look on her face as she stared at his black stretch Rolls-Royce, complete with diplomatic flags, inside the large, modern barn. A uniformed driver leaped to attention, opening the door for them. Sharif indicated for her to go first, something that made his bodyguards look at each other behind their aviator sunglasses. Well, let them wonder about the breach in protocol. Sharif didn't care. He climbed in beside her.

Irene's mouth was wide as she looked around the backseat of the limousine in awe. Seeing him, she kept scooting, pressing herself against the far wall.

"Are you so afraid to be near me?"

"Um." She stopped, looking uncertain. "I was making room."

"Room?"

"For all the bodyguards."

His lips curved. "One of them will sit up with the driver. The rest will follow separately."

"Oh." She paused. "But there's plenty of space. This car is ridiculous."

"I'm glad you approve."

"I didn't say *that*." She stretched out her legs in illustration. "You could fit a football team in here. This space is big enough to be used as a house for a family of—five…"

Her voice trailed off as she caught him looking at her bare legs, and realized that her hemline had pulled halfway up her thigh. Exhaling, she quickly sat up straight, yanking down the hem like a prim Victorian lady. He hid his amusement because he knew by the end of the night he would have stroked and kissed every inch she was trying to hide from him now. And she would have stroked and kissed every inch of him. Her defenses would fall and she would succumb to her own desire. The passion he sensed beneath her facade, once unleashed, would burn them both to ash. Let her try to hide from him now all she wanted. It would just make conquest all the sweeter.

"What are you smiling about?" she said suspiciously.

"Nothing," he said, still smiling. As the limo moved down the ribbon of road, he turned his head to look at the beautiful Italian countryside. Brilliant golden sunlight brushed his face, dappled with the shadows of clouds passing across the blue sky. He was aware of every movement Irene made in the seat beside him, and relished the hot anticipation building inside him. He couldn't remember the last time he'd wanted any woman so much.

In a few minutes, the limo and following SUV pulled up

in front of an officious-looking Italian building clinging to the edge of a cliff, tightly between the lake and the main road through town. Without even waiting for the driver to open her door, Irene opened it herself and jumped out. Standing on the sidewalk, she blinked up at the building, then glanced back doubtfully.

"Are you sure this is the place?" she asked Sharif.

"It is the address."

Hesitantly, she followed him into the building. The bodyguards hung back in the hall as Sharif and Irene found the small, gray, official-looking room where the ceremony for Falconeri and his housekeeper bride had just begun. Quietly, they took the last seats in the back, behind the rest of the guests, and watched the couple marry in the civil ceremony.

Even Sharif had to admit the bride looked radiant, in a simple cream-colored silk suit and netted hat, holding her cooing baby son in her lap. The groom looked even more joyful, if that were possible. The Falconeris were the only bright light in a rather gray room.

"They look so happy," Irene whispered.

"It's beautiful," he agreed sardonically.

She flashed him a glance. "It's different from the ceremony last night, that's all."

He gave a low laugh. "Last night was about romance. This is about marriage. The legal, binding contract." A hollow feeling rose in his gut. "Trapping them. To each other. Forever."

Irene's eyes lifted in surprise. Then she scowled. Leaning over, she whispered in his ear, "Look, your royalness, I get how you're deeply uninterested in any sort of emotion that doesn't end up in a one-night stand, but seeing as Cesare is your friend—"

"My business acquaintance," he corrected.

"Well, Emma is my friend, and this is her wedding. If you have any rude thoughts about marriage in general or theirs in particular, keep them to yourself."

"I was just agreeing with you," he protested.

She stared at him, then sighed. "Fine," she said, looking disgruntled. "This setting isn't completely romantic."

Sharif looked at her.

"Unlike you, Miss Taylor," he said softly. "You, I think, are the last truly romantic woman of a cold modern age." He tilted his head. "You really believe, don't you? You believe in the fantasy."

She looked away, staring fiercely at the happy couple.

"I have to," she said almost too softly for him to hear. "I couldn't stand it otherwise. And just look at them. Look at what they have…"

Sharif looked at her. He saw the yearning on her face, the wistful, almost agonized hope.

As the bride and groom spoke the final words that would bind them together forever in the eyes of Italian law, Sharif silently reached for Irene's hand and took it gently in his own. This time, he wasn't thinking about seduction. He was trying to offer comfort. To both of them.

And this time, she didn't pull away.

CHAPTER THREE

"Now, THIS—" IRENE sighed, leaning back on the blanket as she felt the warm Italian sun on her face a few hours later "—is lovely."

"Yes," Sharif's low voice said beside her. "Lovely."

Just the sound of his voice made her heart beat faster. Opening her eyes, she looked at him, lounging beside her on the picnic blanket on the hillside. He'd abandoned his jacket on the way back to the villa. She'd intended to return with the rest of the guests, but he'd convinced her otherwise.

"You're not going to make me go back alone, are you?" he'd asked. "And desert me for a bunch of people you don't care about?"

She'd hesitated, and when she saw that Emma had already left the town in a luxury sedan with Just Married written in a sign on the back, she'd found it impossible to say no.

The truth was that she was starting to…like him. It didn't mean anything, she told herself. After all, it was only natural that she'd find his company slightly more appealing than that of the rest of the wedding guests, none of whom she knew. Why wouldn't she feel more relaxed around Sharif, especially now that he'd traded the formidable native dress of the Emir of Makhtar for a tailored European suit that made him look exactly like every other man?

Well. Maybe not exactly like every man. And maybe *relaxed* was not the precise word to describe her feelings around him.

Irene shivered.

Stretched beside her on the blanket, Sharif emanated sex appeal, looking impossibly handsome in a gray vest and tie and tailored gray trousers. She licked her lips as her eyes dropped to the sleeves of his white shirt, rolled up to reveal the dusting of dark hair over his tanned forearms.

Just seeing that much of his skin made a bead of sweat break between her breasts that had nothing to do with the warm Italian sun.

He lifted a dark eyebrow, and she realized she'd been staring. And cripes, had she just licked her lips?

"It's…warm for November…isn't it?" she said weakly.

His dark gaze looked amused. "Is it?"

"Haven't you noticed?" She sat up abruptly on the blanket. She was relieved to see the rest of the wedding party and guests picnicking in the post-wedding luncheon farther down the hill. Golden sunlight danced across the field of autumn flowers, in the meadow on the Falconeri estate. Picnic lunches had been arranged for all of them by the picnic butler. Honest to God, a picnic butler. Shaking her head at the memory, Irene reached for the big wicker picnic basket. She licked her lips again, trying to act as if she'd been thinking about only food all the while. "You must be hungry. When I'm hungry, I can't think about anything but cream cakes. You're hungry, right?"

"Starving," he said softly, his dark eyes tracing her. "And you're right. When a man is hungry, everything else stops. Until his craving is satisfied."

Irene had the sudden feeling he wasn't talking about food. A tremble went over her body as she looked at him.

He gave her an innocent smile with his full, sensual lips.

No man should have lips like that, Irene thought. It shouldn't be legal. She suddenly wondered what it would feel like to be kissed by those lips.

No! She couldn't let herself be tempted, not even for a moment. Virginity, once lost, was lost forever. She couldn't let herself be lured by desire, not when the cost for that momentary pleasure would be the life—the committed love—that she really wanted!

She forced herself to look down at the basket. She took out Italian sandwiches on fresh crusty bread, antipasto and fresh fruit salad, all of which she put on elegant china plates before handing one to him, along with a fine linen napkin and a fork she suspected was made of pure silver.

"Thank you," he said gravely.

"Don't mention it," she said, looking away. She noticed the four bodyguards at a distance, in strategic locations on the edges of the meadow. "They really follow you everywhere, don't they? I know you're emir and all, but how can you stand it?"

Sharif used a solid-silver fork to take a bite of antipasto off his elegant china plate. "It is part of my position that I accept."

She shook her head. "But the loss of privacy...I'm not sure it's a great trade-off. Wealth, power, fame. But also four babysitters dogging your feet wherever you go."

"Six." The corners of his lips tilted upward. "The other two are keeping an eye on my room at the villa."

Irene stared at him. "Right." Her voice was heavy with irony. "Because you never know when there might be a sudden attack on *Lake Como*."

"You never know what the world will bring to your door."

"It's obvious, even to me, that six guards is overkill in a place like—"

"My father was shot down in broad daylight, twenty years ago, while vacationing with my mother." He took a bite of pasta salad. "Shot down by an ex-mistress. In a private, gated villa on the French Riviera."

Irene gave an intake of breath, then set down her forkful of fruit salad. She lifted her tremulous gaze. The hard lines of his face held no emotion.

"I'm so sorry," she whispered. "What…happened?"

"His mistress turned the gun on herself. She died at once. My father bled out on the terrace and died ten minutes later. In my mother's arms."

It was all so horrible, Irene felt sick inside. "I'm so sorry," she said again, helplessly. "How old were you?"

"Fifteen." His mouth pressed into a grim line. "At boarding school in America. A teacher pulled me out of class. Two men I'd never met before bowed to me, calling me the emir. I knew something must have happened to my father but it wasn't until I arrived back at the palace that I discovered what it was." Reaching out with an unsteady hand, he poured a bottle of springwater into one of the glasses. He drank it all in one gulp, then looked away. "It was a long time ago."

She felt awful, needling him about bodyguards when his own father had died in a situation every bit as apparently safe as this. "I'm sorry…you…I'm such a…I can't even imagine…"

"Forget about it." Sharif looked at the rest of the wedding party farther down the meadow. "As you said, today is a day for celebration. What's this?" Reaching into the basket, he pulled out a bottle of expensive champagne. "And still chilled." His lips curved as he looked at the label. "Now, *this* is the right way to endure a wedding."

Endure? She wondered at his choice of words. Then, she could hardly blame him for thinking so ill of romance, love or marriage, when his own parents' marriage had ended as it had.

He looked up, his dark gaze daring her to ask him more about it. Her mouth went dry.

"It's a little early for champagne, isn't it?" was all she could manage.

Without answering, Sharif popped the bottle open and poured it into two crystal glasses. He held one out to her, with a smile that didn't meet his eyes.

"Surely you, Miss Taylor, with your romantic nature," he drawled, "would not refuse a glass of champagne to celebrate your dearest friend's happy day?"

When he put it like that… "Well, no." She took the glass. "And for heaven's sake. Call me Irene."

Sharif looked down at her across the blanket.

"Irene," he said in a low voice.

Sensuality and power emanated from him in a way that fascinated her. In a way that was dangerous. Her eyes fell to his lips. To the slight shadow of scruff on his sharp jawline. To his neck.

Forcing herself to look away, she drank deeply from her glass. She'd never tasted champagne before, and it was every bit as delicious and bubbly and intoxicating as it looked in the movies. Sitting here in the meadow, beside a sexy Makhtari emir, overlooking a two-hundred-year-old Italian villa with the blue sparkling lake beyond, Irene felt as if she, too, had been transported into a movie, or a dream.

They ate in silence. With no words to fill the air, she was even more aware of Sharif's every movement. She looked at him sideways through her lashes, at the gleam of golden sunlight against his tawny skin. The thick shape of his throat above his white collar and blue tie. His long, muscled legs beneath the well-tailored trousers. She felt a cool breeze on her own overheated cheeks and the bare legs peeking out from her dress. But just as she was desperately trying to think of something to talk about, he abruptly spoke into the silence.

"So, you live in Paris?"

It was such a small-talk sort of salvo, it surprised her. Irene suddenly wondered if, in spite of Sharif being a powerful, rich sheikh, he might also be a person, who himself might have been trying to think of conversation, just as she had been.

"I had a job there. As a nanny for the Bulgarian ambassador's children."

"Had?"

She ate some fruit salad. "I was, um, fired."

He looked shocked. "You?"

"I loved the children, but…their parents and I had some creative differences." She took a big bite of sandwich and chewed slowly, but after she swallowed, he was still waiting patiently for her to continue. She sighed. "I've never been good at holding my tongue. I felt the parents were spending too much time at parties and entertaining, and were neglecting the emotional needs of their girls and needed to get their priorities straight."

He lifted his eyebrows. "And you—said this—to them?"

"I've always had a problem with telling the truth."

"You mean the problem is that you actually tell it?" He gave a low laugh, and she loved the sound. So sexy. So warm. It made his dark eyes light up in a way that melted her inside.

"Don't laugh," Irene said. "You're a billionaire and a

king. I bet no one tells you the truth about anything. They're too scared."

"I doubt that very much." He gave another laugh, but this time there was no warmth in it. "I wish some of my servants were a little more afraid, to tell you the truth. My sister has a companion who—"

He cut himself off.

"You have a sister?"

"Yes." He looked away.

Birds sang above them, echoing plaintively across the valley. Feeling awkward, Irene lifted her glass to her lips to take a fortifying drink of champagne, only to discover she'd finished it already. How had that happened?

"Allow me." Sharif brought the bottle to her glass. Placing his hand over hers, to steady her hold on the crystal stem, he tilted the bottle against the lip and poured deeply into her glass. Irene felt his larger hand over hers, felt the warmth of his palm against her skin, and a deep shudder went through her.

She looked up at his darkly handsome face.

"So where are you working now?" he asked.

She licked her lips. "I'm, um, not."

"Taking time off?"

"I'm sadly between jobs," she said lightly. "It's been six months. I'm running out of money."

Sharif frowned. "Can't Mrs. Falconeri arrange a job for you at one of her husband's hotels?"

"She probably could, if I asked her. But I won't."

"No desire to work in the hotel business?"

"It's not that. I wouldn't dream of presuming on our friendship that way. It wouldn't be right."

He was staring at her as if she were crazy. "What are you talking about?"

She glared at him. "I'm not that kind of person, okay?

Feelings are feelings, friends are friends, and I'm not going to use any relationship for financial gain. I won't. I'm not like—"

Like my family, she almost said, but cut herself off just in time.

Or maybe she didn't. Sharif was looking at her with consternation. As if seeing her for the first time.

"What happened?" he said in a low voice. "I thought some man broke your heart. But it's more than that, isn't it? Or else why wouldn't you ask a good friend for help finding a job? Why would you be afraid?"

"I'm not afraid!" Her cheeks flamed. "I just prefer to find a job on my own, that's all. I don't need Emma's help." She wouldn't let him see into her soul. She wouldn't. "Don't worry about me, Your Highness," she said coldly. "I'll be fine."

He looked as if he didn't believe her. His lips parted, as if he was about to ask her questions she wouldn't want to answer.

Looking down across the meadow, she rose unsteadily to her feet. "Let's pack up. I'm done."

But after they'd silently packed the dishes and he'd folded the blanket, as she started to walk ahead of him, Sharif caught her arm.

"Wait." Tilting his head, he gave her an impish, sideways smile. "Before we rejoin the other guests, I have something to show you."

An hour later, Irene was still staring at it in shock.

"You've got to be kidding," she said for the sixth time. She tilted her head, regarding it from the other direction. Nope. It still didn't look real. It was too outrageously huge, too ridiculous to be believed.

Beside her, Sharif tilted his head as well, looking down at it with poorly concealed masculine smugness. "Like it?"

Irene licked her lips, trying to find the words.

"A little too big?" he offered finally.

She looked up at him. "You think?"

"It's purely for your pleasure."

"I didn't ask for anything that huge."

"You didn't ask for anything at all. But I knew you wanted it. Every woman does."

Irene bit her lip, staring at it.

"Touch it," he said encouragingly. "Go on. Don't be afraid. It won't bite."

"That's what you think," she muttered, but finally, the temptation was too much to resist. It was too spectacular not to touch. She wanted to feel it for herself, every hard delicious curve.

Reaching out, she gently stroked her fingertips over the diamond necklace he was holding out in the black velvet case.

The diamonds felt hard and smooth. Especially the center five stones, which had to be well over ten carats...each. They sparkled from the fire inside them.

Just as she did when she was near Sharif.

"Put it on," he said, coming closer. "You know you want to."

Yanking back her hand, she shook her head, setting her jaw. "I couldn't possibly accept."

"Why not?"

She looked at him in disbelief. "You really have to ask? After I told you how I feel about mixing the lines between relationships and financial gain?"

Sharif lifted a dark eyebrow.

"Why, Miss Taylor. Are we in a *relationship*?" he

purred. "Am I to understand you cannot accept my small gift because you've fallen desperately in love with me?"

He'd caught her very neatly.

"Of course not," she said, glaring at him.

"In that case…"

He pulled her to the full-length mirror in his bedroom suite. Removing her borrowed band of Emma's pearls, he replaced them with the diamond necklace from the black velvet box.

She nearly gasped at the cool weight of the stones against her skin.

"You look beautiful," Sharif said softly, standing behind her. "You will be the queen of the ball tonight."

"No one will be queen but Emma," Irene said. "It's her day." Then she swallowed as she looked at herself in his mirror.

Afternoon sunlight was beaming down from the tall windows of his bedroom. She saw her own big eyes, the pink flush on her cheeks, her full, trembling lips. In her borrowed Lela Rose dress, with the diamonds flashing fire against her skin, she did look like a queen. But she couldn't kid herself it was the dress, or even the jewels that made her look so…alive.

It was the man standing behind her now. She couldn't touch him. But she could touch this…

Unthinkingly, she raised her hand and ran it down the thick, hard jewels. "How much did it cost?"

"It's not good manners to ask, is it?"

"How much?" she demanded.

He shrugged. "A minor amount that I can easily afford."

Irene licked her lips, still staring at herself in the mirror. *Take it off this instant*, she ordered herself, but she found her hand wouldn't obey. Instead of reaching back to undo the clasp at her nape, it was stroking the huge jewels as they trailed from her collarbone to the center of her breastbone. *It probably cost as much as a car*, she thought. *A car? A house. A mansion.*

"A loan?" she suggested weakly.

He shook his head. "A gift."

Irene had never seen anything so lavish and exquisite as this necklace, and knew she never would again. Crazy to think she was wearing a million euros around her neck—or more—when she had less than twenty euros in her purse.

But it wasn't a gift, whatever Sharif had said. It was payment in advance. No man gave something for nothing. What was the difference between accepting a diamond necklace from a sheikh or getting a hundred bucks from old Benny who pumped gas as the Quick Mart? No difference at all.

But she found herself still stroking the jewels for another five minutes before she gathered the willpower to reach for the clasp.

He put his larger hand over hers, stopping her. Their eyes met in the mirror.

"They're yours."

"I told you. I can't accept."

"I won't take them back. They were bought for you today in Rome."

"Rome?" she cried. "How?" Then she remembered his newspaper. "It's very wasteful," she grumbled. "Sending private jets all around the world at the drop of a hat. Buying diamonds for a stranger."

"You're not a stranger. Not anymore." He shrugged. "If you don't want the necklace, toss it in the lake. Bury it in the garden. I care not. It's yours. I won't take it back."

"But—"

"I'm bored with this subject. Let's find something fun to do." He gave her a lazy smile. "Perhaps go congratulate the bride and groom on their civil ceremony?"

Guilt flashed through her as she recalled how she'd barely spoken three words with Emma all day. "Good idea," she mumbled.

But for all the rest of the long afternoon, she found herself unable to take off the necklace, or to part company with Sharif, who was continually at her side, whispered shocking things to try to make her laugh, and then laughing himself when she whispered her own shocking things in return.

The beautiful, chic supermodel types goggled at them for the rest of the afternoon, and through dinner, too, as if they couldn't imagine what the handsome, powerful Emir of Makhtar could find so fascinating about Irene. Oh, if only they knew. She was insulting him, mostly.

She allowed herself a small, private giggle with her after-dessert coffee. Then her eye caught Emma's worried face across the table.

Irene's smile fell. Looking away, she scowled. Emma should know she didn't need to worry. She knew what she was doing.

Didn't she?

After dinner, alone in her own room for the first time that day, Irene looked down in awe at the beautiful gown Emma had loaned her for the ball that night. It was strapless red silk, with a sweetheart neckline and a very full skirt. The perfect gown for a night that would be the culminating event of the wedding celebration. Tomorrow would be nothing but hangovers and staggered breakfasts, as guests scattered for the airport, for the train, back to their real lives. But tonight—*tonight*.

Tonight there would be fireworks.

Trembling, Irene looked at herself in the mirror, wearing only a red strapless lace bra and panties—and the necklace. Lifting her long dark hair off her neck, Irene bit her lip, turning her head to the left and right.

She'd wear it just a few hours more. Then she'd give it back to Sharif, she promised herself, and no harm done.

Irene brushed her long dark hair, then piled the heavy weight on top of her head in an elegant topknot. She put on black eyeliner and red lipstick. Pulled on the strapless scarlet ball gown. Zipped it up behind her.

Looked in the mirror.

A woman she didn't recognize looked back at her.

Beautiful.

Exotic.

Rich.

An illusion, she thought. Just for tonight. Tomorrow she'd turn back into a pumpkin. She'd face the hollow choice of asking a friend for a job, against her pride and principles, or else going back to Paris to pack her things to return to Colorado, a penniless failure. She'd go back with nothing but the dream that someday, if she worked hard enough and followed all the rules, she'd be good enough. She'd find a good man to love her as she wanted to be loved. She took a deep breath.

But just for tonight, she would forget all that. She'd pretend she was someone else, just like the other women at the villa, wealthy and beautiful and without a care in the world.

Going out into the hall, Irene ducked back when she saw Emma and Cesare, both of them dressed for the ball, coming out of the next doorway. Emma was giving her husband an impish smile as she ran her hand down the front of his tuxedo. Cesare looked at her with a low growl, then gave her a passionate kiss, pulling her right back into their bedroom—next door.

Well, that was one mystery solved. Sharif wasn't the one who'd kept her awake last night with all the noise. Smiling to herself, Irene counted to ten to give Emma and

Cesare time to close their bedroom door before she went back into the hall.

She felt strangely nervous as she went down the sweeping stairs to the ballroom. Her hands were trembling for some reason she couldn't imagine. She touched the diamond necklace again, as if it was some kind of good-luck charm.

Just for tonight, she repeated to herself. *No harm done*.

The gilded ballroom was packed with people. Already, the hum of excited conversation and the music of the orchestra filled the huge room all the way to the high ceilings and the enormous crystal chandeliers. Unlike most of the weekend, which had involved an intimate number of twenty or so guests, tonight's event had brought celebrities and royalty and tycoons and politicians and billionaires, not just from Europe but also from South America and Asia and Africa. There had to be at least five hundred people, or maybe eight hundred. She had a hard time counting, and anyway, she didn't really care, because even though she wouldn't admit it to herself, there was only one person she was really looking for—

"Irene." His low voice behind her caused a thrill of pleasure to rush through her body. "You dazzle me."

Turning with a smile, she got her first look at Sharif in a tuxedo and her heart lifted to her throat. How could he look even more devastatingly handsome? How was it even possible?

Taking her hand in his, Sharif bent and kissed her skin. At the touch of his lips on her hand, the hint of his hot breath, a flush of heat covered her body. Her eyes were wide as he straightened. He smiled at her, then held out his arm.

"Shall we show them how it's done?"

This time, there was absolutely no hesitation before she took his arm. They walked into the ballroom together. Irene was conscious of many pairs of eyes on them as they danced and danced and drank champagne and toasted the happy couple and danced some more. All night, they never left each other's side. They spoke about everything and nothing, and as she smiled up at him, he looked down at her, caressing her with his eyes.

Every word, every moment, seemed filled with magic and a delicious sort of tension, as if the very night were holding its breath. Irene felt dizzy, drunk with happiness. Against her will, she found herself wondering what it would be like to be in Sharif's arms, not just for these few hours, not just for this one night, but for tomorrow as well, and the day after that.

As they swayed to the music on the dance floor, he gave her a sensual smile, brushing an errant tendril of dark hair from her face. Just feeling the soft brush of his fingertips, even though they were in the middle of the ballroom with hundreds of couples around them, made her almost forget to dance. She stumbled, but he caught her smoothly, lowering her into a dip.

"Thank you," she whispered breathlessly, looking up at him.

Sharif's eyes were dark with heat. "My pleasure."

It seemed like minutes or hours that he held her in the dip, almost horizontally, and she wondered wildly if this was the way he would look over her in bed. Her knees went wobbly, but before she could collapse completely, he pulled her back upright, tight against his hard body.

She licked her lips, pressing her cheek to the shirt of his tuxedo. She could feel his warmth beneath the fabric, feel the power and strength of his body towering over her own. She thought she could hear his heartbeat.

He stopped dancing. Took a ragged breath.

"Irene," he said in a low voice.

Terror struck her—or maybe it was excitement—she no

longer knew the difference. She only knew what was about
to happen and that she could not stop it, even if she wanted
to. And she didn't. Slowly, she pulled away from his chest.
She lifted her gaze to his.

Sharif's eyes seemed to burn with dark fire. He ran
his hands over her bare shoulders, softly down her back.
She felt the roughness of his hands, the size of them, the
strength. He ran his fingertips up her arms, to her neck.
He stroked the edge of his thumb softly against her aching
lips, sizzling where he touched, making her yearn, making her *need*.

Cupping her face, he tilted back her head. She felt the
warmth of his breath. Felt the hard heat of his body against
hers. For an instant, time seemed suspended. She forgot
the people around them. Forgot to dance. Forgot all rational thought. Forgot to breathe.

He lowered his mouth to hers, and kissed her.

It was like nothing she'd ever experienced. The memory
of Carter's sloppy kisses of two years ago instantly evaporated, became laughable. Sharif took command, holding her
in his arms, his lips hard and hot and sweet and soft. The
music stopped. She heard only the rush of blood through
her veins, making her dizzy, lost in the riptide of pleasure
that tore through her, body and soul, leaving her weak and
clutching his shoulders as if only this kiss could save her.
As if his kiss were life itself.

She wanted him. She wanted this powerful billionaire
sheikh, who had become simply Sharif to her. She wanted
him. Even if it destroyed her...

"Fireworks! Come out now for the fireworks!"

The words rang out multiple times, in multiple languages. Irene heard the delighted response of the crowd,
felt the rush as people started to leave the ballroom. Sharif
pulled away. Her eyes opened slowly. She felt almost be-

wildered as she looked up at his handsome face, at his dark eyes, half-lidded with desire. Then she saw something else in his eyes.

Smugness. Masculine smugness.

She blinked. Took a deep breath. Eyes wide, she put her hand to her forehead.

"What are you doing to me?" she whispered.

"Don't you know?" Sharif tilted his head as he looked down at her, his black eyes hot with desire. He stroked her cheek. "I am seducing you, Irene."

A shock of awareness blasted over and through her, causing prickles to go up and down her body from her earlobes to her breasts and lower still. "You're—you're *seducing* me?"

"Forget the fireworks outside." Running his hands down the bare skin of her shoulders above her strapless red gown, he lowered his head to her ear. "Come back to my suite and we'll have our own."

He pulled back from her, and she saw in his face that he expected her to say yes. He thought he'd won. In spite of all her protests, he'd always expected to win. Dawning horror rose inside her soul.

"All of our time together—it's just been one long set-up? From the moment we met?"

Sharif twirled a tendril of her long dark hair around his finger. "I've never had to work so hard for any woman. But no woman has ever intrigued me more. Come back to my room, Irene. Let me show you everything the night can be…"

Irene ripped out of his arms, pressing her hands against her temples. *One long set-up.* All the laughter and banter. All the camaraderie and delight. She'd thought it was magic. She hadn't seen the secret work of the magician pulling the strings.

"It was all just to get me into bed?" she whispered. "All our—our friendship was a lie?"

Sharif's smug expression disappeared.

"Not a lie," he said sharply. "A seduction. Surely even you can see the difference."

"Even me?" Pain wrenched through her, the pain of shattered dreams, dreams she should have known better to have but that she'd allowed herself to believe in anyway. "Stupid. Stupid," she whispered, hating herself.

"Irene…"

Looking up at him, she hated him even more. She couldn't bear to meet his black gaze that always saw through her soul. Was he seeing through her now? Did he know what a fool he'd nearly made of her—the fool she'd nearly made of herself, letting herself fall into the magic, believing it to be real?

A sob lifted to her throat. Turning on her heel, she fled the empty ballroom, out into the night.

Outside, hundreds of wedding guests stood across the terraces, their eyes lifted up as the first explosions of colorful fireworks streaked across the sky, across the black mirror of the lake.

Irene fled in the opposite direction, toward the garden, her red silk skirts flying behind her. Only when she was in the dark quiet of the overgrown trees did she exhale. And cover her face with her hands.

She remembered how harshly she'd judged her mother and sister for falling for men's lines, again and again, first for love, then for attention and finally for money. Oh, if only she'd known how it all started! With such breathless, foolish hope!

Sharif's voice was low behind her. "I don't understand."

Trembling, she whirled around.

The moon had gone behind the clouds and in the darkness of night, she couldn't see his face. "It's been fun, hasn't it?" he said. "Why are you reacting like this?"

Fireworks suddenly lit up the sky again, and she saw his face. He looked bewildered. He had no idea what he'd done to her.

Irene was glad for that, at least. She looked down, waiting for the sky to grow dark. Waiting for her voice to grow steady enough for her to speak.

"It's just sex," Sharif said. "It doesn't mean anything."

"It does to me," she said. "Either it's making love with all your heart, or else it's just an empty, hollow shell of what it's meant to be."

He snorted. "You're making a big deal out of—"

"I've waited my whole life for the man I will love. The man I'll marry."

Another boom of fireworks, a distant happy cry from the crowd, and she saw the shocked expression on his face. "You can't be saying what I think you're saying."

She waited for it to be dark again. Then she said quietly, "When I marry, it will only be for love. And our wedding night will be truly about making love. The kind that will last forever…" Her throat caught. "You've accused me of being romantic," she said softly, blinking fast. "I'm just waiting for the One."

"One at a time?" he said weakly.

She shook her head. He scowled.

"What difference does the number of lovers make?"

"To you, it doesn't." Irene looked up. "But it matters to me. Sex is sacred. It's a promise without words. A promise I'll only make to the man who will love me for the rest of his life, and I can love for the rest of mine." Her throat ached as she asked him a question to which she already knew the answer. "Are you that man, Sharif?"

A last blast of fireworks ricocheted across the night like a lightning storm, illuminating his expressionless face.

"No," he said dully.

The ache in her throat now felt like a razor blade. She forced herself to ignore it. To smile. "I didn't think so." Unclasping the necklace was suddenly easy. She blinked fast, and was proud of herself for her clear, unwavering voice as she said, "Thank you for a weekend I'll never forget."

Reaching for his hand, she pressed the heavy diamond necklace against his palm. He looked down.

"It was a gift," he said.

Past his ear, she saw movement on the edge of the garden, his bodyguards hovering at a distance. It almost made her laugh. "Your minders are here." With a deep breath, she reached up and touched his rough cheek. "I wish all kinds of beautiful things for you, Sharif." She tried to smile. "There's lots of magic to believe in. The kind people make for themselves."

But as Irene looked at his stricken black eyes, her throat suddenly closed tight. Without another word, she turned and ran toward the villa. Above her, the fireworks' grand finale exploded across the sky in exquisite bursts of color, like flowers blooming to life then just as swiftly fading away.

She'd passed the test. She'd won.

Irene barely reached her bedroom before her knees collapsed beneath her. Sliding to the floor in a splash of red silk, she covered her face with her hands, and cried.

CHAPTER FOUR

HE'D LOST. FAILED.

Sharif could hardly believe it.

I wish all kinds of beautiful things for you.

Remembering her lovely, anguished voice, he muttered a curse. He stalked through the crowd watching the last fireworks, stomping back toward the villa. Two bodyguards fell in behind him as always. One spoke to him in urgent Makhtari Arabic.

"Your Highness, you should know that—"

"Later," he bit out. His whole body felt tight. For the love of heaven, couldn't they leave him alone, even now? Stomping up the stairs, Sharif paused, looking down the dark hallway toward Irene's room. But what was the point?

There's lots of magic to believe in. The kind people make for themselves.

Furiously, Sharif turned toward his own suite. He could hardly believe that it was ending like this. That after hours of flirting with her, dancing with her, it had still ended with him going back to his bedroom alone.

For the last thirty hours, Irene had been the center of his battle strategy, the intense focus of his every thought. He'd used all his best techniques, the ones that never failed. He'd charmed her, listened to her, given her his complete attention—and not just for an hour, but for the entire day.

More. He'd told her the truth when he said he'd never tried so hard before. He'd forced himself to seduce her slowly, an inch at a time, luring her as a horse trainer would tame a skittish colt.

And this was the result?

He looked down in disgust at the extravagant diamond necklace clenched in his fist. Women could never resist him. So how had she?

I've waited my whole life for the man I will love.

Sharif took a shuddering, incredulous breath. He'd never met a woman like this. She was crazy. But that was also why she'd drawn his interest, that light inside her. The fierce purity.

I don't fail, he'd boasted to her once. Well. He rubbed the back of his head. She'd certainly proved the truth of *that*.

What did he care? he told himself harshly. What was one woman to him, more or less?

He just had never failed before. Not in any arena of his life. When he tried something, he always succeeded.

Until now. And he suddenly felt something for Irene he hadn't felt for any woman in a long time.

Respect. No. More than respect. *Envy.*

Which didn't make any sense at all. After all, *he* wasn't bound by any antiquated, ridiculous rules about sex. He could have it whenever he wanted.

Well, except now. With her.

More irritated than ever, he stomped down his empty hallway. Four bodyguards were waiting near his door, glancing at each other, all of them looking nervous.

"Your Highness," one of them tried.

It took all of Sharif's self-control not to shout in the man's face. "Later," he growled, and pushed past them into his room, nearly slamming the door behind him. *Your minders*, Irene had called them. The symbols of a duty that in this moment chafed him almost beyond bearing. For God's sake, couldn't they leave him in peace, even for a moment?

In the dark bedroom, he tossed the ten-million-dollar diamond necklace carelessly across his desk, hearing it clatter and fall.

Then he heard something else.

"Your Highness," a kittenish voice gasped in the darkness. "I've been waiting for you!"

Irene? But even as the thought flashed through his mind, he knew it wasn't her. And if it wasn't Irene… Coldly, he switched on the bedside light.

To his shock, he saw the beautiful blonde Gilly, his sister's companion, who'd come from a respectable family with such excellent references.

"You sounded tired over the phone…" she purred, sitting up. She was naked, and smiling at him like a cat with a bowl of cream.

Sharif felt suddenly, crashingly weary. "How did you get past the bodyguards?"

"Oh. That." She giggled. "I told them there was an emergency with Aziza and I had to speak with you privately as soon as you left the party."

So that explained why they'd wanted to talk to him. His weariness faded, turned to anger. "And my sister?"

"She's fine," she said hastily, correctly interpreting his glare. "Well, except for counting down the days until her wedding."

"Counting down?"

"You know—with dread."

His jaw became granite. "Her engagement wasn't my idea."

"Yes, well…" Gilly waved her hand airily. "I'm sure it will all work out."

Turning away from her, Sharif sat on the chair by the fireplace and pulled off his shoes, one by one. He'd hired her as Aziza's companion only because, after years spent with an elderly governess, his young sister had begged him for someone closer to her own age. She'd been thrilled when Gilly Lanvin had moved into the palace, with her sophisticated ways and intense love of fashion. But the result for his sister had been nothing short of disastrous.

When Aziza, at barely nineteen, had been sent expensive gifts and flowers by the aging sultan of a neighboring country, Gilly had turned her head with fairy-tale dreams of being a queen. His sister had begged and pleaded with Sharif to allow her to accept the proposal. Finally, with some reluctance, he had. It was a good match politically, and if his sister truly was so sure…

Except Aziza's certainty had now melted away as the wedding approached, and she realized she was about to become the wife of a man forty years older than herself, a man she barely knew beyond his excellent taste in Louis Vuitton handbags and Van Cleef & Arpels earring sets. She was desperate to get out of it now, but it was too late. Sharif had signed the betrothal. Some choices, he thought grimly, you just had to live with. He knew that better than anyone.

"…I knew you were hoping I would surprise you. I could tell." He realized Gilly was still talking, crooning in a really annoying singsong voice. "If you'll just come over here, Your Highness—*Sharif*—I'll rub you down, make you feel so good—"

"Get out," he said flatly.

She gasped. "But—"

"Get. Out."

Rising to his feet, he opened the door and spoke coldly to his bodyguards in the hall. "Miss Lanvin is returning to Beverly Hills. Get her last paycheck and put her on the next plane."

The bodyguards glanced at each other as if they knew they all had a good chance of being fired.

"Now," Sharif said tightly.

The next second, the bodyguards were at his bed, and as one of them lifted the naked, whining woman from the mattress, another efficiently covered her with a thick white terry-cloth bathrobe from the en suite bathroom. Within thirty seconds, they were carrying her down the hall and down the stairs and permanently out of his life—and Aziza's.

So the bodyguards were of some use after all. Sharif leaned back against his door, almost smiling to himself as he thought of using this point against Irene. Then his smile faded as he realized it was unlikely he'd ever talk to her again. The thought made him hurt a little inside. Why? Simply because he was too proud to accept failure? Surely he couldn't be so childish as that?

Pulling off his tuxedo and silk boxer shorts, he stepped into the shower.

Irene wanted to wait for love and marriage. So be it. Even if he didn't agree with her idealistic sentiment, he could respect it. He had no choice but to respect it.

His own life and ideals were different. When he married, love would have nothing to do with it. In fact, once he and his future wife had a child to be heir and another as requisite spare, he fully expected he'd avoid her for the rest of his life.

Climbing naked into bed, he gave a suspicious sniff. He could still smell Gilly's flowery perfume on the sheets. It irritated him. He was tempted to call the villa's housekeeping staff and have them change the sheets, but that seemed like more trouble than it was worth. Not to mention likely to cause a scandal. He could just imagine what Irene would say if she heard. Some scathing remark about the promiscuous nature of selfish, coldhearted playboys.

Getting up, he opened the large oak wardrobe, found some clean sheets and changed the bed himself. He'd never done such a thing before, as from birth all of his needs had been attended to by servants. He'd mostly been raised by an American nanny and Makhtari tutors who taught him history and languages, along with fencing and fighting and riding. Even at boarding school, someone else had changed his sheets. So cleaning up after himself, even in this small way, was new. His fingers were clumsy as he did it.

Finally, Sharif stood back from the bed, surveying his work with satisfaction. Just because he'd never done something before didn't mean he couldn't learn the skills. Again, he wished he could show Irene. Again, he reminded himself he'd never see her again.

There's lots of magic to believe in. The kind people make for themselves. Her dark eyelashes had trembled against her pale cheeks.

Climbing into bed, he closed his eyes into a hard, dreamless sleep. He woke early, with the sound of his phone ringing.

It was his chief of staff, back at the palace. He was needed in Makhtar. His European vacation was over. No more pleasure. No more distraction. All that awaited him at home was cold hard duty and a young sister in tears at the mess she'd made of her own life. He'd have to find her a new companion to hold her hand for the remaining three months until her wedding.

Rising from the bed, Sharif yawned, rubbing the back of his head. He reached his arms upward, stretching his naked body before he dropped to the floor and did a few quick push-ups, just to wake up and get some of the adrenaline out of his bloodstream.

Find Aziza a companion? The situation seemed hopeless. He needed a woman who was both young, for Aziza's sake, and old, for his. He needed someone he could trust, someone who wouldn't jump into Sharif's bed, someone who would be professional enough to put Aziza's needs before everything else. Someone who...

Sharif's spine snapped back as his eyes went wide. He picked up his phone again. He read through business emails, made a few additional calls. Without hurry, he dressed in his traditional Makhtari garb and, leaving others to pack his suitcases, he went down to the breakfast room, bodyguards falling into line behind him.

He walked straight through the pale yellow room, ignoring all the women who tried to catch his eye. He offered an absentminded "good morning" to the host and hostess, then saw the person he'd been looking for. Pushing past all the rest, he went straight to Irene, who was sitting at the table with a plate loaded with pastries and scrambled eggs as she poured a great deal of cream into her coffee. He stopped right in front of her.

"I want you to come work for me," he said. "At my palace in Makhtar."

Irene's eyes still felt scratchy from a night of crying. She'd prayed she'd never have to face Sharif again. Foolish hope.

It had taken her hours to fall asleep, hours of running worried circles in her mind about the choice she'd make today. Would she take her first-class flight back to Paris, where she had only a few days left of paid rent, and then the open-ended economy ticket back to Colorado, to the rickety house on the wrong side of the tracks? Would she go back in penniless humiliation to the place where Carter had told her she'd never be remotely good enough for a man like him?

Or would she ask Emma to find her a job in one of her husband's luxury hotels around the world—using a friendship for her own financial gain?

In her darkest hour, Irene had bitterly regretted her pride, which had made her spurn Sharif's lavish gift of the diamond necklace. If she'd kept it, she and her family could have been wealthy—set for life!

But at what cost?

No. She'd done the right thing. He'd made her want him. Dazzled her with romance. But she'd resisted the temptation, and she'd never see him again. So the damage wouldn't be permanent, either to her heart, or to her soul.

So how could she abandon her principles now, and ask Emma to arrange a job for her?

But how could she not?

Anxious and unsure, feeling exhausted and alone with her heart still aching over the coldhearted way Sharif had tried to seduce her, the way he'd *kissed* her, Irene had finally gotten out of bed. She'd taken a shower and dressed. No fancy designer clothes this time, but her own plain cotton T-shirt and hoodie and jeans fit for traveling. Going down to the breakfast room, she'd filled her plate with a mountain of food. She'd numbly sat down alone at the table.

Then she'd felt a shiver of awareness behind her. Without turning, she knew who'd just come into the breakfast room. A dark shadow came across the table in front of her.

"I want you to come work for me. At my palace in Makhtar."

It was the same husky voice that had haunted her dreams. Irene looked up from her plate of food. A shiver went through her body as she met Sharif's dark eyes, a hard aching tingle across her lips, which he'd bruised every bit as thoroughly as her heart.

He was once again dressed in his full sheikh regalia,

with his bodyguards hovering behind him, the full presence of the Emir of Makhtar. And he'd never looked so handsome. The ultimate male figure of every woman's romantic fantasy. Or at least hers.

Wrong, she told herself fiercely. Her ultimate fantasy was a smart, funny, loyal man who would mow the lawn of their little cottage, read books to their children and love her forever. A man who would notice if a little neighbor child walked past the house, crying after her first day of school. A man who would roll up the sleeves of his old shirt, pull down his cap and go up to the school to make sure it never happened again. Her mother hadn't done it. She'd never known her father, either. Irene had been an accident, a mistake. Her mother had told her that all her life. *Stupid condom didn't work. Don't know which one.*

But after the first day of kindergarten, Dorothy Abbott had been the mother who'd comforted her, Bill Abbott the father who'd protected her. *That* was the house Irene wanted to live in. The parents she would someday give her own children.

There would be no accidents. Because until she met the right man, there would be no sex. No matter how she might be tempted.

"Work for you?" Irene repeated. She hated the weak sound of her voice and tossed her head, intending to give a sharper retort along the lines of *Immature as you are, your worshipfulness, I don't think you exactly need a nanny,* then she remembered all the eyes upon them. That type of banter was private, between her and Sharif, not between Irene Taylor, the American nanny, and the Emir of Makhtar. The banter was in the past, anyway. It was when Sharif had wanted to seduce her, and when she'd nearly given him the chance.

"I was not aware you had any children, Your Highness," she said coldly.

A half smile twisted the edges of Sharif's lips. She had the feeling he knew exactly how she'd felt forced to choke back her real reaction. He'd probably set up this meeting in public for exactly those reasons, damn him.

"I have a younger sister," he said.

Her lips parted. She tried to keep her expression impassive as she said, "Tell me about the position," as coolly as if she had already had five job offers today and fifty thousand dollars in the bank.

He lifted a dark eyebrow. "I would be pleased to give you further details, Miss Taylor. Shall we talk outside?"

She nodded. Rising to her feet, she followed him out of the villa, to the very same terrace where they'd first danced. It already seemed so long ago.

The blue skies and warm autumn sun had evaporated. Winter, too long held at bay, had finally arrived full force into northern Italy. The lowering sky was gray, and mist covered the tips of the distant hills across the lake. A cold blast of wind made her shiver in her comfy pink hooded sweatshirt and old jeans.

Irene looked pointedly at the bodyguards who'd followed them outside. With a sigh, Sharif gave them a glance, and they backed up to the villa wall, out of earshot.

"Why are you asking me to work for you?" she hissed. "What kind of trick is this?"

"No trick." He tilted his head, his eyes dark. "I've recently had reason to sack my sister's current companion."

"What happened? Let me guess. You fired her for talking back? If that's the case, there's no point hiring me. You know that I—"

"She showed up here last night. In my bed."

Her cheeks went pink. "Oh," she said faintly. "Delivery service. How nice for you."

"No," he said sharply. "I don't sleep with employees. I

threw her out. Now my sister needs a trustworthy companion until her wedding three months from now."

"*Wedding?* How old is your sister?"

"Nineteen."

Someone else getting married so young. It made Irene feel suddenly ancient at twenty-three. "Why would you choose me?"

Sharif's dark eyes met hers.

"Because I feel I can trust you to look out for my sister," he said quietly. "And I know I won't find you unexpectedly naked in my bed."

He sounded so sure of that. He didn't know what turning down his offer last night had cost her. Irene shivered in her thin cotton hoodie, looking out at the gray lake. She thought of what was waiting for her in Colorado. What was waiting for her in Paris.

"When is the wedding exactly?" she said.

"Late February."

"And the salary?"

"Ah." He relaxed, tilting his head as he gave a shrug. "For a trustworthy person of this nature, you understand, no price would be too great."

"How great is great?"

"Name your price."

Name your price? That was something people said in movies, not in real life. "You can't be serious."

"Try me."

Irene licked her lips. Recklessly, she thought of a huge amount, more than a whole year's salary working for her previous families in either New York City or Paris. She opened her mouth to ask for that amount.

Then she snapped it shut.

She mustn't be hasty. She'd read in a book once that women never valued themselves highly enough—that they were afraid to negotiate salaries out of a fear of being turned down, or even more ridiculously, of not being liked. Well, she didn't care if Sharif liked her, did she? And he was making it plain she had him over a barrel. If there was ever a time to value herself highly, it was now.

She thought of what it would cost to send her mother to the best rehab facility in Denver. The cost of moving to a brand-new apartment in a brand-new city, of paying rent for the next five years so her sister could go to community college and never again be tempted to go looking for some sugar daddy in a bar. Irene thought of the cost of making sure none of them would ever have to go back to that sad little house by the railroad tracks again. A new life not just for Irene, but for her mother and older sister.

So she took that first number and exploded it, like turning a single-story building into a skyscraper. Taking her heart in her hands, she kept her face expressionless and looked him straight in the eyes. "A hundred thousand dollars."

"Agreed," he said, before she'd even finished the last word.

Oh, no! She'd blown it! The fact that he'd agreed so quickly meant she hadn't asked for nearly enough!

"Per *month*," she added quickly.

He gave her an amused smile. "Naturally."

"Fine," she said, wishing she'd had the guts to ask for more.

"Fine. I will have my people pack your things."

"Thanks, but I prefer to pack my own stuff. I already did it in any case."

"Of course you did. Independent and responsible as you are." He smiled again, and his dark eyes seemed to caress her face, causing an answering spark of awareness to light like a match inside her. Match? That match had been lit from the moment he'd found her standing alone at the moonlit lake that first night. It had turned into a simmering fire that was waiting at any moment to explode.

She wouldn't let it. She'd already passed the test, hadn't she? She'd resisted her attraction to him and for the sake of the three hundred thousand dollars, more money than she'd ever seen in her lifetime or would ever expect to see again, she would resist it again.

Fortunately, she knew he wouldn't pursue her romantically again. Obviously, he'd been just trying to amuse himself with a bit of slumming during his friend's wedding weekend, but they were returning to real life now. To his home country.

Holy cow. Sharif was Emir of Makhtar. He'd made her forget. Once they were in Makhtar, though, she'd likely never see him in the palace, not until the day he paid her. Likely not even then. Paying the help? He had people to handle that sort of thing.

"So when do we leave?" she asked awkwardly.

He smiled. "As soon as we say our goodbyes and get the suitcases in the car."

Two hours later, they were boarding his enormous private jet.

"So what did Mrs. Falconeri say when you told her you were coming to work for me?" Sharif asked as they crossed the tarmac.

Irene blushed. "I, um, never told her."

He gave a low laugh that was way too knowing. She changed the subject. "What's it like? Your home?"

"An oasis on the Persian Gulf. Sparkling new city, palm trees, a bright blue sky, warm, friendly people."

She looked at him skeptically. "I already agreed to the job. You don't have to sell the place like a tourist-board representative. I want to know what it's really like."

Sharif stopped, looking at her. "It's the best country in the world. I would do anything for Makhtar. Sacrifice anything."

His love for his country shone in his face. She'd never seen such passion, idealism, vulnerability in his dark eyes. She had to look away.

Fortunately, it was easy to find something astonishing to look at. The inside of his private 747 looked nothing like any of the flights she'd been on. Not even that first-class flight. The front cabin of his plane was wide and gleamed with light and comfortable white sofas and seats, with a bar on one side and a large flat-screen television against a wall. It looked like the contemporary interior of an expensive New York restaurant.

Overwhelmed, she sank into the closest seat. "I guess I should call you *Your Highness* now."

"And from this moment, you are Miss Taylor," he agreed.

Biting her lip, she looked out the window. As the jet's engine warmed up, to take them away from Italy and up into the clouds, Irene felt her heart grow suddenly lighter. Thanks to this stroke of fate, she hadn't had to give up her principles. And she'd never need to worry about money again. This would change everything for her family. Everything. With a deep breath, she looked at Sharif.

"Thank you for hiring me," she said softly.

As the bodyguards trailed past him to the rear cabin, he frowned in surprise. "Thank you for solving my problem."

A flight attendant, glamorously attired in a skirt suit and a jaunty blue hat and scarf, served some sparkling water on a silver tray. Taking a sip of the cool water, Irene looked at her new employer.

Sharif looked handsome and powerful in his stark white robes, sitting on the white leather sofa on the other side of the spacious cabin. Taking his own sparkling water off the tray, he smiled his thanks to the flight attendant. Irene sighed with happiness, leaning back against her own plush leather seat.

"I wish all the people who were mean to me in school could see this." A low laugh escaped her lips. "No one would ever have guessed I'd someday be companion to a princess of Makhtar. Especially with my grades in geography. I couldn't have placed Makhtar on a map." Irene wasn't a hundred percent certain she could do it now, but she kept that to herself. "Um, are you still sure about this?"

He set down his glass. His handsome face was inscrutable as he slowly looked her over. "Why wouldn't I be?"

Irene hesitated, feeling self-conscious. "I told you I have a bad habit of talking back to employers. Knowing the kind of woman I am, Your Highness, are you sure you really want me as your employee?"

"I'm sure, Miss Taylor. There can be no doubt." His black eyes met hers as he said huskily, "I want you."

CHAPTER FIVE

IRENE HAD NEVER flown on even a small private plane before, let alone the huge 747 that belonged to the royal house of Makhtar. But by the time the plane landed that evening, she was growing shamefully accustomed to the luxury that accompanied Sharif wherever he went. Even the stretch Rolls-Royce, and the attendant entourage of black SUVs for the guards, was starting to seem almost routine.

There was just one thing she couldn't get used to. One thing that was a shock to her senses, each and every time.

She looked at him beneath her lashes, in the back of the limo. He was busy now, speaking with a young man, his chief of staff, who'd met him at the private airport at the edge of the city. The two men were speaking in rapid Arabic, leaving Irene free to sneak little glances.

Gone was the darkly seductive playboy she remembered. Here, Sharif was the emir. Formal. Serious. And definitely not paying the slightest attention to her. Telling herself she was relieved, she looked out the window, which was tinted against the shock of the hot Makhtari sun.

Makhtar City gleamed from the desert, like a polished, sun-drenched diamond in the sand. It was a new city, still being rapidly built with cranes crisscrossing the blue sky.

She saw prosperous people, families pushing baby strollers on newly built sidewalks to newly built cafés. It had to be almost ninety degrees Fahrenheit, from the blast of heat she'd felt walking across the airport tarmac to the air-conditioned limo. Very different from the chilly morning in the Italian mountains. But Sharif had told her on the plane that this was their winter.

"In November, people finally come out of their houses, as the weather turns pleasant. In summer, it can reach a hundred and twenty degrees. Tourists complain then that swimming in the gulf is like taking a hot bath—no relief whatsoever from the unrelenting heat." He'd grinned. "Makhtaris know better than to try it."

It sure didn't seem like winter to her. The hot sun made her want to rip off her jeans and hoodie in favor of shorts and a tank top. But on the street, both men and women wore clothing that completely covered their arms and legs. They didn't even look hot, strolling with their families. Irene still felt a little sweaty from her four minutes outside. It was way more humid than Colorado, too. She'd have to get used to it.

Still, there was something about this city, this country, that she immediately liked. It wasn't just the gleaming new architecture of the buildings, or the obvious wealth she saw everywhere—luxury sports cars filling the newly built avenues, lined with expensive designer shops and gorgeous palm trees.

It was the way she saw families walking together. The way she observed, on the street, young people holding open doors for their elders. Family was even more respected than money. The wisdom and experience of age was respected even more than the beauty and vigor of youth. It felt very different from the neighborhood she'd grown up in. At least the *house* she'd grown up in.

As a child, she'd wanted so desperately to respect her mother and older sister. She'd wanted a mother who would give her hugs after school, a sister she could emulate and admire. She'd wanted a family who would look out for her.

But by the time she was nine, she'd realized that if she wanted milk in the fridge and the light bills paid, she'd have to take care of it herself. She'd learned how to run a household from watching Dorothy, but sadly there was nothing she could do for her mother and sister beyond that. Any attempt she made to suggest a different career path just made them accuse her of judging them.

Now, for the first time, Irene would really be able to help them. No more just sending them bits and pieces of her salary that didn't really change anything. With such a huge amount of money as three hundred thousand dollars—or whatever was left after taxes—she could change not just her own fate, but the lives of the people she loved deeply, no matter how many times they'd broken her heart.

"Miss Taylor. You are ready?"

They'd arrived in a large, gated courtyard past the palace gate, filled with palm and date trees surrounding a burbling fountain. Sharif was looking at her quizzically.

"Yes, Your Highness."

His eyes widened at her meek, impersonal tone. But she knew how grand households worked. One hint that she was anything but his sister's companion, a single sly suggestion that she was also the emir's mistress, and by nightfall she'd be despised by the entire palace staff.

A uniformed servant opened the door, and she stepped out.

"It's cooler," she said in surprise.

"The palace is on the gulf. And here in the courtyard—" Sharif's eyes seemed to caress her "—you can feel the soft breeze beneath the shade of the palm trees."

She looked up at the towering Arabic fantasy of the palace in front of her, like something out of a dream. "It's just like you said it would be."

"The palace?"

"The whole country."

Sharif paused. "I'm pleased you like it." He turned to his young chief of staff. "Please escort Miss Taylor to her new quarters."

The young man looked at Irene with clear interest. "With pleasure."

Sharif stepped between them. "On second thought," he said abruptly, "I will do it myself."

"Yes, sire," the young man said, visibly disappointed. Sharif swept forward in his robes, and Irene fell into step behind him.

"You shouldn't have done that," she whispered once they were out of earshot. "You can't show any particular interest in me. The other servants will talk."

"Let them talk. I didn't like the way he looked at you."

"Friendly?"

Sharif scowled. "Flirty."

"And that is bad because…he's married."

"No."

"Engaged."

"No."

"A womanizer. A liar. A brute."

Sharif's jaw twitched. "No, of course not. Hassan is none of those things. He is an honorable, decent man. Of course he is. He's my chief of staff."

Irene looked at him from beneath her eyelashes. "So why not let him take me?"

"If any man is going to take you," he said softly, "it will be me."

She stopped, blushing in confusion. Surely he couldn't still be thinking he…

"Your room is next to my sister's. I am headed that way."

She exhaled. "Oh."

The palace was huge, with high ceilings and intricate Middle Eastern architecture. As they passed from room to room, each more lavish than the last, every servant they passed bowed at the sight of Sharif, with obvious deep respect.

So many rooms, so many hallways. Irene grew increasingly worried that she'd ever be able to find her way back again. After they went up a flight of stairs, she expected to see some sort of servants' wing. Instead, the rooms just got more lavish still. A sudden fear seized her.

"Your bedroom isn't in the same hallway as mine, is it?"

Sharif looked down at her with his inscrutable black eyes. "Why, Miss Taylor," he said softly, "are you asking for directions to my room?"

"Yes—I mean, no! I mean..."

He tilted his head. After a full day since his morning shave, there was a dark shadow along his sharp jawline that made him seem even more powerfully masculine. "Your room is close to mine. That won't be a problem, I presume?"

She licked her lips. "I'm not sure that's a good idea."

"Why?"

Because part of her was still afraid she might forget herself some night and sleepwalk naked into his bed, just like hapless What's-her-name who got fired. If Sharif knew the hot dreams she'd had last night, starring him... And he was her *employer* now.

Irene shook her head helplessly. "I just wouldn't want you to think..."

He paused, his sensual lips curved as he looked down at her, close but not touching. "Think what, Miss Taylor?"

Her voice came out in an embarrassing little squeak. "Never mind."

Sharif stared at her for a long moment, then setting his jaw, he turned away with a swirl of robes. "This way."

She followed him down the new hallway, still shaking with the ache of repressed desire. As they went down the marble halls and approached the royal apartments within the palace, the hallways grew more crowded, not just with servants, but also with the emir's advisers, serious men all in white robes, some of whom bowed as Sharif passed, others who merely inclined the tip of their heads. But in the faces of them all, Irene saw the most sincere respect.

"They love you," she said.

He glanced at her. "Don't sound so surprised," he said dryly.

"It's just that—I don't see respect like this for leaders anymore."

His jaw tightened. "They just remember how it was. Before."

"Before?"

"Here we are, Miss Taylor." His voice had gone cold and formal again. He pushed open a door, giving only a brief glance inside before he indicated she should go forward, while he waited in the hall.

Irene stepped into the room.

"Oh," she gasped. She took two steps inside, looking at the enormous bed, the view over the Persian Gulf, complete with her own balcony. The lavishness of the Middle Eastern decor was like nothing she'd ever seen before. She'd thought her room at the Falconeri villa in Lake Como had been spectacular, but it had been like a roadside motel room, compared to this!

"This whole room is for me?" she said faintly.

Sharif did not enter the room.

"Dinner is at nine."

She turned back to face him, her cheeks flooded with

heat as, against her will, she immediately pictured an intimate dinner for two, with total privacy. "I don't know if—"

"My sister will be joining us."

"Oh." Her blush deepened. "Then of course I will be there."

"Of course, since I bid it." His voice reminded her of her place here, and who was king. But his sensual dark eyes said something else.

She had to get a hold of herself!

"Thank you, Your Highness. I look forward to meeting my new charge."

With an answering bow of his head, he left her.

Irene closed the door behind her, sagging back against it as she exhaled. Then she looked slowly around her incredible bedroom. It was twice as big as the whole *house* she'd grown up in. She looked at the silk damask, the fanciful decorations, the gold leaf on the walls. And most surprising of all: her meager possessions from her rented studio apartment in Paris had miraculously been transported here. How the heck had he done that? What was he, magic?

Well. Yes.

If not magic, he was a magician who knew well how to pull invisible strings.

But they had a deal. A business arrangement. Her whole family's future was now riding on it. She couldn't forget that. One slip-up, one indication that she was still desperately fighting her attraction to him—now more than ever— and she'd be thrown out as ruthlessly as her predecessor.

She just had to forget everything that had happened in Italy, that was all. Forget the heat of his skin on hers when he'd taken her hand. Forget his smile. The intensity of his dark eyes. The strength of his body against hers as he'd swayed her to the music. Forget the passion of the kiss that had set her on fire.

She had to forget the huskiness of his voice as he said, *I am seducing you, Irene.*

The Emir of Makhtar, powerful billionaire, absolute ruler of a wealthy Persian Gulf kingdom, had once wanted her—a plain, simple nobody. She had to forget that miracle. *Forget it ever happened.*

Irene put a tremulous hand to her bruised, tingling lips, still aching from his kiss the night before.

But how could she?

Sharif paced three steps across the dining hall.

Irene was late. It surprised him.

So was his sister, but that left him less surprised. He'd briefly spoken with Aziza earlier, after showing Irene— *Miss Taylor*, he corrected himself firmly—to her room. His sister had been glad to see him for about three seconds, before he'd informed her, without explanation, that he'd fired Gilly and hired a new companion.

"But she was going to take me to Dubai tomorrow," Aziza had wailed. "Isn't it bad enough that you're forcing me to go through with this wedding? Do you also have to take away my only friend? I'm trapped here! Like a prisoner!"

And she'd fallen with copious sobs to her enormous pink canopy bed.

Irritated by the memory, Sharif paced back across the dining hall. He leaned his hand against the stone fireplace. It had been built nearly nineteen years before, along with the rest of the palace, in perfect replica of the previous building, which had been left in ruins during the brief dark months of civil war after his father's sudden death.

Aziza could blame him if she wanted for her choice to marry. But he would not go back on his word. He would not risk scandal and instability. Not for his own happiness. Nor even for his sister's.

He heard a noise and whirled around, only to discover his chief of staff. "Yes?"

The man bowed. "I regret to inform you, sire," he said sadly, "that I carry a message from the sheikha. She wished me to relay to you that she is unwell and will not be attending you at dinner, nor meeting her new companion."

Sharif's eyes narrowed. Irritation rose almost to an unbearable level as he pictured his spoiled, petulant little sister coming up with this plan as a way to register her complaint and get her own way. The fact that it shamed him, as host and brother, that she was refusing to appear for dinner and meet her new companion would only make her happier still.

"Did she. Very well," he said coldly. "Please inform the kitchen that no meals are to be brought to her room. Perhaps if she grows hungry, she will remember her manners."

"Yes, sire," Hassan said unhappily, and bowed again.

Sharif watched him go. He'd told Irene the truth. His chief of staff would be a fine choice for any woman to take as husband—a steady, good-hearted man of some consequence, and at twenty-eight, he was probably even looking for a bride. And yet, when he'd seen the young man starting to walk Irene to her room, seeing them together had caused a strange twist to Sharif's insides. He hadn't liked it. At all. It had almost felt like—jealousy. A sensation he wasn't used to feeling.

His body tightened as he remembered how she'd trembled in his arms, when he'd seized her lips with his own. How she'd thrown her arms around him and leaned against his body, kissing him back softly and uncertainly at first, then with increasing force and a passion that matched his own. His one and only failure at seducing a woman. Ironic, since it was the one he'd wanted most. He still ached to possess her.

Sex is sacred. It's a promise without words. A promise I'll only make to the man who will love me for the rest of his life, and I can love for the rest of mine.

He pushed the memory away. He wasn't going to waste any more time hungering for a woman he could not have. He was bewildered by her idealistic decision, yes. But he respected it. And realized now why he'd envied it.

Because love, or even lust, would never coexist with marriage in Sharif's life. That pure lovemaking Irene had spoken of so wistfully would never be in the cards for him.

Few people have that anyway, he told himself harshly. *Lust is brief, marriage is long and romantic love is a fantasy.*

Turning away, Sharif lifted a silver goblet from the polished wood dining table. He took a long drink of cold water. He wiped his mouth.

Irene's nervousness around him, the way she held his gaze for longer than strictly necessary, told him she still desired him. If he truly wanted to seduce her, in spite of her romantic ideals— He cut off the thought. He wasn't that much of a selfish bastard. He would leave her alone. Let her go. Even after that searing kiss. Even though he wanted her more than he'd wanted any woman. He would not allow himself to...

"Sorry I'm late."

Irene's voice was breezy, unrepentant. It caused heat to flash through his body. He turned, but whatever mocking reply he'd been about to make died forgotten on his lips when he saw her.

She was dressed in white, the color of purity. Could her meaning be any more plain? But even if he knew what she was telling him, her plan had backfired. Because the white of her modest dress only served to set off her creamy skin. Her thick black hair looked exotic, her brown eyes mysterious and deep as midnight. She looked like a woman any man would willingly die for.

Her expression darkened as she looked left and right. "Where is your sister?"

Sister? He struggled to remember. Oh yes. "Aziza..." His voice was hoarse. He cleared his throat. "I regret my sister is not feeling well. She will be unable to join us tonight."

Irene glared at him suspiciously.

"Not my idea, I assure you," he said. "But if my sister is not hungry, I certainly am." The understatement of the year. "Come. I'm sure my chef is growing antsy, as his dinner has certainly been ready for a while now."

"Oh." For the first time, Irene looked uncomfortable. "I am sorry. I didn't think of that." She bit her lip. "But just the two of us—I mean, it doesn't really seem appropriate to—"

"To what? To eat?"

"Alone. Just the two of us."

"What would you like me to do to avoid gossip? Invite someone else to join us? Perhaps my chief of staff?" he said coldly.

Her eyes brightened. "Good idea."

He scowled. "Unfortunately he has other duties. He's already gone home to his family."

"To his girlfriend?"

"His mother. You take a great deal of interest in him for someone you just met."

She shrugged. "He's just the only person I've met. Other than the three different people I had to ask for directions to find the dining room, that is."

So that was why she was late. He'd thought she'd done it on purpose, to taunt him. He relaxed as the servants brought out plates of food, stews of chicken and meat, rice, vegetables and traditional Makhtari flatbread. The air around them suddenly smelled of spice, of cardamom and saffron. She sniffed appreciatively.

"Tell me more about your country," she said, digging into her dinner. "It is my home now, at least for the next few months." She took another bite of chicken and sighed with pleasure. "You said it wasn't always like this."

"No." He wasn't sure how much he wanted to tell her. "If you are going to be companion to my sister, you'll be expected to know," he said finally. "When my father died, the country fell into civil war."

The color drained from her face. She set down her fork. "Oh, no."

"My father had held everything together. With him suddenly gone, none of the great families could agree on anything. Except that they didn't want a fifteen-year-old boy on the throne."

"How bad did it get?" she said quietly.

Gripping his silverware, he looked down at his plate.

"Half this city burned," he said. "By the time I arrived back here from boarding school, this palace was ash. One day, I was a boy studying astronomy and calculus and history. The next, my father was dead, my mother prostrate with grief and rage, my home destroyed. And my country in flames."

Silence fell in the shadows of the dining room.

Slowly, Sharif lifted his gaze to hers. He saw tears streaming down Irene's stricken, beautiful face. Strange, when he felt nothing. He'd stopped feeling anything a long time ago.

"What did you do?" she choked out.

"What I had to."

"You were only fifteen."

"I grew up quickly. My mother's brother, and my father's

former adviser, the vizier, were both trying to claim themselves as regent until my eighteenth year. They were destroying Makhtar in their battle. Even at fifteen, I could see that." Feeling that he wanted to finish the topic as quickly as possible, he set down the goblet. "So I made the deal I had to make to save my country. Then I brought Aziza to live with us. She was a baby, a newborn."

"She wasn't living with you before?"

"She was with her mother."

Irene frowned. "But your mother was with you."

"Aziza is my half sister. The day I lost my father, she became doubly an orphan. She lost both her parents."

"You can't mean…" Irene gave a low gasp. "Aziza's *mother* was your father's mistress, who killed him?"

He gave a single nod.

Her hands covered her mouth as if she couldn't bear the pain—but why? Sharif wondered, as if from a distance. It was not her pain to bear. Why was she taking it so personally?

"And you still brought her here? Raised her?"

"Aziza had been left with a paid servant. I couldn't abandon her. She is my *sister*." Setting his jaw, he looked away. His voice was thick as he said, "Nothing that happened was her fault. She needed me."

For a long moment, Irene looked at him.

"You have a heart," she whispered.

He set his jaw. "What else could I have done? Refused to even see her, as my mother did? Leave her to the orphanage or worse? She's a princess of the blood. My sister."

"You love her."

"Yes." No matter how Aziza irritated the hell out of him sometimes, Sharif could never forget the first time he'd seen her, a tiny baby crying so desperately she was nearly choking with piteous sobs. He'd never allow anyone to hurt her.

"You have a heart," Irene repeated quietly. As if she still couldn't quite believe it.

"Anyone would have done the same."

"Your mother didn't."

Sharif felt a lump in his throat. "Don't be hard on her. She'd just lost everything. She barely was able to look at me, either. Her heart gave out. She died a few months later."

"So you were alone—ruling the country—at just fifteen? With a newborn baby sister to watch over?" She shook her head. "How did you do it? At fifteen, I could barely manage a part-time job after school to pay our utility bills. How did you manage to pull your whole country back together? All alone?"

Here it was, then. The one thing she didn't know. The thing he'd been dreading to tell her. The thing that he had been trying to force himself to face.

Sharif put both his hands against the table. "Because even then, I understood human nature." He wouldn't be a coward. He wouldn't. He looked at her. "I encouraged my uncle to believe he would have great influence over me, to make him give up the idea of a regency. And as for the vizier— to him, I made a promise." He said quietly, "I promised to marry his daughter."

Irene stared at him, as if she hadn't heard right. She blinked.

"You…" She swallowed. "You're engaged?"

"Officially, it has not yet been announced." He looked back at the water, wishing for something stronger. In the royal palace he respected his country's long custom and abstained from alcohol. How he wished he did not honor such niceties at the moment. He felt he could have drunk an entire bottle of scotch as he forced himself to say aloud the very words he'd been desperately trying not to think about for months. "But it is time for me to make good on that promise. Our engagement will be announced after Aziza's wedding."

"Do you—" She flinched, then whispered, "Do you love her?"

"It's not a question of love. I made a promise. I cannot go back on my word. Even though I might wish otherwise." He looked away. "When my time comes, I will make the sacrifice."

"*Sacrifice.* You speak of it as if it's a death."

"Because it is," he said in a low voice. "For these last few months of freedom I've tried to enjoy what pleasures I could. But even then, even now, I feel the bars starting to close in."

Irene stared at him for a long moment, and he saw her beautiful face struggle between sympathy and anger. Anger won.

"How could you?" she said. "How could you live like you do—Europe's biggest playboy…"

"My reputation as a playboy might be more than my actions truly deserve…"

"And all along—you've been committed to marry someone?" She rose to her feet, her face a mask of fury. "How could you flirt with me when you were promised to another woman? How could you try to seduce me? How could you *kiss* me?"

"Because I'm trying not to think about it," he snapped, rising to his feet in turn, meeting her fury with his own—except Sharif's anger was cold and deep and edged with despair. "Can you understand what it is like to despise someone to the depths of your soul, and know you'll still be forced to call her your wife? To have a child with her?" He paced by the dining table, his jaw taut as he swiveled to glare at her. "You asked why I was at Falconeri's wedding. I barely know the man! I went because…"

"Because?"

"Because I was trying to accept my fate!" he exploded. Turning away, he forced his voice to calm down, forced his heart to slow. He took a deep breath. "I went because I needed to feel like any ridiculous fantasies I ever had about marriage were wrong. I knew Falconeri was marrying his housekeeper for the sake of their baby. I thought, if I went to the wedding, I would discover the truth beyond their happy facade. I'd discover they could barely tolerate each other. Instead, I saw something different." He lifted his gaze to hers. "And I met you."

Looking at Irene's beautiful, honest, stricken face, emotion filled Sharif's heart. He found himself yearning for what he'd never known, and what he'd never have.

Their eyes locked. Irene's expression became sad, vulnerable, filled with grief. "How could you?"

He looked at her.

"How could I not?" he said in a low voice.

Tears streamed down her face as she shook her head. "Never kiss me again," she choked out, and fled the room.

CHAPTER SIX

SHE SHOULDN'T BE crying.

She had nothing to cry about.

Sharif—*His Highness*, Irene corrected herself savagely as she stomped up the stairs toward her room—was her employer, nothing more. So what if he'd kissed her in Italy while virtually engaged to another woman? It wasn't as if Irene ever thought they might be together. She'd lost absolutely nothing. In fact, she should be glad to be proven right—Sharif was every bit the heartless womanizer she'd first believed him to be!

Though maybe not *completely* heartless…

Can you understand what it is like to despise someone to the depths of your soul, and know you'll still be forced to call her your wife? To have a child with her?

No! She pushed away the memory of his hoarse voice and bleak eyes. She wasn't going to have an ounce of sympathy for him. She was *not*!

I made the deal I had to make to save my country.

Childishly, she covered her ears as she continued to rush down the hall. Things were right and wrong. Black and white. There were no shades or colors between. Only excuses. She wouldn't let herself feel a whit of sympathy. What he'd done was *wrong*!

Irene somehow managed to find her way back to her

room. The dinner that had seemed so delicious was now churning inside her belly. She took a shower, brushed her teeth and caught a look at her face in the bathroom mirror. Her hand trembled as she set down her toothbrush. She wiped her mouth with the back of her hand. Then froze.

She still felt his kiss there. She touched her lips with her fingertips. She could still feel his mouth on hers, the way he'd claimed them so passionately as his own on that night of fireworks in Italy. She could still feel the way she'd kissed him back, with a lifetime of pent-up loneliness and need. With intoxicating hope.

Irene dropped her hand. She couldn't think about that now. Glancing out her window, toward the moonswept Persian Gulf beyond the palace, she swallowed over the lump in her throat. Whatever it had been between them—a lie? a dream?—it was definitely over.

Climbing into her bed in the huge room, Irene pulled the luxurious sheets up to her chin. What would Dorothy have told her to do? She'd have said that Irene shouldn't sell her integrity, not for any price. She squeezed her eyes shut. She'd couldn't remain in Makhtar, under the same roof with him. Not now. She'd take the first commercial flight out of Makhtar City tomorrow morning, back to...

Her eyes flew open.

To where?

To her hometown in southern Colorado, to join her mother, drunk and bitter, and her sister, growing old before her time? She'd give up her newfound joy at the thought that she could take care of them?

Irene took a deep breath. No way.

She wasn't going anywhere. She'd stay here the rest of November, then December and January and part of February. She could do it. She had to do it. So the answer was simple.

She wouldn't be even slightly attracted to her dangerous, sexy, all-but-engaged boss. She'd look into Sharif's face and be cold, cold, cold all the way to her heart...

She thought again of his handsome face, his dark, bleak eyes.

Can you understand what it is like to despise someone to the depths of your soul...

She wasn't going to feel an ounce of sympathy. Why should she, for a man who had everything in the world, who was handsome, rich and powerful, the ruler of a wealthy Persian Gulf nation? The man had everything!

Except love. Or even hope of love, until the day he died...

Exhaling, Irene turned on her other side, squeezing her eyes shut. She would stay here and work, but nothing more. She wasn't going to think of him for another moment, except as anything but her boss. She wouldn't... She vowed, yawning. *Wouldn't...*

Except she saw Sharif standing in the moonlight on the edge of Lake Como, dressed all in black.

What are you doing here? she choked out. He was the last person she'd expected to see.

He turned. The silvery light frosted the edge of his dark hair, illuminating his black eyes.

Don't you know? he said softly, coming toward her. She shook her head. He pulled her into his arms, brushing back tendrils of her hair. His expression was different than she'd ever seen before. He looked tender, hopeful, yearning as he searched her gaze.

I'm seducing you, Irene, he said in a low voice. Their eyes locked. *I've been waiting to seduce you for all my life.*

Waiting for you...for you. The words echoed across the moon-swept Italian lake mockingly, like the plaintive cry of night birds, and each echo caused a new twist in her heart, somewhere between ecstasy and grief, because she knew she'd been waiting for him, too. But all the waiting was in vain.

But why? Weren't they meant to be together? Hadn't they been waiting in their loneliness for the other?

Sharif's expression changed, became stark with need. As if claiming her, he whispered her name. She was breathless, spellbound, as he slowly lowered his mouth to hers.

Come to me, he whispered. *Be with me. Love me.* With every syllable of every word, she could feel the brush of his lips against hers, so close, tantalizingly close. His last two words were so faint she heard them only with her heart.

Save me.

And at that, her soul could no longer resist what her body hungered for. Wrapping her arms around him, she drew him against her and pressed her lips to his. She nearly gasped from the explosive sensation of his mouth against hers. She pulled him down against her, sinking back against the soft bed. Her hands twisted in his hair. She felt the deliciously heavy weight of him pressing her deep into the mattress, and gasped against his lips. She needed to feel more of this, more…

Wait a minute. An alarm went off in the back of her brain.

Mattress?

Irene's eyes flew open. She suddenly realized two things. First: She'd been dreaming about him on the Italian lake. Second: She wasn't dreaming now.

Sharif's body was over hers on the bed. His weight on hers. His lips on her. So hot. So sweet. So impossible to resist…

Then Irene remembered why she must resist, and she pushed him away. Hard.

"What are you *doing*?" she cried.

"What are *you* doing?"

Sitting up furiously, she turned on the light on her bedside stand. Sharif was sitting on the edge of her bed in a dark shirt and trousers.

"I told you never to kiss me again!" she accused.

"You," he replied pointedly, "kissed me."

"Don't be—" Irene paused at the sudden humiliating memory of pulling him down against her on the bed, of pressing her lips to his. Oh, dear heaven, was it possible that she, while lost in her dream, could have—

Irene shook her head furiously. "You shouldn't be in my bedroom!"

"That's not what you seemed to think a moment ago."

"I thought I was dreaming," she retorted, then immediately wished she hadn't.

His dark eyebrow lifted. "Dreaming of me, were you?"

Her cheeks flamed with heat. "It's the middle of the night! What are you doing in here? Get out!"

Sharif rose from her bed, absolutely calm, as if what had just happened hadn't affected him at all—even while it had left her overwhelmed, humiliated, intoxicated and furious. Stupid dreams! She hated them all!

He took a deep breath.

"I need your help," he said quietly. "I need you to come with me. Right now."

She stared at him. "Have you lost your mind? It's—" she twisted her head to look at the elegant, nineteenth-century antique bedside clock "—three in the morning! I'm not going anywhere with—"

"My sister has run away."

Irene cut off her angry words. She looked at his face in the dimly lit room.

"Run away? Are you sure?" She narrowed her eyes. "This better not be some kind of joke—"

"Do you think I would joke about my sister?"

She looked at him.

"No." She sighed as all the anger went out of her, making her deflate like a balloon. Pushing her blankets aside, she stood up. Amusement flickered in his eyes as he looked at her long flannel nightgown, which went up to her neck and down to her wrists.

"Is something funny?" she demanded.

He cleared his throat. "Not a thing."

Sheesh, did no one wear old-fashioned nightgowns anymore? Apparently none of Sharif's lovers. Whatever. Irene liked it. A deliberate choice from all the tight knit camisoles and hot pants her mom and older sister used to lounge around in, on the off chance a current boyfriend might stop by the house for a booty call.

Irene lifted her chin, silently daring him to say something about her choice in sleepwear so she could bite off his head. Wisely, he didn't.

"Aziza took no bodyguards. Only her old nurse is with her. It might be innocent. It might not be. Either way, I need you to help me find her. Quickly. Before any of the servants notice. Because once they do…"

Biting her lip, Irene nodded. Although many employees in a large household were loyal to death and would die before they said anything, others would find the gossip too delicious a currency to resist telling at least a friend or two. From there, rumors would spread like wildfire. "But why would she run away?"

Sharif's face looked grimmer still. "*Why* is irrelevant. What matters is finding her. Quietly. Before the news gets back to her fiancé and the whole wedding is in an uproar."

"But why," she persisted, "would your sister run away from her own fiancé? If I were planning to marry, I'd be counting down the days. Wild horses wouldn't drag me from the man I loved…"

"You are a private citizen. You have freedom that Aziza and I never will."

"But—"

"You don't need to understand. Just get dressed and come with me now."

Was it possible his sister wasn't keen on this marriage? But looking at Sharif's hard expression and the impatient set of his shoulders, Irene knew there was no point in asking. She'd ask Aziza herself, once they found her. "Give me three minutes."

He didn't move.

"Wait outside!"

"Three minutes," he warned her, "and I'm coming back in."

She believed him. As soon as he went out in the hall and closed the door, she flew to her closet, putting on the quickest clothes possible, a casual maxi dress and a jean jacket. She pulled her unruly dark hair into a hasty ponytail and grabbed her purse. Three minutes? She'd done it in two. She opened her door. "Ready."

He'd been leaning against the wall. He straightened, his face shocked.

Now she was the one to be amused. "Surprised?"

"I've never known a woman who could—" He pressed his lips together, then said tersely, "You're different. That's all."

Not totally different, sadly. One of the things that had given her speed was that she didn't want him back in her bedroom. But even now, against her will, she remembered how it had felt to have his body on top of hers. How it had felt to twine her hands in his hair as she pulled him hard against her and kissed him so deep she never wanted to let go…

"Um." Her cheeks turned pink. So much for treating him only as an employer. She'd kissed him. Told him she'd been *dreaming* about him! Trying to pretend the kiss had never happened seemed like the best bet. "Do you have any idea where she might have gone?"

He gave a single abrupt nod, then gestured for her to follow him down the silent hall. Her flip-flops thwacked against the marble floor, so she took them off to pad silently in bare feet.

Once they were out of the palace, he held up his hand harshly. She froze, confused. Then she saw that the gesture wasn't for her, but for the bodyguards outside. For the first time since she'd known him, he was leaving all the bodyguards behind.

"Are we taking a plane?" she ventured.

Still walking, he shook his head. "It would involve too many people. I don't want to take that risk until I know what she's doing. We'll have to travel in a way that no one will look twice at us. In a way that makes us invisible."

Irene followed him across the gated courtyard, the only light the moon, the only sound the burble of the unseen fountain. He stopped in front of a building with large sliding doors. He paused, his hands clenched at his sides. She looked up and saw an expression on his face that truly shocked her to the core.

Fear.

She'd never thought Sharif could be afraid of anything. But she tried to imagine how she would feel if her sister had run away. If her mother was missing and unable to be found. The powerless fear that would grip her heart.

"We'll find her, Sharif," she whispered, trying to offer

comfort. "We will. I'll help you find her." She reached for his hand. "Everything will be all right. You'll see."

For a moment, he looked down at her hand.

"Thank you," he said in a low voice. He pulled his hand away, the brief moment of vulnerability gone, the ruthless air of command returned, and he wrenched open the garage door. "Let's go."

"I still can't believe this is your idea of invisible," Irene grumbled a few hours later.

Sharif gave her a wicked grin from the driver's seat of the insanely expensive red sports car. "Just trying to fit in."

"Fit in," she snorted. She stretched in the passenger seat, yawning. "You—"

Then she saw the bright skyscrapers in the distance. Her mouth snapped shut as her eyes went wide.

She breathed, "Is that—?"

"Yes," he said. "Dubai."

It was still early morning, and though the sun was barely in the sky, already it was growing hot. She'd slept through the first few hours of darkness, and had just a dim memory of a perfectly modern highway across bare, empty desert, and a sky that was inky black with stars.

They'd entered the United Arab Emirates at the Makhtari border, where they were welcomed with deep respect and courtesy that was fit for—well, a king; and yet with discretion that made it clear they understood this was not a state visit. Against her will, Irene had wondered if Sharif had done this trip before, and with whom.

They'd stopped for gas at a station outside Abu Dhabi. She'd gone inside and discovered the station was not that different from the ones at home. Same brand of candy bars, same sodas, same everything—except the labels had Arabic writing on one side and English on the other. Using her credit card, she bought a bag of chewy fruit candy and tucked it in her purse. She also got two coffees and brought them out to Sharif, who'd just finished refueling the flashy red car.

He'd stared at the outstretched paper cup, frowning, as if she were offering him jewels, not an espresso worth ten dirhams. Taking a long drink, he gave a sigh of satisfaction. He looked at her, his eyes deep. "Thank you."

"It's no big deal," she'd said uncomfortably. "It's just coffee." She tilted her head. "Aren't you used to people bringing you stuff?"

"Yes. Servants. Sycophants. But not—" He cut himself off. He looked at the coffee, then shook his head as his lips twisted upward on the edges. "It's not poisoned, right? As a warning to make sure I never try to kiss you again?"

She snorted, then gave a wistful sigh. "I can't really blame you for that. I'm the one who kissed *you* this time."

His eyes met hers sharply, and for a single insane moment, electricity crackled between them.

No! She would not let herself want what she could not have!

Turning, she opened the passenger door. "Your sister," she said.

"Yes." His voice was low. Getting back into the car, he started the engine.

But as they drove north from Abu Dhabi, she'd looked out the window, far too aware of Sharif next to her in the small interior of the sports car. She tried to focus on the gleaming buildings, the desert, the brand-new, immaculate highway with road signs written in Arabic, with English translations beneath.

Now, as they approached Dubai, Irene said, "How do you know she's here?"

"She was angry at me yesterday. For firing Gilly."

"Gilly?"

"Her companion who thought it would be amusing to ambush me while she was naked in my bed."

"Oh."

"Gilly was not a good influence on Aziza. She convinced her that things—luxury handbags, jewels, royal titles and money—would make her happy."

Irene leaned her arm against the window of the Ferrari and said sardonically, "I can see why that would bother you."

He gave her a sideways glance. "She convinced my sister to accept the Sultan of Zaharqin's proposal, because of his lavish gifts and high position. It wasn't my idea. But now I've given my word. I cannot allow her to back out."

"Nineteen-year-olds change their minds all the time."

"If my subjects do not believe my word is inviolate, how can I expect their respect? Their obedience?" Setting his jaw, he stared at the skyscrapers of Dubai ahead of them. "I suspected Aziza might come to our vacation villa here…"

"Vacation villa, huh? For when you're bored with being waited on hand and foot at the palace?"

"The guard called me a few hours ago. He confirmed that my sister's there, with only her nurse as chaperone. I'm grateful it wasn't worse."

"Nurse? Is she ill?"

"Nanny, I guess you would call her. Basimah virtually raised her."

"Why didn't she call and warn you what Aziza was up to, then?"

"Basimah?" He snorted. "She's protective of Aziza like a mother bear to a cub. She sees me as the enemy. Especially since the engagement."

"Hard to believe. So why has your sister changed her mind about the wedding? Did the sultan send her a gift she didn't like? Last season's handbags? The wrong color of jewels?"

He stared grimly forward at the widening highway, as the traffic on the outskirts of Dubai increased. He said reluctantly, "The Sultan of Zaharqin is older than she is."

"How much older?"

He paused. "Forty years."

For an instant, Irene just stared at him, wide-eyed. Then she exploded.

"You are making a *nineteen-year-old girl* marry a man *three times her age*? Are you out of your *mind*?"

"Aziza agreed to it. If she's changed her mind since, her duty is to serve her people," he said coldly. "Just as it is mine."

"It's ridiculous!"

"No, Miss Taylor." Sharif's eyes were focused on the road, but his jaw was tight as he said, "*You* are ridiculous to criticize something you do not understand. You have no responsibility to anyone except yourself and your own family. You do not know what it means to rule a country. It is Aziza's privilege and her duty to protect and defend all of our people. That means doing everything she can."

"But she is only nineteen—"

His hands tightened on the steering wheel. "I was fifteen."

"You grew up early."

"So did you." He gave her a hard, quick look. "You've spent so much time asking why my sister ran away. Why did you?"

She stared at him. "I didn't run away."

"You left your home, went to New York, then thousands of miles across the ocean to take a job in Paris. Then you traveled even farther to the Middle East. What else would you call it except running away?"

"I just needed a job…"

"You had a good job in New York. But you chose to leave, when a position became available working for your employer's cousin in Paris. It's not just about money. You wanted distance."

Her whole body went cold. If he already knew that…

"How much do you know about my past?" she whispered.

Sharif gave her a dark look.

"Everything. You think I would have hired you if I did not? I had a complete dossier on you before the plane even landed in Makhtar."

The chill in her heart became a freeze. "Then you know my mother and sister…" Her voice cracked.

"Yes." His expression changed, became gentle. "I know everything."

"And you don't—want me a million miles from your sister?"

He shook his head.

"But reputation matters so much to you—"

"*Honor* matters to me," he corrected sharply. "And you are not to blame for the choices others have made. Even if they're people you love." His knuckles were white on the steering wheel, and she suddenly remembered that Sharif, too, had good reason to believe this.

They drove in silence. Then he said, "The only thing I couldn't understand from the report is how you got that first job in New York. Why would a wealthy family on Park Avenue choose you from their agency, and send for you all the way from Colorado?"

"I was so young and from a small town in the West." She gave him a sudden impish grin. "They wanted a nanny with a wholesome, sheltered background."

He snorted, then sobered. "You are sheltered in your way," he murmured. "You protect your heart."

"Yes." Her smile faded. "And you're wrong to force Aziza to marry against hers."

Sharif's expression turned to a scowl. "With your beliefs about the sanctity of marriage, I thought you would support me."

Ahead of them, she saw gleaming skyscrapers, with futuristic architecture twisting improbably high, high, high into the blue sky. "Marriage isn't just a bunch of words on paper. The commitment can only come from your heart. From love."

Sharif's lip curled. He turned forward to stare stonily at the road. "Spare me your further thoughts on the subject."

Her cheeks turned hot. "Look," she tried again, "as ruler of your country, I understand your sense of honor, but surely even you can see that—"

"You, Miss Taylor, may lead your life however you want." He tossed her a contemptuous glance. "Make lifelong decisions based on romantic fantasies. Break engagements, marry on a whim, divorce as often as you like. You are free to make whatever self-indulgent, foolish choices you wish..."

"Foolish!" she cried. *"Self-indulgent!"*

"But my sister and I are not." He tilted his head coldly. "Tell me, Miss Taylor. How many happy marriages have you seen in real life? Can you name even one?"

"Emma and Cesare!"

"Too easy. They're newlyweds. Anyone can be happy for four days. Who else?"

She said slowly, "I was virtually raised by an elderly couple, neighbors who lived down the street. They were barely out of high school when they eloped to a judge's office, but they were married for over fifty years. They never loved anyone but each other. They raised children, they took care of each other, grew old together. They died one day apart…"

"After fifty years of marriage, they were probably happy to die."

"Shut up!" Irene shouted. "You don't know what you're talking about!"

"Oh, you can give out the truth, but you can't take it?"

"They loved each other! I saw it! Their house was the only place I ever felt happy or safe in my whole childhood!"

Silence fell.

"Ah," he said softly. "At last. The reason for your iron-clad virginity. You think if you hold out for marriage, you'll be happy and safe for the rest of your life. But it doesn't work like that."

"No? How does it work, then—sleeping around with women you don't even like, that you can't even remember? How is it working for you, knowing you'll never truly have a partner, someone to watch your back, someone to protect and adore? Tell me more about your great life, Sharif, how wonderful it feels to never love anyone, or have anyone ever love you back!" She shook her head, blinking away furious tears. "You're just scared to admit I'm right, because if you did—"

"Enough." He suddenly sat up straight, every inch the arrogant, untouchable Emir of Makhtar. His broad-shouldered anger filled the space of the Ferrari. "I've allowed your honesty, even appreciated it, because it serves my ends. I need my sister to have a companion I can trust. But do not speak to me of *love.*" His low voice dripped scorn. "Love is nothing more than selfish delusion that weak-minded people allow to come before

duty. Before honor. Before even their own good. People destroy their lives, and the lives of their families, over this poisonous thing that you call *love*."

The sports car seemed to be going faster and faster through the heavy traffic, until they were darting around the big trucks and luxury sedans on the road. Sharif turned the car off the highway in a hard right, barely slowing down.

He'd been right about one thing, Irene thought unhappily. Their flashy red sports car fit right in. No one gave it a second glance.

She took a deep breath.

"I told you when you hired me," she said shakily, "that you might regret it. Because I speak the truth."

"It's not truth. It's your *opinion*. One that you are free to have because you have nothing to lose. You do not have the lives of two hundred thousand people depending on you."

"No, but—"

"Share your feelings with me, Irene Taylor. Talk your head off whenever you want. But if you say one word of it to my sister—if you preach to her about love that lasts forever—that is your last day under my employment. You will be sent back home without pay. Do you understand?"

Setting her jaw, Irene looked away.

"Do you understand?"

"Yes." She gripped the edge of her leather seat as he turned the car sharply into a private driveway. Ahead of them, she saw a stucco fence at least ten feet high, with a guardhouse at the gate.

The air in the car, which had crackled with such sensual energy in the gas station outside Abu Dhabi, now seemed frozen over. How was it possible, Irene wondered miserably, that feelings could burn so hot one moment and so cold the next? Just a few hours ago, she'd been crying at the thought of his engagement.

Now, she would have dearly loved to push him out of the Ferrari and leave him in a ditch by the side of the road.

CHAPTER SEVEN

"I CANNOT BELIEVE that you would take such a risk coming here unprotected... Knowing full well that your future husband might hear of this foolish escapade..."

Sharif set his jaw, folding his arms with a scowl as he looked down at his young sister. He'd been lecturing her for some time.

"Of all the selfish, idiotic..."

Aziza sat meekly on an outdoor sofa on the grand terrace of their family's vacation villa, which overlooked an Olympic-size pool and the gleaming brilliance of the Persian Gulf beyond. His sister's eyes were turned down, but he recognized the stubborn set to her jaw. It matched the stubborn expressions of the two women sitting on each side of her.

Old Basimah was on the left, glaring at him with hard beady eyes, her sagging jowls quivering with unspoken fury that he, the elder brother who was merely and unimportantly the emir and absolute ruler of Makhtar, would dare to scold her precious charge.

Ignoring her, Sharif continued harshly, "You must never do such a thing again..."

But at this, the woman sitting on Aziza's other side, holding her hand, looked up sharply.

"She has explained why she came to Dubai, Your Highness," Irene said coolly. "She apologized for not telling you her intention, but surely you would not begrudge the sheikha a simple, discreet weekend vacation." Irene lifted an eyebrow, as if to say, *You, of all people, cannot criticize her for that.* When she saw her mark hit home, she relaxed and gave him a placid smile. "She is not, after all, a prisoner—is she?"

Sharif's scowl deepened. He'd expected that Irene would get along well with his headstrong young sister. He hadn't expected them to become friends so quickly. Or that she would take his sister's side so craftily, in a way he could not easily fight. Aziza knew it, too. There was a reason his sister was arguing in English, not Arabic.

"There are many places to relax," he replied through his teeth, "in Makhtar City."

Irene gave him a sweet smile. "But Her Highness had her heart set on coming here, where she could test her skiing lessons at the indoor ski slope at the Mall of the Emirates." She tilted her head. "She could have requested the use of your private jet, and flown off to a ski resort in Switzerland or Patagonia with an entourage. Instead, she came here simply and privately, at very little expense. Surely her thriftiness should be rewarded, not scolded."

The woman should be in diplomacy, he thought grumpily.

"Of course," he said through gritted teeth. She was not only giving his sister a reasonable defense, she was also obliquely pointing out his lavish spending on his own trips abroad. While not directly giving voice to her disapproval of Aziza's coming wedding, she was undermining his authority and giving his younger sister greater confidence in her decisions, to better fight him later. *Well played*, he thought. But Irene didn't know who she was dealing with.

Sharif looked down at his sister. Aziza's plump cheeks

were still stained with tears, her hands listless in her lap. She was, after all, just nineteen. He himself had first started taking illicit weekends himself at that age as a way to escape from the pressures of the palace. That was what he'd first feared when she'd left—that she was meeting some boy here, some waiter she'd met, or heaven knew what. Thankfully, that wasn't the case. So perhaps—just perhaps—he was being too hard on her.

Sharif took a deep breath. "All I want is for you to be happy…"

Aziza looked up. "How can I be happy?" she cried. "When I'm just waiting, waiting to marry that old man?"

"How indeed?" Irene murmured under her breath.

Thus encouraged, the younger woman glared at her brother and tossed her head defiantly. "It's like having a date with the guillotine!"

Enough was enough.

"You made a promise," he said sharply. "You know your duty. You have yours, just as I have mine…"

"It's not fair! I went from an all-girls boarding school to the palace, and now I'm trapped there until I go to my husband's house, where I'll be trapped for the rest of my life." She shook her head. "You've lived your life for the last nineteen years, Sharif, bossing everyone around as emir, enjoying yourself in London and all over the world. What about me? When is my time to live?"

Sharif looked at the three mutinous feminine faces in front of him and felt momentarily outgunned.

He saw the tenseness of Aziza's trembling shoulders as she sat on the outdoor sofa. Saw the brittle expression on her face. All she'd wanted was a chance to swim and ski and distract herself from the engagement she'd entered into so hastily. He, of all people, could understand this.

"Perhaps in my desire to keep you safe, I haven't given

you enough freedom," he said slowly. "I didn't realize you
felt trapped in the palace, Aziza." He paused. "Shall we
remain in Dubai for a few days? Have a holiday? Perhaps
when you're done skiing, we should go on a shopping ex-
cursion."

"Shopping?" Aziza said hopefully.

"Every bride needs wedding clothes."

"How much can I buy?"

"Anything you want."

Aziza slowly rose to her feet, her eyes wide. "Anything?
Five new handbags? A new wardrobe? Ball gowns? Jewels?"

"Anything and everything."

"Thank you, Sharif! Oh!" she cried, tossing her arms
around him. "You're such a good brother!"

Now, Irene was the one to scowl. And he was the one to
give her back a placid smile, as if to say, *Did you expect to
win so easily? I've been in politics my whole life.*

"It's just what I needed," his young sister said, wiping
her eyes. "It will make me feel so much better."

Sharif smiled at her. This was what he liked best—for
his orders to be met with thanks and joy. But in this case,
he felt he shouldn't take full credit. "Thank Miss Taylor,"
he murmured. "It was her idea."

Irene's lips parted. "It wasn't exactly my—"

"Thank you, Miss Taylor!" Aziza threw her arms around
Irene's shoulders. "You're already so much more fun than
Gilly!" A smug smile crossed the younger woman's face as
she crowed, "Just wait until Alexandra sees all the things
I'm going to buy today—it'll be twice as much as all the
pictures she's been posting from her dorm! I win! I win,
win, win!"

Irene rose heavily to her feet. Sharif saw the sour expression on her face and hid a smile.

He spread his arms wide. "I will have my driver bring the car around. My bodyguards arrived ten minutes ago."

"They did?" Irene said, then: "Of course they did."

Twenty minutes later, the four of them—plus a driver and bodyguard—were in a gray limousine, speeding from the villa to the mall, with the other bodyguards driving SUVs ahead and behind.

Sitting in the back of the limo, Sharif felt Irene's sideways glare. He didn't mind at all. Like his sister, he'd won.

Aziza was settling down, on track to a marriage that would increase the stability and prestige of his small nation. And, he hoped, her older husband would stabilize her. Yes, the Sultan of Zaharqin was older, but he was steady and respectable. It would be a good match. Something that would last, and would in time, as they built their family, lead to mutual respect, Sharif hoped, even affection, between husband and wife.

Stability. Peace. Those were the things he valued, both in his country and in his life. His eyes fell on Irene sitting across from him in the back of the limo.

He wished he could say he felt peaceful now.

They were barreling down the road at a breakneck pace, the driver well accustomed to the traffic laws of Dubai, which were often treated more like suggestions, really, than laws. The battle of wits between him and Irene had his blood flowing. All his senses were aware of her.

Sharif's gaze slowly traveled from the impatient tapping of her foot in those ridiculously casual plastic flip-flops, to the curvaceous outline of her body in the long knit cotton dress. A jean jacket covered her tightly folded arms in the frigid air-conditioning of the Bentley. He saw the angry set of her jaw. The warm creamy hue of her skin. She was staring out the window, her teeth biting down on her full, pink lower lip. She was clearly repressing the words she wished to say, but her body language said it all for her. She'd lost this battle, and she didn't like it.

He couldn't stop looking at her lips, the full sensual lips that had kissed him so suddenly and unexpectedly when he'd gone into her bedroom to wake her. Her beautiful eyes had fluttered open, she'd smiled, whispered something he couldn't hear, then pulled him down hard against her on the bed. His whole body suddenly felt tight, his heart pounding at the memory.

What a woman. If it had been his choice, he would have chosen a woman like this for his queen, angry and sweet, sexy and idealistic and proud. He respected her. Even though it was a pain in his side, he admired the way she'd fought for his sister. Even before she'd met Aziza, she'd been protective of her. She wasn't afraid to fight for what she believed in.

He suddenly wondered what it would be like to fight with Irene every day, having her argue with him furiously over the breakfast table, her deep brown eyes shooting sparks of fire. Then taking her to bed every night, where the fire could explode. It wouldn't always be peaceful. Or stable. And yet it would be, because what was between them, both the good and bad, would always be real...

He cut the thought off. *Real*, he mocked himself. His lip curled. He was starting to sound as bad as Irene. Like a *romantic*. Real?

The promise he had made at fifteen to wed the vizier's daughter was real. His need to protect his people and keep Makhtar prosperous and safe—that was real, too. He would announce his engagement to Kalila as soon as Aziza's wedding was done. Kalila would be his queen, would provide him with the heir he needed.

That was the most real of all. Even if the thought of what he'd need to do to get that heir on Kalila repelled him. She was sly, devious, cold-blooded. It would be like bedding a snake.

Whereas the woman sitting close to him now—

Irene made him feel warm all over. Hot to boiling. She was passionate and alive. Everything she believed, she believed with all her heart. She wore her heart on her sleeve, even if that made her vulnerable, even if she risked looking like a fool. She appealed to him in a way he couldn't explain, not even to himself.

But the longer he knew her, the more beautiful she was. Even now, when she was angry and tapping her foot with self-righteousness, she glowed from within.

He wanted her. Now, more than ever.

Perhaps he'd been too hasty in deciding not to seduce her.

Yes. He straightened in the backseat of the limo, suddenly liking this idea. It was true he had a self-imposed rule about not sleeping with employees. Apart from the risk to the tranquility of his household, it had always just seemed, well, tacky.

But his position on this issue was rapidly evolving.

Just look how distracted he was right now, half out of his mind with desire. His mind was so filled with thoughts, his body so tense with need, that it was probably good he wasn't back at the palace, making decisions that affected the affairs of state. How could he be expected to make rational decisions in the condition he was in?

And Sharif was well experienced sexually. How much worse must it be for Irene, who was not? Every bit of her body language, from her tapping foot, to her teeth biting her pink lip, to her arms crossed tightly over her full breasts, told him that she felt the same overwhelming tension between them.

She wanted to remain a virgin until she was wed. Fine.

But how would she even be able to make a decent choice of husband, in the permanent lifelong decision of marriage, if she was half out of her mind with lust?

He could save her from the bad judgment that a mind clouded by lust could bring. Protect her from rushing headlong into a poorly considered marriage.

For her sake, he could seduce her. For her sake, and for his.

Because he wanted her too much. Even when she was angry. Even when she was blunt. Even when she was annoying him with her wildly wrong ideas. Seducing her, taking her virginity freely given, would help free both of them from this—obsession—so they could each move on with their well-planned lives.

Though he nearly growled aloud at the thought of any future man touching her. He wanted to be her man. He wanted to satiate himself with her, to feel her lips against his own, to fill her, to suckle and taste and caress every inch until she gasped and cried out with pleasure and held him tight, so tight, as if she'd never let him go…

"We're here!" his sister squealed, jarring him from his thoughts. Blinking, he saw they were at the mall entrance.

"Skiing first?" he asked his sister. "Or shopping?"

"Skiing—definitely skiing. Then lunch at the Swiss fondue restaurant with the view over the ski hill…"

"How big is this mall?" Irene said, looking shocked.

"Dubai has the best and biggest malls in the whole world. Everyone knows that."

"Everyone," Irene echoed faintly.

Aziza turned back to him. "Your bodyguards can carry the bags while we shop afterward." She tilted her head, her eyes sparkling beneath her head scarf. "I intend to buy a lot, Sharif," she said warningly. "A lot."

He looked at her. "And I intend not to complain."

"Ah… This is the best day ever." The teenager sighed. Sharif looked from Aziza to the elderly Basimah, whose wrinkled face was almost smiling at him—surely the first time ever? Could a shopping spree really mean so much?

The limo stopped and a bodyguard opened the door. Cooing happily, Aziza and the older woman hopped out.

Irene did not move. She still sat glaring at him, unimpressed. Her foot, still crossed over her leg, was now tapping as if she wanted to do nothing more than give him a hearty kick right out of the back of the limo. "Distracting a teenager from a lifelong decision with a shopping spree at the mall? Isn't that like shooting fish in a barrel?"

"We all distract ourselves in different ways from things we cannot change."

"But she still could—"

"If she was mature enough to accept a proposal, she's mature enough to live with it."

Irene started toward the open car door, then paused just long enough to throw back a glance like a fistful of daggers. "I just hope you're happy."

A gust of hot wind blew inside the car through the open door. Sharif inhaled the lingering vanilla scent of her hair, sensual and warm.

Not yet, he thought. A slow-rising smile lifted his lips. *But I could be.*

Irene floated on her back in the Persian Gulf, staring up at the starry night, feeling the warm water lap against her skin.

After three full days in Dubai, she'd seen everything, she thought. They'd gone to the top of the Burj Khalifa, they'd had high tea at a six-star hotel, the Burj al-Arab, shaped like an enormously high sailboat floating out in the water of the gulf. Now that there was no risk of scandal—

now they had a story of "trousseau shopping" rather than "runaway bride"—Sharif made no effort to hide their presence. Yesterday, they'd taken a private helicopter to Abu Dhabi, where they'd met up with one of Aziza's friends from boarding school and enjoyed Friday brunch with their family at the British Club.

If the other expat families enjoying mimosas on the patio had been shocked to see the Emir of Makhtar invade their quiet club with his entourage, they, being British, had hidden it well and swiftly returned to the pleasures of the morning and talking with their friends.

So much for the sights. Most of the last three days had been spent on one thing: shopping, shopping and more shopping. Irene had enjoyed it at first. It had been a relief to leave the indoor ski slope, after falling on her face again and again in the man-made snow, feeling as ungainly and clumsy as an ox with Sharif's amused eyes on her. At least, she told herself he looked amused. Not smoldering. Not as if he was thinking, every time she fell into the snow, every time he took her hand and pulled her up, that he wanted to kiss her senseless.

Her cheeks still burned when she remembered how she'd kissed him back in Makhtar. Stupid dreams! Look at the trouble they got her into!

She'd tried to keep her distance from Sharif, keeping her focus on Aziza, as they went next to a different mall, where she saw a fish aquarium larger than a building, billed as the largest in the world. There were so many shops, people walking through them dressed in every way from tank tops and shorts to black abayas and face-hiding burqas. Although even they, if you looked closely enough, had high heels peeping out from beneath their hems, and carried ten-thousand-dollar handbags carelessly under their arms.

Watching Sharif buy so many things for his sister,

Irene suddenly regretted she hadn't contacted her mother or sister for a year, other than sending them money from her salary. She bought her mother a floral tea set of bone china and a box of baklava from Lebanon, and for her sister a touristy canvas handbag with DUBAI printed on it with big block letters and pink butterflies. She had it all shipped back home. After buying herself a bag of tasty treats from the biggest candy store she'd ever seen, she was done. Today they'd gone to the Gold Souk, but as Aziza and Basimah pawed through jewelry, Irene's feet had hurt and she couldn't stop yawning. The other two women had shopping stamina that put Irene to shame.

Even Sharif seemed to have infinite patience. He advised his younger sister on her purchases when asked, but always deferred to her choice. Perhaps he wasn't a total disaster as an older brother, she thought grudgingly. Even if he was a total disaster for *her*.

Irene stretched out her body in the warm water, letting all her aches and tensions dissolve, letting her troubles float up to disappear into the soft, humid, starry night. Strange to be alone out here. She'd never imagined that she, Irene Taylor from Lone Pine, Colorado, who'd had her lunch box smashed her first day in kindergarten, and been pelted with insults she hadn't even understood back then, would someday leave that misery behind and live half a world away, in a glamorous villa filled with royalty.

She sighed with pleasure. Aziza had gone upstairs to take photos of her haul to send to friends. Basimah was having a cozy game of cards with the cook. Sharif had disappeared to make phone calls, presumably about affairs of state in Makhtar.

So Irene had pulled on her modest one-piece black swimsuit, wrapped her body in a towel and sneaked outside.

She'd meant only to swim in the villa's enormous pool.

But as the sun had lowered in the sky, she'd found it impossible to resist the streaks of orange and persimmon light sparkling on the gulf. Would the water really feel as hot as a bathtub?

She'd looked around to see if anyone was watching, seen only the distant bodyguards and gates on the edges of the private beach. It seemed like overkill, in a city as bright and modern and safe as Dubai felt to her, but then everything about Sharif's security arrangements always seemed like overkill.

Though when she remembered his heartbreaking story about his parents, she could almost understand why he would go to such extremes for security. And why he would believe romantic love was either illusion, or poison.

Can you understand what it is like, to despise someone to the depths of your soul, and know you'll still be forced to call her your wife? To have a child with her?

Every time Irene remembered his bleak voice, she shuddered. Marrying someone you hated so much, sharing your life with them, your home, your children? It would destroy everything about Sharif. Everything that was, beneath his arrogant bossiness, so bright and alive. The marriage would be corrosive to him as acid.

The thought caused a hard pain in her chest. He would keep his honor. Maintain his country's stability. But at what cost?

Perhaps she'd discuss that with him, convince him that…

No. Bad idea. She needed to try to avoid intimate conversations, not encourage them. The last thing she wanted to do was feel anything more for him than she already did. She couldn't let herself see the emotion beneath his mask. She couldn't let herself feel his feelings, any more than she could reach out to feel him in her arms.

The Emir of Makhtar was not for her, and he never would be. Not in any way she could accept.

In three months, she would go home. She'd take care of her family, go to college. Maybe she'd be a teacher. She wouldn't give up on the life she wanted. Not for a momentary temptation, no matter how strong the temptation might be. When she loved a man, she would give him everything, or else nothing at all…

Lying on her back in the soft waves of the Persian Gulf, she looked up at the stars in the deepening night. If she turned her head one way, she could see the skyscrapers of the Dubai Marina towering overhead. If she looked the other, she could see in the distance the populated, man-made islands that were carved into the shape of a palm tree.

But here, floating in the water, she was totally alone, just her and the moon and the infinite stars in the dark, velvety sky. She closed her eyes, feeling the water caress her skin.

Then she felt a man's hands beneath her. Her eyes flew open and she saw the outline of Sharif's dark head in the moonlight, the gleam of his black eyes. Startled, she fell, putting her feet down in the sand and whirled to face him in the water.

"Sharif," she breathed. "What are you—" She caught herself. "I mean, good evening, Your Highness…"

"We're alone." His eyes burned through her. "You don't have to be polite."

She stiffened, narrowing her eyes. "In that case, I'll say what I've been thinking for the last three days. What the hell are you doing? Distracting Aziza with piles of cheap gifts…just so she can impress her shallow friends—"

"They weren't cheap, I assure you."

"This is her *life* we're talking about." Her eyes filled with tears. "She's too young to realize the choice she's making."

He stood in front of her, his muscular chest tanned and

bare, both of them swayed by the gentle roll of the water in the darkness.

"We become older by the choices we make," he said. "By the responsibilities we take—or don't take. You know this already. How old were you when you started taking on responsibilities for your family—responsibilities that should never have been yours? Was that your choice? Or were you just doing what you had to do?"

She felt the sandy bottom beneath her feet. The water was high—all the way to her chest, and up to his ribs. The water's gentle waves swayed their bodies. One hard wave could push them together. "We're not talking about me."

"We are now."

"You don't understand what you are making her give up. If she marries without love, she'll never be happy, ever."

"And you think you will?" He took a step toward her, his black eyes glittering. "You're so desperate to save your pure body for marriage. But how will you know the difference between love and lust, Irene? You who have never known either one? What will stop you from throwing your life away to the first man who makes your body come alive?"

Every inch of her body felt alive right now. She felt the waves caressing her overheated skin as she looked up at his handsome, angry face. She licked her lips. "I…I'll just know…"

"You *won't* know. That's the whole point." He looked angrier. "You need to be taught the difference. To understand. So you won't promise your whole soul and future away to some man who will never deserve it."

She felt his gaze fall to her lips, and trembled all over. Her mouth tingled, aching for his kiss. Remembering it. But as he started to move toward her, she stepped back in the water.

"Tell me about her."

"Who?"

"Your bride. What is her name?"

His handsome face was suddenly as immobile as stone. "I don't want to talk about her."

"But I do."

"What do you want to know, Irene? She is a poisonous snake who amuses herself with more lovers than drops of water in the sea."

"I know there's a double standard here, but have you considered your own long list?"

"It isn't her lovers. It's the way she relishes flaunting them. Telling me about them. She hates me even more than I hate her. She has—a cruel heart."

Irene's heart twisted at the thought of a woman like this being Sharif's wife, at his side, in his bed. She swallowed. "And this is the woman you want to be queen of your country? The mother of your children?"

His eyes looked dark. "Leave it alone."

"You think I might make a foolish choice in marriage because of lust?" she choked out. "Take a look at your own—because of pride!"

For a moment, she was afraid she'd pushed him too far. Then he looked away.

"It's not pride," he said in a low voice. "I am emir. I do not have the luxury of going back on my word, or offending Kalila's powerful family. I cannot take the risk of Makhtar falling into chaos, into war, ever again. You don't know what it was like." He looked at her, his jaw tight. "I would die first."

Irene looked at his taut shoulders. She thought of how few people she'd known in her life who would sacrifice their own happiness for the sake of strangers. She took two splashing steps toward him, then stopped, staring at his dark silhouette outlined by silver. His body was in shadow, illuminated by dappled moonlight, reflected from the water.

"Sharif." She licked her lips. "I have to tell you something. I…"

He seemed to brace himself. She exhaled.

"I'm sorry," she whispered. "All this time I thought you were a selfish playboy. The truth is you're…noble."

"Noble? No." He shook his head. "I'm just…"

"What?"

"Doing my job."

She felt a rush of admiration—even longing. She tried to push it aside. She couldn't allow herself to feel desire, attraction…infatuation.

"I always knew I would someday be emir. I've known since birth that it was my fate." He looked at her. "But you are free. You should enjoy it."

Free? She'd never thought of it that way. But in some ways, it was true. Sharif, as a billionaire emir, was a prisoner of his people—the servant and slave of his country. While she, who'd grown up with nothing, who'd had to fight just to survive, had always had one thing he did not. The knowledge that the choice of what to do with her life was hers.

"What do you want, Irene?" Sharif said softly. "What will you choose for your future to be?"

The question made her throat hurt. Looking down at the water, she took a deep breath.

"I want to have security for my mother and sister. I want to help my mother go to rehab. I want to be able to pay for my sister to go to college if she wants. I want what I've always wanted. To take care of my family."

"So we're not very different after all. You've made sacrifices, taking responsibility for the people you love, even at a cost to yourself. You and I…" Cupping her cheek, Sharif said fiercely, "We are alike."

Irene looked up at him with an intake of breath. For a moment, they stood together in the warm, swaying waters of the Persian Gulf, their eyes locked in the moonlight. She felt his hand against her cheek.

His gaze slowly fell down her body in the black swimsuit. Beads of water glistened on the tanned skin of his bare, muscular chest. The tension between them changed. His fingertips trailed down her cheek, then moved to tangle in her wet hair. He tilted her head back.

And lowering his head to hers slowly, very slowly, he kissed her.

The kiss was different than any between them before. Slow, and lingering, and deep. She felt the silk of his lips against hers, so powerful and strong, their tongues meeting and twisting and tasting, tangling together, like their souls.

Their nearly naked skin pressed against each other in the sliding waves of the water, pushing them against each other, pushing them apart. She wanted him…oh, yes. And he wanted her. Everything he'd said about lust was true. In this moment, with her smaller body wrapped in his, she wanted all of him, forever and ever. She didn't think she could ever have enough. She wanted not just his body, but his heart.

She abruptly pulled away.

"You promised not to kiss me," she said hoarsely.

"I never promised that. You asked. Then you broke your own rule by kissing me yourself." He tried to keep his voice casual, but she heard the rough edge of his voice. "I still remember how you pulled me on top of you, in your bed."

Her cheeks went hot. "I explained about that—"

"Yes." His sensual mouth curved. "That you were dreaming of me."

"I never said—"

"I thought," he said, running a fingertip along her wet bare skin beneath her collarbone, "you were always going to tell me the truth."

She took a deep, shuddering breath.

"All right," she said in a low voice. "The truth is that I was dreaming of you that night in the palace. I was dreaming of you kissing me. And then suddenly you were there." She lifted her gaze to his. "It was the first time in my life that a dream came true."

Sharif's eyes were wide, as if he'd never expected her to admit so much. He said softly, "I would give anything to do more than just kiss you. If you'd give up the idea of…"

"Of being a virgin when I wed?" She took a deep breath, tried to smile. "It's not just about my body. It's about sharing the same level of commitment. In fact," she tilted her head, "I'd prefer for him to be a virgin as well…"

Sharif's shocked face looked almost comical. "You're joking, right?"

She shrugged. "I just have my standards."

"Impossible ones. Even as emir, even if I were free to choose, I wouldn't expect my bride to be a virgin."

"You don't expect to love her either, so clearly we have different ideas about marriage."

"Clearly," he said, sounding irritated. "I believe in reality."

"And I believe in dreams." Irene looked away. "There's a man out there, somewhere in the world, who will love me for the rest of my life."

"And if he never comes? What then?"

"He will," she whispered. "I have to believe it."

He looked down at her, their faces inches apart. "What if you're wrong?"

Irene shivered, feeling the heat and strength of his nearly

naked body so close to hers in the night. She lifted her gaze to his.

"Then I'll be very sad," she said, trying to smile, "that I didn't sleep with you when I had the chance."

They stared at each other for a long moment in the moonlight.

"So that's it?" he said finally. "I can't change your mind?"

"Can I change yours?"

Wordlessly, he shook his head, and that was that. She exhaled. So did he.

Reaching out, he silently took her hand. He led her out of the water, splashing to the white sand beach.

He paused, looking at her. "A one-piece swimsuit?" His lips quirked. "A bold choice."

"You know I like modest clothes."

"Obviously so. Even Basimah has a bikini, I believe. But then you," he said softly, coming closer, "are an old-fashioned girl."

Irene looked up at him, her heart pounding, wondering if he would kiss her, wondering if she would resist.

Instead, he started walking, pulling her past the enormous pool with all the bridges and grottos and foliage and palm trees. He led her up the sweeping steps toward the villa.

Irene felt as if she was a million degrees hot. In spite of her words, she felt as if she wasn't completely in control of herself, not anymore. Not since the moment they'd met. Her rational brain was shouting at her to do something, but the sound was completely obscured by the rush of blood in her own ears, by the pounding of her heart.

She exhaled when he dropped her hand, bending to pick up the beach towels left carelessly on the lounge chairs. He held out her towel. She took it wordlessly, unable to look away as she watched him towel off every inch of his hard, towering, half-naked body.

"So we are what—friends?"

She nearly jumped, and remembered that she, too, should be toweling off. She did it quickly and nodded. "Friends."

"Interesting." A strange gleam was in his dark eyes, illuminated by the lights of the villa. "I've never tried to be friends with a woman."

"No?"

He paused. "Especially one who's driving me out of my mind."

She protested, "I haven't argued anything about your sister's wedding in at least—"

"That's not what I was talking about."

"Oh." She bit her lip, then blurted out, "You can put that aside, right? We can just be friends? Because I need this job. And I can't wonder if, in a moment of weakness, you might…"

"I won't keep you from waiting for your husband," he said softly. "Whoever he may be." He took a deep breath. "But I wonder if there's something you would do for me."

"What?"

Sharif's jaw went hard, and he looked away. It took him several moments to speak, and when he did, his voice was strained.

"I wonder if…after Aziza is wed, and your job is done… if you'd stay a few extra days. Just until my engagement is announced. Just until—" His voice cut off. He looked at her. "Would you stay with me, Irene, not for money, not as my employee, but just as my friend? Until it's over?"

Beneath his low, rough voice, she heard a hint of isolation, even despair. He was asking for a friend to stand beside him, to wait until the day he was forced to sign his life away. She suddenly realized that being emir, ruler of all but equal of none, must be a strangely lonely experience, in spite of all the servants and palaces and wealth. He was surrounded by people who expected him to be strong. He had to appear powerful at all times. Whom could he ever allow to see any vulnerability or weakness or regret? Who would ever protect *him*?

No one.

If only, Irene thought, *I could be the one to spend my life at his side. We're so different. But maybe we could have been happy just the same.* The thought made a lump rise in her throat. But there was only one thing she could do. She held out her hand.

"Yes, Sharif," she said. "I'll stay till the end."

CHAPTER EIGHT

SHARIF STARED DOWN through the window of his private office, watching Irene and his sister walk together through the palace garden below.

Irene looked up, as if she felt his gaze. He lifted his hand in greeting. But she abruptly turned away, her sensual body swaying like music as she disappeared with his sister through the garden. He dropped his hand.

Did she know?

Had she guessed?

Grimly, Sharif set his jaw. Every time he saw her, it was harder to hide. He honestly wasn't sure how much longer he could keep it from her.

For three months now, Irene had been living in his palace. For three months, she'd slept in the bedroom across from his. He'd spoken with her, laughed with her. Seen how the rest of the palace staff had come to respect and even love her.

Three months of torture. Of having her join him at dinner, of looking across the table and seeing the sweep of Irene's dark eyelashes trembling against her creamy skin, to see the parting of her full pink lips as she ate and drank and smiled.

Three months of wishing that she, and no other, could be his queen. His *wife*.

Sharif's jaw set as he looked out the window toward the vast sweep of the sparkling gulf. His whole body electrified every time he thought of how it had felt to kiss her in the water that last night in Dubai. He wanted her in his arms. In his bed.

Cold comfort to tell himself that at least no one knew his feelings. He wished he didn't know them himself.

Because Sharif could no longer pretend to himself that what he felt for Irene was lust. He respected her too much for that. It wasn't just friendship, either, no matter how he tried to pretend otherwise. The truth of the matter had hit him hard across the jaw last week, when she'd suddenly burst into laughter at something he'd said—he could no longer even remember what it was—but he'd looked into her sparkling, shining brown eyes, and felt something explode in his chest.

He was in love with her.

In love.

Love wasn't just a myth. It wasn't an illusion. It filled him with light and wonder in a way he'd never felt before. The ache in his heart that expanded until he could think of nothing else. He'd known in that moment that he would do anything for Irene's happiness. Kill for her. Die for her.

He was supposed to be reading through some dry legal documents, in preparation for a phone discussion that afternoon with the Sultan of Zaharqin about a joint oil venture, to be funded both privately and with each nation's sovereign fund. Instead, Sharif had found himself just standing here by the window, on the off chance he might see Irene walking in the garden. And now he had, and now she was gone, his knees were weak and he felt like someone had stabbed his heart with a dagger.

He was in love with Irene.

And he could never have her. Not in marriage. Not without marriage. He couldn't have her in any way.

In one week, his sister would be wed. All he had to do was stay away from Irene for the rest of the week, and he could be done with this torture. He wouldn't have Irene stay another day after that, no matter how he'd once practically begged her. The moment the wedding was done, he would send her away. He'd go back to how he'd felt before.

Numb.

His hand tightened on the window.

"Your Highness, Miss Taylor is asking to see you."

He whirled around to see Hassan, his chief of staff, in the doorway of his office.

"Send her in," he said abruptly, then silently jeered at himself. So much for willpower and staying away from her.

Hassan briefly bowed his head, but as he turned to go, he hesitated, then turned back. "If I might ask your advice, Your Highness…would you think it inappropriate if I were to ask Miss Taylor to accompany me to the party after your sister's wedding—"

"You are forbidden." The hard words came out of Sharif's mouth before he even realized what he was saying. Hassan's eyes widened with shock.

"I see," he said slowly. "Is there some reason that you—"

Sharif tried to be calm. To be cool. But a visceral fury went through him that he could not control and he whirled a fierce, black glare on his trusted friend that would have decimated a lesser man.

Hassan blinked.

"Ah," he said quietly. "So that's the way of it. Does she—"

"No," Sharif said tightly. "She doesn't know and she never will. Once my sister is wed, Miss Taylor will return home. That's the end of it."

"I see." He paused. "The staff love her, sire. Though she

was not born in Makhtar, it's clear she loves this country. Your people would joyfully serve her, I think, if you were ever to decide that she—"

"My engagement to Kalila Al-Bahar will be announced next week," Sharif said flatly.

"Oh." Hassan stared at him. He didn't have to say how the palace staff felt about Kalila. After two disastrous visits in the past, Sharif already knew.

"No one must ever know my true feelings for Miss Taylor," he said quietly. "Least of all her. She cannot know. It is bad enough that I do."

"I am sorry," Hassan said. He hesitated. "Shall I still... send her in now?"

Sharif looked at him and shook his head. "It's all over your face." His lip curled. "Go out the back. I will let her in."

Once alone, Sharif took a deep breath. He realized his hands were trembling, so he took a moment to clear the emotion from his heart, from his mind, from his expression. Then he went to open the door.

Irene looked beautiful, he thought, like everything any man could ever want. She was wearing a simple sheath dress in pale pink, the same color she'd been wearing the moonlit November night they'd met. Her hair was twisted into a thick topknot. Her only makeup was red lipstick. Even her new dark-rimmed glasses made her look, in his current demented state, like a sexy librarian.

"You're wearing glasses," was all he could manage in the way of intelligent conversation.

"I know," she said mournfully. "I lost a contact lens this morning. I've ordered a new pair, but they won't get delivered until later today."

"To what do I owe this pleasure?"

She looked at him, then her expression hardened. "You have to call off this wedding."

How did she know how ardently he'd been wishing that same thing? How had she guessed? In a harsh voice he said, "I cannot. It has been a long-held promise..."

"Not that long," she pointed out, frowning. "Just six months, Aziza said."

Six months? It had been nearly twenty years. It had...

He realized Irene was speaking about his sister's marriage, not his. He'd very nearly blurted out something that would have told her everything. He shook his head, trying to clear the fog from his brain. "Aziza wanted you to speak with me? That's why you rushed away when you saw me at the window?"

"She begged me." Irene's cheeks turned a tantalizing shade of pink. "She felt that...you might listen—to me."

Sharif exhaled. His sister was no fool, though sometimes she liked to pretend to be one. If she already knew the influence that Irene had over him, how long would it be before everyone knew—including Irene herself?

"We've been through this already," he said.

"She's realized all those gifts you bought her in Dubai are meaningless, compared to throwing her life away! She should be in college, Sharif. She's a bright girl. She should have the chance to—"

"The wedding is in a week. It's too late." Sharif folded his arms, glaring at her. "So if there's nothing else..."

She sighed. "I need to go anyway, or else I'll be late for—"

She bit down hard on her lip.

"Late to where?" he demanded.

Her cheeks had turned a deeper red. "Nothing. Never mind."

Clearly she was hiding something. He had the sudden flash of Hassan's eager face. "Where are you going?"

"I hardly think it matters to—"

"This is my kingdom. You are the chaperone of my sister." Sharif was conscious he was behaving like a brute, but he couldn't stop himself from thundering, "I have full right to know—"

"All right, all right," Irene said irritably. "You don't need to go Total Emir on me. If you must know—" the blush deepened "—I have an appointment for—*hammam*."

"Hammam?" he repeated in a strangled voice. Against his will, he had the image of Irene totally naked in a steam bath, her body getting slowly rubbed down in the heat, drenched with pails of water, her pink skin invigorated, lightly whipped and wrapped with towels.

"I've heard of nothing else since I came here." She sighed, rolling her eyes. "Apparently it's like having a spa day and a massage and a facial all rolled into one. I promised Aziza I'd go. Since I'll be leaving next week, I'm running out of time."

Her last words hung between them. *Running out of time.* The silence stretched awkwardly, filled with things neither would say.

"Well, I'm off," she said, trying to smile. "Although the thought of getting naked in front of strangers makes me blush."

Naked. Heat pulsed through Sharif's body. All he could think about was how he wished he could be the lucky bath attendant who would touch her, stroke her, caress her naked skin.

He wished he could be free to make love to her.

No. It was more than that.

He wished he could be free to love her.

Turning to go, Irene stopped at the door and looked

back at him one last time, her big brown eyes deep and imploring.

"Give Aziza the freedom that you cannot have for yourself, Sharif," she said. "Set her free."

His soul shuddered to the core as he looked at those feverishly bright brown eyes.

"I will think about it," he heard himself say.

Irene blinked in shock. "What?"

He needed her to leave the room, now, before he lost the last thread of his self-control and did something that would ruin someone's life. Possibly many lives. "Just go."

The roughness of his voice made her look sharply at him. She searched his face, then swallowed, stepping back. He wondered what she had seen. Then he knew.

She'd seen the truth on his face, that he was barely holding back from claiming her as his own, against his honor, and damn the consequences.

"I'll go," she stammered, and fled.

Sharif walked around his large polished wood desk. He leaned his arm against the window, then pressed his forehead against the glass. *Give Aziza the freedom that you cannot have for yourself.*

He closed his eyes, remembering when he'd first met his sister. She'd been a tiny, squalling baby placed unsteadily in his teenage arms. She'd been helpless, so small and sad, an unloved orphan. He'd vowed to protect her with his life. He'd vowed he would always love her and take care of her.

You've lived your life for the last nineteen years, Sharif. He heard his little sister's tearful voice. *What about me? When is my time to live?*

His eyes slowly opened.

He couldn't do it. He was already making the sacrifice of his heart. He couldn't allow his young sister to do the same. She'd made a mistake when she'd agreed to the engagement. But he wouldn't, couldn't, allow her momentary error to become a permanent one.

He would protect her. As he always had.

Turning, he picked up his phone from his desk. He dialed the private number of the Sultan of Zaharqin.

When he reached him, the man was cordial at first, even friendly. But when he realized Sharif wasn't phoning to discuss the potentially huge oil venture, but to cancel the wedding just a few days before the ceremony, the man's voice turned frosty.

"You realize," he said, "that some would consider this affront to be an act of war."

Sharif's body went tight. He had a flash of memory, of his palace burned to ash, of Makhtar City in smoke, of hungry children crying. *No.* But he kept his voice steady. His country had changed. *He* had changed. He was no longer a fifteen-year-old boy. He was now the one in control.

"Makhtar has always been, and always will be, Zaharqin's greatest friend and ally," Sharif said. "As I am yours. But the hearts of teenagers are changeable. It is regrettable, but there it is. You remember when you were that age…"

"Yes," the sultan said stiffly. "I had already taken my first wife."

"It was a different world, when you and I were young," Sharif said, as if they were the same age.

The man snorted. "You're right about that. Young people today do not know the meaning of duty. Their whims drift on the wind. I should know. My own children—"

The sultan stopped. Sensing weakness, Sharif said smoothly, "Exactly so. But what does not change is friendship, between rulers and between nations. Or the solid profit from good business." He paused. "It would be a pity to let plans for our multi-billion-dollar oil venture falter, merely because of this small personal matter…"

"You really expect me to partner with you? After the mortal insult you've just offered me? I should be calling my generals and telling them to roll our tanks into your city."

"You are free to do so, of course. Free to try. Your generals will warn you about our modern, highly trained army and state-of-the-art defenses. But you could try anyway. Such a mess it would be." He sighed. "A shame to cause the deaths of our most loyal servants and friends, for something so silly as a nineteen-year-old girl deciding she was too young for marriage and motherhood."

"I will be mocked. They'll say the nubile young bride left me at the altar. They'll call me old—me, in my prime! Nothing can compensate for the loss of honor."

"No one will mock you when they hear my sister has left you not for another man, but to study science and literature in college. Your people will say you are well rid of a bride who would have been distracted by academic pursuits from the proper affairs of her high royal position." He paused. "But mostly they will say that you cut me raw, eviscerated my insides from my body, with the deal you made in our oil venture."

"Deal?" The sultan cleared his throat. "What deal?"

It was then that Sharif knew he had him.

"The deal where I take all the financial risk, paying billions of dollars in all the expenses of research, development and transport, and you get all the profit."

After that, it was easy. The man's anger faded, lost in greed and the happy thought of the story that would make the rounds, of how the great Emir of Makhtar had been crushed by his good friend in a business deal. They spoke for some time, hashing out the details of the press release. By the end, the sultan was laughing.

"Even my own children have never cost me so much," he said gleefully. "I wish you joy of her. Please send my best wishes to your sister and thank her, from the bottom of my heart."

Hanging up the phone, Sharif groaned a little, putting his head in his hands. The cost of this little escapade would be far more than any mere shopping spree or diamond trinket. This one would hurt, and he'd be taking it out of his own private fortune. It might take twenty years for his net worth to recover. If it ever did.

But he could live with that. What he couldn't live with was Aziza being unhappy and trapped forever in a loveless marriage. Not his baby sister. Not when he'd vowed to protect her.

But if it wasn't for Irene's interference...

Sharif sucked in his breath. He had to see Irene. Now. He had to tell her that the wedding was off. She had to be the first to know.

Sharif nearly ran down the hall, but Irene's room was empty. Then he remembered. *Hammam*. Turning, he rushed with almost indecorous swiftness to the other side of the palace. The female servants' eyes went wide as he hurried past them, but no one dared to stop the emir as he strode into the dark, quiet, peaceful *hammam* of the women's wing.

He stopped.

It took a moment for his eyes to adjust. He'd never been in here before. The large, hexagon-shaped room was filled with shadows. The high dome soaring overhead was interlaced with patterns of stars, which caused star-shaped beams of sunlight to fall softly into the darkness. Brass lanterns with flickering candles edged the floor, and in the center of the room, a blue pool of water reflected illuminated waves of light on the surrounding dark alcoves.

Only one woman was receiving the pleasures of *ham-*

mam, the steam baths, wraps, massage. Sharif's gaze focused on her.

And he suddenly couldn't breathe.

Irene was lying on a warmed marble slab, facedown with her eyes closed, getting rubbed down by the bath attendant, an older woman who had been hired away from Istanbul long ago. Only a single towel covered Irene's body. As he watched, that towel slipped and fell to the tile floor.

His mouth had already dropped. But seeing Irene naked, his knees shuddered beneath him. He forgot the reason he'd come here. Or maybe suddenly, for the first time, he truly knew it.

The Turkish bath attendant looked at him in surprise, her eyes wide. He held his finger to his lips, then motioned for her to leave.

She looked disapproving, but what could she do? He was the emir. For the first time in his life, Sharif used his raw power for his own selfish purposes.

The woman left, and he took over, pressing his hands against Irene's back, massaging the warm, pink skin of her naked, overheated body.

Aziza had told Irene that the *hammam*, or Turkish bath, would be steamy. "A sort of middle place between heaven and hell," she'd said, then added hastily, "but you'll like it. Trust me."

Irene had already sat naked on a marble slab in a dark alcove for an hour, sweating profusely in steam that was thick as mist. Periodically, the female bath attendant had returned to splash Irene's naked body with hot soapy water, dumped from buckets, then used a coarse hand mitt to scrub her skin from top to bottom. After several times of this procedure, Irene had started to feel like her skin was glowing and also slightly raw.

The worst was that she couldn't see anything in the *hammam* except patterns of shadow and light. She'd taken off her glasses, leaving them with her clothes in the changing room. Without them, she felt disoriented, even helpless, but maybe it was all for the best. Getting totally naked in front of a stranger, even one as businesslike as the female attendant, was a brand-new experience. Without glasses, and with no contact lenses either, she couldn't tell if the attendant was judging the shape of her body. Irene couldn't have even said what the attendant's face looked like. Especially in the deep shadows of the *hammam*. The only light came from the enormous dome above, gleaming tiny pinpoints of light, leaving dappled stars onto the white marble. Heaven and hell indeed.

Just like the last three months had been.

She'd seen Sharif every day, lived in the same palace, even the same hallway. Every morning, every evening, she'd sat across from him at the dining table. She'd seen his darkly handsome face, heard his voice. They'd spoken about politics and world affairs; they'd discussed Makhtar's recent international film festival and new art gallery. And that was just in public. In private, when they were alone, they'd teased each other about everything and nothing.

Sharif knew her now. He knew her as no one ever had. He knew her, though he hadn't kissed her since that night in Dubai.

After she'd started learning Arabic with a Makhtari tutor, Sharif had asked her to be his de facto hostess, entertaining ambassadors and heads of state. Breathlessly, Irene had dressed in designer gowns from local boutiques. She'd entered the ballroom on his arm. Once she would have been shy and afraid of strangers, but now, at his side, she was ready to do battle, to do her best to charm his friends and enemies alike. For him. All for him.

She wanted to make him proud. She wanted to make his dark eyes gleam as he smiled at her across the ballroom. And afterward, when they were alone, she wanted to hear him say in his deep, sensual voice, "Thank you, Miss Taylor. You are a pearl beyond measure. Makhtar is grateful for your service."

"I know," she would tease in reply. "You're seriously lucky to have me. All the other emirs keep calling."

He would laugh, then his eyes would turn dark and he would start to say something—then stop himself. Irene would catch her breath and turn away. Without even asking what he could not say. Because she knew.

Heaven had turned to hell. Having Sharif so close, but never being able to touch him, never being able to say what was truly in her heart…it was agony.

How could she bear to stay another day?

How could she ever bear to go?

In a week, whether she was willing or no, Irene would leave Makhtar forever. Aziza would be married to a man three times her age, and Sharif would take as his queen a woman he despised. No one was marrying for love here. All those lives ruined.

Including, she was starting to fear, her own.

"Stop thinking," the bath attendant barked in English, sloughing Irene's shoulders with the rough hand mitt, scrubbing her skin until she flinched. "Too tense!"

"Yes." She sighed, and tried to obey. The woman pulled her to standing and rinsed her with a shock of cold water, then stepped back and made some sort of gesture. She waited expectantly.

"I'm sorry, I can't see," Irene said apologetically for the tenth time.

"Come," the woman said roughly in English, grabbing her hand. "I take."

She led Irene out of the alcove, to the center of the *hammam*, beneath the dome. She gently pushed her to lie down, with her naked belly against the marble slab in the center of the room, on the edge of the illuminated blue pool. Irene sighed as she felt the cool marble beneath her skin. Her backside was covered with a towel, and thick white steam floated beneath the tiny beams of light, between the shadows.

"Close eyes," the attendant said, and Irene obeyed. She tried not to think, not to let herself feel the rising heartbreak inside her, but quiet her mind and soul and just let the attendant's hands massage the aching muscles of her shoulders.

But just as Irene started to relax, the hands were gone. She heard a heavy step, the attendant's intake of breath. Then the hands returned to rubbing her back, even more intently than before.

She tried not to think about Sharif. It was impossible. In just a week, Irene would leave this country, and never see him again... Never feel his eyes on hers. Never feel the heat of his body as he brushed innocently against her in the hallway. Never feel his hand take hers, or the soft innocent press of his lips against her cheek. Never see his smile, or the wicked gleam of his dark eyes.

Cold water was splashed on her naked body in the semi-darkness. She heard the hiss of hot coals. Felt the hard, firm hands slowly kneading into her tense back, going slower, deeper...

Why couldn't she forget Sharif? Why wasn't this working?

She couldn't be falling in love with him. She *couldn't*. He was promised to another. And she'd made promises to herself, to her own future, that she intended to keep.

How she wished there had been another choice. But

there wasn't. Soon, another woman—his bride and queen—would take Irene's place at all those diplomatic dinners.

"Walk with me," Sharif had said quietly last night, as he often did when they were dining just as a family, without all the fuss and pomp of ceremony. For two hours after dinner, they'd been alone, walking together in the moonlight of the garden. But for the first time, there had been no teasing laughter between them. No laughter of any kind.

"What is the emir's future bride like?" she'd asked Basimah wistfully that morning.

The older woman had turned red. "Do not ask me about her."

"But you've met her. Aziza said your sister worked in her household once, was even her personal maid."

"The emir is getting what he deserves, that's all I'll say," Basimah muttered. "Making my poor lamb marry that sultan. If I could do something to prevent his wedding, if I knew something that would prevent it, I still wouldn't lift a finger. That's all I'm going to say about his fine bride with her fine fancy feathers. They deserve each other."

So Irene had been forced to go looking online for pictures of the Makhtari heiress. It didn't make her feel better. The beautiful future queen of Makhtar was all brilliant eyes and severe cheekbones and pouting red lips, skinny as a rail and always dressed in the highest fashion.

She'd seen pictures of Kalila Al-Bahar at a royal polo match… Skiing in Gstaad… Coming out of a club in London, dressed in a fur… Attending a royal wedding. After graduating from an expensive boarding school in Switzerland, she had skipped college to become a full-time jet-setter. She would fit into Sharif's world as she, Irene, never could.

The pressure gentled on her back. Rough fingertips

slid down her naked skin in a way that was distinctively…
sensual. And Irene's eyes flew open.

Twisting her head, she looked back and saw a dark blur.
She couldn't see a face. But she knew.

"What are you doing here?" she choked out. "You aren't
supposed to be in here!"

Sharif's voice was low, even silky. "I rule this country.
I can go where I please."

"Not in the women's bath in the palace!" Sitting up, she
tried to twist around in a way that would hide her body. It
was impossible. She wanted to cover herself with a towel,
but couldn't find it. She was naked, sitting on a slab of marble, in the hot steam of the *hammam*, alone with the man
she wanted most. The man she couldn't—mustn't—have!

"What are you doing here?" she cried again, covering
her breasts with her arms.

She felt, rather than saw, his eyes slowly rake over her
body.

"I came to…" His voice was hoarse. "To tell you…"

His words trailed off. He abruptly pulled her against
him.

"Irene," he whispered against her lips. She felt his hands
grip her upper arms. Felt the heat of the steam room and
the rawness of her pink, freshly scrubbed skin. His hands
tightened. She heard his ragged intake of breath.

And he savagely lowered his mouth to hers.

This kiss had nothing of tenderness in it. It was searing.
Hungry. Demanding. It took possession, hard and deep.

She felt Sharif's lips on hers, and after her three months
of yearning, something snapped inside her. She forgot she
was naked—or didn't care—she just needed him, needed
this, or she would die. Wrapping her arms around him, she
returned the kiss desperately, kissing him back so hard

that it bruised her lips, needing to taste him, to possess him in return.

He shoved her back against the marble, kissing her as if he'd lost his mind, and she kissed him back with equal force, because she'd certainly lost hers. They held each other in a frenzy of mutual passion and need. He roughly started pulling off his clothes, ripping off his shirt, then his trousers. Above the hiss of water dripping against hot coals on the other side of the darkened, domed room, empty of everything except the six-sided marble slab surrounding the illuminated blue water of the pool and the pinpoints of light above, she heard the gasp of his breath as he pulled her back hungrily into his arms. His hands swept down her naked skin, and she touched him all over, realizing he was naked, too. Naked against her, in the hot, steamy *hammam*, suspended directly between heaven and hell.

She kissed him, nibbling on his lower lip, gasping as she felt his hands cup her aching breasts. He licked up her neck, sucked on the tender flesh of her earlobe, then moved down her body, tasting every inch of her as he went down, down to the valley between her breasts.

"I've wanted you—for so long," he choked out. "For months I've thought only of you—"

He pushed her full breasts together with his large hands, pressing his lips in the cleavage between before he moved to suckle her. She cried out. She'd never felt any sensation like this before. Never imagined what it could be.

She twisted on the marble as he moved down her body, his wet, hard body sliding slowly against hers. He gripped her hips, then went down farther. She trembled beneath him as his fingertips traced the outside edge of her body, her waist to hips to knees, all the way to the sensitive soles of her feet, which he kissed, one by one. Then he slowly moved upward, pushing her legs apart—kissing to her inner knees—upward, upward…

He used his powerful hands to part her thighs. He lowered his head. Irene suddenly couldn't breathe, as she felt the warmth and heat of his breath against her most sensitive core. If some part of her was screaming that she had to stop, stop this now, she wouldn't let herself hear it. Later. She'd let herself think later. When her body wasn't on fire with need for him… For only him….

He inhaled, exhaled, as if breathing her into the rhythm of his own heart. Then he moved his head closer and licked her inside thigh. Her eyes squeezed shut, her lips parted in a gasp. He moved up higher, gripping her legs, holding her down against the marble. Finally, with agonizing slowness, he lowered his head.

He took a long, lingering taste between her legs, so deep and slow that her hips bucked with the intense wave of pleasure that crashed over her, nearly drowning her with desire and need.

"Sharif…" she gasped. "You…you can't…"

But he could. And he did. Using his mouth and tongue, he teased her, using her body as if he'd known it all his life. As if he knew it better than she did. She twisted beneath him, side to side, nearly weeping with the weight of her desire. She would do anything. Anything.

As he continued to lick and suckle her aching wet core, she felt him push a single thick fingertip inside her. Then another. He invaded her tight, virgin body, slowly stretching her with his fingertips, as she expanded to accept him inside her. Caught in the onslaught of brutal pleasure she'd never imagined possible, her body went tighter and tighter still, as her hips lifted of their own accord. Her lips parted with a long intake of breath that seemed to go on and on and on, until she felt dizzy beneath the shadows and light of the Turkish bath, beneath Sharif himself, as the world spun around her, and sent her flying.

She hung on to his shoulders with her fingernails as she flew and flew. She heard a scream as the black-and-white world exploded into a million bright colors, and fell, chiming like music.

Sharif moved over her almost instantly, lifting his body so that the thick hardness of him was between her legs, demanding entry.

She lay beneath him, limp with pleasure, unable to resist. *Not wanting* to resist. Any thoughts she'd once had of the future or honor were washed away from her mind, like sand beneath an ocean wave. Who cared about something so unimportant as the future? What was that, compared to this?

He drew back his hips, to plunge inside her.

Her eyes lifted to his face. Even this close, she couldn't see his face. All she could see was shadow.

The moment before he would have entered her, he hesitated. He held himself still.

Then, with a low curse, he rolled off her.

It took several moments before she realized he wasn't coming back. She blinked, struggling to understand, to awaken from the sensual haze.

Something white flew toward her. Looking down at her lap, she saw a towel. He'd thrown her a towel?

"Get dressed," he growled. Bending over the tile floor, he picked up his trousers and pulled them over his naked, hard, unsatisfied body.

Irene's throat suddenly hurt. She looked down at the towel, at her own naked body. She'd thrown herself at him, she realized. She'd been willing to throw everything away for the sake of a single moment—and *he was turning her down*.

"I don't understand," she said in a small voice.

"Don't you?" he said in low fury.

Wrapping herself in the towel, she rose from the marble. She felt humiliated. *She hadn't known.* She hadn't fully realized how overwhelming sex could be, the need that could block out all reason, as primal as the need to breathe or eat or sleep.

Close as she was, without her glasses, she still couldn't see his face. As her cheeks turned hot in shame, she was glad. "I can't imagine what you think of me."

"No. You can't."

She said over the razor blade in her throat, "Was it to teach me a lesson? That I'm nothing more than a naive fool, a prude, with my ridiculous dreams of love and saving myself—"

"No," he cut her off. "It wasn't a lesson." She saw the tension of his shoulders, the set of his body that was like a trap waiting to snap shut. "It was a mistake."

"I never knew it could feel like that." She suddenly felt like crying. "I'm sorry."

"*You're* sorry?" Going to her, he lifted her chin, forcing her to meet his gaze. Now they were so close, she finally saw his agonized dark eyes. "I am to blame," he ground out. "Only me. When I came here, I never meant...but I saw you and—" Dropping his hand, he clawed back his dark hair. "I am the only one to blame."

So it hadn't been a test? Her heart started beating again. "Then why did you stop? I couldn't have stopped you."

"You could have stopped me at any time—just by saying no."

"But I couldn't. The way it felt..." Irene took a shuddering breath. "I lost all control, I lost my mind. If it wasn't a test, then I don't understand. You had me in your power. Why didn't you..."

"Why didn't I take you?"

Wordlessly, she nodded.

Sharif stared at her for a long moment. "You say that you now understand how overwhelming passion can be. I now understand what you were talking about as well. Making love should be an expression of love. Love that lasts forever." Reaching out, he stroked her cheek and whispered, "I won't take your dream away from you."

Irene realized that tears were spilling over her lashes. And it was in this moment that she knew, knew it to her very blood and bones, that if she'd made love with him today it would have only been the expression of what was in her heart.

She loved him. All of him, his honor and ferocity and humor and selfishness, all of him, with every bit of her soul.

"Sharif…" she choked out. *Don't marry that other woman, beautiful as she is. Marry me. Love me.*

"You're getting what you want," he said in a low voice. "That's what I came to tell you."

She gaped at him.

He gave her a smile that didn't meet his eyes. Dropping his hand, he stepped back. "I've canceled my sister's wedding, Miss Taylor. You've won."

"Aziza's free?" Irene closed her eyes as she pictured the young girl's face. She looked at him in gratitude. "Thank you."

"No. Thank you. For reminding me of my place."

"But what about you?"

His expression hardened. His voice was even as he said, "Canceling Aziza's wedding means that my own must go forward as soon as possible. I will be phoning Kalila and—"

"I saw pictures of her," Irene said miserably. "She's beautiful."

"Yes," he said dully. He exhaled with a flare of nostril, looking away. "Very beautiful."

Looking at him, Irene's heart broke.

"Don't do it," she said. "Don't marry her."

"I gave my word."

"Break it," she said desperately.

He gave a low, humorless laugh. "You are saying this? *You*?"

She swallowed, remembering all the times she'd insisted on honor, on love, on the importance of marriage and honesty.

He looked at her. "Even if I could discard my honor so lightly, Kalila comes from a powerful Makhtari family. If I offended her father, it would start trouble. It could even start a war."

"It's not fair," she said tearfully. "You made the promise when you were fifteen—a boy!"

"I knew what I was doing." He pushed back a tendril of her damp hair. "And if I could so lightly break my promise to Kalila, how could anyone ever trust my word again?" Looking down at her, he said softly, "How could you?"

"I could," Irene insisted, even if part of her wondered. She gripped the towel wrapped tightly over her breasts, over her breaking heart. "I know you, Sharif," she said, her voice cracking. "Honor, caring for your family, for your country—that's everything to you. You can't—"

A heavy door banged against the wall. Cold air rushed into the *hammam*, causing the steam to melt away. Irene jumped when she saw the bath attendant rush in. The woman didn't even look at her, just went straight to Sharif and spoke in rapid Arabic. The words were too quick for Irene to understand, but she saw the instant tension of Sharif's body, like a man who'd just been cut with steel.

"What is it?" she asked as the attendant bowed and hurried away. "What's happened?"

Sharif walked to a wall. He flicked on an electric switch,

and the bath was suddenly filled with harsh light, causing all the shadows and mysteries to disappear, leaving only cold reality.

"You need to get dressed." His voice had no expression.

Something was wrong. Something was very wrong. Longing to put her arms around his naked chest, to offer him comfort, she went close to him, trying to see his face. He looked at her. He was once again the powerful emir in control. The vulnerable man she'd so briefly seen beneath the mask had disappeared as if he'd never been.

Emotionlessly Sharif said, "My future bride has seen fit to honor us with a visit."

Irene's lips parted. "You can't mean—"

"Kalila has just arrived unexpectedly at the palace." He turned empty eyes to hers. "Come, Miss Taylor," he said. "Come meet my beautiful bride."

After finding Sharif at the sdfflisdf about losing it her
so the table, gg kngwyoaieao mo onaf lqgal is yon, said
notus also a Lwkid aamoe laida. It on po loix aigaiten
and thaing, wdyr sdigifdfdd. barpaod. I adnmmon
adkeisd io not lottuk ame utnal lvek gjwady rays
beitui a roitei cf e riap dasoame aller all koiktuaa
sdfj thepugg ajmou dfihdg aoeu odkmap faeai aiatutt
puae aatg kalia ahadub Aeifgdit bestyaoajo sfaotnud beid
reeeeetei ithungi, a idsiei tar tray gaioud weih suaea
test ksti aiftediji beoea a agit 1bk yatduyee d foin.

CHAPTER NINE

"You can't trust servants. Any of them." Kalila Al-Bahar's red-nailed hand waved airily over the dining room table. "Thieves and liars, most of them. And the precious few who aren't, well, they're generally stupid and lazy."

Irene blushed, exchanging glances with Aziza, who sat wide-eyed beside her. Kalila seemed completely unaware that the long dinner table was, in fact, surrounded by twelve palace servants, all of them within earshot, all of them stone-faced.

"Oh," Kalila turned to Irene with a saccharine-sweet smile on her sharp red lips, "I do beg your pardon. Of course I didn't mean *you*, Miss Taylor. I'm sure you're... none of these things."

"Of course," Irene said through gritted teeth. Her eyes met Sharif's. He was at the head of the table, in his traditional white robes, as was right and proper for the Emir of Makhtar entertaining the daughter of the former vizier, now wealthy governor of Makhtar's eastern region.

Sharif's handsome face was as expressionless as a statue, but oh, she knew what he was feeling. Her heart twisted painfully.

This horrible woman was to be his wife—the partner of his life—the mother of his children?

Irene had been so nervous to meet the beautiful Kalila.

After leaving Sharif at the *hammam*, she'd rushed to her room, tidied up, showered and dressed. She'd been relieved to see a new box of contact lenses from the local optometrist waiting on her writing desk. Her hands had trembled as she put on red lipstick and a simple black sheath dress, adding a rope of fake pearls around her neck, like armor.

As if any lipstick or fake pearls could make Irene compete with Kalila Al-Bahar. When Irene had first met her at the start of dinner, she'd been overwhelmed with misery. The Makhtari heiress was even more beautiful and thin and impossibly glamorous in person. She had dark eyes lined with kohl, dark hair streaked blond, red lips, long red fingernails, tight red dress. The February weather in Makhtar was pleasantly warm, but she'd still draped herself in a mink coat. She looked like a gorgeous 1950s film star, Irene had thought, crossed with a dash of anorexic porn actress.

Then Kalila had started to speak, and she hadn't stopped since. She had a beautiful, husky, magical voice. But she dominated every conversation with selfish, ugly words.

"If I had my way," she continued now, "I'd bury every servant in the desert, and replace them with—I don't know, anything. Trained dogs. Robots." She sighed. "But robot technology is just so damn slow."

The silence that greeted this bombshell was immediate. Even Kalila sensed something in the air.

"But enough about that." She turned abruptly to Aziza. "I heard you like to shop. I should take you shopping."

"Thank you," Aziza murmured, tossing Irene a panicked look out of the corner of her eye.

"Do not worry," Kalila said kindly. "I can show you where to go and what to buy. Once you are in my hands, in the right clothes, we'll be able to disguise how you're so hideously fat and plain."

Aziza gave a funny little intake of breath.

Irene saw the pain in the younger girl's face, and her lips parted as if she'd taken the blow herself. It was one thing to insult *her*—Irene could take it—but to purposefully hurt someone as sweet and defenseless as Aziza…

Putting her hands on the table, Irene started to rise to her feet, intending to say something sharp and reckless. But Sharif beat her to it.

"Enough, Kalila." He was standing at the end of the table, cold fury on his face. "You will apologize to my sister for your words that are both hateful and untrue."

Glaring at him, Kalila tossed her head. "High time someone told the girl to do something with herself!"

"It's all right, brother." Aziza tried to smile, but her eyes still looked suspiciously moist. "She's right. I have many flaws. I could stand to lose a few pounds." She looked down at her tightly folded hands, all her usual excitement deflated as she whispered, "I am lucky that the sultan even wants to marry me…"

Sharif stared at her.

"No," he said gently. "I meant to tell you. You won't be marrying him, after all."

Her eyes widened, then she said miserably, "Did he change his mind because I'm too fat?"

Her confidence was so shot, Irene wished ardently to slap the cold superior smile off Kalila's face.

"*No.* He wanted to marry you. But I called it off," Sharif said firmly. He glanced at Irene. "Miss Taylor convinced me that college is the proper place for a young woman as bright and determined as you."

"Bright?" Aziza breathed. "Determined?"

Walking to her place at the table, Sharif put his hand on his young half sister's shoulder. "Yes," he said quietly. "And brave and strong. Your whole life is ahead of you. You might become a scientist, an economist, who knows?

There are many ways for a princess to benefit her country." He smiled down at her. "You will do good things for Makhtar in ways I cannot even yet dream. I trust you to find the right path."

"Oh, brother..." Bursting into tears, Aziza rose to her feet and threw her arms around him. "Thank you," she breathed. She shook her head, wiping her eyes. "You won't regret this."

Watching them, Irene had a lump in her throat.

"You're throwing away her only chance for a good marriage," Kalila said, looking down at her red-tipped nails. "No man will ever want to marry a fat, smart girl."

It was the final straw. Throwing her hands against the table, Irene jumped to her feet. "You horrible, dreadful woman!" she cried. "You, be queen of Makhtar? You're not fit to even clean the palace bathrooms!"

Kalila looked at her, all cold, thin, glamorous beauty.

"Ah, so the claws come out at last," she murmured, "of the famous Miss Taylor that half this city has fallen in love with." She narrowed her eyes, and Irene suddenly wondered if she'd heard rumors—if she was the reason that Kalila had come here so abruptly. Tilting her head, the heiress said with venomous sweetness, "But with Aziza's wedding canceled and her leaving for college soon, there is no reason for you to remain here anymore as her companion, is there? I will thank you to leave my table."

Irene shook with rage. "*Your* table?"

"Yes. My table," she said coldly. She waved her skeletal arm. "This palace will be mine. The country will be mine." With a hard smile, she looked straight into Irene's eyes. "Sharif will be mine."

Kalila's vicious words sliced through Irene's heart, causing her to stagger back.

The other woman watched her reaction with spiteful

pleasure, then turned to Sharif and said sweetly, "I have finally decided to set a date. With your sister's engagement off, we will officially announce our engagement tonight."

"No…" The word was a barely audible whisper, coming unbidden from Irene's heart.

Sharif stood beside his sister, his shoulders tight, as cold and expressionless as a statue.

"Well?" Kalila said.

He glanced at Irene. For an instant, she saw the flash of pain in his dark eyes. Then he turned to Kalila with perfect manners and no emotion whatsoever.

"As you wish. It will be arranged within the hour."

"And since all our country is expecting a royal wedding at the end of the week…" She waved her arm, causing her diamond and platinum bangles to clink together loudly. "It would be a waste of money not to take advantage of the arrangements already in place, don't you think?"

A dawning horror rose in Irene's heart.

Sharif's expression sharpened. "We cannot simply switch my sister's wedding for ours, Kalila. Royal protocol must be followed."

"*You* are emir. *You* set the protocol." Kalila tilted her head. "Unless you have changed your mind. Surely you do not wish to disappoint our people, Sharif? Surely—" her voice took an edge "—you do not wish to insult my father?"

Brief hatred flared in his eyes, then died.

"No," he said dully. "I do not."

Irene grabbed his arm desperately. "Sharif," she gasped, too stricken to realize she was calling him by his first name in front of everyone in the dining room, "Please. You cannot…"

He looked down at her.

"My bride is right," he said coldly. "We no longer need you, Miss Taylor."

"What?" Irene whispered, dropping her hand. He was staring at her as if she were a stranger. As if they hadn't spent all these months together. As if, just a few hours before, he hadn't nearly made love to her. As if she were nothing and no one.

She swallowed, blinking fast. She shook her head.

"But I can't…" she choked out. *I can't leave you.* Then she looked around the dining hall, at Kalila staring at her smugly, at Aziza with big eyes in her pale face, at the servants who were trying and failing to pretend they weren't hearing every word.

Turning away from them, Irene looked at the handsome face of the man she loved.

"But I love you," she whispered.

Sharif seemed to flinch, as if he'd taken a bullet to the heart. But his expression was granite as he looked at her.

"Thank you for your service," he said, making the words meaningless and cold. "You will be paid the entire amount, as agreed." When she did not move, his jaw hardened. He grabbed her wrist. "It is time for you to leave."

Without another word, he physically pulled her from the cavernous dining hall. Once in the hallway, he dragged her hard along with him, speaking sharply in Arabic to his bodyguards as they passed. The bodyguards fell into place behind him, one of them speaking into his earpiece to someone else unseen. Irene looked at Sharif's face. "What are you doing?"

He looked at her. "I'm sending you away. To the future you deserve."

Irene wondered how she could have not known immediately, beneath the pretense of the playboy she'd first seen in Italy, exactly who he was. A good-hearted man. She should have loved him from the moment he'd first pursued her on the shores of Lake Como. Fighting back tears, she shook her head. "I won't leave you."

He looked away, tightening his grip on her arm, pulling her rapidly down the long hallways of the palace. "You must."

"Not like this," she choked out. "Not with *her*."

Sharif stopped, his face grim. He signaled to his bodyguards, and they moved ahead without him. Once alone, he cupped her cheek, looking at her urgently.

"Kalila will be my wife. I've always known this. From the very day I met you, Irene, at the wedding of someone I barely knew, I was trying to accept my fate. I couldn't then. But—" he took a deep breath "—I can now."

"What?" she said, stricken.

He looked down. "Because of you," he said in a low voice. "Because of what you taught me."

"I never taught you to marry someone you hate, someone who is horrible like that—to make her the queen of your country—"

"You taught me how to believe again." He looked up. "You taught me to love. For the rest of my life. As I will love you."

Their eyes locked in the shadows.

Then a sob escaped her as she flung her arms around him, pressing her cheek against his chest, against his white robes. "I can't leave you. I won't. It's too soon—"

Fervently, he kissed her forehead, her hair. "Better now than later. Before anything happens that we both—regret."

Tears were running openly down her face. "I regret only that I didn't let you make love to me every single day." Looking up at him, she shook her head. "I should have let you kiss me, from the night we first met—"

"Shh." He put his finger on her lips. "It is better this

way. You'll find someone who can make you happy. Who can give you what I never could."

"Another man?" The thought was like death. "How can you even hope that for me?"

His black eyes looked infinitely deep and sad. "Because I need your happiness more than my own."

A bodyguard came back and gave him a nod. Sharif turned back to her and said simply, "It is time."

Gently taking her hand in his own, he pulled her out a side door and into the warm night. She heard the burble of the fountain, the soft cry of night birds. She saw the black outline of palm trees swaying against a violet sky scattered with stars. She loved everything about this country. Somehow, it had become home to her. Every part of it— especially its emir...

Then she saw a limousine waiting to take her to the airport.

"No!" she cried, backing up desperately. She tried to think of an excuse to linger, just ten minutes more. Five. "My clothes—I need to pack my things…"

"It will be arranged. Here is your bag. Your passport." He snapped his fingers and a bodyguard gave him something. Sharif held out her purse. "My plane is waiting to take you home. Your final paycheck will be transferred to your bank account in Colorado before you land."

This was really happening. "How can you do this to me?"

"Do it to you?" He took a deep breath. "It's *for* you that I'm doing this."

"At least let me stay the week. I will stay here with you until the bitter end. Even—" she lifted her gaze to his "—after…"

His lips parted with shock. "You mean, even after I am wed, you would—"

Her voice was small. "I won't leave you. Not even then."

Sharif stared at her, then shook his head fiercely. "*No.* Even if you were willing to give up all your dreams, I wouldn't let you." Pulling her into his arms, he searched her gaze. "Don't you understand? I have to believe in something. Something more than just cold duty to my country. And it's you."

Her legs were trembling. She clung to his shoulders, barely holding on. She wanted to fall to her knees and wrap her arms around him and beg him not to make her leave, at any cost.

"Don't marry her. Marrying someone you hate will ruin your life."

"It is already ruined," he said softly, looking at her, and suddenly tears were choking her as she read everything in his eyes.

"Sharif—"

"I love you, Irene," he said. "For the first time in my life, I understand what that means. Because my love for you will last for the rest of my life." He cupped her cheek. "You were right."

A sob escaped her. "No—"

"Be happy," he whispered. He kissed her one last time with all his passion, his lips tender and yearning and full of grief and love. Then he let her go. He held up his hand, and two bodyguards came forward to escort her into the limo.

"Sharif," she screamed, fighting them. "Sharif!"

But they pushed her into the backseat of the car, and the door was slammed shut behind her. As the limo sped away, Irene looked back with a sob through the rear window. She saw Sharif's forlorn figure get smaller and smaller in front of the palace, until he disappeared altogether and all she had left of him was that last image of his stricken face, burned forever into her heart.

* * *

Long after the limo had disappeared past the palace gate, Sharif remained immobile, staring at the clouds of dust on the road. He closed his eyes, still seeing Irene's tear-stained face as it had looked through the rear window. He knew he'd never see her again.

"Your Highness?"

He opened his eyes bleakly to see Hassan standing in the side door of the palace. "I have the head of the top Makhtar PR agency on the phone," he said. "He's saying he received an urgent message. I can of course take a message if you—"

"No," Sharif said, and barely recognized his own voice. Kalila must have called them immediately—but then, she knew all the angles. She'd probably already announced their engagement on her social media accounts, making it all sound romantic, making everyone envious of their *great love*. "Ask him to come to the palace at once. We're going to announce our engagement."

"You and Miss—"

"To Kalila," he cut him off.

"But—Miss Taylor?"

"I sent her home."

"But you…I thought…" He hesitated. "When the rumor swept through that you'd rushed to see her in the women's *hammam*, the whole staff greatly hoped…"

"Speak to me no more of Miss Taylor," he said harshly. He turned away. "Let's get this over with."

"Get what over with, exactly, Your Highness?"

"My engagement. My wedding." *My life.*

After they returned to the palace, his chief of staff and bodyguards went their separate ways, as each man's duty required. And so did Sharif.

He walked slowly down the hallway, back toward the dining room. But with every step farther away from Irene, the strength seemed to leave his body. He felt like an old man. No. He felt as if he'd already died.

He stopped.

Irene. Her name was like a prayer in his heart. He pressed his fists hard against his eyes. She would have everything he could not give her. A man who would love her, marry her, have children with her. All her dreams would come true, even without him. He had to believe he'd done the right thing. Loving her, remembering the brief moments they'd shared, would have to be enough to sustain him for the rest of his life. The memory of her, and the knowledge that she'd someday be happy with someone else...

Bleakly, he went back to the dining room. It was empty. His sister had left. His servants had cleared the table.

Only one person remained, standing by the open window, smoking a cigarette. She turned to face him.

"So you tossed her out," Kalila said. "I confess you surprised me. I did not expect you to let this one go so easily."

"What do you want, Kalila?" he said wearily.

She gave him a hard smile. "Your assurance that, after we are wed and I give you your heir, you will leave me alone, with all the same rights to play that you have."

Sharif stared at his future bride in the shadows of the empty dining hall. "We are not yet wed, and you are planning how you wish to be unfaithful?"

She gave a cold laugh. "Don't take that outraged tone with me. I'm not one of your doe-eyed little virgins." She took another elegant drag off her cigarette. "Not like *her*."

He jolted. "You knew we were never lovers?"

"Of course, I could tell. Stupid little virgin, hanging on your every word, staring up at you with those big needy eyes." She took another puff. Her fingers were almost as thin and white as the cigarette. "Have her, if you want. And

I intend to have my own fun. I don't care if you hate me. Our marriage is about power, not *love*."

She made the word a sneer. Just as he once had.

"When you are my queen," Sharif said tightly, "I expect you to rule with respect and dignity for our customs and laws."

She shrugged her skinny shoulders. "I'm no fool. I'll be discreet."

"This I doubt."

She snorted. "More than you have been," she said pointedly, "sneaking around with your sister's companion. Even if you weren't lovers, I heard whispers about your—*relationship*—all the way to New York. My father was the one who called me."

Sharif's lips twisted sardonically. "So that is why you raced here? Because you feared I wouldn't keep my word—that I would marry her?"

Kalila looked away abruptly, then lifted the cigarette to her lips with trembling fingers. "I should have nailed this down a long time ago." Looking out the window, she said in a low voice, "I won't let one mistake keep me from everything that should be mine."

Sharif's eyes narrowed. "She wasn't a mistake."

"What? Oh. Yes. Miss Taylor. But she's gone now. And we understand each other, do we not?" She jerked her chin with glittering eyes. "We'll be wed next week in your sister's place. Then we will consummate the marriage…as often and frequently as we must…"

He tried not to flinch.

"Once you get me pregnant, I do not care what you do. Bring your precious Miss Taylor back. Install her in your bed, for all I care." Kalila abruptly put out her cigarette on the windowsill, leaving a burn mark before she dropped the cigarette carelessly to the floor. He watched the lingering ashes fall against his tile floor like gray snowflakes. "It means nothing to me."

Staring at her, Sharif had a sudden flashback to shining brown eyes. *When I marry, it will only be for love. And our wedding night will be truly about making love. The kind that will last forever.* He remembered the tremble of Irene's voice just an hour before, when she'd told him she loved him.

"Our marriage is nothing but a means to an end," Kalila said. "Something to endure, and ignore, until we both are dead."

He abruptly focused on her face, on those black eyes with fake black lashes, beautiful, yes, but so cold, with an almost reptilian stare. So different from loving, warm brown eyes that glowed at you with the heat of summer, like the warmth of an embrace. He looked at his fiancée's hollow cheekbones, so different from the healthy rose-dusted cheeks that blushed with modesty or shyness or even anger.

Kalila didn't seem to feel anything, care about anything, so long as she had two things: money and power. She wanted the prestige of being Her Highness, the Sheikha of Makhtar, the mother of the future heir—and the pleasure of enjoying herself with any man she pleased during the length of their marriage.

She was shallow. Terminally shallow.

And once, Sharif suddenly realized, he'd been just like her. Oh, he'd always cared about doing his duty by his country, and by his family. But other than that, he'd cared for nothing and no one. He'd wasted endless days on meaningless love affairs, trying to distract himself from his own empty soul.

Then he'd had the grace and fortune to meet Irene. It was the miracle of his life.

And the tragedy.

"Not a word in reply?" Kalila took a step toward him, frowning. "What has changed in you, Sharif?"

"What are you talking about?"

"You're different somehow. You…" She sucked in her breath, covering her hand over her mouth with an astonished giggle. "But wait. Don't tell me you're actually in love with her?"

"Be quiet," he snapped.

"Your sweet virgin. So tender. So true…"

"She's worth a thousand of you," he said.

"You love her." Kalila cackled a laugh. "The great Emir of Makhtar is chained down at last. How very amusing to see you caught this way. Just like—"

"Like what?" he said, expecting an insult. She looked away.

"Nothing," she muttered. "It's just funny, that's all. Your precious Miss Taylor—"

He grabbed her wrist.

"Don't ever," he said in a low, dangerous voice, "speak her name again."

Kalila blinked, then gave another low laugh. "Have it your way." She ripped her bony arm from his grasp. "Keep your sweet memories. I will take my throne." Her eyes were feverishly bright. "I think this marriage will suit me very well."

CHAPTER TEN

FIVE DAYS LATER, Irene was in Colorado, kneeling on the ramshackle porch of her old house, boxing up the last items to take north to their new place in Denver. There was surprisingly little to pack. Some of her family's old possessions, worn clothes like her mother's pink terry hot pants with the word *Tasty* emblazoned across the backside, had gone straight into the trash. A few other things had gone to the local charity shop. But her sister and her mother had already taken the things they cared about when they'd left here four days ago.

Her sister, Melissa, was already unpacking boxes in the brand-new condo in Denver that Irene had leased, right between the local community college and Colorado's best private rehab facility, where their mother had checked herself in two days ago. Melissa was studying to take her GED test, to compensate for never having graduated from high school, and looking eagerly through the college course book. A rough road might still lie ahead, Irene knew, but it was going to work out. They were going to be settled and secure, and have the chance to be happy.

"Thank you, baby," her mother had said, openly weeping when she hugged Irene close, the last moment before she went into rehab. "I wanted to be a good mother to you.

I tried. But I didn't know how." She wiped her eyes hard. "I'm going to learn."

Melissa had cried, too—when she first saw the luxury condo on a lovely, tree-lined street in Denver, and the college book sitting on the kitchen counter. "You remembered how I used to talk about becoming a dental assistant?"

Irene nodded.

"Do you know how much they make per hour?" Melissa demanded, then she, too, wiped her eyes. "Plus, they hang around with handsome single dentists all day…"

"You'd be a great assistant. Or you could be a dentist yourself."

"Me?"

"Sure." Irene had shrugged. "Let all the sexy male dental assistants come to you."

"You think I could?" her sister had breathed as if considering the idea for the first time. "And you'd pay for me to go to dental school?"

"Any kind of school you want." Irene had reached out and taken her sister's hand. "I believe in you."

Melissa blinked back tears. "I always thought you judged me…"

"I did," Irene said. "I did and I'm sorry. I didn't understand then how powerful sex and love can be. Or that sometimes, no matter how hard you try—" she looked down "—dreams don't always come true…"

"Dreams don't come true?" Melissa's voice changed. She shook her head. "You're wrong about that, Reena." She smiled, her eyes shimmering with tears. "Just look around me right now."

The words still rang in Irene's ears when she'd driven back to Lone Pine today, to finish packing and close down the house. Her last stop on the way out of town would be to return the key to the corpulent landlord, who'd be sad to see the two older Taylor women leave after twenty years of paying him rent, not always in cash. Irene had been taping up the last box when the air in the tiny house, with its stained carpets and peeling wallpaper, had suddenly become thick with the haze of neglect and poverty and bad memories. Putting a hand to her throat, she'd run outside, onto the crooked wooden porch to take a staggering breath of cool, clear air.

Now, leaning against the rough wood, Irene stared out at the dark spring night. On the edge of town, between the railroad tracks and the forest, patches of snow still lay on the ground. In the distance, she could see the roof of the tiny house where the Abbotts had once served her cookies after school. Irene pulled her cashmere cardigan a little tighter over her body. She told herself she'd been lucky, really, to have known love, even for such a short time. But if she was lucky, why did it hurt so much?

She'd gotten six different calls from Makhtar since she'd left, all of them from different members of the palace staff who were desperate to have Sharif's wedding to Kalila called off. Well, get in line, she thought. But the latest call had been particularly painful. Aziza had called her at three that morning, waking her up.

"How can I be happy," she'd wailed as greeting, "when both of you are going to be miserable forever?"

"We're not miserable," Irene had lied. "We're fine, and—"

"Fine? You should see my brother right now!"

Irene's throat had ached, and she closed her eyes against the flash of blinding pain. "There's nothing I can do."

"But you said you loved him. How could you love him, and leave him to that woman?"

"He gave me no choice."

"You haven't even called him! Even Basimah is surprised. She told me, since you didn't call after my wedding was canceled, you must not love Sharif at all."

The knife twisted a little deeper in Irene's heart.

"Aziza," she'd gasped in the dark, empty bed of her condo, "please…"

"No, forget it!" she'd snapped. "Don't even try to save him—just enjoy your life and forget all about us!"

She'd ended the call, leaving Irene weeping for the next three hours in the dark.

She missed Aziza, and Makhtar, and everyone in the palace. But most of all, she missed Sharif. His absence was a hole through her body, leaving everything hollow and devoid of meaning. She felt as if she was dying without him.

Irene's gaze fell on her car.

Her last suitcase had arrived from Makhtar yesterday. It was still in the trunk of her rental car. She hadn't wanted to open it because once she did, the last possible link between her and Sharif would be gone. As long as she didn't open it, she could hope he'd left her some note, some letter to read and treasure for the rest of her life. She'd tried to put it off as long as she could.

She couldn't wait another minute. Grabbing her suitcase from the car, she dragged it up to the porch. With a deep breath, she flung it open.

All she saw were the clothes she'd left behind. Clothes. Just clothes. Kneeling forward, she started pawing through them more desperately.

Then she saw it.

A note.

With a gasp, she picked it up. She opened it. Her heart

pounded as she recognized his jagged handwriting. But the note had only two words: *Unpack thoroughly.*

That was it? She looked at the back. Blank. *That was it?*

Still on her knees, she crushed the note to her chest. All that hope for nothing. She leaned her head against the rough, splinter-covered wood of the porch. She wanted to burst into sobs.

"I heard you were back in town."

Irene looked up through a shimmer of tears to see Carter Linsey standing in front of the ramshackle cottage, wearing a dark vest over a white shirt. Carter, the crush of her teenage years, the supposed heartache that had driven her abroad.

"Carter?" Wiping her eyes, she rose unsteadily to her feet. "What are you doing here?"

"I wanted to see if it was true about you. And it is." He rubbed his jaw, looking her over. "Wow. Your time in Paris really...wow."

Irene looked down at her pearls, sleek cashmere sweater set and slim-fit gray trousers. A little dressy for packing up boxes, but since she hadn't wanted to open that last suitcase, she'd had nothing else clean to wear today. She wore contact lenses instead of glasses now, and she'd probably lost weight, too, since she'd lost her appetite beneath the weight of her grief. She suddenly realized she looked different from the girl who'd left over two years ago. Maybe even fit for the Linsey Mansion, as she'd once dreamed. "Um. Thanks."

"So, your family is really moving, huh?" He tilted his head, his eyes smoldering in the way that had once made her heart beat faster. "It's a shame. Because I was kind of thinking maybe...you'd give me another chance."

She stared at him. "You what?"

"Yes." He ran his hand through his tousled dark blond hair. "I think I made a mistake. About you."

She stared at Carter, wondering how she could have ever thought she loved him. The truth was, she'd never even known him. He'd been just a symbol to her. A way of getting out of an unhappy life.

"Oh, Carter. I'm afraid…I must decline your kind offer."

He blinked. "I thought you had a thing for me."

She gave a low laugh. "I thought so once, too." She looked away. "I thought if I could get a man like you to love me, it would mean I was worth something. But that's not love."

"Then what is?"

"It's not about trying to feel better about yourself," she said slowly. "Love is about *protecting the other person*." Her throat went dry. "It's about doing everything you can to give the person you love the life they deserve…" Irene's voice trailed off as she remembered how Sharif had done exactly that.

And she'd left him. In that woman's clutches.

But there was nothing I could have done! She told herself desperately. It wasn't as if she had any kind of control over Kalila—or way to stop her from—

The emir is getting what he deserves. Basimah's voice came back to her. *If I could do something to prevent his wedding, if I knew something that would prevent it, I still wouldn't lift a finger.*

Irene stared off in the distance, her lips parted. Basimah had said that long ago, but she'd been too distracted with her own jealousy and misery to pay attention to the words. How had she missed it? How had she not heard?

Even Basimah is surprised, Aziza had said. *She told me, since you didn't call after my wedding was canceled, you must not love Sharif at all.*

"Irene?"

She focused abruptly on Carter's handsome, pouting face.

"Excuse me," she said. "I need to make a phone call. Thanks for stopping by."

"You're—throwing me out?" he said incredulously.

"I'm wishing you all the best. But not with me. Sorry. I'm in love with someone. And he needs me now."

Scratching his head, Carter threw her one last sorrowful, disgruntled look and left. But Irene had already turned away to dial a number in her phone.

"I was wondering why you didn't ask me about it days ago," Basimah said sourly a few minutes later. "I all but told you everything. After he set my lamb free, canceling her wedding, I expected you would ask. But you didn't, you just left, and I decided you must not have loved him as much as I thought. Although abandoning him to that Al-Bahar woman seemed cold…"

"Tell me everything," Irene begged, kicking herself. She listened to Basimah's story, and her heart was suddenly in her throat.

"Go to Sharif. Tell him everything!"

"Me? Get involved in a palace scandal? No. I keep my head down. And so does my sister. That's how we've kept our jobs so long."

"Tell Aziza, then. She can go to her brother and—"

"I'm not having her involved, either. Poor lamb has suffered enough. And she has enough to think about, applying to colleges and preparing to face the big wide world. No. You love him, you save him yourself."

"But he'll never accept this without proof."

"So get it."

Irene wetted her lips. "That would take money. More money than I can even imagine. If he's been blackmailing her for so long, he'll never let that go for cheap. Even if I gave him every penny I have left, he'd just laugh—"

"Do what you want. I'm out of it, and so is my sister, and so is Aziza. It's your problem now," Basimah said simply, and hung up.

Clutching her phone, Irene sank to the rough wood floor of the porch in despair. She'd just been handed the key to everything. But it was too late. It came down to a problem of money. And time. The wedding was in two days, half a world away.

If only she'd kept that diamond necklace Sharif had tried to give her in Italy, she suddenly thought. She gave a half-hysterical laugh. She hadn't realized then she was throwing away her future. And worse: his.

If you don't want the necklace, toss it in the lake. Bury it in the garden. I care not. It's yours. I won't take it back.

But he had. She'd forced him to take it back, pressed it in his hands, and he'd never had another chance to…

Unpack thoroughly.

Irene sat up straight, covering her mouth with her hand. Wide-eyed, she stared across the porch at her open suitcase.

With a gasp, she flung herself toward it.

The day Sharif had dreaded for half his life had come at last. Today was his wedding day.

He was almost glad to get it over with.

In his finest royal robes, of shining white, Sharif walked down the hallway toward the throne room where he would sign his life away.

As was traditional in Makhtar, the bride herself would not be there for the formal signing ceremony. For that small favor, he was glad. He'd already endured enough of Kalila's company this week. Today would be simple and private. All he had to do was go to the throne room where he and the bride's father would sign the papers and conclude the legal formalities, in front of a few witnesses.

So perhaps, if he closed his eyes very tight, he could pretend it was someone else he was marrying today. Someone bright and beautiful, soft and loving.

Against his will, he pictured Irene, with the warmth of a smile glowing in her eyes.

Sharif's footsteps faltered against the marble floor of the hallway, then stopped. He closed his eyes, hearing the roar of blood in his ears. In this moment, he would have given thirty years of his life—forty—if, instead of a billionaire emir who ruled a wealthy nation, he could just be a common goat farmer of the far south, barely able to feed his family each month on a pittance, if only he could have the most basic freedom of all: being with the woman he loved.

"Sire?"

He saw Hassan in front of him.

Sharif tried to speak, had to clear his throat. "Yes?"

"Your bride's father is awaiting you in the throne room, along with the officiant and the witnesses."

Time to face the blade. "I would like you to witness as well."

The man bowed his head. "I am honored." His voice was stilted. He lifted his head with pleading eyes. "But it is not too late…"

"It's nineteen years too late," Sharif said wearily.

"Miss Taylor…"

"Don't say her name," he ground out. "I don't want to hear it. If she's tried to call again, I don't want to—"

"She's here."

Sharif stared at him. He felt all the blood leave his face. "Here?"

"She showed up ten minutes ago at the palace gate. I did not let her through," Hassan added unhappily. "With your standing order, I had the bodyguards detain her. But I thought—" he bit his lip "—maybe you'd changed your mind and—"

Imagining Irene so close to him now, on the day of his wedding, emotion slashed though Sharif.

"No," he choked out. He put his hand to his forehead. If he saw her face now, today of all days, there was no way he'd be able to go through with this wedding. Promise or no promise, he'd cast honor aside and let his country's fate fly as it would. Let the whole nation risk dissolving into chaos and war, if he could just feel Irene's arms around him again—

"There you are, Your Highness." Sheikh Ahmed Al-Bahar, the former vizier and current governor of Makhtar's eastern region, was standing in the doorway of the throne room. He bared his teeth in a smile. "You are late."

"Yes," Sharif said listlessly. "Forgive me. I am coming now."

The man gave an impatient nod and disappeared back into the throne room. Sharif walked toward it as if walking toward his own execution. Each step was more difficult and required more courage than the one before.

He'd given his word.

He had no choice.

Kalila would be a toxic wife, but perhaps she would still be a good queen, and good mother. Perhaps she…

No, he couldn't even make himself believe that. His stomach twisted at the thought of his future child being raised by her. It felt wrong, so wrong. He didn't want to raise a child with her. Or even create one with her.

There was only one woman he wanted as his wife. Only one he wanted in his bed. One woman to be the mother of his children. And he would never have her.

"Sharif."

He heard Irene's soft, worried voice behind him, and knew he was dreaming. Clenching his hands at his sides, he closed his eyes, enjoying the dream just for one last moment, before he went into the throne room and gave it up forever.

"Sharif!"

The voice was louder now. He frowned, opening his eyes. And turned around.

Irene stood before him, her beautiful face pale. Her lower lip was chapped as if she'd spent the last day chewing on it. Dark circles were beneath her eyes, as if she hadn't slept in days. But she was smiling. And so were the six bodyguards behind her.

His trusted bodyguards had let her into the palace? Against his express orders?

"I don't understand…" Sharif breathed. His heart lifted to his throat but he tried to ignore it, to force it down. He couldn't allow this to happen. He couldn't let himself love her. "You can't be here, Irene. You have to go…"

"No." Irene's eyes were glowing. "You can't make me leave you ever again."

Slowly, afraid of making the dream disappear, Sharif lifted his hands to touch Irene's upper arms. He felt the warmth of her through her cotton blouse. She was really here. He shuddered.

"Please," he whispered. "This is killing me. Seeing you today, when I must marry another…"

Kalila's voice came sharp behind him. "What the hell is *she* doing here?"

He turned to see her in the wide hallway, dressed like a beautiful royal Makhtari bride, covered with colorful silks and brocades and literally dripping in jewels.

"What am I doing?" Looking at her, Irene suddenly gave a warm smile. "I'm stopping this wedding." She turned to

Sharif. "Kalila Al-Bahar cannot marry you. Because *she is already married.*"

It was a dream. It had to be.

His grip tightened. Then he shook his head. "It is impossible. She would never do such a thing."

But her smile only lifted to a grin. "I knew you wouldn't believe me. So I can prove it."

And she stepped aside to reveal the young, extremely muscular man standing behind her.

Kalila's jaw dropped. A mixture of fear, rage and hatred suddenly emanated from her kohl-lined eyes. "Get out of my palace!"

"No," Irene said, so powerful and calm that Sharif did a double take. "*You* will get out of mine."

With a cry, Kalila rushed toward them, as if she intended to claw Irene's eyes out with the red talons of her henna-covered hands. As Sharif stepped protectively in front of Irene, servants started popping their heads out of doorways. Kalila's father came out of the throne room, his own entourage gathering behind him.

"What is going on?" he demanded. He looked at his daughter. "Kalila…?"

But she was looking only at the muscle-bound man. "Don't say it, you piece of trash. Don't even *think* of—"

"Sorry, babe," the man said with a shrug. "She had a better offer."

Sharif whirled to face Irene.

"Tell me," he said urgently.

"Five years ago, in New York, Kalila married her *personal trainer.*" Triumphantly, she held up a piece of paper. "I have the marriage license to prove it."

With a shriek, Kalila tried to reach for it, but Sharif was faster. Grabbing it from Irene's hand, he looked it over. Then silently handed it to Ahmed Al-Bahar.

The man read, and his face turned scarlet.

"It's a lie—all a trick—" Kalila gasped. "I would never throw my life away on a *servant*—"

"Letters in her own hand." Irene held up a stack of envelopes, bound together with a black ribbon. "Love letters. Notes she sent with the blackmail money, begging him to come back to her."

"Women always fall in love with me," the personal trainer said with a smirk. He shrugged. "I can't help it if she let me take advantage…"

"Dirty blackmailer!" she screamed.

"Lying bigamist," he retorted.

"Aah!" She turned to Irene with murder in her eyes. "And you—how did you know? Who talked?"

"Yes," Sharif breathed. He looked down at Irene. "How did you do this?"

"Let's just say I have my sources." She smiled at him, tears of happiness glistening in her eyes. "I knew you wouldn't believe me without proof. So I bribed Rafael with the diamond necklace you'd hidden behind the liner of my suitcase."

"The necklace?" he echoed.

She lifted an eyebrow. "You said it was mine to do with as I pleased. And I found what I wanted to do with it." Reaching up, she stroked his cheek as tears now streaked down her face. "I wanted to save the life of the man that I loved."

A lump rose in his throat. It was true. She'd saved him.

He took a deep, shuddering breath.

"Does this mean," he whispered, "that you will marry me?"

With a horrendous shriek, Kalila collapsed in her wedding dress in a dead faint.

"Your Highness," her father said behind him, "my

daughter has dishonored us. And if not for her—" he glared at Irene "—the dishonor would have been greater." He bowed his head, even as his whole body was tense. "I will deal with Kalila later. For now, I await your punishment."

Silence fell.

"My punishment," Sharif said, "is that you will take her away to live in peace far, far from Makhtar City. And in return—I will say nothing of her betrayal when I announce my change in wedding plans."

The man slowly straightened. His wrinkled face was filled with awe. "You will say nothing of our shame?"

Sharif nodded. "I will say the reason for my change of bride is a personal matter. I will say it's because I've fallen in love for the first time in my life, and there's only one woman I want to be my partner on the throne. Only one woman fated to be my wife. Only one I want to be the mother of my children. I will give this explanation to our people today, but only on one condition." He looked at Irene. "If you agree to marry me right now."

"Say yes," the older man gasped.

"Say yes," Aziza cried from a short distance down the hall.

"Say yes!" cried Basimah and Hassan and all the rest of the palace servants who'd gathered to watch from the ends of the hall.

Irene looked at him, her beautiful pink-cheeked face shining with love.

"Yes," she whispered.

It was the single sweetest word Sharif had ever heard. As he pulled her into his arms, he dimly heard the servants and courtiers burst into spontaneous applause and cries of approval. But all he could think about was the moment his lips would touch hers.

And then...they did.

* * *

"Feel married yet?"

Sharif's voice from the bedroom of their Denver hotel suite was equal parts wry and frustrated. Irene smiled at herself in the bathroom mirror. She couldn't blame him for feeling a little impatient. They'd been officially married in Makhtar two days ago, but had yet to have a wedding night.

It had been a hasty, very formal ceremony. Since she had no official father or male representative, Sharif had abruptly changed the law and decreed that from now on, the marriages would be signed and arranged only by the bride and groom themselves. They'd signed the contracts, then before they'd even had a chance to kiss, the two of them had been forced to part for a full day of wedding celebrations, with the traditional separate feasts for women and men. Irene hadn't been thrilled about attending any six-hour party without Sharif at her side. But as the new sheikha of the land, she'd done it anyway.

Her first royal obligation hadn't been all bad. The women at the feast had come up to her, some shyly, some happily, but all of them relieved to have Irene as the new queen in Kalila's place, even—perhaps especially—the heiress's cousins and distant relatives. Irene was truly touched by their kind words and gracious welcome. Of course, Aziza was over the moon about it, bouncing with joy she didn't even try to disguise. Privately, Irene had thanked Basimah with tears in her eyes. Basimah had demanded that she never mention it again, but then sniffed and wiped her eyes and said she hoped Irene would be a good ruler, loyal and kind.

Irene had still been in shock. She, a nobody from Colorado, the girl who had been mocked and tormented through school about her poverty and family's scandalous past, was now the honored queen of one of the wealthiest nations in the world. She just wished her family could be here to see it...

Her family.

The instant Sharif had arrived at the women's feast to give the groom's traditional greeting, she'd grabbed his arm. "We need to go to Colorado right away," she'd said anxiously. "My sister and mother missed the wedding. They need to be part of it, too..."

"I'll send my plane and bring them here," he growled. He'd stroked her cheek. "I want you in my bed tonight. *Right now...*"

She'd trembled from his touch but remained stubborn. "My mother can't leave Colorado, she's just started rehab. But she might be able to leave for just an hour or two and meet us for a quick ceremony in Denver. Please, Sharif," she'd whispered. "Please."

He'd looked mutinous, then sighed. "Of course, your family must be part of it."

"And," she said thoughtfully, "I could maybe invite Emma—and Cesare..."

An hour later, they were on Sharif's private jet, heading for Colorado. Irene would have been more than willing to have their wedding night at cruising altitude, to join the Mile High Club on their way to Denver, which was nick-named the Mile High City. But this time Sharif was the one to grumpily refuse.

"You haven't waited all your life for your wedding night, to have it haphazardly on some random plane." He'd kissed her, and said softly, "We'll have only one first time, you and I, and it's going to be done properly. In a honeymoon suite at the best hotel in the city, after your family has seen us well and truly married." He'd sat down on the white leather sofa, looking very pained as he muttered under his breath, "Even if it kills me."

Emma and Cesare had flown in with their baby at the last minute, joining Irene's mother and sister, who all had happily cried as they watched Sharif and Irene quietly get married again in Denver, in the privacy of a judge's chambers downtown, with no paparazzi and no fuss. Dorothy and Bill Abbott would have approved, Irene had thought with tears in her eyes.

"So now you know," Cesare had informed Sharif smugly after the ceremony, "how irresistible the right woman can be."

He'd laughed good-naturedly. "Yes." He'd looked down at his new bride. "If I'd met Irene sooner, I'd have gotten married a long time ago."

Now, their family and friends were gone. After the quick ceremony was done, Sharif had heartlessly refused to even allow them even a wedding dinner afterward. "A man only has so much willpower, wife," he'd informed her darkly. "We're going to the hotel."

Now, it was just the two of them. Married. Alone.

Nervously, Irene bit her lip as she looked at herself in the mirror of the marble bathroom of the finest suite in the historic, luxurious Brown Palace Hotel. Her cheeks were rosy after the glasses of champagne the manager had given them upon arrival. Her lips were red from her nervous chewing. Her heart was pounding.

Her sister had slyly given her this lingerie as a wedding gift. Irene had never worn anything like it in her life. The white corset pushed up her full breasts, barely covering her nipples, making her waist tiny. She had tiny white lace panties, partially covered with a naughty white garter belt that held up thigh-high white stockings and white satin kitten heels.

"Modest *and* naughty," her sister had chortled with glee. "Perfect for you, Reena!"

Yes, it was. And she could hardly believe she was about ready to leave this bathroom and let Sharif see her in it. But he was her husband now. Her husband, who would know every part of her, as she would know every part of him, for the rest of their lives.

"Irene?" Sharif called hoarsely from the adjoining bedroom.

"Almost ready." Hair up or down? Her hands shook as she held up her dark hair. Then she let the dark waves tumble over her bare shoulders. Her legs were trembling as she went out into the bedroom of the enormous, elegant hotel suite.

Sharif was stretched out across the enormous four-poster bed, still wearing the black suit from their ceremony. He turned toward her, smiling. "Finally—"

His voice choked off when he saw her in the white corset and garter belt. He sat up, his expression pale.

Irene faltered. "Do you not like it?"

"Like it?" he said hoarsely.

Never taking his eyes off her, Sharif rose unsteadily to his feet and walked to where she stood trembling on the blue carpet. For a moment, he just looked down at her with his dark eyes, the infinitely deep gaze that saw every part of her and loved her in spite of her flaws, as she loved him in spite of his. He cupped her face.

"I nearly died just looking at you. I nearly had a heart attack. If I didn't know you were mine…"

"But you do," she said as her heart started beating again. She smiled at him. "Yours now. Yours forever."

"I love you, Irene, my beautiful wife. I will love you until I die."

She put her hand over his. "You're trembling."

Sharif's lips lifted into a crooked smile. "Sorry." He

took a deep breath. "But you see, in a way, it's my first time, too…"

She licked her lips. Then, lifting on tiptoe in the white heels, she kissed him very, very softly on the lips, then whispered five words in his ear.

"Take me," she said. "Take me now."

Her husband kissed her hungrily, savagely, and lifted her in his arms. Never breaking the kiss, he carried her to their wedding bed, and there, they shared their private, final vow, the one she'd waited for all her life, in the sweet promise without words that would last not just tonight, not just tomorrow, but forever.

* * * * *

SAVED BY THE CEO

BARBARA WALLACE

To my fellow Calanetti creators for making this project so fun to work on.
And to Carol, Val, Darlene and Michelle, who always make me feel like a rock star.
Thanks.

CHAPTER ONE

"I THINK I'M in love."

Louisa Harrison bit off a piece of *cornetto*, moaning as the sweet cake-like pastry melted like butter on her tongue. Crumbs dotted her chin. She caught them with her finger, not wanting to waste a drop. "Seriously, Dani, how do you not weigh a thousand pounds living with this man?" If she were married to a chef as wonderful as Rafe Mancini, she'd be the size of her palazzo, the grounds and the vineyards combined.

Her best friend laughed. "Trust me, it's not easy. Fortunately, running around the restaurant all day keeps me in shape. Especially now. Ever since the royal wedding, we've been slammed with requests for reservations. Everyone wants to eat at the restaurant that fed Prince Antonio and his bride."

"As well they should." Danielle's husband, Rafe, entered the restaurant dining room brandishing a coffeepot. "You make it sound as though Mancini's is some ordinary royal wedding caterer."

"I'm not sure there is such a thing as an *ordinary* royal wedding caterer," Dani replied, kissing him on the cheek, "but you're right, Mancini's is anything but ordinary. Once people taste Rafe's food, they are desperate to come back."

"Only they can't for at least eight weeks. My beautiful bride is right—we are booked solid through the harvest festival."

"That's fantastic," Louisa replied helping herself to a cup of coffee. Rafe Mancini not only created wonderful food, he made the best American coffee in Tuscany.

That was Dani's doing. She'd insisted Rafe add a few New World touches to his traditionally Italian menu to placate US tourists. One of many small changes she'd implemented over the past few months. It hadn't taken long for her friend to establish herself as an equal partner both in the relationship and the business. But then, Louisa had heard there were men in this world who actually liked when their wives had minds of their own. Not to mention lives.

She just hadn't married one.

"Mancini's isn't the only place that's doing well," Dani continued. "Business has been up all around the village. Donatella told me sales at the boutique are up over 40 percent from last year."

Louisa wasn't surprised. Over the past nine months, Monte Calanetti had gone from sleepy Tuscan village to must-see tourist destination. Not only had they been selected to host Halencia's royal wedding—considered the wedding of the year in most circles—but art experts had recently discovered an unknown fresco masterpiece hidden in the local chapel. Now it felt as if every person in Italy, tourist or resident, made a point of driving through the town. That they arrived to discover a picture-perfect village *and* an Italian *Good Food* rated restaurant owned by one of Europe's premier chefs only enhanced the town's allure.

"Quite a change from when you and I arrived here, huh?" she noted. It'd been an early spring day when the two of them had met on the bus from Florence. Two expatriates, each on her own quest to the Tuscan Valley. For Dani, the tiny village represented a last adventure before deciding on her future. Louisa, on the other hand, had taken one look at the terracotta roofs rising from the valley and decided luck had granted her the perfect place to escape her past. A place where she could heal.

"I knew as soon as I stepped off the bus that Monte

Calanetti was special," Dani said. "There's something magical about this town. You can feel it."

More like her friend felt the attraction between her and the man she eventually married; there'd been sparks from the second Dani and Rafe had laid eyes on each other. Louisa kept the thought to herself. "The royal wedding planner certainly thought so," she said instead.

"Unfortunately, we can't ride the wedding momentum forever. Once harvest season ends, people will be more interested in the ski resorts." Rafe said.

"People will still seek out Mancini's," Louisa said.

"Some, yes, but certainly not the numbers we've been enjoying. And they certainly won't spend time visiting other businesses."

True. So much of Monte Calanetti's appeal revolved around being able to stroll its cobblestone streets during the warm weather. It would be hard to make a wish in the plaza fountain if the water was frozen. There was a part of Louisa that wouldn't mind the crowds thinning. She missed the early days when she could walk the streets without worrying that some American tourist would recognize her. Another part, however—the practical part—knew the village needed more than a seasonal income. Prior to the wedding, several of the smaller businesses had been on shaky ground.

A third part reminded her she needed income, too. Till now she'd been surviving on the money the royal family had paid her to use her property, and that was almost gone.

"It won't matter if Mancini's is the best restaurant in the world, if it's surrounded by empty buildings," Rafe was saying. "We need something that will encourage people to spend time here year-round."

Funny he should say that. Louisa sipped her coffee thoughtfully. The practical part of her had also been kicking around an idea lately. It was only a germ at the moment, but it might help the cause. "It would be nice to see the village continue to prosper," she had to admit. Even though she, like Dani, was a relative newcomer, she'd already come to consider the place home, and nobody wanted to see their home suffer economically.

"What do you have in mind?" she asked him. He obviously had something up his sleeve or he wouldn't have put on this breakfast.

Pushing up his sleeves, the chef rested his forearms against the edge of the table and leaned close. "I was thinking we could start some kind of committee."

"Like a chamber of commerce?" Did they even have those in Italy? They must.

"Nothing so formal. I'm picturing local business leaders brainstorming ideas like the harvest festival that we can put on to attract traffic."

"And since the palazzo is such a big part of the village…" Dani started.

"You'd like me to be on the committee." That made sense, especially if she carried through with her own idea. "Count me in… What?"

Her friend and her husband had suddenly become very interested in their breakfast plates. "There's one problem," Dani said.

"Problem?" Louisa's fingers gripped her fork. "What kind of problem?" As if she didn't know what the problem would be. Question was, how had they found out?

"I want Nico Amatucci on the committee, as well," Rafe answered bluntly.

Oh. Her fear vanished in a rush, replaced by a completely different type of tension. One that started low in her stomach and moved in waves through her. "Why would that be a problem?"

"Well," Dani said, "we know the two of you haven't always gotten along…"

Memories of wine-tinged kisses flashed to life. "That's in the past," she replied. "We worked together on cleaning up the plaza, remember?"

"I know, but…"

"But what?"

The couple exchanged a look. "At the wedding, you two looked like you'd had a falling-out."

Louisa would have called it a momentary loss of her senses. "It's no big deal." And it wasn't. Beneath the table, her fingers tapped out a rhythm on her thigh. In comparison to what she thought they were going to say, her "falling-out" with Nico amounted to nothing.

She barely remembered, she thought, tongue running over her lower lip.

"Working together won't be awkward, then?" Rafe asked.

"Don't be silly—Nico and I are adults. I'm sure we can handle sitting on a committee together."

"What committee?"

As if waiting for his cue, Nico Amatucci strolled into the dining room. If he were someone else, Louisa would accuse him of waiting to make a dramatic entrance, but in his case dramatic entrances came naturally.

"Sorry I'm late," he said. "We've been working around the clock since the wedding. It appears people can't get enough of Amatucci Red." The last part was said looking straight at her. As Louisa met his gaze, she forced herself to keep as cool an expression as possible and prayed he couldn't see how fast her heart was racing. This was the first time she'd seen him since the wedding. The vintner looked as gorgeous as ever.

He'd come straight from the fields. The ring of dampness around his collar signaled hours of hard work, as did the dirt streaking his jeans and T-shirt. Louisa spied a couple smudges on his neck, too, left behind after wiping the sweat from his skin. She'd say this about the man: he worked as hard as his employees. Something he, as the owner of one of Tuscany's finest boutique wineries, didn't have to do. Probably did it to make up for the fact he was arrogant and presumptuous.

A frown marred his Romanesque features as he pointed to the coffeepot. "American?"

"That a problem?" Rafe asked.

"No." His sigh was long and exaggerated.

Rafe rolled his eyes. "There's no need to be dramatic. If you want espresso, just say so."

"Make it a double," Nico called after him with a grin. "I've been up since sunrise."

Despite there being three empty seats on the other side of the table, he chose to sit in the one his friend had just vacated, which positioned him directly next to Louisa. "I trust I didn't keep you waiting too long," he said to her. His crooked smile made the comment sound more like a dirty secret. But then, that's what Nico Amatucci did. He used his charm to lure people into bending to his will. When they didn't bend to his authority, that is. His sensual mouth and sparkling dark eyes could worm their way past a person's defenses, trapping them in his spell before they knew what was happening.

He reached for a *cornetto*, his shoulder brushing against Louisa's as he moved. The hours of hard work had left him smelling of fresh-tilled dirt and exertion. It was a primal, masculine scent, and though Louisa tried her best not to react, her own basic instincts betrayed her and she shivered anyway. To cover, she ignored his question and took a long sip of coffee.

Nico countered by taking a bite of pastry. "Has everyone recovered from the wedding?" he asked, licking the crumbs off his thumb. Louisa narrowed her eyes. She swore he was purposely trying to make the action erotic.

Especially when he added, "I know I'm still feeling the aftereffects. Are you?"

Again, he looked straight at her. Louisa lifted her chin. "Not at all," she replied with a crispness that made her proud.

Apparently it wasn't crisp enough, since he reacted with little more than an arched brow. "Are you sure?"

Dani jumped to her feet. "I'm going to go see if Rafe needs help. Marcello rearranged the pantry yesterday, and you know how he gets when he can't find things."

Who did she think she was fooling? Rafe wouldn't allow anyone to rearrange his pantry without supervision.

"Subtle," Nico remarked when Dani was out of earshot. "One would think she was trying to give us time alone."

"One would think," Louisa muttered in return. "Though I don't know why."

"Perhaps she thinks we need to talk."

"Well, she would be wrong. We don't need to talk about anything."

"I see. Is that why you're avoiding me, *bella mia*?"

His beauty indeed. *I'm not your anything*, she wanted to snap. She didn't belong to anyone. Not anymore. And especially not to someone like him. Bad enough she let herself fall under his spell at the wedding. "Who says I've been avoiding anyone? Maybe I've been busy. You're not the only one who's had a lot to do since the wedding."

"My apologies. You're right." His chair made a scratching noise on the floor as he angled it so they were facing one another. Taking the last *cornetto* from the center of the table, he tore the pastry in two and divided the pieces between their plates. "So tell me, what have you been up to that has kept you so busy?"

Louisa glared at the fluffy delicacy in front of her. "Things," she replied.

"Things?" His chuckle was smooth like syrup. "That's a very broad category."

"I'm a very broad person."

"Ah, *bella mia.* 'Broad' is definitely not what I would call you." His hand moved forward. Thinking he was about to brush the bangs from her eyes, Louisa jerked back, only to turn red when he picked up his half of the pastry. "I wanted to talk about what happened at the wedding."

"I told you, there's nothing to talk about. We made a mistake, that's all. Why don't we forget it ever happened?"

Sounds from the kitchen drifted into the restaurant as Nico chewed his pastry. Louisa listened, trying to determine how far away she was from rescue. There was an uneasy familiarity to the way they sat with Nico's leg close but not touching hers.

Slowly his eyes lifted to meet hers. "What if I don't want to forget?"

"One double espresso as ordered!" Rafe announced. The chef returned to the dining room carrying a gold-rimmed demitasse. Behind him trailed Dani, who shot Nico a look. From their mutually taut expressions, Louisa wondered if there hadn't been a disagreement over interrupting the conversation. She offered a silent thank-you to whichever one of them had won.

First thing Dani did when she sat down was to try to catch Louisa's eye, but Louisa continued to stare at the tablecloth and prayed that the floor might swallow her up. She hated scrutiny. Hated the feel of people's eyes upon her. Trying to look inside her. Thinking they could read her thoughts. Her fingers crept to her neckline to tug the suddenly too-tight collar.

"Will there be anything else, your highness?" Thank God for Rafe. Again. He set the cup on the table with a flourish, forcing Nico's attention back to the business at hand.

The vintner's bronze fingers wrapped around the handle. "This will do for now," he replied.

"You do know that when I said 'your highness,' I meant it sarcastically, right?"

"Yes, but you wait on me all the same." Nevertheless, Nico saluted his friend with the cup before taking a sip. "So," he said after he swallowed, "you said something about a committee?"

"You *were* listening," Rafe replied. "Yes, I want to create a committee for developing tourism."

"Monte Calanetti already has a person in charge of tourism." Nico explained. "Vincenzo Alberti."

"Tell me you're joking. Everyone knows Vincenzo did nothing and that the only reason we hosted the wedding was because your brother was in town to write the proposal. It could have just as easily gone to some place in Umbria."

"True. Vincenzo is rather useless."

"What I'm talking about is something independent and more grassroots. I'm certain if the local businesspeople put their heads together, we can come up with a host of ideas to increase tourism. Not to mention run them better."

"I certainly won't complain about increased business, especially during the dormant months," Nico said. Leaning back, he hooked an arm over the back of his chair. "Who else do you have in mind besides the four of us? I assume it is the four of us, since we're all sitting here."

The two men began tossing names back and forth, some of whom Louisa recognized, some she didn't. She wasn't surprised when, as the conversation progressed, the dynamic between the friends shifted with Nico slowly taking the reins. That was something else Nico Amatucci did. No matter how commanding others might be—and Rafe certainly qualified as commanding—Nico was always the one in charge.

Her ex-husband had been the exact same way. Minus

the rugged sensuality that is. Steven had been painstakingly glossy, his looks created from the pages of fashion magazines whereas Nico was more earthy. The kind of man who got his hands dirty from actually working with them, not from helping himself.

She remembered the roughness of Nico's calloused hands as his thumbs had fanned her cheeks...

And how effortlessly he'd managed to dance her into a secluded corner without her realizing. In charge till the end, just like Steven.

"We need to make it clear to everyone involved that we don't want to be too commercial," she heard him say. "It's one thing to increase tourism, it's another to lose the very thing that makes Monte Calanetti special."

Rafe agreed. "Absolutely. Ideally, we want events or attractions that highlight our traditions and Old World charm. That's what the tourists want. Maybe there's something we can do around the *Madonna and Child* painting in the chapel. Something historical."

"I read the other day that Santo Majorca is building a spa around its underground springs. Too bad we can't unearth a spring here."

"Wouldn't that be nice?"

"Ow!" Louisa jumped as pain shot up from her shin. Damn it, but Dani wore pointy shoes. That kick would leave a bruise.

The two men turned to look at her. "Everything all right?" Nico asked.

"Fine," she said, rubbing her leg. Beneath her index finger she could feel a small divot. There was definitely going to be a bruise.

Across the table, her friend didn't even have the decency to look apologetic. She was too busy gesturing with her eyebrows for Louisa to say something. Louisa replied with a shake of her head.

Why not? Dani mouthed.

Because of a zillion reasons. The concept was still too vague and unformed, for one. She wasn't ready for people to start poking holes in her idea. Or take it over, she thought, sliding a look in Nico's direction. She wasn't sure she was ready period.

"Did I miss something?" Nico asked.

Of course he would say something. Those sharp brown eyes didn't miss a thing, not that either she or Dani were being very subtle.

"Louisa's been working on a terrific idea," Dani said.

"Really?" He turned to face her. "What is it? If it's something that will help, by all means tell us."

"It's still at the very beginning stages. I haven't worked out all the details yet."

"But the general idea is brilliant. She wants to turn the palazzo into a hotel."

Some of Nico's enthusiasm faded in favor of concern. "What kind of hotel? You're not planning to alter the property, are you?"

"Nothing drastic, I assure you," she said as she shot a narrow-eyed look in Dani's direction. Why couldn't she have found an unenthusiastic best friend? "I was thinking of something more like a high-end boutique hotel."

"Isn't that a great idea?" Dani piped in, clearly unfazed by Louisa's glare. "People love to stay in historic buildings. Remember that couple last month who told us they were staying at Palazzo St. Rosa? They couldn't stop raving about the place."

"She's right, they couldn't," Rafe said. "No matter how hard I tried to make them."

"They showed us the photos, and the place can't hold a candle to Louisa's."

"That's because Palazzo di Comparino is special." Intended as both a compliment and a warning, Nico's comment made Louisa bristle. It'd been nine months since she'd moved in and he still acted as though the palazzo was his responsibility. And Dani wondered why she didn't want to talk about her plans.

"Special, yes," she replied, "but it's also very large and expensive for one person to keep up." Especially if said person had no other source of income. "Opening it to the public is one way to cover some of the expenses." As well as help her stay independent. Being in charge, having total control of her life again, seemed almost too good to be true.

Maybe she could finally put the past behind her.

No sooner did the thought form than her old friend insecurity came rushing in to take its place. "Of course, the building needs a lot more upgrading before I can do much of anything, and I still have to secure financing. Who knows how long it'll take before anything happens."

"Well, I agree with Dani—I like the idea. A high-end hotel is exactly what Monte Calanetti needs," Rafe said as he warmed both her and Dani's coffee. "If you need anything, let us know. Nico and I will be glad to help. Isn't that right, Nico?"

"Absolutely." The vineyard owner slid his empty cup across the table for a refill, which Rafe immediately provided, remembering Nico preferred espresso. There was a roguish gleam in his eyes as he smiled. "As the two of us have proven, we make a good team, do we not?"

A good team. In a flash, Louisa's mind traveled back in time…

The Royal Wedding

"Ask and you shall receive. Your cake, *signorina*." Nico's exaggerated bow as he handed her a slice of cake made Louisa laugh. The wedding had brought out the lightheartedness in everyone, even her. It felt good, laughing. She'd faked happiness for so long that she was afraid she'd forgotten how to truly enjoy herself.

"Grazie," she replied with her best regal nod before noticing he'd returned with only one plate. "No slice for you? Don't tell me there isn't enough." She saw the cake; it was large enough to feed all of Italy.

"Ah, but it's more fun to share, don't you think?" From his breast pocket, he produced two forks. "To commemorate our successful partnership. We make a good team, do we not?"

"Surprisingly, yes." If anyone had told her that one day she and the vineyard owner would be civil to one another, let alone work together, she would have told them they were crazy. But the two of them had organized the massive village cleanup in preparation for today's wedding. As a result, the palazzo and the plaza had never looked lovelier—a pretty big achievement considering the village had started out picture-perfect.

And now, here they were enjoying each other's company at the wedding reception, as well. Things between them had definitely thawed since Louisa's first day in town when he'd demanded to see her ownership papers. Or maybe she was the one who was starting to thaw?

It certainly felt as though something inside her was shifting.

She focused her attention to the cake Nico was sliding toward her.

"If we're toasting, shouldn't we be raising a glass?" she asked, taking one of the forks.

"We've been raising our glasses all day. I thought we could use a change of pace." He moved his chair so that they were sitting side by side, close enough that his elbow nudged hers. Cutting off a bite of cake, he raised it in the air like a glass. "To teamwork."

"To teamwork."

Louisa moved to cut her own piece of cake, intending to salute him back, only to have him press the cake to her lips before she could. "The lady should always have the first bite," he said, his low voice.

A warm tightness moved through her as the fork slid between her teeth. Chocolate and raspberry melted on her tongue.

"Good?" he asked.

"Amazing." She ran a tongue over her lower lip, chasing the hint of frosting that had been left behind. "Try some."

With what could only be called a wicked smile, he did, and when the fork disappeared into his mouth, the tightness in her stomach intensified. A hint of chocolate remained on her lips. Though tempted to lick the taste away, she reached for her napkin instead. After that display, running her tongue over her lips seemed too much like answering in kind and the summer air already felt thick and stifling.

While she'd never let him know it, Nico was quite possibly the most handsome man here, even more handsome than the crown prince. Months of working outdoors had left him with a permanent tan that gave everything else about him—his smile, his eyes, his crisp white shirt—a kind of brilliance the other men couldn't match.

Why on earth was he sitting here eating cake with her? Giving voice to her thoughts, she said, "I have to admit, I was surprised when you suggested we attend together." Handsome, rich...she assumed he had a black book of supermodels at the ready for occasions like this.

"Made sense, did it not? We're both here because our businesses are involved in the celebration.

"Why?" he asked with another grin. "Is there someone you would rather be sitting with?"

"Well, the best man is sort of attractive."

"The best man is only interested in the wedding planner. Face it, *bella mia*," he said, stretching an arm across the back of her chair. "I am the best offer you have."

Another laugh bubbled its way from her chest. She must have had too much wine because his arrogance was sounding damn sexy at the moment.

The room grew quiet. "*Signore e signori*, his Royal Highness Prince Antonio and his bride invite you to join them in this, their final dance of the evening."

"Wow," she said, "last dance already? Time goes by fast."

"Looks like my company was good after all."

Louisa cut another bite off the cake. "Don't get too carried away."

"Come on, admit it." He nudged her shoulder. "You had a good time."

"Yeah, I did." And for the first time in years, she meant it. This had been her first black-tie event since the divorce, and she'd feared the memories of her old life would prove too much to deal with, but Nico had proved a wonderfully entertaining companion. She was actually sorry to see the evening end.

"We need to dance," Nico said, setting down his fork in a way that made it sound more like a command. "One doesn't refuse an invitation from a future king."

Apparently not. All around the room, couples were making their way to the dance floor to join Antonio and his bride, Christina. A few feet away Dani and Rafe were already wrapped in each other's arms, as were Nico's brother, Angelo, and his fiancée. Even Nico's extremely pregnant sister, Marianna, was swaying to the music.

She looked back at the hand Nico was holding out. Such strong capable hands, she thought, the tightness giving way to an internal shiver. "I haven't danced in a long time," she warned. "Your feet might want to be prepared."

"Consider them forewarned."

She needn't have worried. As soon as Nico's arm entwined her waist, she forgot all about being rusty. Their bodies moved together like two synchronized pieces of a whole.

Nico's eyes swept the length of her. "I've been meaning to tell you how beautiful you look. You outshine the princess."

"Careful, talking like that could be considered treason in Halencia." She tried to brush off the compliment with a smile. Flattery had lost its meaning to her a long time ago. Looking good had been part of the requirements when she was married. Looking good, behaving properly, doing what she was told…all part of the job.

"I'll take the risk," he said as he pulled her close. Louisa's eyes locked with his as they moved across the floor. They were darker than she'd ever seen them, the pupils giant pools of black. While Steven always expected her to look beautiful, he never looked at her with such blatant appreciation. The glint in Nico's eyes made her feel like a bite of wedding cake, waiting to be sampled. The thought should have frightened her. Instead, hot shivers danced along her spine.

God, but it'd been a long time since she'd felt like a woman instead of a possession.

The orchestra faded away, drowned out by the sound of their breathing and the rasp of his jacket as it brushed her sequined bodice with every rise and fall of his chest.

She wasn't sure who leaned in first. Once his mouth closed over hers, who had made the first move didn't matter, not when his lips were moving against hers as if he were trying to kiss his way inside. She kissed him back just as hungrily, too many passionless years making her desperate. They kissed hard and deep, only stopping when the need to breathe became too much.

Blinking, Louisa slowly remembered where they were. "I—"

"Shh…" He pressed a kiss to the corner of her mouth. "It's okay, *bella mia*."

Bella mia. My lovely. *Mine*. Louisa stiffened.

"Don't worry," he said, misreading the reaction for embarrassment. "No one can see us."

Turning, she saw that they were in a secluded corner, just outside the ballroom door. While she'd been lost in his spell, Nico had steered them safely away from prying eyes.

How thoughtful and practiced of him. But then, men like Nico didn't do anything spontaneously, did they? They were always in control. Like hunters stalking prey, only instead of bullets they used smiles and seduction. Their victims were trapped in their gilded cages before they ever knew what was happening.

Except Louisa did know. And she was never ever going to be trapped again.

Pushing just enough so as to not make a scene, she stepped out of his embrace. "The bride and groom will be leaving shortly. I better make sure everything is set for their departure." She left him standing in the corner without turning back…

"Louisa?"

Yanked from the memory by the sound of Dani's voice, she saw the three of them staring at her. "You okay?" her friend asked.

"I'm fine," she lied. Part of her was still back on the dance floor, lost in a pair of dark eyes. "You were saying?"

"I was saying that as far as financing your hotel is concerned, I would consider investing…"

"No." She didn't mean for the word to come out so strongly, but Nico was looking straight at her while he spoke and the memory of how those eyes distracted her was so fresh…

Just as well, though. Better to be blunt than let him think he had a chance. As an investor or anything else.

Monte Calanetti was her chance at a new life. No way was she going to let someone sweep in and mess things up.

Not this time.

CHAPTER TWO

NICO SQUINTED AND double-checked the line on the refractometer. "Twenty-two point four."

"Is that on schedule?"

"Close." Pulling the battered leather journal from his back pocket, he flipped through the pages until he found last year's data. "One hundredth of a point off," he reported before turning the page and making note of today's measurement. Even better than he expected. He'd been afraid the easy summer had accelerated the ripening process. So far, however, the sugar levels were holding close to previous years, which boded well for this year's vintage.

"When will you harvest?"

He turned to the young man at his elbow. Mario, a viticulture student from the university was hanging on his every word. "Depends upon the weather and the variety, but for Amatucci Red, I like the Brix level to be between twenty-five and twenty-six. A hair shy of precocious, as it were," he added with a chuckle.

Mario nodded as he took notes. Nico would never admit it out loud but he enjoyed being seen as a master. It made him feel as though he'd achieved what Carlos had hoped for him. "Precocious?" he asked. "I've never heard that winemaking term before."

"That's because it's not really a winemaking term, just something Carlos Bertonelli used to say. 'Grapes are like children. You want to raise them to be sweet, but not so sweet they overwhelm you.' In other words..."

"A hair shy of precocious."

"Exactly." Tossing a grape into the air, he caught the

plump berry in his mouth. "Carlos was full of sayings like that," he said crushing the skin between his teeth. The juice was tart on his tongue; a ways to go before preco-ciousness. "His version of Old World wisdom."

"Signor Bertonelli is the man who used to own these vineyards, right? The ones surrounding the palazzo?"

"*Si.* He was my mentor. Taught me everything I know about winemaking." Nico's heart ached a little every time he thought of the old man, which was often.

"Is that why you're still maintaining the vineyards? Out of respect for him?"

"Out of respect, and partly because Monte Calanetti wouldn't exist without these vineyards. I don't want to see part of our tradition disappear."

There was more to the story, naturally—the truth was always complicated—but Mario didn't need to know how Carlos had kept him grounded when life got crazy. With his even, unflappable demeanor and vat full of wisdom, the old man had been mentor, grandfather and safety net all rolled into one.

When he was a little boy, Nico wondered if the stork hadn't delivered him to the wrong house. That he should have been dropped in the Bertonelli fields instead of his own family's. Truth was, Carlos had been so much more than a mere mentor. Not a day went by that Nico didn't miss the man.

If he were alive, perhaps he could help Nico under-stand his grandniece better. Looking over the vines to the palazzo, he spied Louisa's platinum-blond hair reflecting the sun as she watched them from the terrace. He nodded hello only to have her move out of view. Still avoiding him. She'd been doing so since the wedding.

Never had he met a woman who was so difficult to read. Cold one moment, warm and tender the next. He'd thought they'd turned a corner at the wedding. A very satisfying corner at that. He smiled, remembering the press of her mouth against his. So soft, so receptive. Then suddenly—poof!—everything changed, and they were back to those frigid early days when she barely gave him the time of day.

"Signor Amatucci?"

Mario was staring at him, obviously waiting for a response of some kind. "Nico," he corrected. "Not *Signor*."

"Sorry. Nico. I was wondering what you wanted to do next."

Figure out what's going on in my blonde American's head. He doubted that's what Mario meant, though. "I want to gather a few soil samples from the southern fields," he said. "Why don't you head back to the winery and begin testing the grapes we've collected?" It was standard practice to double-check the field readings using the equipment at the lab. Unlike his mentor, Nico liked to have solid data to corroborate his taste buds.

"Are you sure?" Being on the field must truly be making him nostalgic, because the way the kid straightened with the prospect of responsibility brought back memories of the first time Carlos had given him a task to complete on his own. Had he looked that earnest? "I suggested it, didn't I?"

"Yes. Of course. I'll leave the results on your desk."

"Along with your recommendations. I'm eager to hear your suggestions."

The kid nodded again, wide-eyed and serious. "Absolutely."

Of course, Nico would repeat the tests himself later on—the crops were far too valuable to trust to a university student—but there was no need to say anything. Better for Mario's confidence if he believed he was operating without a safety net.

He started packing his test gear back in his canvas

satchel. The faded bag had been with him since his days
with Carlos, and looked older than that. "If you have any
problems, talk to Vitale. I'll be back later this morning."

"How are you getting back? Do you want me to come
back for you?"

"No need. I'll hop the wall. There's a low spot," he
added when the student frowned. "The Amatuccis and
the Bertonellis have been cutting back and forth through
these properties for years." At least this Amatucci had.
His brother and sister had found other ways to escape.

Once Mario's taillights disappeared in the dust, Nico
shouldered his bag and headed south. Above him, the sun
lit a cloudless blue sky. The air was ripe with fruit and
olives, and if the breeze hit just right, you could catch
the faint undertone of lavender. Another perfect day, he
thought, wiping the sweat from his forehead.

He was by himself, walking the terraced hill. Back
when he was a little boy, these fields had been filled
with workers. He remembered the first time he ventured through the archway that divided the properties, a
stressed-out, scared boy looking for a place where doors
didn't slam and voices were calm. Stepping into the fields
of Comparino had been like finding paradise. There was a
tranquility in the steady tick-tick-tick of the sprinkler, the
low hum of the insects. And it never changed. Oh, there
were storms and blights. Natural disasters that caused
temporary disruption, but no matter what, Nico knew that
come summer, the sounds would be there. Grapes would
grow and wine would get made the same as it had for
hundreds of years. How he loved the predictability; so
unlike the world on his side of the arch, where he never
knew from one day to the next whether his parents were
together or apart.

Such is the price of grand passion, Carlos said once,

after one of his parents' explosive breakups. *It's either sun or storm. No in between.*

Nico wouldn't know. His passion didn't run that deep.

The vines in the south garden had grown thick and tangled with neglect. Left unmolested, insects had nibbled holes in the leaves. Ignoring the bee buzzing near his ear, Nico knelt in the shade. Using his utility knife, he churned the hardened topcoat, unearthing the moist soil beneath. Then he carefully shoveled several inches of the rich black dirt into collection jars. He was wiping the residue on his jeans when a flash of white caught the corner of his eye. He smiled. Part of the reason he'd picked this morning to test the soil was because the southern fields abutted the verandah. This time of morning, Louisa would be having breakfast outside, the way she always did, and while she might be avoiding him, she wouldn't be able to resist spying on what he was doing. Pretending to study the overgrown rose bush marking the end of the row, he kept his back to her. "Careful, *bella mia*," he said, breaking into English, "people might think you are interested in what I am doing."

"I'm always interested in what people do on my property," came the deliciously haughty reply.

Slowly, he turned around. Louisa stood at the railing, a mug cradled between her palms. Despite the early hour, she was fully dressed in jeans and a soft flowing shirt. She hadn't done her hair yet, though. Instead of being pulled tight in her signature severe hairstyle, the strands hung long and loose around her shoulders. If she knew that was how Nico preferred she wear it, she'd no doubt tie it back tighter than ever.

"Do you plan to scrutinize your hotel guests with the same intensity?"

The mention of the hotel was ignored. "I was out here

having breakfast. You're the one who crossed into my field of vision."

Apparently they were also going to ignore the fact she'd been watching him earlier. At least she'd answered him. Did that mean they were back on speaking terms?

Only one way to find out. "Breakfast, you say. I don't suppose there is enough coffee for two?" When she didn't immediately answer, he grabbed the terrace balustrades to haul himself up and over the wall.

"I thought you despised American coffee."

"It's growing on me. Like a lot of American things," he added with a smile.

He nodded his head toward the bistro table that held the rest of her meal, including a tall thermal carafe. "Should I drink from the container?"

"Please don't. I'll get you a cup."

She didn't ask him to leave. Did that mean she was thawing again?

"You know that you are going to have to learn how to make a proper espresso if you plan to open a hotel," he said, following her inside.

"I didn't realize you were also an expert on hotel management."

"No, just an expert on being Italian."

As they passed through the glass doors into the room that had been the *piano nobile*, he instinctively paused. "I'll wait here." When Louisa frowned over her shoulder, he lifted his dusty work boot. If Carlos had been alive, he would have walked across the floor without a second thought, but Louisa seemed more the clean and orderly type. The last thing he wanted was to ruin their fragile accord by tracking dirt across the clean terracotta tiles. The gesture must have been appreciated because she nodded rather than arguing the point. "I'll be right back."

The palazzo looked good. Louisa had accomplished

a lot over the past few months. The dated furniture had been replaced by comfortable modern pieces but the Old World elegance remained. The intricate coffered ceiling and carved archways gleamed they were so clean. Hard to believe it was the same property. Carlos had never seemed to care about his living conditions, especially after his wife died. And then, of course, there were the years it had sat unclaimed. If Nico hadn't kept an eye on the property, Carlos's legacy would have fallen into even greater shambles.

Louisa never did say why she'd ignored the property for so long. He asked her once, but she told him it was none of his business. And now, after years of neglecting her inheritance, she was breaking her back attempting to return the palazzo to its former glory.

His American was definitely a confusing and complicated woman.

"If you want pastry, you'll have to go home," Louisa said when she returned. "Today is market day."

"Coffee is fine. Thank you." It didn't escape him that she held the cup at arm's length, keeping a healthy distance. Things might be warmer between them, but not completely thawed.

"I'd offer milk, but I know you prefer it black."

"I'm flattered you remember."

"Hard to forget black coffee." She brushed past him, leaving behind a soft memory of Chanel.

"May I ask what you were doing digging in the dirt?"

"Taking soil samples."

"Why?"

For a chance to talk with you. "To determine what needs to be done to make the dirt suitable for new vines." Depending upon the soil levels, he planned to recultivate the field, with canaiolo or cabernet sauvignon, if he was feeling untraditional. "Since it will take a few years before the plants yield a usable harvest, I want to replant sooner rather than later."

"Is that so?" She tossed him a cryptic look before turning to the hills. "Funny. I don't remember selling you the property."

She had to be joking. She was going to claim sovereignty now? "That's funny, because I don't remember you complaining about my maintaining it on your behalf."

"On my behalf and to your benefit. Or are you going to tell me you didn't double your vineyard without paying a penny?"

"No," he replied with a shrug. "Why deny the truth?" He had benefited from using Carlos's land. Carlos would have wanted as much. "You chose to stay away, and I saw no sense in letting good land go to waste."

"I didn't choose, I..." Whatever she was going to say was swept aside by a deep breath. "Regardless, that doesn't give you the right to do what you want. No matter how good you are at it," she muttered into her cup.

"Good at vineyard management or doing what I want?" Her side eye gave him his answer. "Fine. You're the owner. If you don't want to recultivate, what would you like to do with your neglected vineyards?"

"I'll let you know," she said, jutting her chin for maximum haughtiness.

They both knew he would replant; she was being stubborn for stubbornness' sake. He wondered if she knew how attractive she looked when she was being argumentative. Maybe that was why he enjoyed pushing her buttons. Like a person with a stick poking at a hornet's nest and getting off on the risk, provoking her to annoyance had excitement curling low in his stomach. And damn if it wasn't easy to push her buttons. Seemed as though all he had to do was breathe and her eyes were flashing.

Those eyes were flashing brightly at the moment. Reminding him of how she'd looked right after they kissed.

Ah. Clarity dawned.

"This isn't really about recultivating, is it?" he asked, stepping closer. "This is about what happened at the wedding."

She whipped around to face him. "I told you I didn't want to talk about that."

And yet the moment hung over them begging to be mentioned. "Come now, *bella mia*, don't tell me you expect us to pretend it never happened?"

How could they possibly ignore such an amazing kiss? Surely he wasn't the only one who lay awake at night remembering how perfectly their bodies fit together. The way her breath quickened when he'd stepped closer, told him he wasn't.

"Don't call me *bella mia*, and I'm not asking you to pretend about anything. It's simply not worth talking about. We drank a little too much wine and let the romantic atmosphere get to us, that's all."

"Really?" He leaned in, angling his head near the curve of her neck. "That's all it was? A drunken mistake? I'm not sure I believe you." Especially when her skin flushed from his proximity.

"Why not?"

"Because..." Nico let his gaze take the path his fingers wanted to take. "For one thing, I wasn't drunk."

This time it was Louisa who closed the distance between them, her eyes ablaze from the confrontation. "Maybe you weren't, but that doesn't mean I wasn't. Much as your ego would like to think otherwise."

Oh, how his little hornet's nest enjoyed poking him as much as he enjoyed poking her. "Trust me, *bella mia*," he said, "my ego doesn't need stroking. Go ahead and call it a drunken mistake if you have to. Same way you can tell yourself that you wouldn't enjoy a repeat performance."

Louisa's lips parted with a gasp, like he knew they would. With a smile curling his own, Nico dipped his head to claim them.

Just as their mouths were about to touch, she turned her face. "Okay, fine, I admit it was a great kiss, but it can't happen again."

"Why not?" Again, he didn't understand. Two people obviously attracted to one another; why shouldn't they explore the possibilities?

"For a lot of reasons. To start with, I'm not looking to get involved in a serious relationship."

All the better. "Neither am I." *Serious* came with certain expectations, and as history had proven, he lacked the depth to meet them.

"And—" she dodged his outstretched hand "—we're neighbors, plus we'll be working on that committee Rafe is creating. We'll be around each other all the time."

"Perhaps I'm misunderstanding, but doesn't that make things easier?"

"It will make things awkward."

"Only as awkward as we let it be," he replied.

Her sandals slapped softly against the floor as she returned to her breakfast table, a position, Nico noted, that put a barrier of glass and wrought iron between them.

Of course, she already knew that, or else her hands wouldn't be gripping the chair back so tightly. Nico knew the cues; she was working up to another reason. "Look, right now I can't be involved with anyone seriously or casually. I need to concentrate on taking care of myself. Do you understand?"

"Si." Better than she realized. The last woman who'd said those words to him had been suffering from a broken

heart. Was that Louisa's secret? Had she come to Monte Calanetti because some bastard had let her down?

If that was the case, then far be it for him to add to her injury. One woman was enough to have hurt in a lifetime. There were other women in Monte Calanetti whose company he could keep, even if they weren't as enigmatically fascinating. "Consider the kiss forgotten," he told her.

Louisa's back relaxed as she exhaled. "Thank you," she replied. It felt good to clear the air between them. She'd been acting like a complete brat the past couple of days, stuck between wanting to stand up for herself and being afraid of succumbing to the attraction. She'd treated Nico like the enemy rather than the neighbor she'd come to know and respect. But now that they were on the same page...

Maybe she could finally stop thinking of how much he reminded her of Steven. Her ex-husband's kisses had made her head spin, too, she recalled. The first time she'd been kissed by a man who knew what he was doing.

Feeling Nico's dark eyes studying her, she added in a low voice, "I appreciate your understanding."

"I am nothing if not agreeable."

The joke broke the spell and Louisa laughed. They both knew he could be as stubborn as she could. "Yes, I've seen how agreeable you can be." He'd been particularly "agreeable" earlier this year when his sister, Marianna, had announced her unplanned pregnancy. Louisa had had to talk him out of staking the baby's father in the garden.

"I brought a smile back to your face, did I not?" His smile was crooked and way too sexy.

"I'm glad you said something," he added in a more serious voice. "I did not like that our friendship had turned awkward again."

He was being kind. "I was being a bit irrational, wasn't I?" *Bitchy* would have been a better word.

"A bit. But I may have egged you on."

She laughed. "You think?"

"A bit. How about if we both promise to be on our best behavior?"

"Sounds like a plan."

"Good." To her surprise, there wasn't an ounce of seduction in his smile. If anything he looked genuinely happy. Damn if that didn't make her stomach flutter.

"But," he continued, changing topics, "you should do something about these fields. It is a waste of good cropland."

Not to mention bad business. Guests weren't going to pay to stay at a nonworking vineyard.

Shoot. She was going to have to let him replant, wasn't she? "As soon as I finalize the plans for the hotel, I'll make some decisions." He might be getting his way, but he would get it on her schedule.

"How are your plans going?"

"They're coming along." Only last night she'd put the finishing touches on a preliminary marketing plan.

"Glad to hear it. You know—" he set down his cup, the contents of which, Louisa noticed, were untouched "—my offer still stands. If you need investors…"

Louisa tensed before remembering she'd promised to behave better. It wasn't his fault his offer set her teeth on edge. "I won't need investors," she told him. "I've got a meeting with the bank this afternoon to discuss opening a line of credit. If plans go as I hope, I might be able to open on a limited basis this winter."

"That soon?"

"I did say limited. Waiting until the palazzo is fully renovated could take years, and I want to move fast enough that I can capitalize on the royal wedding." She sounded defensive, the way she used to whenever Steven questioned her. *But he's not Steven, and you don't need any-*

one's permission anymore. "I figured I'd concentrate on upgrading the infrastructure, plumbing, electrical, that stuff, and make sure the front half of the palazzo is in perfect working order, before expanding into the back."

"Sounds smart."

"I think so." She did *not* feel a frisson of pleasure at the compliment. "Now I just have to hope the bank comes through with financing quickly." And that the loan officers would take the palazzo for collateral without looking too far beyond the fact she was Carlos Bertonelli's grand-niece. Her post-divorce financials were sketchy at best. And heaven help her if the bank looked into her former life. She'd never get financing.

"Who are you meeting with?" Nico asked.

"Dominic Merloni."

"I know him. He's a smart businessman. When I get to my office, I'll call—"

"No. Thank you."

"I don't mind. I'd do the same for any friend."

"Did you do it for Rafe when he opened the restaurant? That's what I thought," she said before he could answer. Rafe would have had his head if he'd interfered.

So would she. "Look, I appreciate your wanting to help, but it's very important to me that I do this 100 percent on my own."

"I understand," he said. Except that he didn't. Louisa could tell from how his brows knit together. He was studying her, looking for the reasons behind her need for independence. Louisa said nothing. She'd already revealed more about her past than he needed to know.

"But," he added, "I hope, if you need a reference, you won't hesitate to give Dominic my name. I'm told I have influence in this town. With some people, that is."

Louisa couldn't help but return his smile. "With some people."

They chatted for a few more minutes, mostly about superficial things. Rafe's committee, plans for the harvest festival. A series of nice safe topics that would prove they'd put the awkwardness of the kiss behind them. Nico had just started describing the traditional grape-stomping ceremony when his cell phone rang.

"Mario, the student who is working for us this summer," he explained when he hung up. "He's finished with the task I assigned him and wondering if I'm coming back before lunch."

"Is it that late?" Louisa looked to her bare wrist. They'd let time get away from them. Her bank appointment was in the early afternoon.

"Only for people who had breakfast before sunrise," Nico replied. "The rest of the world is safe."

"Good to know, seeing as how I just finished breakfast."

"And my second."

"Such as it was." She nodded to his untouched coffee. "Guess you're not as fond of American coffee as you claimed."

"I must have confused it with something else American, then. Good luck with Dominic." With a parting wink, he jumped over the walk.

He was lucky he didn't break his leg leaping off terraces like that, Louisa thought as she watched him disappear into the vines. She decidedly didn't think about how graceful he looked when he moved. Or about how firm and muscular his arms looked while supporting his weight.

She always did have a weakness for men with nice biceps, she thought with a shiver.

Too bad Nico Amatucci was every mistake she'd vowed not to repeat. She'd had her fill of charismatic, dominating men, thank you very much.

She checked her bare wrist a second time. Her Rolex

was long gone—sold to pay off bills—but the habit remained. Didn't matter—Nico's comment about lunch told her the morning was getting on. If she wanted to be prepared for her meeting, she'd best get her act together.

Gathering her plate and the coffee cups, she headed into the palazzo, where the latest draft of her business plan lay spread on the coffee table. Nico must not have noticed, because he wouldn't have been able to resist commenting if he had.

Pausing, Louisa scanned the numbers on the balance sheet with a smile. A solid, thorough plan, but then she'd always been good with numbers. Sadly, she'd forgotten how much she enjoyed working with them. Once upon a time, she'd had a promising career in finance. Until Steven had talked her into staying home shortly after their marriage, that is. Cajoled, really. For appearance's sake, he'd said. People were already gossiping about how the CEO was dating his extremely young employee. Made sense not to add fuel to the fire. "Besides," he'd told her, "as my wife, you have far more important things to focus on."

Like making sure she looked and behaved perfectly at all times. She should have seen the signs then, but she'd been too in love to notice. Lost in her personal fairy tale. The little nobody Cinderella swept off her feet by the silver-haired billionaire Prince Charming.

It wasn't until the feds took him away that she wondered if he hadn't been afraid she'd figure out what he was up to.

Oh well, that was in the past now.

It had taken her a while to settle in at the palazzo, but over the past few months, she'd developed a very comfortable routine. First came breakfast on the terrace, where she would practice her Italian by reading the local papers. The language immersion tape she'd bought in Boston had turned out to be useless—fluent in two weeks, ha!—but nine months in, she was getting pretty comfortable. After breakfast, she would go online to catch up on the American news and check her email. Usually her inbox didn't contain more than a handful of messages, a far cry from the days when she would get note after note. Now her messages were mostly from Dani, who liked to forward jokes and pictures of baby animals. On the plus side, she didn't have to worry about whether the message was some kind of ruse arranged by Steven to catch her in a lie.

At first she didn't look twice at the internet alert, the helpful online tracker she'd created to stay on top of the news. Another reference to the wedding, she assumed. Every day brought two or three mentions. It wasn't until she was about to log off that she realized the alert was one she'd set up before leaving Boston. The words *Louisa Clark* leaped from the screen in boldface type.

Her heart stopped. A year. A whole year without mention. Why now?

She slid her fingers to the mouse. *Please be a coincidence*, she prayed.

And she clicked open the link.

CHAPTER THREE

Scam King's Ex Hosts Royal Wedding
Is Luscious Louisa Looking for a New Partner?

After nine months under the radar, Louisa Clark,
the blonde bombshell who seduced and ultimately
brought down bogus financier Steven Clark has
reappeared. This time in Europe under the name
Louisa Harrison...

A BIG FAT PHOTO of her smiling at the royal couple ran
under the headline.

The article went on to list her as the owner of Palazzo
di Comparino and suggested that hosting the wedding had
been her way of snagging a new billionaire husband. Because, after all, that was how she'd landed Steven, right?
She was the young femme fatale employee who'd seduced
her older boss, only to sell him out when the feds began
closing in. Never mind that the narrative didn't remotely
resemble the truth. That she was the one who had been seduced and betrayed. Just as long as the story sold papers.

Louisa tried to breathe, but an invisible hand had found
its way to her throat and was choking the air out of her.
The site even used that god-awful nickname. *Stupid headline writers and their need for memorable alliteration.* No
way would this be the only article. Not in the internet era
when every gossip blog and newspaper fed off every other.

Sure enough. A few shaky keystrokes later, the search
results scrolled down her screen. Some of the stories focused on rehashing the case. Others, though, created all-

new speculation. One politician in Florence was even demanding an investigation into the al fresco discovered in the palazzo chapel last summer, claiming it could be part of an elaborate art fraud scheme. Every page turned up more. Headline after headline: Ponzi Scheme Seductress Turns Sights on Tuscany *and* Italy: Lock Up Your Euros! and Royal Scandal! Is Halencia's Financial Future at Stake?

Oh God, Christina and Antonio. She'd turned their fairy-tale wedding into a mockery. They must hate her. Everyone must hate her. Dani. Rafe. *Nico.* They loved Monte Calanetti; all they wanted was for their village to thrive, and she was tainting the town with scandal. How could she ever show her face in town again?

The phone rang. Louisa jumped. *Don't answer it. It could be a reporter.* Old habits, buried but not forgotten, kicked right in.

Not a reporter, thank goodness. The bank. The name appeared under the number on her call screen. One guess as to why they were calling. Forcing air into her lungs, she answered.

"Signorina Harrison?" an unfamiliar female voice asked.

"Y-yes." Louisa fought to keep her voice from shaking, and lost.

"I'm calling for Signor Merloni. He's asked me to tell you he can't meet with you today. Something has suddenly come up."

"Right. Of course." What a surprise. A lump formed in her throat. Only pride—or maybe it was masochism—made her hang on the line and go through the motions. "Did...did Signor Merloni give you a new date?"

"No, he did not," the woman replied. "I'm afraid his calendar is full for the next several weeks. He's going to have to call you when a time becomes available."

And so the ostracism started. Louisa knew the drill. Signor Merloni wouldn't call back. No one would.

They never did.

Phone dropping from her fingers, Louisa stumbled toward the terrace doors, toward the fresh air and rolling hills she'd come to see as home, only to stop short. Paparazzi could be lurking anywhere, their telephoto lenses poised to snag the next exclusive shot of Luscious Louisa. They could be hiding this moment among the grapevines.

So much for going outside. Backing away, she sank into the cushions when her calves collided with the sofa. What now? She couldn't call anyone. She couldn't go outside.

It was just like before. She was a prisoner in her own home.

Damn you, Steven. Even in prison, he was still controlling her life.

The Brix level matched the portable reading exactly. Nico wasn't surprised. When it came to grapes, he was seldom wrong. *Of course not. Making wine is the only thing you really care about.*

The voice in his head, which sounded suspiciously like his former fiancée's, was wrong. Making wine wasn't the *only* thing he cared about; there was his family, too. And tradition, although tradition involved winemaking so perhaps they were one and the same. Still, while he found great satisfaction in bottling the perfect vintage, if Amatucci Vineyards collapsed tomorrow, he wouldn't collapse in despair. That was his parents' domain. If he couldn't make wine anymore, he would cope, the same way he'd coped when Floriana had walked out on him, or whenever he'd come home to discover his parents had broken up—again. Dispassion, when you thought about it, was a blessing. Heaven knew it had saved him from going mad when growing up.

If the trade-off for sanity meant living a life alone, then so be it.

Why was he even thinking about this? Louisa's comment about needing time for herself, that's why. Someone had hurt Louisa badly enough that she'd fled to Italy. Her pain was too close to the mistakes he'd made with Floriana. Poor, sweet Floriana. He'd tried so hard to want her properly, but his tepid heart wouldn't—couldn't.

Was the man who'd broken Louisa's heart trying to be something he wasn't, too? Hard to believe a man would throw her over for any other reason.

"Mario, could you turn down the volume?" he hollered. He could hear the television from in here.

Leaving the beakers he'd been measuring on his lab table, he left his office and walked into the main processing area where Mario and his production manager, Vitale, stood watching the portable television they had dragged from the break room.

"Last time I checked, football didn't need to be played at top volume," he said. With the equipment being readied for harvest, it didn't take much for the noise to reverberate through the empty plant. He motioned for Giuseppe to hand him the remote control. "I didn't know there was a match today."

"Not football, *signor*, the news," Mario replied.

"You brought the television in here to watch the *news*?" That would be a first. Football reigned supreme.

"Si," Giuseppe replied. "Vitale's wife called to say they were talking about Monte Calanetti."

Again? Nico would have thought they were done discussing the royal wedding by now. "Must be a slow news…" He stopped as Louisa's face suddenly appeared on the screen. It wasn't a recent photo, she was far more dressed up than usual, and it showed her with a man Nico didn't recognize. A very handsome man, he noticed, irritably.

The caption beneath read Luscious Louisa—Back Again?

Luscious Louisa?

"Isn't that the woman who owns the palazzo?" Vitale looked over at him.

Nico didn't answer, but the news reader droned on. "…key witness in prosecuting her husband, Steven Clark, for investment fraud and money laundering. Clark is currently serving seventy-five years…"

He remembered reading about the case. Clark's pyramid scheme had been a huge scandal. Several European businessmen had lost millions investing with him. And Louisa had been his wife and testified against him?

No wonder she'd run to Italy.

Another picture was on the screen; one from the royal wedding. Nico gritted his teeth as a thousand different emotions ran through him. The presenter was talking about Louisa as if she were some kind of siren who'd led Clark to his doom. Had they met the woman? Alluring, yes, but dishonest? Corrupt?

His ringtone cut into his thoughts. Keeping his eyes on the television, he pulled his phone from his back pocket.

"Have you seen the news?" Dani asked when he answered.

"Watching it right now," he replied. On-screen, the presenter had moved on to a different headline.

"The story's on every channel. It's all anyone in the restaurant can talk about."

It's untrue, he corrected silently. The ferocity of his certainty surprised him. He had not one shred of evidence to support his belief, and yet he knew in his bones that Louisa wasn't guilty of anything. One merely had to look in her eyes to know that whatever the press said, they didn't have the entire story.

"Did you know?" he asked Dani. Rafe's wife was Louisa's closest friend. If Louisa had told anyone of her past…

"No. She never talks about her life before she got here," Dani answered. "Hell, she barely talks about herself."

Nico's gut unclenched. Silly, but he'd felt strangely hurt at the idea of Louisa sharing her secrets with someone else.

"There are reporters all over town," Dani continued. "One even came in here asking questions. I've been trying to call her since the story broke to see if she's okay, but she's not answering her phone."

"Probably avoiding the press."

"I'm worried, though. She's so private, and to have her life story plastered all over the place…"

Terrifying. "Say no more," he replied. "I'll head right over."

Louisa had lost track of the time. Curled in the corner of her sofa, away from the windows, she hugged her knees and tried to make her brain focus on figuring out the next step. Obviously, she couldn't stay in Monte Calanetti. Not without tainting the village with her notoriety. And going back to Boston…well, that was out of the question. What would she do? Go to her mother's house and listen to "I told you so" all day long?

Louisa hugged herself tighter. Ever since seeing the media alert, there'd been a huge weight on her chest, and no matter how hard she tried to take a deep breath, she couldn't get enough air. It was as though the walls were closing in, the room getting smaller and smaller. She didn't want to leave. She liked her life here. The palazzo, the village…they were just starting to feel like home.

She should have known it wouldn't last. Steven's shadow was destined to follow her everywhere. For the rest of her life, she would be punished for falling in love with the wrong man.

"…you're doing?" A giant crash followed the question. The sound of tinkling glass forced Louisa to her feet. Running to the terrace door, she peered around the corner of the door frame in time to see Nico dragging a stranger across the terrace toward the wall. The crash she'd heard was her breakfast table, which now lay on its side, the top shattered.

"Hey, what do you think you're doing?" she heard the stranger gasp. "This is my exclusive."

"Exclusive this," Nico growled. Holding the man's collar in one hand, he yanked the expensive camera the man carried from around his neck and hurled it over the wall.

"Bastard! You're going to pay for that."

"Be glad it was only your camera." Nico yanked the man to his feet only to shove him against the railing. "Now get out. And if I ever see your face in the village again, you'll find out exactly what else I'm capable of breaking, understand?" He shoved the man a second time, with a force that made Louisa, still hidden behind the door frame, jump. Whatever the reporter said must have satisfied him, and Nico released his grip on the man's shirt. Louisa stepped back as the man started toward the stairs.

"Where are you going?" Nico asked, his hand slapping down on the man's shoulder. "Leave the way you came in."

"Are you kidding? That's a five-foot drop."

"Then I suggest you brace yourself when you land." The two men stared at one another for several seconds. When it became obvious Nico wasn't backing down, the reporter hooked a leg over the railing.

"I'm calling my lawyer. You're going to pay for that camera."

"Call whoever you'd like. I'll be glad to explain how I'm calling the police to report you for trespassing on private property. Now are you leaving, or shall I throw you over that railing?"

The reporter did what he was told, disappearing over the rail. Slowly Louisa stepped into the light. Nico's shoulders were rising and falling in agitated breaths, making her almost afraid to speak. "Is he gone?" she asked in a soft voice.

"Is he the first one?" he asked, voice rough.

He turned, and the dark fury Louisa saw on his face had her swallowing hard to keep the nerves from taking over her throat. She nodded. "I think so."

"He was climbing over the wall when I got here. Probably saw your terrace door was open and thought he could catch you up close and off guard."

"In Boston, they preferred using telephoto lenses."

"You're not in Boston anymore."

"I know." She should have realized how ruthless the press would be. After all, this was Italy; they'd invented the word *paparazzi*.

"At least you won't have to worry about this one trespassing again. That is, if he's smart."

"Thanks."

"Can't promise there won't be more, though," he said brushing past her. "You'd best be prepared."

More. He was right, there would be others. It was all she could do not to collapse in a heap where she stood. Those months of hiding in Boston had nearly destroyed her. She wasn't up to another go-round. The stranger on her terrace was proof enough of that. If Nico hadn't shown up when he did...

Why had he shown up? Returning to her living room, where she found her neighbor searching through the bookshelf cabinets. "What are you doing?"

"Carlos kept a stash of fernet tucked in back of one of these cabinets. Do you still have it?"

"Two doors to the left." She hadn't gotten around to finding a better location. "I meant why are you here?"

"Dani called me. She saw the news on television."

"Let me guess, she's horrified to find out who she's been friends with and wants me to stay away so I won't drag the restaurant into it." Seeing the same darkness on Nico's face that she'd seen a few moments ago, it would seem her neighbor felt the same way.

"What? No. She and Rafe are trying to figure out what's going on. A reporter came to the restaurant asking questions." He paused while he pulled a dust-covered bottle from the cabinet. "She said she tried calling you a half dozen times."

That explained some of the phone calls then. "I wasn't answering the phone."

"Obviously. They asked if I would come over and make sure you were okay. Good thing, too, considering you were about to have an unwanted visitor."

He filled his glass and drank the contents in one swallow. "This is the point in our conversation where you suggest that I'm an unwanted visitor."

"What can I say? I'm off my game today." She sank into her corner and watched as Nico drank a second glass. When he finished, he sat the empty glass on a shelf and turned around. He wore a much calmer expression now. Back in control once again.

"Why didn't you say anything about your former husband?" he asked.

And say what? *My ex is Steven Clark. You know, the guy who ran the billion-dollar investment scam. I'm the wife who turned him in. Maybe you've read about me? They call me Luscious Louisa?* She plucked at the piping on one of the throw pillows. "The idea was to make a fresh start where no one knew anything about me," she replied."

"You know how unrealistic that is in this day and age?"

"I managed it for nine months, didn't I?" She offered up what she hoped passed for a smile. Nine wonderful months. Almost to the point where she'd stopped looking over her shoulder.

When he didn't smile back, she changed the subject. "You said a reporter came into the restaurant?"

"This morning. That's how Dani knew to turn on the television."

She could just imagine the questions he'd asked, too. "Tell them I'm sorry. Things will die down once they realize I'm not in Monte Calanetti anymore."

Nico's features darkened again. "What are you talking about?"

"I'm catching the bus to Florence tonight."

"You're running away?"

He made it sound like a bad thing. "I certainly can't stay. Not anymore."

"But the palazzo... What about all your plans for restoring the property and turning it into a hotel? Surely, you're not planning to abandon Palazzo di Comparino *again*?"

His voice grew harsh on the last word, causing Louisa to cringe. His feelings regarding the palazzo were no secret; to him, the fact she allowed the property to sit unclaimed for so long was as big a crime as anything Steven had done. Of course, she had good reason for the delay, but he didn't know that.

"Have you seen what they are writing about me?" she asked him. The stories would only get worse. "That guy you threw off my terrace is probably down in the village right now trying to dig up dirt. And what he can't find, he'll make up. Whatever he can do to sell papers."

"So?"

"So, I'm doing Monte Calanetti a favor by leaving. The town is on an economic high. I don't want to do anything to take that away." Unable to stand the way his eyes were bearing down on her, Louisa pushed herself to her feet and walked toward the rear corner of the room, as far from the windows—and Nico—as possible. A tapestry hung on the wall there, and she focused on the intricate weave of brown thread. "Better I leave the palazzo empty than stay and let the town become branded as the home of Luscious Louisa," she said.

"How noble of you, running away without saying goodbye to your friends. I mean, that's what you were going to do, no? Leave without saying goodbye?"

"Like people would care." Rejection hurt enough when it was people you didn't like. The idea of walking down the street and seeing disdain in the eyes of people she cared about made her sick to her stomach. "Trust me, everyone will be more than happy to see me gone."

"Happy? Did you say we would be happy?" There was the sound of footsteps, and suddenly a hand was on her shoulder, yanking her around and bringing her face-to-face with a pair of flashing brown eyes. So angry; so ready to correct her.

It was instinctive. The corner of her vision caught his hand starting to rise, and she couldn't help it.

She flinched.

Madonna mia, did she think he was going to strike her? As he raked his fingers through his hair—completing the motion he'd started before Louisa recoiled—Nico felt his hand shaking. What scared him was that he did want to hit something. Not Louisa. Never Louisa. But something. The wall. That miserable paparazzo's face. So much for the liquor calming his nerves. The swell of anger that he'd been fighting since seeing the news was pushing hard against his self-control. Mixing with another emotion, one he couldn't identify but that squeezed his chest like a steel band, the feelings threatened to turn him into someone he didn't recognize.

How could she just leave Monte Calanetti? For nine months they'd treated her as one of their own, made her part of their family, and she didn't think they cared? Did she truly think so little of them?

He felt betrayed. "If you think so little of us that you believe we would let a few gossip articles sway our opinion, then perhaps you should go somewhere else," he said. "After all these months, you should now have realized that people in Monte Calanetti are smarter than that."

"That include Dominic Merloni?"

The banker? What did he have to do with anything?

"He canceled our meeting as soon as the news broke. He won't be the only person to cut me off. Just the first."

"Dominic Merloni is an arrogant bastard who thinks everyone in the village should worship him because he once played football for Genoa."

"That's not what you said about him this morning."

"This morning I was being polite." But if she was going to be irrational, then there was no need to keep up the pretense. "I'm talking about the people who matter. Like Dani, your supposed *best friend*. You think she is so petty?"

"Of course not," she replied. "But Dani loves everybody."

"Yes, she does, but you were going to leave her without saying goodbye anyway."

"I already told you, I'm—"

"Yes, yes, doing the village a favor. Let us start organizing the benediction. Saint Louisa the martyr. Abandoning Palazzo di Comparino for the good of the people."

Louisa stood with her arms wrapped around her as though they were the only thing holding her up. As far from the woman he'd come to know as could be. Where was the haughty American who challenged him on every turn? The hornet who threatened every time he poked her nest? "I don't know why you care so much," she muttered.

Nico didn't know either, beyond the emotions that continued squeezing his chest. He shouldn't care at all. He should accept the change in circumstance as another one of life's upheavals and move on.

He couldn't, though. All he could think about was how the more he watched her retreat into herself, the more he wanted to grab her by the shoulders and shake the fight back into her. He wanted to...to...

He stalked back to the bookshelf. Grabbing a clean glass from the bar, he poured two more glasses of fernet and walked back to her. "Here," he said, holding one of the glasses out. "Drink. Maybe you'll start thinking more clearly." Maybe he would, too.

"I don't need to think clearly," she replied. Nonetheless, she took the drink. "I need to leave town."

"And go where?"

"I don't know. Africa. New Zealand. Someplace where they can't find me. I'll figure something out. I just know I have to leave.

"No, damn it!" he said, slamming the bottle on the shelf. "You can't!"

The air between them crackled with tension. Nico looked at Louisa cradling her glass with trembling hands and grew ashamed. Since when did he yell and slam objects?

Taking a deep breath, he began again, this time making sure his voice remained low and level. "Leaving town is the worst thing you can do."

"How can you say that?"

Again, Nico wasn't entirely sure. Several answers came to mind, but none of them felt completely whole or honest. The true, complete answer remained stuck in the shadows, unformed.

"Because the town needs you," he said, grabbing the first reason that made sense. "You've become an important part of our community. Whether you believe in them or not—" she turned away at his pointed dig "—the people here believe in you."

"Besides," he added in a voice that was even lower than before, "if you run away, the press win. People will believe what's written—the stories will start to sound true. Is that what you want? To give Luscious Louisa life?"

"No."

"Then stay, and show the world you've got nothing to hide. That what the press is saying is nothing more than gossip."

He let his reasoning wash over her. For several minutes, she said nothing, all her concentration focused on an invisible spot inside her drink. When she finally spoke, the words were barely a whisper. "What if you're wrong?"

"I'm not." It hurt to hear the doubt in her voice. Damn her ex for killing her trust. "Whatever happens, you already have three people on your side."

"But last time..." She shook her head.

"Last time there was a trial, no? This time it is only gossip. In a few days the press will have moved on to a new scandal and forgotten all about Luscious Louisa. Then you go back to your life. Surely, you can handle a few days of whispers, can't you?"

"You have no idea how many whispers I've handled in my lifetime," she replied, looking up at last.

Finally, there was a spark. A bit of the fire he'd come to expect. "Good. Then, it's settled. You're staying here, where you belong."

Louisa had opened her mouth to reply but stopped abruptly. He heard the sound of rustling outside on the terrace. She'd heard it, too, because the fingers holding her glass grew white with tension.

For the third time in less than an hour Nico could feel his temper rise. At this rate he would need an entire case of fernet to keep him from murdering the entire Italian media corps.

"Wait here," he mouthed, then held an index finger to his lips. Moving as softly as possible, he headed toward the terrace door, which they'd accidentally left propped open, and peered around the corner. There was another rustle, followed by a flutter before a lark flew past his face. Nico started at the sudden movement, his cheeks turning hot. "Just a bird," he said unnecessarily.

"This time," Louisa replied.

She was right. This time. Sooner or later the paparazzi would get their shot. "Maybe you should stay with Dani and Rafe," he said.

"I thought you didn't want me running away."

"I don't, but I also want you safe." He didn't say it, but it wasn't only the paparazzi he was worried about. There were also those unhinged few who would want to see if Luscious Linda was as sexy as the gossip pages implied. Until the story died down, trespassers were a real threat.

"I don't know..."

Surely they were past her insecurity at this point, weren't they? "What's the problem? As long as you are staying with them, you won't have to worry about the paparazzi. Rafe will make sure no one bothers you." Nico would make sure he did.

"Rafe and Dani have a business to run. I'm not going to ask them to waste their time babysitting me."

"No one is babysitting anyone."

"Aren't they? If they have to spend their time protecting me from all the paparazzi in town then it's babysitting," Louisa replied. "I'm better off grabbing the bus." She took a sip of her drink and grimaced. "What is this stuff?"

"Fernet-Branca."

"I hate peppermint," she replied, and set the glass on the coffee table.

"It is an acquired taste." Her change of topic wasn't going to work. She could complain about the drink all she wanted, he wasn't going to let her leave Monte Calanetti.

Tossing back his own drink, he slapped the glass down before the liquor even started cooling his insides. "If you don't want to stay with Rafe and Dani," he said, "then you'll just have to stay with me."

"Excuse me?"

If the situation weren't so serious, he'd laugh at the shock on her face. It was the perfect solution, though. "You will be able to avoid the paparazzi in the village, plus you'll be close enough to keep an eye on the palazzo. Can you think of a better location?"

"Hell. When it freezes over."

This time he did laugh. Here was the feisty Louisa he was used to.

"I'm serious," she said. "If I don't want Rafe and Dani playing babysitter, I sure as hell don't want you doing it.

She was being stubborn again. It wouldn't work any more than trying to change the subject had. "Fine. If it makes you feel better, you can work while you are staying with me."

"Work?"

"Yes. I told you, since the wedding, we've been inundated with orders for Amatucci Red. I can barely keep up as it is, and with the harvest and the festival coming up, I'm going to need as much help as I can get. Unless you don't think you can handle filing invoices and processing orders."

"You—you'd trust me to do that?"

"Why wouldn't I?"

"What about Luscious Louisa?"

God, how it hurt to see her looking so vulnerable. Tears

rimming her eyes and her lower lip trembling. Silently, he damned Steven Clark for dragging her down with him.

He might have promised to keep his distance, but at this moment, he couldn't stop himself from closing the space between them. He brushed his thumb across her quivering lip.

"Like I told you before, anyone who has spent time with you knows you're not the icy seductress the press makes you out to be."

"Thank you." A tear slipped out the corner of her eye and he fanned it away with his hand. So vulnerable and so beautiful. It shocked him how badly he suddenly needed to keep her safe. But then, this afternoon had been full of shocking reactions he'd never experienced before.

There was one reaction he recognized, though. The stirring in his jeans as he breathed in her scent. He brushed the hair from her face, the strands reminding him of corn silk. Promise be damned. He wanted to kiss her. Quickly, he stepped away before he could take action. Now was not the time to push his luck. "Go pack a bag," he told her. "We'll leave before the paparazzi realize you're gone."

You made the right decision, Louisa reminded herself on the way upstairs. Hiding out *was* better than running away, and Amatucci Vineyards did make the ideal hiding place. Plus she would be earning her keep. It wasn't as though she was going to become Nico's kept woman. She'd insist on the entire arrangement being professional and platonic.

Why, then, was her stomach in knots? Maybe, she thought as her eyes fell on the suitcase in the corner, because she'd gone from leaving town to working for Nico in less than an hour without knowing how she made the journey.

Or maybe it was because saying yes had become a whole lot easier once Nico had brushed her cheek.

CHAPTER FOUR

LUSCIOUS LOUISA'S LATEST CONQUEST?

"TOO BAD THEY couldn't find a proper synonym. *Conquest* spoils the alliteration." Nico said, turning the newspaper over.

Louisa didn't share his sense of humor. The headline screamed across the front page along with a photograph of her and Nico cropped from one of the official wedding shots. Apparently the photographer Nico kicked off her balcony had done some research following the altercation. The article described how the "enraged" vintner had come to her rescue and implied the two of them had been an item for weeks. Or, as the article put it, she'd managed to charm the richest man in town.

This was exactly what she didn't need after a restless night. There was still a large part of her dying to grab the first bus to Florence. Screaming loudly, in fact. She couldn't stop thinking how easily she had agreed to Nico's idea. Sure, he had a point about staying and proving the press wrong, but to put herself in his care like this? It reminded her of how things had begun with Steven. He'd liked to swoop in and take care of everything when they were dating, too. *Only you're not dating Nico*, she reminded herself, staring down at her breakfast pastry.

And unlike with Steven, this time she had age and hindsight in her favor. She may have agreed to stay here, but she would keep her bags packed. That way if the situation changed and the walls started closing in, she could be out of here in a flash.

Meanwhile, her breakfast partner was enjoying his pastry as though he didn't have a care in the world.

"I don't know how you can be so cavalier," she said watching him chew his pastry. Anyone would think he liked being dragged through the tabloid mud.

Nico shrugged. "How am I supposed to act?"

Indignant, perhaps? Angry? Some *show* of emotion. He'd practically exploded when he discovered the paparazzo yesterday, and that had nothing to do with him. These headlines were personal. "The article makes you sound like a lovesick fool."

"Which anyone who knows me will immediately recognize as a complete fabrication. I'm not and have never been the lovesick type."

A fact that should comfort her, seeing as how she was now sleeping under his roof. It didn't, though. Instead, she felt a dull ache in the pit of her stomach.

"So what was yesterday? An anomaly?"

He looked away. "Yesterday I caught a man breaking into your home. I was upset for your safety. This," he said as he waved his cup over the tabloid "is entirely different."

"How? It's still an invasion of privacy. And the things they wrote about us…" As though Nico were some kind of fly trapped in her web. She shivered. "Surely you care what people think."

"I already told you, anyone who knows me will recognize it for the garbage it is."

"Why is that?" Not that she wasn't glad, but she wanted to know why he was so certain.

A strange shadow appeared behind his eyes, turning them darker than usual. "Like I said, I'm not the lovesick kind," he replied. "Now, the fact they referred to me as the 'royal vintner'? That is something I hope people *will* believe. You cannot buy better publicity."

"Glad you're happy." One of them should be.

She took a look around the surroundings that were
to be her home away from home for the next few days.
Worn out and uncomfortable last night, she'd insisted on
being shown straight to her room. Nico's rust-and-green
kitchen was warm but dated, like the kitchen of a man
who didn't spend too many meals at home. Did that mean
he didn't entertain much either? Would people notice he
had company?

A sudden, horrifying thought struck her. Now that Nico
had been identified, the press would start stalking him,
too. For all they knew, a telephoto lens could be trained on
them right now. Reflexively, she looked over her shoulder
at the kitchen window.

"Relax," Nico told her. "I drew the curtains when we
got home last night. No one can see you."

Sure, they couldn't see her now. But eventually... "This
was a mistake. I'm better off just going to Florence."

"No one is going anywhere except to the winery."
Nico's hand reached across the table and grabbed her
wrist, preventing her from standing. "Trust me, everything is going to be fine. In a few days, another scandal
will erupt and the press will forget all about you."

Louisa looked down at the bronzed hand gently encir-
cling her arm. His thumb brushing her pulse point, the
tiny movement as soothing as a caress. That his slightest
touch could calm her was disturbing in itself.

Slipping free, Louisa reached for the newspaper and
flipped it back over. The picture on the front page showed
the two of them with their heads together in quiet conversation. Arm slung casually over the back of her chair, he
was leaning forward as she spoke in his ear, her hand resting lightly on his forearm. She remembered the moment.
The orchestra had started playing, and she'd moved closer
so she could comment on the song selection. Thanks to

the angle, they looked more like a couple who had eyes only for each other.

A second photo greeted her when she turned the page. The two of them dancing. No need to mess with the angle this time. Their gazes were locked; their bodies pressed together like lovers'. Must have been taken only moments before Nico had kissed her.

What if there was a photo of them kissing? Louisa's stomach dropped. The blogosphere would have a field day. Her horror must have shown on her face, because when she looked up, Nico was watching her. "If they had a photo, they would have used it," he said, reading her mind.

He was right, Louisa thought, letting out her breath. "The one they used is bad enough. Did we really look like that?" Like they couldn't get close enough.

"Considering what followed, I would have to say yes."

That's what she was afraid of. Louisa dropped her head on her arms with a groan. "It's only a couple of photographs," he said, patting the back of her head. "We'll survive."

He didn't understand. Any photograph was one photograph too many. "Believe it or not," she said, lifting her head, "there was a time when I liked having my picture taken." She remembered her first public date with Steven and how the local press surrounded them. She'd felt like someone had dropped her on a Hollywood red carpet. "I thought being featured in the paper was the coolest thing ever."

Letting out a long breath, she balanced her chin on the back of her hand. "After Steven was arrested, reporters started camping out in cars across the street. They'd call my name each time I left the house, and I would hear the cameras snapping. Click-click-click-click. It never stopped. After a while I stopped going out unless it was to go to court. I had my food delivered. I kept the curtains drawn.

I swear Steven had more freedom in prison." Out of the corner of her eye, she caught Nico's gaze slide toward his windows and the green linen drapes blocking the view.

"Did you know, I couldn't even take out my garbage, because they would go through the contents?" she asked. "I had to let it pile up in the basement until after the trial was over." If she concentrated, she could smell the stench. The horrible sour smell that drifted up the stairs every time she opened the basement door. "I actually dreamt once that the bags overflowed and buried me alive."

"Bella mia..." He reached for her hand.

Louisa pulled back with a shake of her head. No more comforting touches. "I wasn't trying to make you feel sorry for me." Honestly, she didn't know why she'd told him at all. The memory had simply popped out and it had been the first time she shared the secret with anyone. She supposed it was because the situation was repeating itself again now.

"Well, I promise no garbage here."

How was it he knew the way to make her smile no matter how aggravated or sad she got? "Well, if there is," she said, "you're responsible for taking it out."

"Agreed." Nico smiled, and the warmth in his eyes was as reassuring as any embrace. For that moment, anyway, Louisa felt as if everything would be okay.

Seeing Louisa smile cheered him. It was strange how important seeing her smile was becoming to him. Nico tried to imagine what it must have been like for her during the trial, trapped inside her home while the wolves with their cameras gathered around in wait.

It made him doubly glad that he had lied about the photographs not bothering him. He would never tell Louisa, but seeing the pictures actually bothered him a great deal, although not for the reason she thought. It was his expression in the photographs, a dazed, trancelike appearance that upset him the most. He'd been photographed by the press dozens of times, but never could he remember seeing a shot where he could be seen looking so intently at his partner. Then again, he couldn't remember ever sharing a dance as memorable as the one he shared with Louisa either. Looking at the photograph had brought every detail back into focus, from the softness of her silk gown to the floral scent of her hairspray as she curled into his neck.

Unfortunately, Louisa's reaction was far different. Even though he expected her to get upset, he was surprised at the disappointment her response left in his stomach. Clearly, being the one who usually kept the emotional distance, Nico wasn't used to a woman's disinterest.

Sensing her attention about to return to the headlines, Nico gathered the newspaper and folded it in two. "No more gossip," he said, slapping the paper on the countertop. "We move on to better topics. You need to finish your breakfast. Today is a workday. If you're serious about earning your keep, then we need to get to the winery."

"Are you always this bossy with your houseguests?" she asked, the smile staying in place.

"Only the Americans," Nico countered. What would she say if she discovered she was the first woman to be one of his houseguests? Not even Floriana had been given such an honor. Since his parents had moved away, Nico had preferred the house to remain a place of peace and tranquility, something it had never been when he was a child.

And didn't Louisa, with her damp hair and bare feet, look as if she belonged to the place. The novelty of having company, he decided. Other women would look equally at home, if he ever bothered to invite them.

But would other women engender such a strong desire to protect them? Last night, he'd literally found himself patrolling the house, and again first thing this morning.

Frankly, he was surprised he hadn't stood guard outside Louisa's bedroom door to keep her safe.

Keep her safe or keep her from leaving? The dread that gripped him when she mentioned going to Florence was no less today than it had been yesterday. He wished he understood why her leaving Monte Calanetti disturbed him so much.

He looked past her shoulder to the back door and the thin dark line scored in the wood just to the left of the doorknob. A reminder of the time his mother had thrown a carving knife at his father's disappearing back. "Did you sleep well?" he heard himself ask.

"Okay," she said. "It's never easy sleeping the first night in a new place and all."

"Perhaps, after a full day's work, tonight will be better." For both of them. Wiping his mouth, he tossed the napkin onto his empty plate and stood up. "Speaking of... we have a busy day. Get your shoes on and I'll show you what you'll be doing for me."

Beyond the vineyards themselves, Amatucci Vineyards had two primary sections. There was a medieval stone villa that housed the store and wine-tasting rooms as well as a modern production facility. It was to the second building that Nico and Louisa headed, cutting through the rear garden and vines. Something else Louisa had been too stressed out to appreciate yesterday. Unlike the villa, which was stately and ripe with family heirlooms, Nico's garden was a breathtaking display of natural beauty. The vines draping the pergola beams had minds of their own, their branches dipping and weaving into a unique overhead tapestry. Likewise, urns had been placed around the terracotta terrace, their roses and olive plants spiraling up cedar trellises with stunning wildness.

"I like to be reminded of how rugged the hills can be,"

Nico said when she complimented him. *Rugged* was a good word and fit him perfectly, she thought, dodging a low-hanging branch. Nico was earthy and independent. Civilized, but not completely.

"Most of the employees are in the field at this time of day," Nico told her as he unlocked the facility door. "I'll set you up in one of the back offices so you'll have maximum privacy. I also sent an email to the staff last night reminding them that I expect professionalism and discretion at all times, and that I won't tolerate gossip."

"Sounds like you've thought of everything." *Swooping in to take control...* A tightness found its way into her stomach, which she immediately pushed aside. *Not the same thing*, she silently snapped. *Stop comparing.*

The door opened into a small receiving room dominated by filing cabinets and a cluttered metal desk at which a lanky young man too big for his chair sat reading. Behind him a glass window looked out over a warehouse-sized room full of gleaming stainless-steel processing machines.

He practically jumped to his feet when he heard Nico shut the door. "*Signor!* I was just—just—" Seeing Louisa, he stopped midsentence and simply stared. This morning's newspaper lay open on the desk, the photo of her and Nico on display.

"Good morning, Mario. I'd like you to meet Louisa Harrison from Palazzo di Comparino. She's offered to help us fulfill shipping orders so we can get ready for harvest."

"Hello."

"Mario is studying viticulture at the university. He wants to learn how to become a great vintner."

Mario was doing his best to look anywhere but at her. Still, if Nico could breeze in here and act as though there wasn't a suggestive photo of them lying a foot away, then so could she. Mustering up some fake confidence, she flashed the young man a smile. "Pleasure to meet you, Mario," she said holding out her hand.

"Um, yes. Likewise," Mario muttered. Still avoiding her gaze, he hurriedly shook her hand before picking up a stack of paperwork. "I'd better finish getting these field readings recorded into the system," he said. Clasping the papers to his chest, he rushed out of the office.

"Told you people would have problems with me," she said once the young man disappeared.

Nico's mouth was a thin tight line. "I will talk to him. Let him know that kind of behavior is unacceptable."

"Don't. It's not his fault."

"But of course it is. I won't have my employees treating you poorly. He needs to know that."

"Please." She grabbed his hand as he headed toward the door. "I don't want to make a scene." Mario's behavior was nothing compared to what she'd endured in Boston. What she didn't want was to feel as though she was under an even bigger spotlight. "Just show me where I'm supposed to sit and let me get to work."

"You're going to stay, then? I don't have to talk you out of leaving?"

"For now." She was here. She might as well try to tough it out for a little while. After all, there was always the chance Mario was just shy or something, right?

The way Nico's face brightened helped, too, as did his softly spoken "I'm glad."

"But, before I bring you to your office," he added, "I want to show you the facility. You should know your way around the building if I'm not here and you need to find something."

The office exited into the main plant. Standing on the landing just outside the office door, Louisa was shocked to see the facilities empty.

"Where is everybody?" she asked.

"I always close right before harvest. Gives the employees time with their families and lets me make sure the equipment is in working order. Enjoy the silence while you can. Come next week this building will be so loud you won't be able to hear yourself think."

"I bet." She didn't have a clue what any of the machines did, but simply given the sheer number of machines she'd expect a lot of noise. "It all looks so modern," she remarked. "Not quite how I expected wine to be made."

"No doubt you pictured a dark cavern full of oak casks where a group of Italian gypsy women crush the grapes by foot?"

"Nothing that dramatic."

"Are you sure? That's what the tourists believe. Why do you think my store is in the oldest building on the property? To continue the myth."

Meanwhile, their Old World wine was being produced in the finest of twenty-first-century stainless-steel and concrete surroundings. "So no grape stomping at all, then?" Louisa asked as she followed him down the stairs and onto the plant floor.

"Only at the harvest festival."

Ahead, they caught the flash of a pale blue work shirt near one of the machines. "Vitale," Nico called out. "Is that you?"

A silver head appeared. "Yes, *signor.* I was replacing the timer belt." Just like Mario had, the man avoided looking in her direction. "You were right, *signor*," he said. "It had worn thin. We shouldn't have any more problems."

"Good. Good. Vitale, I'd like you to meet Louisa." Once again, Nico forced an introduction, and again Louisa was acknowledged with a nervous smile and a nod before Nico offered Vitale an excuse to leave.

"Give them time," Nico told her when she started to comment. "They'll warm up to you."

Sure they will, she thought with a sigh. "People are going to believe what they want to believe, Nico." Sometimes even when the truth was right in front of them—the way she had with Steven. "And in this case, the headlines have had way too big a head start."

"Headlines be damned. Once they get to know you, they'll realize what is written in the papers is garbage. In a few weeks no one in Monte Calanetti will even care about Luscious Louisa."

"From your lips…"

While they were talking, he'd moved closer, narrowing the space between them until he stood no more than a foot away. Close enough she could see the dark hair peering out from the open collar of his shirt and smell the spicy citrus of his aftershave. "Louisa," he said, his gentle voice sounding as though he were stating the simplest of truths. "It doesn't take a rocket scientist to see the truth about a person."

"Don't be so sure. There's an entire town back in Massachusetts that could prove you wrong."

Nico chuckled. Despite the gap between them, his fingers had somehow found their way into her hair and were combing the strands away from her face. "You're being dramatic, *bella mia*. I'm sure your true friends knew better."

"They might have, if I'd had any."

"What are you talking about?"

"Nothing." Distracted by his touch, she'd opened a door she hadn't meant to open. "Like you said, I'm being dramatic."

He didn't believe her, but Louisa didn't care. She'd revealed enough secrets for one day.

"I'm tired," she said instead. "It's making me say silly things."

"You should get some rest, then."

Easier said than done. True *rest* had eluded her for years. The last time she'd relaxed—truly relaxed—had been when? The first few months of her marriage? Such a long time ago.

Dear Lord, but she was tired of being on guard, and Nico's touch felt so wonderfully comforting. With a soothing brush of his hand, her resistance slipped a little further. It felt so good having someone on her side. Nico's shoulder was right there. Broad, capable, strong. Would it be so bad if she leaned on him for just a little bit? She was so very tired of being alone.

With a soft sigh escaping her lips, she curled into him.

"It's all right," she heard Nico whisper as his arms wrapped around her. "I'm here. I'll take care of everything."

This was a first for Nico. Taking a woman in his arms without any intention of making love to her. But as he drew her close, her sweet floral scent wrapping itself around him, his only thought was of reassurance. He knew why, of course. Louisa's cool and distant mask had slipped, and the vulnerability he saw deepened the queer sense of protectiveness she'd awakened in him. Every time, the depth of what he was feeling shocked him. What was it about this blonde American that made him want to fly to America and strangle every reporter in the country personally for causing her such pain?

At least he could make sure the European press didn't copy their American colleagues, even if he had to physically throw every paparazzo in Italy off his property. Cradling her head against his shoulder, he whispered. "It's all right. I'll take care of everything."

Instantly, she stiffened. "No," she said pulling out of his embrace. "Don't."

Nico opened his mouth to argue, expecting to see the

same indignant expression he'd seen at the wedding, the last time she reacted this way. The color had drained from her face, turning her so pale her skin nearly matched the white blond of her hair. Her eyes were pale, too, as though she were struggling to keep fear from invading their depths.

If he didn't know better, he'd say she seen a ghost.

What had he done? Or had something else happened in Boston, something more than the paparazzi trapping her in her home?

She blinked and the expression disappeared. Back was the Louisa he knew best. Distant and guarded. "It was wrong of me to lean on you like that," she said. "I lost myself for a second. It won't happen again."

"There's nothing wrong with turning to a friend when you're upset." He wondered if the word *friend* sounded as wrong to her ears as it did his. Surely holding a friend didn't feel as good as holding Louisa did. There was an amazing rightness in the way her body connected with his.

"I know, but…" She looked past him, to the window that looked into the front office. Inside, Vitale and Mario could be seen talking. "You've already done enough, letting me hide here."

That wasn't what she was going to say. She was worried what others would think.

"You are not hiding; you are working. Believe me, it is you who will be doing me the favor."

"Do you invite all your employees to stay at your house?"

"Only the beautiful ones," he teased. When she didn't share the joke, he turned serious. "No one will know that you're staying at my house."

"You don't think they'll figure it out?"

"Only if we tell them," he replied. "I've never had much taste for airing personal business in public."

Finally, she smiled. "Nico Amatucci, the model of discretion."

"Something like that."

"Just in case, now that I am working here, I think it's important that you treat me the same as any other employee. Especially considering today's headlines. No sense feeding the gossip."

"You're right." A voice in his head, though, told him gossip was only part of her reason. There was something more to her distance. And not the need to spend time alone, as she'd claimed the other day. It was as if she feared the attraction simmering between them. He supposed he couldn't blame her; the desire was stronger than anything he'd experienced before, as well.

"A regular employee," he said, echoing her words. Now was not the time to push for more. "I'll leave the hugs to your female friends. Speaking of, have you spoken to Dani?"

Louisa shook her head. "Not yet."

"Why not?" *Of course.* The way she looked away said everything. She was embarrassed. In spite of his lecture yesterday, she still worried her friends thought less of her.

If I had friends. Her comment from earlier came rushing back, and his insides tensed with anger on her behalf.

"You should call her," he said. "She's worried."

"I will. After I've settled in."

"Good." If she didn't, he would tell Dani and the others to come visit. She needed to know she had friends on her side, that the people of Monte Calanetti cared what happened to her.

As much as he did.

They spent the rest of the morning touring the winery. Nico explained the entire winemaking process from when the lifts brought freshly picked fruit to the loading dock to the fermentation stage, when the wine aged in oak barrels, just as it had for hundreds of years.

Occasionally, they passed an employee who would murmur a quick hello and rush away. While Louisa pretended not to mind the chilly reception, the words *if I had friends* repeated in his head. All he could picture was her barricaded in her house, surrounded by garbage she was too afraid to take outside while the world stared at her in judgment. He refused to let that happen again, not while she was under his protection.

By the time they finished and she was settled in the rear office with a stack of orders that needed fulfilling, his anger was at the boiling point. He marched back into the processing room and straight toward Mario and Vitale. "You will be friendly and polite to Louisa," he growled. "Is that clear?"

Both men nodded rapidly. He never raised his voice unless trying to yell over the machinery. "Good. You let the rest of the company know, as well. If I hear of anyone showing her disrespect, they will answer to me personally."

The people of Monte Calanetti would warm up to Louisa, even if he had to make them.

CHAPTER FIVE

"I DON'T BELIEVE IT. You really *are* working here."

Louisa froze in her chair at the sight of Marianna, Nico's sister, standing in the doorway wearing a decidedly vexed expression. "When Dani told me, I thought she was joking," she said.

Dani worked fast. Louisa had only called her best friend a few hours ago. Clearly the youngest Amatucci had rushed right over the second she got the news.

"It's only a temporary arrangement," she said. She managed to keep the defensiveness out of her voice, Barely. "I'm helping with order fulfillment."

The brunette waved away the answer as she stepped into the room. Being in her third trimester, her pregnant belly entered a full step before her. "He better not be making you work for a free dinner the way he used to make me. I don't care how wonderful a chef Rafe is, he's not as good as euros in your pocket."

She wanted Louisa to get paid? That was her concern? Louisa didn't know what to say. "You mean you don't mind my being here?"

"Why should I?" She eased herself into a nearby chair with a sigh. "Oh," she said seeing Louisa's expression. "You mean because the press said you two were dating."

"Among other things."

Again, the woman waved her off. "Who believes anything the newspapers say? Are those wine orders?" She motioned to a spreadsheet of names and addresses on the desk.

"Yesterday's telephone orders." Louisa grabbed the

change of topic with more gratitude than she thought possible. "I haven't printed out the internet orders yet."

"Wow, Nico wasn't kidding when he said the business was doing well."

No, he wasn't. Wine vendors, restaurants, tourists—everyone was eager to stock Amatucci Red. "No surprise," Nico had remarked, winking in her direction. "Once they have a taste, they want more."

Louisa had poured herself a glass before bed last night, and it was as delicious as she remembered. *When it had been a lingering flavor in Nico's kiss,* she recalled with a shiver. Between the wine and yesterday's embrace, it was no wonder she'd dreamt of him all night.

Once they have a taste, they want more.

"At this rate he won't have much stock left for the harvest festival," Marianna said, dragging Louisa back to the conversation at hand. "Unless he bottles more."

"I don't think the next vintage is ready." As Nico explained yesterday, the liquid needed to ferment at least five years before it was considered ready for bottling. "He said something about relabeling the remaining stock as Amatucci reserve."

"Relabeling and jacking up the price to reflect the reduced supply," Marianna mused aloud. "An old winemaker's trick, although few pull it off as well as my brother does. There's a reason he's won the country's Winemaker of the Year two years in a row."

"He has?"

"You didn't know?"

"No." She'd had no idea. "I knew the winery was successful." The sheer scope of his operations said as much. "But I didn't know how much so."

"Much as we tease him, my big brother has done very well with our family business. He's considered one of Italy's brightest wine stars."

"Careful, Marianna. Keep saying things like that and I'll believe you mean them." The subject of their conversation strolled in wearing a cocky grin. As Louisa had come to expect over the past couple of days, he already bore the evidence of hard work in the sun. The sight of his glistening biceps made her stomach flutter.

He nodded in her direction. "Although I hope you're suitably impressed."

"I am," she replied. "Very." Smug as the man was, the only awards he'd ever mentioned were the medals various vintages had won over the years, and those he attributed to the grapes, not to himself.

Now that she thought about it though, he didn't need to trumpet his accomplishments. His self-confidence said everything. "I was telling your sister that you planned to relabel the Amatucci Red," she said.

"Nothing wine lovers love more than to think they are getting something unique. And in this case they are."

He smiled again, straight at her this time, and Louisa found herself squeezing the arm of her chair. Who knew legs could give out while you were sitting? When he turned on the charm, it was all a person could do to keep her insides from turning to jelly. What her ex-husband could have done with magnetism like Nico's... *With a little charm, a man can sell anything*, Steven used to say.

Only Nico didn't just sell, he *made* wine. Good wine that he worked hard to produce. He came by his success honestly. That was what she found impressive.

Across the way, his baby sister offered a disdainful sniff. "Don't compliment him too much, Louisa. His head is big enough as it is."

"Not as big as your belly," Nico replied. "Are you supposed to be out in that condition?"

"You're as bad as my husband. I'm pregnant, not an

invalid. I'm also bored stiff. Ryan is in Melbourne until tomorrow."

"So you came here looking for entertainment."

"Isn't that what big brothers are for?" the brunette asked, winking in Louisa's direction.

Louisa felt herself smile in return. Marianna's openness had her flummoxed. She was so certain she would be furious at her for involving Nico in her scandals. Yet here she was, joking as if none of the stories had ever happened.

"If you're going to stay, you're going to have to work," Nico told his sister.

"You want me to pick grapes?"

"No, we—" waving his arm, he indicated himself and Louisa "—can pick your brain. That is the reason I am here," he said. "We need to decide what the winery is going to do for the festival."

"You haven't decided yet?" Eyes wide, Marianna pushed herself straight. "Little last-minute, don't you think?"

"In case you haven't noticed, I've been busy. We still have time." He sounded confident, but Marianna rolled her eyes nonetheless.

"What kind of contribution are you talking about?" Louisa asked. More important, what did Nico expect from her?

"All the major businesses in Monte Calanetti are expected to build a float for the festival parade," Nico explained. "Something that celebrates the harvest or Tuscan heritage."

"Decorated with native foliage," Marianna added. "Grapes, olives, flowers."

"Wow." Louisa hadn't realized the festival was so elaborate. In her mind, she'd pictured a street fair similar to the St. Anthony's Feast in Boston's North End. "Sounds like a lot of fun."

"It is," Marianna told her. "Everyone works together to

decorate and all the businesses compete to see who can outdo the others. The winner gets to display the harvest festival trophy. Amatucci Vineyards came in second last year. We created a miniature version of the plaza, complete with a working fountain." Pulling out her phone, the woman tapped a few buttons before turning the screen toward Louisa. "See?"

The photo showed Nico standing in front of the fountain, hands upon his hips. His smile dripping with pride. He looked like a superhero.

"Impressive," she murmured. Bet whoever took home the trophy didn't look nearly as good.

Marianna assumed Louisa meant the float. "Well, we started planning early. It's nearly impossible to assemble a prize-winning contribution at the last minute."

"Nearly, but not completely impossible," Nico retorted. "All we need is a good idea."

"Don't forget time," Marianna added.

Her brother waved her off, the same wave, Louisa noticed, his sister had used when dismissing the newspaper articles. "We will keep the design simple. It's not about being complicated, it's about being memorable. Like an Amatucci vintage."

His sister rolled her eyes again as Louisa stifled a snort. She was beginning to think some of his audacious behavior was on purpose. To see what kind of reaction he could elicit.

As far as the parade float went, however, he might have a point. She tried to remember the New Year's parades she used to watch on television as a kid. Most of the floats were a blur of colors. "Is there a theme?" she asked.

"Oh, there's always a theme," Nico replied. "But no one pays attention."

"No one meaning Ni—"

All of a sudden, Marianna gasped and clutched her

stomach. Louisa and Nico were on their feet in a flash. The brunette held up a hand. "No need to panic. The baby kicked extra hard, is all. Going to be a little football player, I think. Uncle Nico is going to have to practice his footwork." Her face radiating maternal tranquility, she rubbed her swollen stomach. "Are you ready to play coach, Uncle Nico?"

Louisa's heart squeezed a little as the image of Nico and a miniature version of himself chasing a soccer ball popped into her head.

"I'm not sure I'd be the best coach," Nico replied. It was an uncharacteristically humble comment.

"I suppose you'd be happier if he or she wants to pick grapes."

"I—I just think we shouldn't be making plans for the child's future yet. It's too early. You don't want to court bad luck."

Funny, Louisa wouldn't have pegged Nico as the superstitious type. She supposed it came from being a farmer. No counting on the harvest until it happens or something like that.

Marianna acknowledged his reluctance with a frown. "Fine," she said. "We'll wait until he or she is born before making plans.

"Although I still think she's going to be a football player," she said under her breath.

They brainstormed ideas for a while, until a problem in the wine cellar drew Nico away. Louisa and Marianna continued for a little while longer, but it was obvious the pregnant woman was beginning to tire, despite her protests.

"Story of my life," Marianna said with a yawn. "I can't do anything for more than a half hour before needing a nap."

"Might as well enjoy it while you can," Louisa told her. "Who knows when you'll get this much sleep again?"

The brunette nodded as if she'd delivered some great wisdom. "So true. I'll call you tomorrow and we can talk more about the project."

The two women walked to the front door. As usual, the few employees in the production area watched as they passed by. Marianna waved to each one with a smile while Louisa tucked her hair behind her ear and tried to act nonchalant. The past hour, watching Nico and his sister tease each other back and forth, had been the most relaxed she'd felt in forty-eight hours. She hated the idea that as soon as Marianna left, the atmosphere would go back to being tense and awkward.

They'd reached the door to the front office when Marianna suddenly turned serious. "May I ask you a question?" she asked.

Louisa's stomach tensed. Things had been going so well. What would change Marianna's mood so abruptly? It didn't help to see the other woman looking over her shoulder for potential eavesdroppers. "Of course," she said. "Anything."

"Is it me, or was Nico strangely disinterested when we were talking about the baby?"

Now that she mentioned it, Nico's reaction had been odd, especially considering how invested he had been when Marianna had first announced her pregnancy. Of course, at the time Marianna and her husband had been estranged and he had been worried about his sister's future. "You heard him; he doesn't want to court bad luck," she said.

"I know, but he's never been superstitious before," Marianna replied with a frown. "If anything, I'd expect him to tell me superstition was a bunch of nonsense. He used to hate it whenever our mother saw one of her omens."

"Your mother saw omens?"

"Oh, all the time. Usually after a fight with my father telling her they should make up."

Interesting. "Well, this is the first baby in the Amatucci family. Maybe it's making him tap into his roots."

"Maybe. He does like tradition."

"Plus, he's probably distracted. He has been super busy, between harvest and helping the town get ready for the festival." *And finding time to help her.*

"That is true. He does seem more distracted than usual these days." Marianna's frown quickly turned into a smile that was disarmingly similar to her brother's. "At least some of those distractions are good distractions, no?"

She didn't think that Louisa and he... The brunette's eyes sparkled, causing Louisa's stomach to tumble. "You said you didn't believe the papers."

"Oh, I don't believe the stuff about Luscious Louisa, but you and Nico... I saw that photo of the two of you dancing." She nudged Louisa's shoulder. *"Molto romantico."*

"It was just the camera angle," Louisa said, shaking her head. "The two of us are just friends."

"Friends, eh? Did he really throw a photographer off your balcony?"

Louisa sighed. "Yes, but again, it's not what you think. He was helping me out. You know your brother. If there's a situation that needs handling, he automatically takes charge."

"Hmm. I do know my brother," Marianna said with an odd smile.

"What does that mean?"

"Nothing. You are completely right. My brother does like to take charge. And in this case, I couldn't be happier."

Meaning she still thought they were involved. Louisa would have to have Nico set his sister straight. Still, it was nice to know her friend didn't think Louisa was out to seduce Nico for his money. Her trust meant a lot.

"You really don't care about what they said about me...

about what happened in Boston? What they implied I was doing here in town?"

"Don't be silly. You're not responsible for what your ex-husband did. And you're the last person I'd call a temptress. I mean, look at what you're wearing…" She gestured at Louisa's jeans and green cotton sweater. "I'm dressed more seductively."

"It's the stiletto heels. They make everything seductive." Louisa tried to punctuate the remark with a laugh, but tears sprang to her eyes anyway. Marianna would never know how much her faith meant. Unable to form the words, she threw her arms around the pregnant woman's neck.

"Don't you know you're not supposed to get teary around a pregnant woman? My hormones won't be able to take it and I'll start crying, too." The young woman squeezed her tight, then released her with a watery grin. "I'll call you tomorrow."

Wiping her own eyes, Louisa nodded. "Do you mind if I don't walk you any farther? There might be reporters hiding across the street."

"Of course, I understand. And Louisa?" The brunette reached out to squeeze Louisa's hand. "I'm glad you and my brother are such good friends. He doesn't have that many."

Not many friends? "You're kidding right? We are talking about the same Nico Amatucci, aren't we?" The man with charisma to spare.

"Those are acquaintances, not real friends. He doesn't open himself up to many people. That makes you special."

Special. Right. Marianna's hormones were definitely out of whack.

A sound caught her attention. Looking across the room, she spied Nico talking to an employee by the wine cellar doorway. Almost as if he knew she was thinking about him, he stopped what he was doing to look in her direction. He smiled and, for a moment, Louisa swore the entire winery tipped on its axis. *That makes you special...*

Apparently, Marianna wasn't the only one out of whack.

Louisa was upstairs asleep when Nico got home. He'd planned it that way. Following their embrace the day before, he decided it made sense for them to keep as much distance as possible, so he made a point of working as late as possible, along with heading into the fields before sunrise. The idea was for the long hours to make him too tired to remember the way her body had fit against his, allowing him to sleep without disturbance.

He didn't count on Marianna stopping by and stirring up other disturbing thoughts.

His sister was having a baby, he thought as he poured a glass of Chianti. Despite knowing this for months, it hadn't truly dawned on him until she'd called him Uncle Nico that she was starting a family of her own. Both she and his brother, Angelo, were moving forward with their lives, while here he was in the ancestral home maintaining the past. He, who was so determined never to repeat the madness of his parents.

Settling back on the sofa, he stared in the dim light at the dark square of the unlit fireplace. In his head, he could hear the sound of his parents laughing and clinking glasses. When they were happy, they laughed a lot, but when they stopped laughing... At least his father stayed in nice hotels when Mama threw him out.

All highs and lows, Carlos used to say. *No in betweens.* He never understood how that worked. How people could go from hot to cold to hot again in the blink of an eye. He once told Floriana that it was one thing to have passion in the bedroom, but it was quite another to have passion rule your life. Right before Floriana left, she told him that he had no passion, period.

She'd made a strong argument. He'd barely blinked when she'd said it.

He wondered what she would have said if she'd seen him throw that photographer off the balcony? Probably that she didn't recognize him. Again, she would have a point; Nico barely recognized himself the past couple of days, he was behaving so out of character.

Maybe Louisa really was a siren like the tabloids said. The thought made him chuckle into his glass.

"Nico? Is that you?"

The object of his thoughts appeared at the top of the stairs, a backlit silhouette. It took about two seconds for Nico to become aroused. Another thing that was out of character for him was how he couldn't seem to stop wanting her. Usually, when a woman said she wasn't interested, he moved on. No sense knocking on a door that wouldn't open. With Louisa, however, he didn't want to just knock, he wanted to kick the door in.

"Sorry to wake you," he said. "I was just having a glass of wine before bed."

"Long day?"

"Harvest takes a lot of preparation. Did Mario get you home all right?" He'd ordered his intern to escort her in case there were photographers lying in wait.

"He did. I hope you don't mind, but I got hungry and made some dinner. Puttanesca. There are leftovers in the fridge."

The notion of her at home in his kitchen caused a curious end-over-end sensation in the center of his chest. "Thank you."

"No problem. Good night," she said. Her silhouette hesitated. "Will I see you at breakfast?"

He thought of how good she looked drinking espresso across from him, and the sensation repeated itself. "Afraid not. I have to be in the fields early."

"Oh. Okay. I'll see you at the winery then."

Any disappointment he heard in her voice was pure imagination. As he finished his Chianti, he made a note to take the newspapers with him again when he left tomorrow. The "Royal Wedding Scandal," as they were calling it now, continued to dominate the tabloids, and he wanted to protect Louisa from the exposure.

Is that the argument you're using? Not that you don't want her leaving town? The very thought of her getting on the bus made his heart seize.

Out of character indeed.

The newspapers were missing again. For the second day in a row, Louisa came down for breakfast to discover both Nico and the papers gone from the house.

Who did he think he was, censoring her reading material?

She tracked him down in the fields and asked him that exact question.

"Keep your voice down, *bella mia*," he replied. "Unless you want people to know about our living arrangement." He nodded down the row where a pair of farm hands were watching them with curiosity. "And to answer your question, I wasn't aware I was 'censoring' anything."

"Then where are the newspapers?"

"I took them with me to read over coffee."

"Read about the Royal Wedding Scandal, you mean."

"Where did you hear about that?" The mask of indifference he'd been wearing slipped, proving his deception. Louisa glared at him. "Princess Christina called me this morning to ask how I was doing. She wanted me to know she and Prince Antonio didn't care what people were saying."

"See? Didn't I tell you that your friends would stand by you?"

Yes, he had, and Christina's phone call had meant more to her than she could say. That wasn't the point at the moment, however. "Don't try to change the topic. This is about you keeping information from me."

Nico sighed. "I was trying to protect you from useless gossip."

"Useless or not, you don't have the right to decide what I read and what I don't read." She rubbed her arms. Despite the sun beating down, her skin had turned to gooseflesh. She felt as though she'd had this conversation before with Steven. Only then the argument had been in her head because she'd not dared to speak her mind. Today was the first time she'd said the words aloud.

"I'm sorry. You were so upset by the headlines the other morning, I wanted to save you further distress." While talking, he pulled a grape off the vine and crushed it between his fingers. "I hate seeing you sad," he added, staring at his stained fingers.

The sweetness behind his answer dispelled a little of her anger. Only a little, however. "That's not your call to make, Nico. It's not your job to protect me from the headlines."

"No, just the paparazzi," he replied.

Louisa winced. He had her there. She was using him for protection, making her indignation over the newspapers sound more than a little hypocritical. "Do you want me to move back to the palazzo?"

"Do you want to move back?"

She toed the dirt with her sandal. Short answer? No. She liked having him nearby. Which meant maybe she should move back. "I don't know."

"Oh." He grabbed his satchel, which sat on the ground by his feet, and headed down the row.

She followed him. Thankfully the workers had moved

to another row, leaving them in privacy. "That's all you're going to say?"

"You're not a prisoner, Louisa. You can do whatever you want."

Though cool, she could still hear the hint of hurt in his voice. Problem was, what she wanted scared her. She wanted the security she felt when she was wrapped in Nico's arms. *Which is exactly the opposite of why you came to Italy in the first place. What happened to standing on your own two feet for a change?*

"So what did the headlines say anyway?" she asked.

"You mean you didn't go online and look?"

"No." Her cheeks burned. Going online would have been the easy solution, but she'd been too busy being indignant to turn on the computer. "I came looking for you instead."

"Well, you didn't miss much," Nico replied.

"Apparently I did, or you wouldn't have taken the papers." And he wouldn't be studying the Sangiovese leaves so intently. The winemaker had two very distinct stares, she'd come to realize. His intense "never missed a beat" stare that made her skin tingle, and his "I'm not telling you the whole story so I'm going to look at something else" stare. "Tell me."

"No doubt Christina told you about the royal wedding part. Halencia's government is afraid you might try to entice the royal family into making dubious investments."

"She told me." That wasn't the whole story, though. Not based on how Nico continued to stare at the vines. He took a deep breath. "They also interviewed my former fiancée."

CHAPTER SIX

"OH." IT WAS not the answer Louisa expected. She had suspected the papers would continue plumbing their erstwhile romance, but, in her self-involved haze, she hadn't thought about them digging into Nico's past. Dozens of questions came to mind, but the only words she could manage to say out loud were "I didn't realize you'd been engaged."

He shrugged. "It was a long time ago."

But not so long ago the memory didn't bother him. "Did she say something bad?" Was that why he continued to avoid her eyes?

"Actually she was surprisingly diplomatic. But then, Floriana was—is—a very good person."

If she was so good, why then why was she an ex? Louisa tried to picture the kind of woman Nico would propose to. Someone beautiful, no doubt. And smart. She would have to be smart to keep up with him. More questions came to mind, like what had kept them from the altar? From the shadows filling his expression, the decision hadn't been his, at least not completely.

Her annoyance from before all but forgotten, she reached out to touch his arm. "I'm sorry if it dredged up a lot of bad memories."

At last, he shifted his gaze, turning from the grapes to where her fingers rested on his forearm. As always happened, when his eyes fell on her, the attention made her body tingle. "Not everyone is made to get married."

True or not, his answer, with its lonely, resigned tone, hurt her to hear. Louisa found it hard to think of Nico as ever being lonely—the concepts *Nico* and *alone* seemed like polar opposites. But lines had suddenly appeared around his mouth and eyes as he spoke, lines that could only be etched from sadness.

"Sometimes we just pick the wrong person the first time around, is all," she said, thinking of her own mistake.

"Sometimes. I should check the Brix content on these vines." Pulling away from her touch, he reached for his satchel.

He didn't want to talk about it. Fine. If anyone understood the need to bury past mistakes, she did, and if changing topics took the sadness away from his eyes, all the better.

Nico wasn't the only one who hated to see another person sad.

"Are they ready for harvest?" she asked.

"You tell me." Picking a grape, he pressed it to her lips. Louisa could taste the sweetness the moment she bit down. Once she moved past the feel of his fingers on her lips, that is. "Mmm, delicious."

"If the sugar content matches up, I'll tell the foreman to have his team start working this field tomorrow. By the time we finish, the other fields, yours, should be ready."

"You mean they aren't all ready at the same time?" She stole another grape. The fruit was still sweet, but it didn't make her lips respond like the one he fed her had.

"Grapes on the northern side of the vineyard always ripen sooner. They're on a slope angled to get the most sun throughout the day. Carlos used to call Northern grapes *favorito della Natura* because they got the most sunshine."

"Nature's favorites?"

"He had names for all the fields. The ones in the southern field he called *scontroso*—grumpy—because they were often slow to ripen."

"Wouldn't you be grumpy, too, if the other field was the favorite?"

"That's what I used to tell him."

Louisa smiled, imagining the two men walking the rows, nicknaming the plants. "Carlos sounds like a character."

"He was a very wise man. A born winemaker."

Whose fields would be ruined, but for Nico's care. Guilt kicked at her conscience. If only she could have claimed her inheritance sooner. "I had no idea any of the Bertonellis even existed," she said. "My mother never talked about my father's family." Never talked about her father, period, actually. Geoffrey Harrison was a smooth-talking liar best left unmentioned.

"Don't feel bad. I never knew he had relatives in America."

"Tight family bonds, huh?" she said. The sarcasm came out more bitter than she meant.

"Trust me, family bonds aren't always so wonderful. They can get in the way, too. Like baby sisters deciding you need to entertain them when they are pregnant and bored."

Who did he think he was kidding? He'd loved Marianna's visit yesterday and they both knew it.

"I would have killed for a brother or sister," she said. "Most of my life, it was just my mom and me. We used to joke it was us against the world."

"Must be upsetting for her to see her daughter being lambasted in the press. Have you talked to her?"

"No. She…um…" It was her turn to study the grape vines. How did she explain that she'd screwed up the one good relationship in her life? She'd love to blame Steven again, but this time she had only herself to blame. "I don't want to bother her."

Just as she recognized his evasion tactics, Nico recognized hers. "You don't think your mother's aware of what's going on?" he asked.

"I'm sure she is, but…" But Louisa was too embarrassed to call and talk about it. "The two of us were estranged for a while. I don't want to spoil things by bringing up bad news right as we're getting on better footing."

This wasn't the direction she planned for their conversation to take. Seemed as though whenever the two of them talked lately, she found herself sharing some facet of her past she'd sworn to keep secret. Frightening, how easily she exposed herself to him, more frightening than her desire to lean on his shoulder, and yet at the same time, the words tumbled out without pause.

Perhaps it was because Nico accepted what she said without pushing for more. Like now, he simply nodded and, hands in his back pockets, began sauntering down the row. Made her feel, in spite of how easily the information came out, that she was in control of the information she chose to share.

Mimicking his posture, Louisa headed after him, and the two of them walked in silence for several feet.

"Carlos taught me to appreciate the art of winemaking," he said after a moment, returning to their earlier conversation. Again, Louisa silently thanked him for not pushing. "He never let me forget that ours is a centuries-old craft, and as such we have an obligation to make the best wine possible."

"And your father? He was a vintner, too, was he not?" Strange that Nico's allegiance would be to his neighbor and not the man who raised him. "Did Carlos teach him, as well?"

"My father made wine, but not like Carlos. He was, shall we say, too distracted by other things."

Distracted how? Dying to know, Louisa had to bite her tongue to keep from asking. After all, she owed Nico the same courtesy he showed her when it came to privacy.

He answered anyway. "My mother, for one thing.

Women who weren't my mother, for another. Don't worry," he added before she could offer sympathy. "Mama gives as good as she gets."

"They're still together?" She didn't know why that surprised her, but it did.

"They have what you would call a fiery relationship," Nico replied. "They've separated and reunited more times than I can count, swearing to God every time that they cannot live without each other, and they can't, for about a year or so. Then the plates begin to fly again." The early-morning sun caught his eyes as he cocked his head. Even when sad, he was beautiful. "You could practically hear the clock ticking between breakups."

"I'm sorry."

"Why are you apologizing? You didn't do anything."

No, but she felt as though she needed to say *something*. She knew that feeling of heavy expectancy all too well, the horrible sense of foreboding as you waited—and waited—for some undefined disaster to strike. "Is that how you ended up at the palazzo?"

"The palazzo vineyards were my escape. No chaos, no drama. Just peace and quiet." He took a long, deep breath, making Louisa wonder if he wasn't trying to internalize those very same qualities now. "At first I just went and watched the workers. Then one day Carlos came by—I think the workers told him about me—and he understood.

"My parents' reputations were well-known," he added with a smile. "Anyway, after that, he said if I was going to spend time in the vineyards, I was going to learn about them."

"You're very lucky," Louisa said. How often had she wished she had an ally like Carlos, only to end up hating herself because her isolation was no one's fault but her own?

"I know."

It dawned on her that Carlos Bertonelli had rescued them both, albeit in different ways. Shame rolled through her as she thought about how long it had taken her to claim her inheritance. She'd nearly let her sanctuary fall to pieces because she'd foolishly let herself be convinced there was no escaping her marriage.

"I'm sorry I never got to meet him," she said.

"Me, too." His lips curled into a smile. "He would have liked you a lot, you know," he told her. "The old man always had a soft spot for beautiful women. Right up to the end."

Louisa blushed at the compliment. "He must have loved Marianna, then."

"Of course he did. After his wife died, he would ask her to play the role of harvest queen. He used to tell people it was easier than choosing someone different each year, but everyone knew it was because he had a soft spot for her."

"There's a festival queen?"

"No one told you?"

"No." Although she could certainly picture the beautiful Marianna being selected as queen no matter her age.

"Oh yes, it's a tradition for the local nobility to lead the festivities." Nico told her. "If the nobleman wasn't married, then he would select a maiden from the village to act as his queen for the day. Although in those cases, I suspect there were a few other duties involved, as well." He grinned. "You seriously did not know?"

Louisa shook her head. The thing about Monte Calanetti's traditions running so deep was that everyone assumed they were common knowledge. "It's not something that normally comes up in conversation," she said. "Who took over as the festival king after Carlos died?" The sunburn on Nico's cheeks grew a little darker. "Why am I not surprised?" She could only imagine the crowd clamoring to play his queen.

"Someone had to," he said. "Of course, now that you're here I will gladly abdicate the title."

She laughed. "Oh sure. People would love to see me lead the harvest parade. I can see the headlines now— Luscious Louisa Reigns from on High."

Why wasn't Nico laughing? Granted, it wasn't the funniest joke but he could at least smile at her attempt to make light of her problems. "Actually..." he began.

"You're joking." He was joking, right? "You're suggesting I play the role of harvest queen?"

"It's not a suggestion," he replied.

"Good."

"It's what's expected."

"Excuse me?" Did he say *expected*? The word ran down her back. She didn't do *expected* anymore.

"It's tradition," Nico continued. "As owner of Palazzo di Comparino, *you* are the local nobility. Therefore, people will expect you to take Carlos's place."

"No, they won't." Nico was the town nobility, she was merely notoriety.

"Yes, they will," he quickly retorted. "It's tradition."

Again with tradition. As if that justified everything. Who cared if it was tradition or not? Had he forgotten about the paparazzi, the whole reason she was hiding out at the vineyard? "I'm trying to avoid having my picture taken, remember? Not encourage the papers by parading down the middle of the street."

"You won't be encouraging anything. The festival isn't for another week. By that time, the scandal will have gone away," he said.

Says you. "Scandals never go away," she shot back. They were like weeds, going dormant only to crop up during another season. "People have long memories. Just because the headlines fade, doesn't mean they will have forgotten who I am. The people here aren't going to want to expose Monte Calanetti to ridicule."

An aggravated growl vibrated deep in Nico's throat. *"Madonna mia,"* he said, gesturing toward the heavens, "I thought we were past this. You have got to have faith in the people you live with."

"Oh sure, because the world has been so supportive up until now." She couldn't go through another round of sneers and whispers. She *wouldn't*.

"Monte Calanetti is not Boston."

"Maybe, maybe not," she said. That didn't matter. "What's the big deal anyway? So I don't lead the parade. Traditions can change, you know. There's no law that says everything needs to stay exactly the same."

"I know," he spat.

Then why were they even having this foolish argument? He knew she wanted to stay under the radar. "Look, it's not just the risk of gossip," she told him. Why she was bothering to add to her argument, she didn't know, but she was. "Even if you're right, and people don't care about the headlines, I'm not living that kind of life again."

"What do you mean, 'that kind of life'?"

"The whole socialite thing. I played that role long enough when I was with Steven." She was done with plastic smiles and faking happiness. With being told when and where and how.

He frowned. "So you don't care that when Carlos passed on the palazzo, he passed along the responsibilities that came with it?"

"No, I don't." She'd come to Italy to live *her* life and no one was going to make her do anything different.

"I see," Nico said, nodding. "Now I understand."

"Do you?"

"Si. Comparino is merely a piece of property to you. No wonder you ignored its existence for so long."

Ignored? *Ignored?* Oh, did he just say the wrong thing. Louisa's vision flashed red. "Don't you dare," she snarled. "I didn't ignore anything. From the moment I opened the lawyer's letter, I wanted to be here." He had no idea how badly. How many nights she'd lain awake wishing she could board a plane and escape.

"Of course you did. Your desire to be here was obvious from all those months you left the place to ruin."

"I was testifying against my husband!"

Her shout sounded across the vineyard. If the field workers didn't know her business before, they certainly knew it now. Let them. By this point, the damn trial was public knowledge anyway. What was another mention? Taking a deep breath, she added in a lower voice. "I couldn't leave the country for an entire year."

The explanation might have been enough for some, but not Nico. Crossing his arms, he positioned himself in front of her, his broad shoulders blocking the path. "You ignored us for over *two* years, Louisa, not one," he reminded her. "Or did the authorities refuse to let you leave the country before the arrest, as well?"

Not the authorities. Damn it all. How had she ever let the conversation turn in this direction? To the one secret she hoped to never have to say aloud.

"It's complicated," she replied. It would be too much to ask for Nico to continue accepting her terse answers at face value. Not this time. He was angry; he would want answers.

Sure enough, his eyes burned dark and intense as he stood, arms folded, waiting for her to continue. Louisa's skin burned from the intensity. She thought about lying, but she'd never been very good at it. Pretending, masking her emotions, sure, but out-and-out lies? Not so much. Looking back, it was a wonder she'd managed to keep Comparino a secret at all.

"I didn't have a choice—I had to stay in Boston. If Steven had known I had property in my name—property of my own—he would have..." Angry tears threatened. She looked down so he wouldn't see them.

"He would have what?" Nico asked.

"Taken it," she replied, choking on the words. "He would have taken the palazzo the same way he took everything else I had."

At last, the ugly truth was out in the open and Nico would never look at her the same way again. How could he? She was a stupid, gullible fool who let a master manipulator ruin her life. Shame rose like bile, sour and thick in her mouth. She didn't dare raise her eyes to look into his face. She couldn't bear to see pity where there'd once been admiration. There was only one thing she could do.

Spinning around, she took off down the path.

What the—? Nico stared at Louisa's retreating figure before sprinting after her. "Louisa, hold up!"

"Leave me alone," she said. "I have to get to the winery." She sounded as though—was she crying?

It didn't take long for him to close the distance between them. When he did, he touched her shoulder hoping to slow her pace, only to have her tear free of his grip so fiercely you'd think he was physically restraining her. She turned and snarled, "I said leave me alone."

She was crying. Tears streaked her cheeks. Their tracks might as well have been scratches on his skin, they hurt that much to see. This was about more than her thief of a husband stealing property. "What did that bastard do to you?"

"Nothing. It doesn't matter. Forget I said anything."

She tried to surge ahead again but he had height to his advantage. It was nothing for him to step ahead and block her path. Not unexpectedly, she shoved at his shoulder trying to make him move. "I said forget it."

"I can't," he said, standing firm. Not after seeing those tears. "Talk to me."

"Why? So you can laugh at what a stupid idiot I am?"

Idiot? Nico shook his head. "I could never think that of you."

"Then you're a bigger fool than I am," she said, jaw trembling. "And I'm…I'm…"

Her face started to crumble. "I'm a damn big one."

CHAPTER SEVEN

LOUISA BURIED HER face in her hands. Nico stood frozen by the sight of her shaking shoulders, wanting to comfort her but afraid his touch might make her run again. Eventually his need to hold her won out, and he wrapped her in his arms. She sagged into him, fists twisting into his shirt. His poor sweet Louisa. Steven Clark should be glad he was in prison because otherwise Nico would... Heaven knows what he would do. He pressed his lips to the top of her head and let her cry.

After a while, the shaking eased. "I'm sorry," she said, lifting her head. "I didn't mean to lose it like that. It's just sometimes I think, no matter how hard I try, Steven will always be there, taunting me. That I'll never completely escape him."

Suddenly all her comments about needing to be on her own took on new meaning. She was running from more than scandal and a failed marriage, wasn't she? He could kick himself for not realizing it sooner. He risked another brush of his lips against her hair before asking, "Did he hurt you badly?"

"You mean physically?" She shook her head. "He never laid a hand on me."

Thank God. Not all abuse was physical, however. Emotional abuse was insidious and painful in its own way. His parents played mind games all the time, driving one another to madness out of revenge or jealousy. "But he hurt you all the same, didn't he?"

"Yeah, he did," she said, giving a long sigh. Backing out of his embrace, she stumbled just far enough to be out of reach, wiping her tears as she walked. "It's my fault, really. The signs were all there from the very beginning, but I chose to ignore them. Love makes you stupid."

"He was also an accomplished liar," he reminded her, his nerves bristling when she mentioned the word *love*. From everything he'd heard of the man so far, Steven Clark didn't deserve Louisa's affection, and he certainly didn't deserve her self-recrimination.

If his underlying message made it through, it wasn't evident in Louisa's answering sigh. "He certainly was. But he was also incredibly charming and romantic, and I was twenty-one years old."

"Barely an adult."

"True, but I was certain I knew everything."

"What twenty-one-year-old isn't?" he replied.

His attempt to lighten the moment failed. Tired of standing, and suspecting getting the entire story would take some time, Nico motioned for her to follow him a few feet ahead, to a small gap between plants. He sat down beneath the branches, the dirt cool and damp through his jeans, and patted the space beside him. Louisa hesitated for a moment before joining him.

"How did you meet him?" he asked when she finally settled herself. He told himself he was asking because he wanted to understand what happened, and not because of the burning sensation the man's name caused in his chest.

"At work. My first job out of college. I was so psyched when I got the job, too," she said, in a voice that still held lingering pride. "Clark Investments was the hottest business in the city at the time. Steven was a rock star in Boston financial circles."

A rock star with twenty years on his starry-eyed employee, Nico thought, gritting his teeth. "You must have been very good to get the job."

"I was."

There was such gratitude in her smile, as if it had been a long time since someone had acknowledged her abilities. Nico laid the blame at the feet of her ex-husband. "Anyway, I met Steven a couple months after I started— on the elevator of all places—and all I could think was *Steven Clark is talking to me.* Later, he told me he was so impressed he had to ask me out."

That, thought Nico, might have been the most honest thing Steven Clark had ever said. What man with two eyes wouldn't be impressed by her?

"I felt like Cinderella. Here I was, a girl from a single-parent family in a blue-collar town while Steven was sophisticated and had experienced things I'd never dreamed of doing. Things like skiing in the Alps and diving with sharks." She scooped a handful of dirt and let it sift through her fingers. "I should have known then, the stories were too outrageous to be true, but like I said, love—"

"Makes you blind," he finished for her. Why that phrase bothered him so much, he didn't know. Of course she'd loved the man; he was her husband.

"He flew us to Chicago once because I said I liked deep dish pizza. Who wouldn't fall for a gesture like that?" she asked. "I thought I'd met Prince Charming.

"My friends didn't think so. They said he made them feel uncomfortable. Steven said it was because they were jealous."

"Perhaps they were."

"My mother, too?" she asked. "She didn't like him at all. Called him a slicker version of my father and said she didn't trust him."

That was why they were estranged. Nico could guess what happened. Her mother didn't approve, and Steven took advantage of the disagreement to push them further apart.

"We had this awful fight," she told him. "I accused

her of not wanting me to be happy, that because she was alone and miserable, she wanted me to be alone and miserable, too. When I told Steven, he said, 'that's all right. I'm all the family you need now.'" The fresh tears in her eyes had Nico moving to take her in his arms again. She shook him off, getting to her feet instead. "I didn't talk to her for almost five years. She could have died and I wouldn't have known."

"That's not true." She was letting her guilty conscience color her thinking.

"Isn't it?" she replied, turning around. "Who would tell me? I cut myself off from everyone I used to know. Because they didn't fit with my new life."

And Nico could guess who had put that thought in her head. A chill ran through him as he slowly began to understand what she meant by Steven taking everything from her.

She'd turned away from him again, her face turned to the foliage. Nico could see her fingering the edge of one of the leaves. Her hands were shaking.

"You tell yourself you're too smart to fall for someone's lies," she said. "You read stories of women trapped in bad relationships and you can't understand how they can be so foolish. That is, until it happens to you."

"Louisa, don't…"

"Don't what? Blame myself? Tell the embarrassing truth?"

Don't tell me at all. Rising to his feet, Nico walked behind her and curled his hands atop her shoulders to steady her. There was no need for her to go on; he'd heard enough.

Unfortunately for both of them, Louisa had unsealed a bottle that insisted on being emptied because she immediately shook her head. "I think maybe I need to tell someone," she whispered. "Maybe if I say the words aloud…"

Nico could hear her breath rattle with nerves as she

took a deep lungful of air before she began to speak. "When it first started, I barely noticed. When you're in love you're supposed to want to spend every minute with each other, right?"

"Yes," Nico replied. His hands were still on her shoulders, and it was all he could do not to pull her tight against him.

"And then, after we were married, when Steven suggested I stop working to avoid gossip, well that made sense, too. It was expected I would be with him at corporate dinner parties and charitable functions. Could hardly do that if I was working full-time."

Lots of women managed both, thought Nico. Louisa could have, as well. But that would have meant having a life of her own, and it sounded as though having an independent wife was the last thing Steven Clark wanted.

He honestly could strangle the man. Here was one of the things that made Louisa such a treasure. Challenging her was exciting. If Nico had a woman like her in his life, he'd do everything in his power to aid in her success, not pin her down like some butterfly under glass. Steven Clark was an idiot as well as a thief.

"When did you realize…?"

"That I was trapped?"

"Yes." Actually, he hadn't known what he'd meant to ask, but her question was close enough.

"I skipped a charity planning committee to do some last-minute Christmas shopping. One of the other members told Steven, and he lost it. Demanded to know where I'd been all day and with whom." She pulled the leaf she'd been playing with from its branch, sending a rustling noise rippling down the row. "To this day I'm not sure what frightened me more. His demand or the fact there were people reporting my actions to him."

Neither aspect sounded very comfortable. "You stayed, however." Because she loved him.

"Where was I supposed to go? None of the assets were in my name. I'd alienated everyone I used to know, and Steven didn't have friends so much as business associates. I couldn't trust those people to help me, not when Steven was handling their money. I couldn't go anywhere. I couldn't talk to anyone. I was stuck."

The proverbial bird in a gilded cage, Nico thought sadly.

"Surely your mother or your friends…"

"And have to listen to them tell me how right they'd all been? I couldn't." Nico wanted to smile despite the sad situation. That was his American. Stubborn to the end, even when it hurt her.

"Discovering I'd inherited the palazzo was torture. Here I had this safe haven waiting for me, and I couldn't get to it. Even if by some miracle I did find a way to evade Steven's radar, with his money and connections, he would have eventually tracked me down."

The leaf she'd been holding fluttered to the ground as she sighed. "In the end it was easier to go along to get along."

"You mean accept the abuse," Nico said.

"I told you, it wasn't abuse."

They both knew she was lying. Steven might not have hit her or yelled insults, but he'd abused her in his own despicable way. He'd stolen her innocence and her freedom and so much more. Nico could feel the anger spreading through him. If it was possible to kill a man by thoughts alone, Steven Clark would be dead a thousand times over.

Arms hugging her body, Louisa turned to look at him with cavernous eyes, the white-blond curtain of her hair casting her cheeks with shadows.

"The day I stumbled across those financial reports was the best day of my life, because I knew I could finally walk away," she said.

Only walking away hadn't been as easy as she made it sound.

The truth wasn't as simple as she described. Walking away was never easy. The details didn't matter. Her story explained a lot, however. Why she balked every time he offered to help, for example. It definitely explained why she feared her friends would cut her off.

"Do you still love him?" It was none of his business, and yet he could not stop thinking about her words before. Love makes you blind.

"No. Not even in the slightest."

If he shouldn't have asked the question, then he should definitely not have felt relief at her answer. He did, though. To save her heart from further pain, that was all.

"I'm sorry," he said.

"I told you before, I don't want your pity."

Her voice was rough from crying, the raw sound making him hate Steven Clark all the more. "I don't pity you," he told her truthfully. He didn't. He *admired* her. Did he know what kind of strength it took to pull herself free from the hell she had become trapped in? Not only pull herself free, but to begin again?

"What I meant was that I am sorry I accused you of abandoning the palazzo," he said.

"Oh." The tiniest of blushes tinged her cheekbones as she looked down at her feet. "Thank you," she said. "And I'm sorry I lost my temper."

"Then we are even." Funny, but he'd forgotten why she'd lost her temper in the first place.

By silent agreement, they started walking toward the production facilities. They'd been in the field most of the morning, Nico realized, or so said the sun beating on the back of his neck. His employees would be looking for him. Wasn't like him to ignore the winery for so long. Add another uncharacteristic behavior to the growing list.

Even though Louisa's confession answered a lot of questions, Nico found his mind more jumbled than before. Mostly with vague unformed ideas he couldn't articulate. Finally, because he felt the need to say *something* while they walked, he said in a quiet voice. "I'm glad you made it to Italy."

The sentiment didn't come close to capturing any of the thoughts swirling in his head, what he wanted to say, but it was enough to make Louisa smile.

"Are you really?" she asked.

She sounded so disbelieving.

"Yes, really," he replied. More than he'd realized until this moment. The town wouldn't be the same without her. The palazzo and Monte Calanetti needed her. He…

The thought lingered just out of reach.

He knew he was taking a risk, but he closed the distance between them anyway, reaching up with his hands to cradle her face. "I can't imagine Monte Calanetti without you."

Her trembling lower lip begged for reassurance or was it that he begged to reassure her? To kiss her and let her know just how glad he was to have her in Monte Calanetti.

Cool fingers encircled his wrists, holding him. Stopping him. She was backing away yet again. "Thank you," she said, slipping free.

This time when she began to walk, Nico purposely lagged behind.

CHAPTER EIGHT

"May I borrow you for a moment?"

Louisa was in the middle of attaching mailing labels to boxes when Nico appeared in her doorway. As soon as she looked in his direction, her stomach somersaulted. She blamed it on the fact that he'd startled her.

Along with the fact he looked as handsome as sin in his faded work clothes. How did the man do it? Look so perfect after being out in the fields for hours. None of the other workers wore hard labor as well. Of course there was always the chance he was supervising more than actually working, but standing around didn't seem his style. More likely Mother Nature wanted to make sure Nico looked a cut above all the rest.

Mother Nature did her job well.

Nico arched his eyebrow, and she realized he was waiting for a response. What had he asked? Right. To borrow her. "Sure," she replied. "What do you need?"

"Follow me to the lab."

Louisa did what he asked, her heart pounding in her chest. She couldn't blame being startled this time. Your palms didn't sweat when you were startled.

It'd been two days since their conversation in the vineyard, or rather since Louisa had bared her soul regarding her marriage. They hadn't talked since. Nico continued to leave the house before breakfast and didn't return until late. To be honest, Louisa wasn't sure he came home at all. After all, the dinner plate she left last night hadn't been touched. If it wasn't harvest season, she'd worry he was purposely avoiding her.

Oh, who was she kidding? She still worried, just as she was worried how to behave around him now. Strangely enough, however, it wasn't her meltdown—or her confession—that had her feeling awkward. It was the memory of Nico holding her close yet again.

Since arriving in Italy, Louisa could count on three fingers the number of times she'd truly felt safe and secure. All three had been in Nico's arms, and they were as engrained in her memory as any event could be. If she concentrated, she could feel his breath as it had brushed her lips when he'd said he couldn't imagine Monte Calanetti without her. The simplest of words, but they made her feel more special than she'd felt in a long time. With his touch gentle and sure on her cheeks, she'd wanted so badly for him to kiss her.

Still, the last time a man had made her feel special, she'd wound up making the biggest mistake of her life, and while she might be older and wiser, she was also a woman with desires that had been neglected for a long time. The idea of giving herself over to Nico's care left a warm fluttery sensation in the pit of her stomach—a dangerous feeling, to say the least. Thank goodness she managed to keep her head.

Thank goodness, too, that Nico understood. In fact, seeing his relaxed expression, she'd say he'd managed to brush the moment aside without problem.

Louisa was glad for that. Truly.

Nico's "lab" was located at the rear of the building a stone's throw from where the grapes were stored after being picked. Now that harvesting had begun, the rolling door that led to the loading dock was left permanently open so that the forklifts could transport the containers of grapes from the field trucks to the washing area. Louisa breathed deep, taking in as much of the sweet aroma as she could.

"Do you mind if I close the door?" Nico hollered. "It'll be easier to hear each other."

She shook her head. Out here the sound was much louder than by her office, where the machines were still dormant.

There was a click and the decibel level was suddenly reduced by half. "Much better," Nico said.

Better was relative. In addition to being small, the room was stuffed with equipment making the close space tighter still. Standing near the door, Louisa found herself less than a yard away from Nico's desk, and even closer to Nico himself. He smelled like grapes. To her chagrin, the aroma made her stomach flip-flop again.

Trying to look casual, she leaned against the door, arms folded across her midsection. "What is it you needed to talk about?" she asked him.

"Not talk. Taste."

He pointed to the equipment on his worktable. "I need a second opinion regarding this year's blend."

"This year's blend?" She knew that super Tuscans were wines made by combining different varieties of grape, but she assumed that once the formula was created, the blend stayed the same.

"Every harvest is different," Nico replied. "Sometimes only subtly, but enough that the formula should be tweaked. Mario and I have been playing with percentages all day, but we're not quite sure we've achieved the right balance."

"I see." Speaking of the university student, she didn't see him.

Nico must have seen her looking around because he said, "Mario has gone home. He was a little too enthusiastic a taster."

"You mean he got a little tipsy."

"Don't be silly. He needed a break, is all." He'd gotten tipsy. "Anyway, I think I'm close, but I could use a fresh palate."

"Wouldn't you be better off asking someone else? I'm not much of a wine connoisseur." If he wanted to know about finish and undertones, she couldn't help him.

"You don't have to be," he told her. "You just have to know what you like."

Stepping to the worktable, he retrieved two beakers containing purple liquid and a pair of wineglasses. "Fancy bottle," Louisa joked.

"Good things come in odd glass containers," he joked back. He poured the contents from each into its own glass and set them on the edge of his desk. "Tell me which one of these wines you like better."

"That's it?"

"That's it."

Simple enough. Picking up the first glass, she paused. "Am I supposed to smell it before I drink?"

"Only if you want to."

Louisa didn't. Things like that were better left to someone like Nico who actually understood what they were looking for. "And do I spit or swallow?" She vaguely remembered there was supposed to be some kind of protocol.

"Drink like you would a regular glass of wine. If you normally spit…"

She returned his smirk. "Fine. I get the point."

The contents of the first glass tasted amazing. Sweet but not overly so with just enough tang to make it stay on your tongue. Delicious. "Mmm," she said, licking her lips.

She was about to declare the choice easy until she tasted the second glass and found it equally delicious. "You're kidding," she said, setting the glass down. "There's supposed to be a difference?"

"Don't focus on finding the difference. Tell me which one you like better."

She tasted each one again, this time with her eyes closed in order to really focus. Took a couple of sips, but in the end, the first glass won out. "This one," she said, finishing the glass with a satisfied sigh. "Definitely this one."

When she opened her eyes, she found Nico watching her with an unreadable expression. His jaw twitched with tension as if he was holding back a response. "Tha…" He cleared his throat. Nevertheless his voice remained rough. "Thank you."

"I hope I helped."

"Trust me, you helped me a great deal."

"Good." Their gazes stayed locked while they talked. Louisa never knew there could be so many different shades of brown. The entire color wheel could be seen in Nico's irises.

"Would you like some more?" she heard him ask.

Wine. He meant more wine. Louisa blinked, sending everything back into perspective. "Better not," she said. "I'm not as practiced a wine taster as you are. Or are you purposely trying to send me home like Mario?"

Nico slapped a hand against his chest, mimicking horror. "Absolutely not. We're shorthanded tonight as it is."

The float-decorating party. It was Marianna's idea. With so many of the employees working long hours, she didn't think it fair to ask them to help decorate the winery float, as well, so she'd convinced a group of friends to do it instead. Louisa had been the first person she'd recruited.

It would be Louisa's first public appearance since the headlines broke.

"Maybe I will have another glass," she said reaching for the beaker.

Nico's hand immediately closed around her wrist, stopping her. "There is no need to be nervous," he said. "These are your friends."

"I know." What amazed her was how much she meant

it. A week ago she'd have been a crumbling basket of
nerves, but not so much now. Partly because the story
was winding down.

And partly because the man next to her was scheduled
to be there, as well. Her personal protector at the ready,
his presence made being brave a lot easier.

After much back and forth, it was decided the vineyard
would have to give up on trying to win any awards and instead design as simple a float as possible. Something that
could be assembled with minimal manpower in as short a
time as possible. Nico was the one who came up with the
idea. Some of the parts of last year's float, namely the fountain, were in storage. All they needed was fresh foliage.
While it was too late in the day for the fountain to spout
water again, they could easily recycle it into a different design. And so it was decided they would recreate the royal
wedding. Two of his employees would play Prince Antonio
and Princess Christina while others played wedding guests.
The couples would waltz around the fountain, pretending
to dance beneath the stars. It might not be an entirely ac-
curate representation, but it would do the winery proud.

As she watched Nico and Mario retrieve the fountain
later that afternoon, she couldn't help wondering if the
idea reminded Nico of the kiss they'd shared. The one
she'd told him to forget had ever happened. Which he apparently was having much better luck doing than she was.

Marianna's party attracted a crowd. In addition to Dani
and Rafe, who came on their day off, there were several
other couples Louisa had met at Marianna's baby shower
and other events. There was Isabella Benson, one of the
local schoolteachers, and her new husband, Connor, along
with wedding planner Lindsay and her husband, Zach
Reeves, who'd just returned from their honeymoon. Louisa
chuckled to herself, remembering the jokes she and Nico
had made at the royal wedding about Lindsay and Zach's

obvious adoration for each other. Even Lucia Moretti-Cascini, the art expert who'd worked on the chapel restoration and who was in town visiting her in-laws, was there. Having appointed herself the unofficial design supervisor, she sat on a stack of crates with a sketch pad while swatting away suggestions from her husband, Logan. In fact, the only person missing was the organizer herself.

Not a single person mentioned the tabloid stories or Louisa's history in Boston. The women all greeted her with smiles and hugs, as if nothing had changed. After years of phony smiles and affection, their genuine embraces had her near tears. Only the reassuring solidity of Nico's hand, pressed against the small of her back, kept her from actually crying. "Told you so, *bella mia*," he whispered as he handed her a glass of wine.

In spite of Marianna's absence, the work went smoothly. In no time at all, the old pieces were in place and covered with a plastic skin, ready to be decorated.

Louisa and the other women were put in charge of attaching the foliage while the men assembled the foam cutouts that would make the frame for the palazzo walls.

"This is a first," Dani said as she pressed a grape into place.

"Hot gluing fruit to a chicken-wire nymph. Are we sure this is going to look like marble?"

"Lucia says it will, and she's the art expert," Louisa replied.

"Art expert. There aren't too many museums who deal with produce."

"They used grapes last year," Isabella reassured them, "and it looked wonderful."

"She's right. I saw pictures," Louisa said, remembering the photograph of Nico that Marianna had shown her. "Hopefully we'll do as good a job. I'd hate to embarrass the vineyard."

"I'm sure we won't, and if it does turn out a disaster, Nico can always keep it locked in the garage."

"True." Louisa reached for a grape to glue into place only to pick up her wineglass instead. Something had been nagging her since the party began and she needed Dani's perspective. "Did you know that as palazzo owner, I'm supposed to play the part of festival queen?" she asked as she took a drink.

"Really?"

"Nico told me it's a tradition."

Dani's eyes flashed with enthusiasm. "How exciting. Do you get to ride on the back of a convertible and wave to a crowd like a beauty queen and everything?"

"I have no idea." Although Dani had painted an image she'd rather not contemplate. "I wasn't planning to do it at all."

"Why not, if it's tradition? Sounds like fun." Dani asked. "I always wanted to be the homecoming queen, but the title always went to some tall cheerleader type."

"I was a cheerleader."

Her friend took a sip of wine. "I rest my case."

"Hey, less drinking, more gluing," Isabella said, her dark head poking over the nymph's outstretched arm. "Do not make me come over there and take your wineglasses away."

Chastised, the pair ducked their heads, though Dani managed to sneak one more sip. "Seriously though," she said, reaching for the glue gun. "You should totally do it. You'd make a gorgeous festival queen."

"I'd rather be part of the crowd," Louisa replied. "I've had enough of the spotlight for one lifetime."

"That I can understand." Dani said, putting another grape in place. "I didn't want to bring up a sore subject, but how are you doing? You sound a lot better than you did when I spoke to you on the phone."

"I feel better," Louisa answered.

"You have no idea how worried I was when I saw those headlines. Rafe told me how brutal the paparazzi can be, and I was afraid one of them might try something scary."

"One did try," Louisa said, "but Nico scared him off."

"So I read in the papers. Thank goodness he showed up."

"Thank goodness is right." Not giving it a second thought, Louisa looked to the other side of the truck bed where he was arguing with Rafe over the foam placement. Sensing he was being watched, he looked over his shoulder and grinned.

She dipped her head before he could see how red her cheeks were. "I'm only sorry his help dragged him into the gossip pages, too," she said to Dani, hoping her friend didn't notice the blush either. "He's a good man."

"Rafe wouldn't be his friend if he wasn't," Dani replied. "I don't know if you've noticed, but my husband can be a little hard to please."

"A little?" Rafe Mancini's demanding reputation was legendary. He'd been known to toss vendors into the street for selling him what he considered subpar products.

And yet, the same chef and his wife had accepted Louisa without question. Louisa felt the swell of emotion in her throat again. Swallowing hard, she did her best to make her voice sound lighthearted "Have I told you I'm really glad we met on the bus from Florence?"

"Is this your not so subtle way of thanking me for being your friend?" Dani asked.

"Maybe."

Her fellow American gathered her in a hug. "I'm glad we're friends, too," she said. "Although if you get hot glue in my hair, I will kill you."

"And Lindsay and I will kill you both if you do not get

to work," Isabella scolded. "We are not gluing all these grapes by ourselves."

"Jeez, I'm glad I'm not one of her students," Dani whispered.

"I heard that."

Louisa snorted, almost dropping the grape she was putting into place. The teasing reminded her of old times, when she and her college friends would get together and giggle over cocktails. Steven had hated that.

"You too, Louisa," Lindsay admonished. "Just because you're dating the boss doesn't mean you get to slack off."

Dating—? The newspaper photographs. Just when she thought she'd actually put them behind her. The only saving grace, if there could be one, was that at least these women didn't consider her some kind of financial predator. Like Marianna the other day, they saw it as a potential romance. "Nico and I aren't dating," she told them.

"Are you sure?" Isabella asked. "Those pictures—"

"Were pictures, that's all," she said, cutting her off. "The two of us are just friends."

"Sure, just like Zach and I are friends," Lindsay replied. She and Isabella exchanged smirks.

"Something tells me the lady protests too much," the teacher replied.

Louisa stared at the grape-covered plastic in front of her and reminded herself the women were only teasing. Nevertheless, that didn't stop her skin from feeling as if it was on fire. Not because she was embarrassed or ashamed, at least not in the way she expected to be. She was embarrassed because they were right.

She *was* protesting too much.

"I didn't realize you found the gluing of grapes so fascinating, my friend."

Nico did his best to look annoyed at his best friend, but

the heat in his cheeks killed the effort. "Checking to see how much progress they are making, that is all."

"Not as much as there would be if you waited longer than thirty seconds between looks," Rafe replied.

He inclined his head to where the women were laughing and topping up their wineglasses. "It's all right, you know. She's a beautiful woman."

"Who? Your wife?"

"Of course, my wife. But I'm talking about Louisa. I saw the photograph of the two of you in the newspaper. Very romantic."

"We were at a wedding. Everything about weddings looks romantic."

"This was different. You were looking at her like…"

"Like what?"

"I don't know," his friend replied honestly. "I've never seen you look at a woman that way."

Perhaps because he'd never met a woman like Louisa before. "She's different," he said.

"Because she's an American. They have a different kind of energy about them. It's very…captivating."

Captivating was a good word. He felt as though he was under a spell at times, what with the uncharacteristic moods he'd been experiencing. He could feel his friend's eyes on him. "It's not what you think," he said.

"You aren't attracted to her?"

"Of course I am attracted. Have you looked at her?"

"Then it is exactly what I think. And, if that picture is to believed, the feeling is mutual. And yet the two of you…" His friend set down the foam block he was holding to give Nico a serious look. "You are not together. Since when do you not pursue an interested woman?"

"I told you, Louisa is different." Other women hadn't been traumatized by an emotionally abusive Prince Charming. "She's not the kind of woman you toy with."

"So don't toy."

Rafe made it sound so easy. Problem was Nico wasn't sure he could do anything else. "Not everyone is made for commitment like you are, my friend."

A warm hand clapped his shoulder. "What happened with Floriana was a long time ago. People change."

"Sometimes. Sometimes they don't." More often than not, they were like his parents, repeating the same mistakes over and over. With everything she'd been through, Louisa deserved better. "I've already broken the heart of one good woman," he said.

"And haven't you punished yourself enough for it?" His friend squeezed his shoulder. "You can't be afraid to try again."

Nico wasn't afraid, he was trying to be kind. Rafe meant well, but he didn't know everything. There were secrets Nico couldn't share with anyone.

Almost anyone, he amended, eyes looking at Louisa. He'd certainly shared about his parents.

It was a moot point anyway. "You are assuming the decision is 100 percent mine to make," he said. "Louisa is the one who is not interested. It was Louisa's choice to keep our relationship platonic." If she went through with selling the palazzo, they wouldn't even have that.

"That's too bad."

"Yes, it is." Why lie about his disappointment? He watched as Louisa laughed with her friends. She had her hair pulled back, and there was purple staining her fingers. Beautiful. Seeing her relaxed made him happy.

"But," Nico said, "you can't force emotions." If anyone knew that, it was him.

His cell phone rang, saving him from any further rebuttals. "About time," he said as the caller ID popped onto the screen. "It's Ryan," he told Rafe. "You tell my sister she better have a good reason for skipping out on her own party. The rest of us have been here for hours working on this float."

Ryan's reply came back garbled. The building and its terrible service. "Say it again?" he asked.

"I said, would a girl be a good enough excuse?"

"What do you mean 'a girl'?" Nico straightened at Ryan's announcement. "Are you talking about a real girl, as in—?"

"A baby, yes." His brother-in-law gave a breathy laugh. "The most beautiful girl you'll ever see. Seven pounds, nine ounces and as perfect as her mother."

Nico's jaw dropped. He didn't know what to say. "Congratulations!" he finally managed to get out.

No sooner did he speak than Rafe nudged him with an elbow. "Baby?" he asked. Nico nodded, setting off a small cheer in the garage. Immediately, both Dani and Louisa dropped what they were doing to join Rafe by his side. "Boy or girl?" Louisa asked.

"A girl," he whispered back. It was hard to believe his baby sister was a mother herself. "How is Marianna?" he asked Ryan. "Is she all right?"

"She's fantastic. Amazing. When you see what a woman goes through to give birth…" Admiration laced every word Ryan said.

Nico felt a pang of jealousy in the face of such love and devotion. His eyes sought Louisa, who waited for details with folded hands pressed to her lips and eyes turned sapphire with anticipation. Like everyone else, her emotions showed on her face. Everyone but him, that was. His insides were numb as he struggled to process Ryan's news.

The gulf that separated him from others in the world widened. *See?* He wanted to tell Rafe. *People don't always change.*

He certainly hadn't.

CHAPTER NINE

MARIANNA WORE MOTHERHOOD as though it was a designer dress. Sitting on the living room sofa of her villa, wearing pajamas and a terry cloth robe, she'd never looked lovelier. Every time she looked down at the bundle sleeping in the bassinet, her face glowed with contentment. "We named her Rosabella," she said to Louisa, who was sitting next to her. "Rosa for short."

"She's beautiful," Louisa said. As peaceful as an angel, her little lips parted in slumber. It was all Louisa could do not to run her finger along a downy cheek.

"The nurses said not to be fooled by how much she's sleeping," she said. "In a day or two she'll be wanting to nurse all the time."

"Then we'll be wishing she'd sleep," Ryan added. He looked as smitten as his wife.

"What do you mean, *we*? I'm going to be the one doing all the work. You'll probably just roll over and go back to sleep."

"Ah, *amore mio*, you know I'd help nurse if I could. It would let me bond with the baby."

"Then it's a good thing I bought you this," Louisa said, reaching for the pastel pink gift bag she'd set on the floor. She'd almost said "we." Living and working with Nico the past week had her thinking of them as a pair.

"A breast pump!" Marianna announced with what could almost be described as evil glee. "Thank you, Louisa; it's perfect. Looks like you'll be able to bond with the baby after all, *amore mio*."

"Yes, Louisa," Ryan said, much less enthusiastically. "It's exactly what we needed."

They were both exaggerating for effect. From the moment he'd learned of the pregnancy, Ryan had been determined to be as active a father as possible. Louisa had no doubt he would be awake every time no matter who did the actual feeding. She looked over at Nico, to see what he was thinking. The man had barely said a word since their arrival. In fact, he'd been unusually quiet since Ryan had called to announce little Rosa's arrival. Currently, he stood next to the bassinet, staring down at the sleeping baby.

"She's so tiny," he said.

"Not for long," Marianna replied. "She's got her father's appetite. Would you like to hold her, Uncle Nico?"

At his sister's suggestion, Nico paled. "I wouldn't want to wake her…"

"You won't, and if she does wake up, she'll probably fall right back to sleep. The little angel has had a busy couple of days. Haven't you, Rosa?" Adoration beaming from every feature of his face, Ryan ran the back of his finger along his daughter's cheek. "You might as well get used to being hands-on," he said to Nico. "No way is your sister going to let you get out of babysitting."

"Absolutely. With Angelo living in the States and Ryan's family in Australia, you're the only family she has in Monte Calanetti. Now hold her. I want a photo for her baby album."

"Better do what your sister says," Ryan said.

The vintner's face was the picture of anxiety as Ryan placed the swaddled baby in Nico's arms. Looking as if he'd rather be doing anything else, he balanced Rosa's head in the palm of one hand while the other held her bottom.

"She's not a bottle of wine," Marianna admonished.

"Hold her close. And smile. I don't want her first memory of her uncle to be that he's a grouch."

"Forgive me; I've never held a baby before," Nico replied. But he did what he was told.

It made for a beautiful photo. Nico with his bronzed movie-star features, baby Rosa with her pink newborn skin. Something was off, though. Louisa couldn't say exactly what, but something about Nico's eyes didn't fit. For one thing, they lacked the sparkle she'd come to associate with his smiles. They looked darker—sad, even—and distant. Not unlike the way they'd looked the other day when Marianna visited.

Did his sister notice? Probably not, since the new mother was too busy directing the photo session. "Go stand next to Nico," she ordered. "We need one of the three of you."

"Um… You want me in your baby album?" Louisa wasn't sure that was a good idea.

"Of course. Why wouldn't I?" Marianna waved at her to move. "Go."

"Sooner you do it, the sooner she'll be done taking photos," Nico said.

She took her place by Nico's shoulder, and wondered if she would ever get used to being welcome. It didn't dawn on her until after Marianna showed her the pictures on her phone that she was in her most casual clothes and not wearing a stitch of makeup. The woman smiling back at her from the view screen looked like someone she used to know a long time ago, before she ever heard the name Steven Clark. Someone she hadn't seen in a long time. Maybe she'd stick around a little while.

"You make an attractive family," Marianna teased. "Maybe I should sell it to the papers."

"You do, and I'll return my breast pump." That she could have such an exchange without blanching spoke volumes about how well she was recovering from the scandal. She turned her attention back to the phone screen, her gaze moving from her face to Nico's to Rosa's and back to Nico's. There was definitely distance in Nico's smile...

Meanwhile, Ryan had retrieved Rosa, who hadn't woken up, and was tucking her into her bassinet. "I meant to tell you," he said, "the cradle fits the space perfectly."

"I'm glad," Nico replied.

"Nico had the family cradle restored," Marianna explained.

"He did?" She hadn't known, although knowing his respect for tradition, the gesture didn't surprise her.

"It has been in our family for generations," he replied, eyes still on the baby. "Made sense that it be used by the first member of the next generation."

"The piece is almost too beautiful for Rosa to sleep in," Ryan said.

"Come with me; I'll show you."

After casting a protective glance into the bassinet Marianna led her toward the nursery. "You know, I almost took the baby monitor with me," she said as they walked up the stairs. "But I thought that might be overprotective."

"With Ryan sitting five feet away from her, I would say yes," Louisa teased. Her friend's extreme mothering was adorable. Might not be so cute when Rosa was older, but seeing as how Marianna had only been a mother for two days, she couldn't help smiling. The Amatuccis didn't do things halfway, did they?

The room was a baby's paradise. The couple had forgone traditional baby colors in favor of restful lavender, browns and greens. The Tuscan hillside, Louisa realized. Stuffed animals and books already filled the shelves, and there were, not one, but two mobiles, one hanging over what looked to be a small play area in the corner.

On the back wall hung a large landscape of the vineyards with baby animals playing peek-a-boo among the vines. Louisa spied a rabbit and a kitten straight off. "Logan Cascini's wife, Lucia, painted it as a baby gift," Marianna told her. "There are supposed to be eleven different baby animals hiding in the fields. So far Ryan and I can only find eight."

"It's amazing." This was a gift that would amuse a child for years to come. Something Louisa would want for her own child. "Makes my breast pump look lame," she said.

As exquisite as the painting was, however, it paled in comparison to the cradle below it. Ryan hadn't exaggerated. It was gorgeous. It wasn't that the piece was fancy; in fact the design was actually very modest, but you could feel its history. The tiny nicks and dents told the story of all the Amatuccis that had slept safe in its confines. She ran her hand along the sideboard. The restorer had done a great job, polishing the olive wood to a gleaming dark brown without destroying what made it special.

"My great-grandfather built this when my grandfather was born. According to my father, it was because my great-grandmother demanded he not sleep in a drawer. Baby Amatuccis have slept in it ever since."

Louisa tried to picture Nico as a baby with his thick dark curls. Bet he had a smile that could melt your heart.

She wondered why he hadn't told her what he was planning. But then, why would he? No doubt the idea came to him when Marianna had announced her pregnancy. If she recalled, the two of them had hardly been friends at the time. Not like they were now.

Actually she wasn't sure what they were to each other anymore. Did a friend lie in bed listening for the sound of footsteps in the hall, relieved yet disappointed when the steps didn't draw near her door? Did a friend watch her friend while he worked, wondering what it might feel like to run her hands down his muscular arms? Louisa doubted it. Yet she had done both those things the past couple of days.

Then there was the fact she was continuing to stay at the vineyard. The headlines had stopped. There was little reason she shouldn't return to the palazzo and start figuring out what she wanted to do for the future.

So how come the two of them were continuing to cohabitate as though they were a couple?

"...godparents."

She realized Marianna was talking. "I'm sorry," she said. "I was thinking about something else."

"Here I thought I was the one with distractions," the brunette teased. "Please tell me you'll pay better attention to your goddaughter."

"G-goddaughter?" Was Marianna asking what Louisa thought she was asking?

"Ryan and I were hoping you would be Rosabella's godmother."

Godmother? She had to have misunderstood. In Italy, a godparent was expected to play a huge role in a child's life. More like a second parent. And they were asking *her*?

That's why they'd insisted on including her in the photograph. "Are—are you sure?" she asked. "There isn't someone you want more?" Her brother Angelo's wife, for example.

"Ryan and I can't think of anyone we'd want more," the brunette said, reaching over and resting a hand atop hers.

"But the scandal?"

"Who cares about the scandal? The scandal is what makes you so perfect. We want our daughter to grow up knowing that doing the right thing isn't always easy, but that truly strong people find a way to make it through."

Louisa couldn't breathe for the lump in her throat. Marianna and Ryan...they thought her brave? Talk about ironic. She'd felt nothing but fear from the day she discovered Steven's duplicity. "All I did was tell the authorities the truth." And seize an opportunity to escape.

"You did more than tell the truth. You paid a price publicly. It couldn't have been easy being destroyed by the press the way you were. That's the kind of person I want to help guide my daughter. A woman who's strong enough to bounce back."

Had she really, though? Bounced back? There were still so many fears holding her back. She wasn't sure she'd ever completely escape Steven.

Still, the invitation meant more than Marianna would ever realize. Louisa felt the tears pushing at her eyes. Seemed like all she did was tear up lately. "You just want me to give you a better baby gift," she said, sniffing them away.

Marianna's eyes were watery. "So is that a yes?"

"Yes!" Louisa didn't stop to think twice. "I would be honored."

"Perfect. I'm so happy." The brunette clapped her hands together the way a child might when getting a special gift. "This will be perfect. You can teach Rosa how to be strong and gracious, and her godfather will teach her how to be smart and respect tradition. Along with wine-making, that is."

Wine? "Who are you going to ask to be godfather?" she asked. As if she didn't know. There was only one man who fit that description.

Her friend looked at her with surprise. "Nico, of course."

Of course.

"Is that a problem?"

Only in the sense that she and Nico would be bound together for the rest of Rosa's life. Flutters took over her insides.

"No, no problem," she said.

Marianna's reply was preempted by a high-pitched wail coming from downstairs.

"Looks like I didn't need to bring the monitor after all," the new mother said. "Rosa has inherited my lungs."

"Ryan and Marianna are going to have their hands full fending off the boys when Rosa's older, that's for sure," Louisa said as they crossed the plaza a short while later. "I won't be surprised if Ryan decides to ship her off to a convent when she's older just to keep them away."

"Yes," Nico replied. "Because naturally Italy is full of convents where the residents can hide their children."

"It's an expression, Nico."

"I know what it is." He tightened his grip on the shopping bag he was carrying, the plastic handle threatening to snap in two from the pressure. The knot at the base of his neck had been tightening since they'd left Marianna's villa, fed by his companion's continual gushing over baby Rosabella. How beautiful, how sweet, how tiny, how wonderful. Every adjective reminding him of his shortcomings, because he felt *nothing*.

"I'm sure Ryan will deal with the onslaught of suitors when the time comes," he told her.

"I'm sure he will, too." She looked at him with a frown. "What gives? You've been in a bad mood all morning. Is everything all right?"

No. Everything was horrible. How else could it be when the world decided to remind you of unvarnished truths? "I have a lot to do at the winery, is all."

"You sure that's all it is?"

"What else would it be?" he asked, in a casual voice. Thank goodness for his sunglasses. He wasn't sure his eyes looked nearly as impassive as his voice sounded.

"I don't know. I was wondering if it had something to do with baby Rosa."

He stumbled over a cobblestone. "Contrary to what you think, the birth of baby Rosa is not the biggest event taking place in this town."

"No, but it is the biggest thing to happen to your family. I would think you'd be happy for Marianna and Ryan."

"I am happy for them." Granted he hadn't been thrilled when he'd first discovered Marianna was pregnant by a man she barely knew, but since then Ryan had proven himself devoted to both his sister and their child. "I hope Rosa is the first of many children."

"Good, because back at the villa you looked like you didn't want anything to do with the baby."

On the contrary. He turned to look at her. "I wanted plenty."

If Louisa caught the pointedness in his comment, she let it pass. They'd reached the town center. It being only a few days until the festival, tourists crowded the cobblestone square. Camera phones at the ready, they posed in front of the fountain and raised them to snap pictures of brightly decorated balconies. Many carried shopping bags like his. Monte Calanetti's economy was still going strong. Rafe would be happy. A lot of these people were no doubt eating at Mancini's this evening.

As though by mutual agreement, he and Louisa stopped in the square where they'd had their first kiss. He wondered how often she thought of that afternoon. As often as he did? Thinking of their kiss had become practically an obsession.

He wasn't sure if nature was trying to soothe him by pointing out that he could at least feel physical passion, or if she were mocking him by giving him a pointless attraction.

To rub salt into his wounds, he stole a long look at Louisa's profile. The way her hair turned white in the bright sun was something he'd never grow tired of studying.

He loved the way her hair wasn't one color but a collection of platinum and gold strands woven together to create a shade that was uniquely Louisa. It was her hair, no doubt, that had caught Steven Clark's attention on the elevator. Had his fingers itched to comb through the colors the way Nico's did?

Louisa turned in his direction, and he quickly looked away.

"Did your sister tell you she asked me to be Rosabella's godmother?" she asked him.

"She did?" He hadn't known, but he wasn't surprised. Marianna had told him how much she'd come to care about Louisa these past months.

"She said she picked me because I could teach her daughter about being strong. Funny, but I don't think of myself as strong."

Because she didn't give herself enough credit. "You're stronger than you think."

"Maybe," she said, looking away. The knot at the back of Nico's neck returned as he guessed what her next comment would be. "She told me they asked you to be the godfather."

"They did." For some insane reason, they actually wanted him as a backup parent. The question had caught him so off guard he couldn't answer.

"It's not going to be a problem, is it?" Louisa asked. "Being paired with me? I know it's a big deal here, and if you'd rather stand up with someone else…"

"What? No." He hadn't stopped to think that his unenthusiastic answer might sound like an objection to her. "I think you'll be a wonderful godmother. It's me that I'm worried about."

"If you're afraid you're going to drop her…"

"No, I'm not afraid of dropping her."

"Then, what's the matter?"

"It's complicated," he replied. Hoping she'd drop the subject, Nico walked toward the fountain.

Monte Calanetti's famed nymph reclined across her rocks, the clamshell in her hand beckoning to all who wanted to toss a coin. Based on the silver and gold coins shimmering beneath the water, a lot of tourists had tried today. "Have you ever wished on the fountain?" he asked when he felt Louisa standing behind him. A silly question. Everyone in Monte Calanetti had tried at least once to land a coin in the clamshell.

"Sure," she replied. "My coin missed the shell, though."

"Mine always missed, too."

"And I thought you were perfect."

She was joking, but Nico grimaced all the same. He was most definitely not perfect.

So much for changing the subject. "Didn't matter. My wish came true anyway," he replied.

"What did you used to wish for?"

"That I wouldn't be like my parents. In and out of love. Jumping from one drama to another. I would not live on an emotional roller coaster."

Her hand came to rest between his shoulder blades, the warmth from the contact reaching through his linen shirt. "Can't blame you there," she said "Who would?"

No one, or so he'd thought, which was why he'd stood here as a little boy and tossed coin after coin. He could see himself, standing at the fountain's edge, his jaw clenched with determination. "Unfortunately, it worked too well," he said, with a sigh.

"You're confusing me."

Of course he was. Louisa felt things deeply. He saw the warmth in her eyes when she looked at Rosa, the immediate affection. His sister couldn't have picked a better woman to help guide his niece through life. She would love Baby Rosa like her own. Unlike…

Fear gripped his chest. "Everyone sees me as some kind of leader," he said. "A man they can count on."

"Because you are. You certainly hold Monte Calanetti together. Not to mention the vineyard, the palazzo."

"Those are things, businesses. Anyone can manage a business. People, on the other hand…" He took off his sunglasses, wanting her to see how serious he was regarding his question. "What if I let her down?"

"Who?"

"Baby Rosa. What if she can't count on me? What if I can't love her enough to be there emotionally when she needs me to?"

"You're serious? That's why you kept pulling away when we talked about the baby." She sank to sit on the fountain wall. "Do you really believe you won't be able to care about your own niece?"

"Care about, yes, but care enough?" He shook his head. "I've already proven I can't."

"When? Oh, your fiancée."

"My fiancée." Taking a space next to her, he let his shopping bag rest on the ground between his feet. Thankfully the noontime heat had chased many of the tourists to the shade, leaving them momentarily alone.

"Floriana was a wonderful girl. Smart, beautiful, kind. We shared all the same interests. We never ever argued."

"She sounds perfect."

"She was," he said, staring at his hands. "We were perfect for each other." The answer tasted sour on his tongue. In a way, singing Floriana's praises to Louisa felt wrong.

"What happened?"

"Simple," he said. "I broke her heart."

There had to be more to the story. Something that Nico wasn't telling her. The man she knew wouldn't carelessly break a woman's heart.

Although wasn't that exactly the kind of man she'd thought he was when she'd met him?

Yes, she had, but she knew better now. Knew him better now. "Surely it's not as simple as that," she said.

"Ah, but it is," he replied. "As perfect as Floriana was—as we were for each other—I couldn't love her. Not truly and deeply, the way a person should be loved. That's when I realized I'll never be like my parents or like Angelo or Marianna. I don't have it in me."

"It?"

"Passion. Real, deep emotion.

"It's true," he said when Louisa opened her mouth to argue. "Angelo and Marianna, they are like my parents. They feel things. Highs. Lows. Excitement. They thrive on it, even. But me...I don't want highs and lows. I want calm. I want..."

"Consistency," Louisa supplied. Certainty. To know when he walked through the door that his world hadn't been turned upside down. She had the sudden flash that Nico had been as trapped by his parents' chaos as she had been by Steven's control.

"Consistency is one way of putting it, I suppose. Much better than saying I lack depth."

"Is that what Floriana said? She was wrong."

"Was she?"

"Just because you don't throw plates like your parents doesn't mean you're not capable of passion." It killed her to hear him beat himself up so needlessly. Couldn't he see how impossibly wrong he was about himself? She'd witnessed his passion plenty of times. In the vineyards when he talked about Carlos. When he talked of Monte Calanetti's traditions.

When he'd kissed her. She'd never felt such passion before.

Nico stared at his hands as if they held the argument

he needed. "Then why didn't I feel anything today?" he asked. "The three of you—Marianna, Ryan, you—you couldn't stop oohing and aahing at Baby Rosa. Meanwhile, the only thing going through my mind was that she looked…small."

"What did you expect to think? She's three days old. It's not like she's going to be filled with personality."

"But everyone else…"

Okay, now she wanted to shake him and make him see sense. For a smart man, he was being incredibly stupid. "Marianna and Ryan are her parents. If she wrinkles her nose they think it's a sign of genius."

"And you…"

"I'm a woman. I'm programmed to think babies are adorable. You, on the other hand, are a guy. Until babies actually do something, you don't see the point.

"Look," she said. Grasping his face between her hands, she forced him to look her in the eye to make sure he heard what she was saying. "Just because a person seems perfect doesn't mean they are. Believe me, I know. You're going to make a wonderful godfather. The very fact you're worrying about doing a good job shows how much you care.

"Besides," she added, "I refuse to do this godmother thing without a good partner. Last time I looked, we made a pretty good team."

The worry faded from around his eyes. Giving her a grateful smile, Nico rested his forehead against hers. His hands came up to cup her face. "Thank you, *bella mia*," he said, the whisper caressing her lips. Louisa closed her eyes and let the sensation wash over her.

They sat entwined like that for several minutes, neither in a rush to break the moment. As far as she was concerned, she could sit there all afternoon. She didn't even care if there were paparazzi watching.

CHAPTER TEN

THE NEXT DAY, a cold front invaded the valley and everyone feared the harvest festival would be threatened by rain. "The tourists will still come," Nico had said as they gathered to finish the float. "We've never failed to attract a crowd, rain or shine."

"But sun brings a better crowd," Marianna had been quick to point out, "and this is the one year when we can count on the crowd being especially large."

Turned out Nico's sister needn't have worried. The morning of the festival, Louisa woke to see the sun brightening a cloudless blue sky.

"Luck is on our side," Nico had remarked over coffee before adding, "Perfect day for playing festival queen."

"Nice try," she'd answered, "but no." With the headlines diminishing daily, why court trouble?

Nevertheless, she agreed to accompany him to the parade's staging ground to give their float a proper send-off. While he was in the shower, she snuck over to the palazzo and got out a tiered skirt and peasant blouse from her closet. A peace offering. She might not be queen, but she could dress in the spirit of the occasion.

The thought didn't occur to her until she was ducking through the archway leading to Nico's villa, that if she was comfortable enough crossing the fields alone, she could move back home.

Tomorrow.

For so many years her thoughts had revolved around escaping—escaping Steven, escaping Boston, escaping the paparazzi—and suddenly here she was focused on staying.

Something had shifted between her and Nico that day at the fountain. There was a depth to their friendship she hadn't felt before. An openness brought about by shared fears. Whereas before there had been attraction, she felt pulled by an attraction of a different sort. Didn't make sense, she knew. But there it was.

"Wow," Nico said when stepped back into the kitchen. "Like a proper Tuscan peasant."

Appreciation lit his eyes, turning her insides warm. She hadn't done all that much. "Thank you. I figured when in Rome, or in this case Tuscany…"

"You look just like a proper Tuscan gypsy." And he, a proper Tuscan vintner in his jeans and loose white shirt. Louisa had never seen him look more appealing. He offered his hand. "Shall we?"

The festival itself was to be held in the plaza. Last night Nico and several of his employees had gone into town to set up a quintet of large half barrels around the fountain, and so she assumed that was where they were heading for the parade, as well. To her surprise, however, he turned his truck toward Comparino. "We start at the palazzo," he told her, "and head into town, recreating the route the farmers took back when the *mezzadria* system was in place. That's when the sharecroppers would present the landowners with their share of the harvest. Back then the Bertonellis would have used the grapes to make wine. Today we use a lesser quality crop and put the fruit in the vats for stomping."

"I can't believe people still stomp grapes." Louisa thought the tradition was reserved only for movies and old sitcoms.

"Tourists come from all over the world to see Old World traditions. The least we can do is provide them."

She bet Nico loved every minute of them, too, lover of tradition that he was. In fact, there was a special kind of glow about him this morning. He looked brighter, more alive. His body hummed with energy, too, more so than usual. Standing by his side, she found it impossible not to let it wash over her, as well.

They turned a corner and drove into a field that had become a makeshift parade ground. In addition to the floats, Louisa spied dozens of townspeople dressed in costume. There were women wearing woolen folk dresses and large straw hats and men dressed as peasant farmers. She spotted musicians and what she guessed were dancers, as well.

"Later on, they'll demonstrate the *trescone*," Nico said. "Everyone present is invited to join in."

And here she thought the festival was just an excuse to eat and drink.

"Can I ask you a question?" she asked once Nico had parked the truck. "Why is tradition so important to you?" She suspected she already knew the answer, but wanted to hear it from him.

"I don't know," he replied. "I suppose it is because tradition helps define who we are and what we do. There's a sacred quality to knowing that you're walking in the footsteps of generations that came before you. Time has passed, but the traditions, the core of who we are, doesn't change."

In other words, he loved the consistency. For a man whose entire life had been fraught with chaos, tradition— like Carlos's vineyard—never let him down. No wonder he'd been so adamant that she lead the parade.

And yet, he was willing to let go of tradition to make her feel more comfortable. Once again, he was rushing to her rescue.

Maybe it was time she returned the favor. "I'll do it," she said.

"Do what?"

"I'll lead the parade."

If everything else went wrong today, the way Nico's eyes lit up would be reason enough for her answer. "Are you sure?" he asked her.

"Absolutely." What were a few miles, right? She could do it. "But only if you'll walk with me."

"Are you asking if I'll be your king?"

Dear Lord, the way he said the sentence... Her insides grew warm. "Don't be literal," she said, trying to hide her reaction by making light of the comment. "More like a royal companion who's there to help me when I screw up."

Damn if the way he brushed a tendril of hair off her cheek before speaking didn't turn her inside out. "It would be my pleasure, *bella mia.*"

Royal companion wasn't the right term at all. Nico was a king. Smiling brightly and waving to the crowds, he belonged at the front of the parade far more than Louisa did. The town loved him.

Or maybe Monte Calanetti was just full of love today. The streets were lined with revelers who laughed and cheered them along as they wound their way slowly down the cobblestone streets. Behind them, the costumed men carried baskets of grapes while the women tossed bags of sugared nuts they had stored in the pockets of their aprons. If photographers were there, they were hidden by the throngs of tourists who, it was clear, were only interested in enjoying the day.

"Signorina! Signorina!" A little girl wearing a dress the colors of Italy, ran into the street carrying a crown made from ribbons and roses. *"Per voi la Signorina Harrison,"* she said, holding it in her hands. *"Una corona per la regina."*

Louisa beamed her. A crown? For her? *"Grazie,"* she said, placing the flowers on her head. The wreath was too big and slid down to her ears, but Louisa didn't care. She grinned and flicked the ribbons over her shoulder.

There were more children. More flowers presented. Too many for Louisa to carry, so she began giving them to the women behind her, running from the front of the parade to the rear and back again. It became a game between her and the children, to see how fast she could run the gamut before another flower appeared. By the time they reached the fountain, she was laughing and gasping for breath.

"Told you the town wouldn't care," Nico whispered in her ear. She turned to discover his eyes glittered with laughter, too. "This is amazing," she told him.

"You are having fun, then?"

Was he joking? What she was feeling at this moment was so much more than amusement. She felt free. All those years of being the outsider were but bad memories. She'd found a place where she'd belonged. A home.

To think, if Nico hadn't gone to the palazzo the day the headlines broke—if he hadn't insisted she stay—she might still be looking.

What would she have done without him?

"I'm having a wonderful time," she said. She moved to throw her arms around him in a hug only to be thwarted by the enveloping crowd. Having emptied their baskets into three oversize half barrels, the marchers stood clapping rhythmically. "They're waiting for you," Nico told her. "The queen is the first to stomp the grapes."

As though they'd been waiting, two of the men wearing medieval costumes appeared at her elbows and began guiding her forward. "Wait, wait," she said, laughing. "I still have my shoes on."

"Just kick them off," a familiar voice hollered. Looking left, she saw Dani waving from a few feet away. "I'll grab them for you," her friend said.

She made her way to the front barrel that, despite its size, was overflowing with large bunches of purple grapes.

"I'm not doing this without my royal companion," she said, looking over her shoulder.

Evidently the crowd thought this a wonderful idea, because a second later, Nico was pushed into the circle. As he stepped closer, his laugh faded to a mischievous gleam. "Now you've asked for it, *bella mia*."

Grabbing her by the waist, he lifted her in the air and plopped her feetfirst into the barrel.

Louisa shrieked as the grapes squished between her toes. "It's cold!"

"You expected a warm bath?" he asked with a laugh. Stepping into the barrel with her, he took her by the hands. "Be careful, it's slippery."

No kidding. The crushed grapes and skin quickly stuck to the bottom of the container, creating a layer of slickness. Twice already, she would have lost her balance if Nico hadn't been holding her up. Still, as cold and slippery as the grapes were, it was fun marching in place. Particularly with Nico's hands sending warmth up her arms.

A few minutes later, the rest of the crowd joined them, kicking off their shoes and crowding into the vats. Laughter abounded as everyone was eager to take their turn mashing the grapes to a pulp.

"I can't believe this is how people used to make wine," she said to him over the noise. "They must have had incredibly muscular thighs."

"Not really." Nico had leaned in to speak. His breath floated over her collarbone leaving goose bumps. "Italian winemakers have used presses to crush grapes since the middle ages. This is just for the tourists."

"You mean there is no Old World tradition?"

"Not that I know of."

"I'm up to my ankles in pulverized grapes because of a gimmick? You—"

He laughed and she gave his shoulder a shove, only to have her feet slide out from beneath her.

"Careful!" Nico scooped her up into his arms just as she was about to fall bottom first into the mashed fruit. "We wouldn't want you to be trampled," he said, smiling down at her.

No danger of that now. With her arms wrapped around his neck, and his arms holding her tight, Louisa had never felt safer. "I'm not worried," she said. "You'd rescue me."

His smile faded. "Always."

Louisa's breath caught at the seriousness in his voice. Just as it had at the royal wedding, the world receded, leaving only the two of them and the sound of their breathing. Nico's eyes grew heavy lidded, his attention focused on Louisa's mouth. Slowly she ran a tongue over her lower lip, an action for which she was rewarded with the tightening of his hand on her waist. "Louisa…" His voice was rough and raw.

He wanted her. But he was holding back to let her make the first move. That she held the power was all Louisa needed to reach a decision.

She pulled his head down to meet hers…

Dear Lord, how on earth could she have gone so long without kissing him? Nico might have given her the power to decide, but once their mouths joined, he took control, kissing her so deeply Louisa couldn't tell where she ended and he began. She didn't care. She was too swept away by the moment.

It was the cheer rising from the crowd that finally broke the moment. "I think the crowd approves," Nico said, rubbing his nose against hers.

Heat rushed to Louisa's cheeks. Let the crowd cheer,

she decided. She held his gaze and wondered if her eyes looked as blown and glazed over as his.

"Why don't we go someplace more private?" he said. Without giving her a chance to answer, he carried her out of the barrel and through the crowd.

Nico pressed a kiss to the head resting on his shoulder. Louisa and he were in his garden, ensconced on a lounger beneath the pergola. Insects could be heard buzzing in the foliage above, their soft droning working with the wine to make him comfortable and drowsy. An interesting sensation, since only an hour before he'd been consumed with lust. Once alone, the urgency had receded. The best wines were made with patience. So it was with lovemaking, as well. They had all night. Why rush when you could draw out the pleasure?

Besides, strange as it seemed, being close to Louisa like this was pleasure itself.

"What was she like?"

Her question came out of nowhere. "Who?" he asked, fingers playing with the tendrils of her hair.

"Your fiancée."

"Floriana? Why do you ask? Are you jealous?" That she might be gave him a jolt of satisfaction.

"I'm curious. What made her so perfect?"

He thought back. "I told you, she liked the same things I liked, she had the same sense of humor. Plus we wanted the same things out of life."

"Which were?"

"To create wine and live a life free of drama."

"I take it you never threw a reporter off her balcony."

"She didn't own a balcony,"

"You know what I mean."

"Yes, I do." Floriana would never need to take refuge in his winery to avoid scandal. Rational to a fault, she would never have fallen for a man like Steven in the first place. On the other hand, she also never ignited a fire in the pit of his stomach the way Louisa did. Standing in those grapes, with that silly floral crown falling about her ears and her clothes wrinkled and damp from the heat, Louisa had been the most gorgeous thing he'd ever seen.

"She sounds like someone Steven would have liked. Whenever I found an interest Steven didn't like, he would find a way to suck the fun out of it."

"I don't understand." The American colloquialism threw him, although he could wager a guess.

"Well…" She shifted so she could prop herself up on one elbow. "He would either get condescending and make me feel like it was silly, or he'd suggest it wasn't the kind of thing 'Mrs. Steven Clark' should be doing."

The man was a bully. Nico was glad they'd put him in prison. Her ex deserved to be locked up in a cell as lonely and sad as he'd made his wife.

"He didn't deserve you. You know that."

"When we met, I thought I didn't deserve him."

A most foolish notion. If anything Steven Clark must have known from the start that he'd discovered a treasure and that was why he'd insisted on wrapping her up so tightly.

"What's sad is how I was so impressed by something that wasn't real. I mean, all his power and breeding. Turned out he wasn't any better than me."

"You were the better one," Nico said. "To begin with, you weren't a thief."

Louisa smiled. "Thanks, but I meant background-wise. He was just some guy from the Midwest. His fancy family history was as phony as his investment scheme. When I contacted the feds, the whole house of cards came tumbling down. The only truly real thing that survived was the palazzo." She nestled back against the curve of his neck, her hand coming up to play with the edge of his shirt collar.

"Thank God, I never told him about the place or it would be gone, too."

Prison was too good for him. "The bastard is lucky he wasn't the one on your balcony," he muttered.

"Might have been interesting if he was. I think I'd have liked to see you throw him over."

"Satisfying, too," Nico said. Propping himself on an elbow, he smiled down at her face. "What is it about you that incites me to violence?"

"I don't know."

Neither did he, and he'd been looking for the answer for the past few weeks. All he knew was that the idea of Louisa hurting made him see red. He wanted to punish Steven and the others for making her life so hard.

Come to think of it, Louisa made him feel a lot of strong emotions. He didn't just want to kiss her, he wanted to kiss her senseless. And he didn't want to enjoy her company, he wanted to spend every moment he could spare with her.

Where on earth did these feelings come from? He'd never behaved this way around Floriana. Or anyone else for that matter.

Could it be that this—Louisa—was what he'd been missing all these years?

He turned on his side until they lay face-to-face. All it took was one look into her blue eyes and his pulse started racing again. "Thank you," she whispered.

"You don't have to thank me for anything."

"But I do. Did you know," she asked as he freed a stray petal from her hair, "that this past week was the first time in years that I've felt like I truly belonged."

"I'm not surprised. Monte Calanetti loves you."

"No, Monte Calanetti loves you. I'm just lucky to have won approval from its favorite son."

"Oh, you have more than my approval, *bella mia*." She'd awakened a part of him he didn't think existed and now it belonged to her forever.

Suddenly, his desire couldn't wait any longer. Slanting his mouth across hers, he drank in her sweet taste. This—this—was perfection, he realized. All these years he believed his soul was incomplete, it had merely been in hibernation, waiting for his blonde American to move in next door.

"Louisa, Louisa, Louisa," he chanted, his lips raining kisses down her throat. "I've waited for so long."

He paused when he reached the lace neckline blocking the rest of her skin from exploration. The top button strained to be released. All it would take was a flick of his fingers.

His hand hovered. The memory of her pushing him away at the royal wedding forced him to slow down. "Are you sure?"

Looking up, he saw eyes more black than blue, the pupils wide with desire. Out of the corner of his own eye, he saw a shaky hand reaching toward her blouse. She smiled, and a moment later, the button was undone.

It was all the answer Nico needed and he crushed his mouth to hers. Later, as his fingers made short work of the remaining buttons and as Louisa breathed his name, he wondered if maybe it wasn't only Monte Calanetti that was in love…

"You are a lying lie-face. I hope you know that."

What the heck? Louisa blinked at the nightstand clock and decided it was far too early to decipher what Dani meant.

"I just want you to know that I forgive you," her friend continued.

"Forgive me for what?" She brushed the hair from her eyes.

"For telling me nothing was going on between you and Nico, of course. You're not going to keep insisting the two of you are only friends after what we saw yesterday."

Louisa smiled, thinking about what Dani and the others hadn't seen. "No."

"Good. Because unless you let all your friends literally sweep you off your feet, no one would believe you," Dani told her. "By the way, Rafe and I completely understand why the two of you wanted to keep things private for a while. Especially given the circumstances."

"Thank you." No sense explaining how she and Nico weren't together until yesterday. Like Dani said, after the way she'd kissed him in the plaza, no one would believe her anyway.

Nico had swept her off her feet, hadn't he? *In more ways than one.* Her stomach dropped a little at that.

He's not Steven. This was a different kind of affair.

"Louisa, are you there?"

She yawned and pushed herself to a sitting position. "I'm here," she said, pulling the sheet up.

"Good. I was afraid Nico might be distracting you."

"Nico isn't here. He went to see how the harvest was going." *I'll wake you when I get back*, he'd whispered upon kissing her cheek. So much for that fantasy. Maybe she could pretend to be asleep. "Is there a reason you're calling this early," she asked, "or did you just want to call me a liar?"

"I have your sandals. You left them in the plaza, in case you were looking for them." Oh, right. Now that she thought about it, Louisa didn't remember Nico getting his shoes either. Definitely wouldn't be able to sell the idea of friends.

"Thank you," she replied, sheepishly.

"Also now that the festival is over, Rafe wants our economic development committee to start meeting in earnest. Can you ask Nico if he's available next Tuesday morning, since you'll probably see him before any of the rest of us will?"

Wow, the little blonde was really enjoying this wasn't she? Louisa shook her head, despite Dani's not being able to see her. "I'll try to track him down."

As if on cue, no sooner did she speak than the bedroom door opened and Nico strolled in wearing a shirt that should have been tossed several washes ago as it was at least a size too small. The fabric clung to his biceps and flat stomach.

When he saw her sitting up, he gave an exaggerated pout. "Dani," she mouthed. Her breath was too short to talk anyway. That shirt left nothing to the imagination, especially to a woman who knew exactly what lay beneath the cotton.

She watched him putter around the bedroom only half listening while Dani talked on about the meeting. Finally, guessing that a pause meant the conversation had ended, Louisa told Dani she had to go.

"What did Dani want?" Nico asked, when she tossed the phone aside.

"To give me grief for not telling her about our affair."

"But we weren't having an affair until…"

"I know," she replied. "And you didn't think people believed the tabloids."

"People will definitely believe them now," he commented. Hard to call them liars, that was for sure. "Does it bother you?"

He looked so serious, standing there smoothing the

wrinkled duvet. "Don't have much of a choice now, do I?" she replied. "I mean, the time to object would have been before I kissed you, and if I recall…"

She rolled onto her stomach, and hugged his pillow beneath her, grinning to herself at how the movement left her shoulders and back exposed. "As I recall, I wasn't doing all that much objecting at the time."

"That is true. I did not hear an objection," he replied. To her surprise, however, his smile didn't last. "I hope I don't hear one today."

An odd question considering she lay naked in his bed. "What could I possibly object to? That yesterday wasn't perfect enough?"

"This."

Louisa sat up as Nico pulled a rolled-up newspaper from the back of his waistband. The pages had been folded to a gossip column. Near the bottom of the page, she saw a brief mention of her holding court at the harvest festival with her latest millionaire boyfriend. Two lines. No more. Her fifteen minutes of notoriety was fading. A weight lifted from her shoulders.

"Looks like I've been replaced by bigger news." Finally. Heaven help the poor person who took her place, whether they deserved the attention or not.

"So you don't mind the mention?" Nico asked.

Honestly? She'd rather they not mention her at all, but given how bad things had been? "Two lines on page thirteen I can handle."

At last, a true smile broke across Nico's face. "Good. I'm glad. I was concerned…"

"About what? That I would freak out?"

"You did before." He pressed a knee to the edge of the bed, and leaning close, cradled her face in his palm. "I never want anything to hurt you that badly again."

"*Never* is a very big promise," she told him.

"Not where you're concerned. If I have to buy up every newspaper in Italy to keep the paparazzi from hounding you, I will."

A shiver ran down Louisa's spine. *He's just trying to make you feel safe and special.* Even so, when he said things like that she couldn't help thinking of Steven.

"No need to do anything so drastic. I'll settle for your arms around me."

"Ask and you shall receive, *bella mia.*" A twinkle appeared in his eye. "Is a hug all you need?"

Well, when he looked at her like that... She grabbed the neck of his T-shirt and tugged him forward. "Now that you mention it, I might have a few other requests."

Following their lovemaking this morning, he'd wanted nothing more than to burrow with her beneath the sheets and, maybe after some rest, make love again. Unfortunately, Louisa insisted they needed to make an appearance at the winery before the gossip got too out of control.

As he leaned back against the bed watching her dress, he marveled at how light and full his chest felt. Never in his entire life could Nico remember feeling this way. It was as though overnight the entire world had grown brighter: every color more brilliant, every smell and sound more pronounced. And Louisa—beautiful, beautiful Louisa— he couldn't get enough of her. Not sexually, although making love with her was amazing, but of *her.* Her company, her presence, her happiness. It overwhelmed him how much he wanted to keep her close and protect her.

Suddenly, it hit him. He was in love.

For the first time in his life, he, Nico Amatucci, was truly, madly and deeply in love. The knowledge swelled inside him, inflating his heart until he thought it might burst.

To distract himself from the desire to haul her down the hall and back into his bed, he pretended to check the messages on his phone. Comprehension was difficult, what with his beautiful American standing a few feet away clad only in jeans and a bra.

"You should move your clothes into the closet," he said as he watched her taking a shirt from her suitcase. This long under his roof, and she hadn't unpacked? They would need to remedy that.

"Actually," Louisa said, "I was thinking it might be time for me to move back to the palazzo."

What? He sat a little straighter. "So soon?"

"It's hardly soon, Nico. I've been here two and a half weeks. This was only supposed to be until the press died down, remember?"

He remembered. He didn't want her to go. Her decision felt too much like her deciding to leave Monte Calanetti. How could she want to leave when they were only just were discovering their feelings.

It took all his effort to keep his voice light and not spoil the moment with his panic. "I suppose," he said, heaving the most dramatic sigh he could muster, "if you prefer to sleep alone in a cold palazzo than in my warm bed…"

"I never said I *preferred* the cold palazzo." She mocked his exaggerated voice with one of her own. "But I will have to go back eventually."

"I know. Not tonight, though?"

"Well…" He could tell from the sparkle in her eyes that she was only pretending to hesitate. "Okay, not tonight. But soon."

"Soon," he said, with a smile. He was surprised at how strongly he wanted her to stay. This new passionate self was going to take some getting used to.

Returning his attention to his phone, he noticed a message from Rafe. Agenda Items for Next Tuesday, the subject line read.

"Did Dani say any more about what Rafe wanted to talk about at this meeting?" he asked Louisa.

"Just that he wanted to get plans rolling on some type of event to attract visitors now that the harvest is wrapping up." She was buttoning the same silk blouse she'd worn when moving in. "He was thinking maybe something in February," she said. Around Valentine's Day."

"A holiday that will attract couples to his restaurant. Why am I not surprised?"

"Well, it is a romantic time of year. What could be more romantic than candlelit dinners with fine wine?"

"True." No sooner did she say the words than the image of the two of them nestled together in a corner table came to mind. "Very romantic indeed," he murmured.

"You could relabel one of your wines for the occasion. The winery must have something bubbly. A prosecco maybe?"

She was on to something. The winery had a very nice prosecco they produced on a limited basis. He could easily convince the local businesses to incorporate it into any plans they came up with.

Tossing his phone aside, he got up and, giving in partially to his desire, wrapped his arms around her waist. "Beautiful and brilliant," he said, kissing her neck. "You are definitely a prize worth keeping."

"Glad you think so."

Was it his imagination or did she tense slightly before breaking the embrace. She had a smile on her face, so he must have.

"Isn't Valentine's Day when you were hoping to open the palazzo to guests?" Since she obviously wasn't going to leave Monte Calanetti now, she could put her project back into motion.

To his surprise, she answered his question with a very sarcastic laugh. "I'm pretty sure those plans bit the dust when Dominic Merloni canceled our appointment."

Dominic Merloni. That shortsighted idiot. "He is not the only financier in Italy. There are other banks. Other sources of funding," he reminded her.

Louisa set down the hairbrush she was using to look at him. "Who's going to lend Luscious Louisa money? It was naive of me to think I could slide by on my maiden name. Too much of my past financial history is tied to Steven's."

"There is still the investor route. I'm sure there are plenty of people who would be interested. I've already said I would—"

"No." Her refusal was sharp and sudden, cutting him off. The reaction must have shown on his face, because her voice immediately softened. "We've already had this conversation Nico. I can't take money from you."

"Yes, but…" But that was before they became lovers. Surely, the situation had changed. Why not let him help?

"The whole idea of the hotel was to create something of my own," she said, cutting off his protest. "If I take money from you, then it won't feel that way. Especially now. The papers claim I'm dating you for your money," she added, picking up her brush.

"I thought you no longer cared what the papers said."

"I said I could deal with a small mention. What I don't want to do is give them more ammunition."

"So, what are you going to do? Give up on your plan?"

"I'm not 'giving up' on anything. The palazzo is going to make a wonderful hotel. Just not as soon as I hoped, is all. In another year or so, maybe, when I've had time to build a better financial profile."

Hearing Louisa put her dream on hold broke his heart. It wasn't right, her suffering another setback because of that cretin she'd married. Especially when he had the wealth and connections to make things happen.

Maybe… He looked down at his phone. Maybe she wouldn't have to wait too long. Wouldn't hurt to make a few phone calls and see if he could open a few doors, would it?

CHAPTER ELEVEN

MORE THAN A few heads turned when Louisa and Nico entered the winery together. Dozens of pairs of eyes all staring knowingly in her direction.

Suppressing the old, familiar apprehension, Louisa nodded hello to everyone. "Looks like our secret is out," she said. The din of the machinery forced her to holler directly into Nico's ear.

He turned and looked at her with such concern, her heart wobbled. "Will you be all right?" he asked.

"I'll be fine." Even if she wouldn't, there was no way she could tell him that when he was looking at her so tenderly. "If I was worried about discretion, I wouldn't have kissed you in front of the whole village, would I?"

Nico looked about to reply when one of the workers called his name.

"Duty calls," he said. He flicked the hair from her eyes with his index finger. While not a kiss, the gesture was still intimate enough that, if there had been any employees who didn't suspect their affair, there weren't anymore.

Trying her best to look nonchalant, Louisa headed toward the back office. She was nodding hello to the women at the destemmer when she noticed the two men behind them exchanging euros.

"They've been placing bets ever since the picture of you and Signor Amatucci appeared in the paper," Mario said, appearing at her shoulder.

Bets. Her stomach churned a little at the news. "On what?"

"On you and Signor Amatucci. Half the staff believed

the two of you were just friends; the other half was convinced the two of you had been together for months."

"Months? You must have heard wrong." Up until the royal wedding, she and Nico had only crossed paths when necessary, and half the time they'd butted heads.

The young man shrugged. "I only know what people told me."

"Which side were you on?" she asked.

"I don't like to place money on anyone who is writing me a reference."

"A smart man," she replied.

"For what it's worth," Mario continued, following her into the office "the majority were hoping the rumors turned out to be true."

"They were?" Come to think of it, while people stared, nobody seemed particularly acrimonious. There were no cold shoulders like in Boston. In fact, Louisa realized, some of them had amusement in their eyes.

"Public consensus seems to be that it was high time Signor Amatucci had a serious relationship."

"It is, is it?"

"At least among the older female employees."

"I see." She wondered if Nico knew he had a mothering contingent. Probably.

Feeling slightly better, she sat down at her desk. Today's order list wasn't as long as previous days' as most people had purchased their bottles in person at the festival. She counted fewer than two dozen names.

"Those should be the last of the orders," Mario said. "We'll be out of Amatucci Reserve after today."

"Guess that means my job will be finishing soon, as well. No wine, no need to fulfill orders." With the headlines dying down and the wine gone, it was definitely time to go home.

"That's too bad," Mario replied. "You'll be missed."

"I know. What will people have to bet on?"

"I'm serious. I'll admit, when you first arrived some of us were concerned. We didn't know what to expect. But then we got to know you, and we realized what Signor Amatucci said at the staff meeting was true…"

"I'm sorry." Louisa put down the paper she'd picked up. "What staff meeting?"

"Right after you started. *Signor* held a staff meeting and told us the headlines were all exaggerations and that we should make a point of getting to know you."

So that's why Mario and the others had warmed up to her. Because Nico had told them to. "How very kind of him," she replied. Inside, she wanted to wring Nico's neck.

"Well, like *signor* said, once we got to know you, we'd realize we shouldn't believe everything we read. At least I don't believe it."

"Thank you." She did her best to keep her voice calm and kind. The young man was being sincere. Besides, her annoyance wasn't with him, it was with his boss.

"This reminds me…" Palms pressed to the desk top, she pushed herself to her feet, deliberately moving slowly so as to stay calm. "There's something I wanted to ask Nico about today's orders. Do you mind?"

"Not at all. I saw him and Vitale heading toward the wine cellar."

Perfect. They could talk without being overheard.

Cool and dark, the wine cellar Nico had proudly told her about on her first day had changed little from when the Amatuccis first started making wine. The stone walls and floor were the same ones against which his great-grandfather had stacked his wine barrels. At the moment the tradition meant little as she stalked the floor-to-ceiling stacks looking for Nico.

She found him in the farthest room, clipboard in hand.

Soon as he saw her, a smile broke across his face. "Now here is a pleasant coincidence. I was just imagining what it would be like to bring you down here and have my way with you."

"You'll have to keep imagining," she replied, sidestepping his grasp.

Immediately his smile turned into a frown. "Is something wrong?"

"You tell me. Did you really tell your employees they had to be nice to me?"

"Where did you hear that?"

"Mario told me about your staff meeting." Not that it mattered who'd told her. The way he was avoiding looking her in the eyes told her it was true.

The irritation she'd been tamping down, quickly roared to life, making it a herculean effort for her not to snatch the clipboard from his hands and toss it on the ground then and there to make him look at her. She settled for spinning around and slamming the door shut. "I can't believe you did that," she hissed once she had his attention.

"Did what?"

"Forced your employees to be my friends. Who do you think you are?"

"Their boss," he replied, sharply, eyes flashing. "And I did not force anyone. I told them to treat you with respect, something I thought you were sorely in need of at the time. Or don't you remember how upset you were on that first day? When you told me about the trial?"

And broke down in his arms. "I remember," she said. All too well. Like so many times, Nico had been the rock she so desperately needed.

"That doesn't entitle you to go around speaking on my behalf." Hearing the complaint aloud, it sounded a lot less egregious than it had when she came marching down here. Still, she pressed on. There was some merit to her grievance. "I needed to win people over on my own, not because of your influence."

"And you did," Nico replied. She rolled her eyes. "Look, I simply told people to give you a chance. That if they got to know you, they would see that what the newspapers were saying was nothing but a load of garbage."

Exactly what Mario said.

"I assure you, *bella mia*, any goodwill you received you earned on your own." With a duck of his head, he offered a small smile. "You are irresistible, you know."

In spite her annoyance, Louisa's stomach gave a little wobble. He wasn't getting off that easily, though. "Regardless, you should have told me what you were planning. I don't like the idea of everyone talking behind my back."

"They were already talking; I wanted to make sure they talked correctly. Besides, if I had mentioned my plans, you would have told me not to, making your job twice as hard."

He had a point, even if the logic didn't sit completely well with her.

"What else did you tell them?" she asked.

"Nothing. I swear."

She believed him. Knowing she could verify whatever he said, he had no reason not to answer truthfully.

His index finger hooked her chin. "My only intention was to make sure people treated you fairly," he said, thumbing her lower lip. "When you told me how badly your 'friends' treated you in Boston, I… I swore I wouldn't let you suffer like that again. I just wanted to erase the hurt from your eyes."

He gazed at her from beneath lowered lids, the black of his eyes obscured by thick dark lashes. Louisa found herself lost in them anyway. He had the power to distract her with a single touch, no matter how slight. Being with Nico was unlike anything she'd ever experienced. Not with Steven or any other man. It was as if she'd been stuck in darkness her entire life and had finally stepped into the light. Nico made her feel beautiful and smart and special and a thousand other adjectives she couldn't name. The sensation scared her to death.

And yet she couldn't stop herself.

"I hate seeing you sad," he whispered. "All I want is to make sure you are happy. I'm sorry if I overstepped."

"Your heart was in the right place."

"It was." He wanted to help her by encouraging her co-workers to get to know her. A far cry from trying to isolate her, the way Steven had done.

"Then I suppose I can forgive you. This time."

Smiling, Nico leaned in to kiss her. *"Grazie, bella mia."*

Oh, but she was so weak, Louisa thought to herself. One brush of Nico's lips, and she was ready to forgive everything. Forgot everything. He could betray her a thousand times and with one touch, she'd be his again. Heart and soul. The thought would terrify her, if Nico hadn't started kissing the patch of skin right below her jaw, obliterating all coherent thought.

From the way the clipboard just slipped from Nico's grasp, she wasn't the only one about to lose control. "What have you done to me, *bella mia*?" he whispered.

Precisely the question Louisa was asking herself. But then Nico kissed her deep, and she was swept away.

"Absolutely not," Louisa said, shaking her index finger. "I'm not letting you talk me out of it again."

Oh, but the spark in her eyes said he was welcome to try. They were discussing Louisa's moving back to the palazzo. The past two nights, Nico had managed to convince her she should postpone her departure. Not that she needed too much convincing.

Tonight, however, Louisa insisted she was sleeping in her own bed.

"Fine," he told her.

"Really?" Nico chuckled at how high her brows rose. She'd been expecting an argument. After all, as they'd both discovered, the persuasion was half the fun.

"Sure. You may sleep wherever you like. Of course," he said, trailing a finger down the back of her neck, "you won't be sleeping alone."

She made a soft strangled sound in her throat that made him want to kiss her all over. He loved how easily she responded to his suggestion and how she stubbornly fought to keep him from knowing. Her eyes would flutter shut and she would bite her lower lip. Inevitably her reaction would leak out anyway, and then he would be the one fighting to hide how she affected him. Surely, she knew how crazy she made him. He would give her the world on a silver platter if she asked.

So if she wanted to go back to the palazzo, to the palazzo they would go. The only reason he kept persuading her to stay was because he didn't want to spend a night without her.

Frightening how much he needed her. Frightening and exhilarating. Was this how his brother and sister felt when they fell in love? Or his parents? If so, perhaps he finally understood them a little bit better.

Although he would never throw a plate at Louisa. Of that he was certain.

"You never told me what you thought of dinner," he said, slipping an arm around her shoulder. The two of them had played guinea pig for Rafe's fall menu.

"It was delicious," she replied. "I've never had rabbit before. And don't try to change the subject."

"*Bistecca alla fiorentina* is a Tuscan specialty. And I'm not changing the subject. I already agreed to let you win."

"Let me, huh?" She reached up and entwined her fingers with the ones on her shoulder, a move that brought her face into perfect kissing proximity. Nico had no choice but to brush his lips across hers.

"Always,' he murmured.

"Except when you don't. Like the past two nights."

Recalling how they'd spent those two nights, Nico felt a satisfied groan rise in his throat. "I like to think we both won those arguments," he replied.

It was early still; the stars had yet to appear in the sky. Nevertheless, the fountain spotlights were already on. The brightness bounced off the coins scattered in the basin.

Reaching into the water, he picked up the first coin he saw and held it up. "A halfpenny for your thoughts," he said.

She laughed. "I was thinking about how much things have changed since I arrived in Monte Calanetti."

"Good changes, I hope."

"Some very good ones," she replied.

She looked so lovely, with the light framing her face. An angel to rival the nymph of the fountain. All those people tossing money and making wishes. He already had his wish standing before him. A fierce ache spread from the center of Nico's chest, giving birth to emotions that begged to be released. "I love you," he told her, the words bursting out of him in a rush.

Louisa's heart jumped to her throat. Of all the things he could have said, why did he have to say those three words?

"Nico—"

"I know," he rushed on, "it's too soon. It's too fast. Too... Too many things, but then again, it's not." His hand trembled as he stroked her cheek. "I think I have loved you for a very long time. Since long before the wedding."

Louisa wasn't sure if she wanted to run or cry. He was

right; it was too soon. If she said the words back, it would mean accepting the fact she had once again fallen in love without thinking things through.

Even if it was already true.

That he seemed to know what she was thinking made the panic worse. "It's all right," he said, pressing his fingers to her lips. "I understand if you're not ready to say the words back. I just needed to tell you."

She was about to tell him she needed time—a lot more time—when a voice interrupted from behind them. "Nico! I thought that was you."

A wiry man with slick black hair approached them with a smile. "And Signorina Harrison. How lucky that I should run into you. Saves me the trouble of tracking you down by phone."

"Me?" She looked at Nico for help.

"I'm sorry, I should have introduced myself. I'm Dominic Merloni."

"From the bank?" Apparently he'd decided she was worth talking to after all.

If the banker noticed the chill in her voice, he was unfazed. "Yes, I wanted to apologize for canceling our meeting so abruptly the other day. There was a family emergency that took me out of town."

"How terrible," she said, not sure she believed him. "I hope everything's okay now."

"Better than ever, thank you. Anyway, since I didn't know when I would be returning, I told my secretary not to reschedule anything. Now that I'm back, I'm looking forward to sitting down and hearing more about your project. You are still thinking of turning the palazzo into a boutique hotel, are you not?"

"Yes! Definitely."

"Wonderful. Call my office tomorrow and we'll pick a time."

This was unbelievable. Here she'd convinced herself that her plans would need to wait another couple of years.

"Um…" She still didn't want to get her hopes up yet. Signor Merloni might be willing to listen, but that didn't erase her weak credit history. "I think before we meet, you should probably know that I'm recently divorced. My personal credit history is relatively new."

"Oh, I don't think that will be a problem," the banker said. "I'm sure you'll be a solid risk." His gaze darted to Nico as he spoke.

She should have known it was too good to be true.

"Well, it looks like we have occasion to celebrate," the winemaker said as they watched him walk away.

"Really?" she asked, narrowing her eyes. Whatever elation she was feeling had vanished, wiped out when the banker had tipped Nico's hand. "And what exactly do you want to celebrate? The fact that you talked Dominic into meeting with me or the fact you're a controlling jerk?"

As she hurled the words at him, Nico stiffened. "Louisa…"

"Don't try to deny it," she said. "I saw Dominic looking at you. He was about as subtle as an elephant. The guy might as well have come out and said you were backing the loan."

"I'm not backing anything."

He also wasn't denying his involvement. "You did talk with him, though."

"I told him I thought the project had potential."

The Amatucci seal of approval. Which, as everyone in Monte Calanetti knew, was as good as a guarantee. Louisa could tear her hair out. No, correction. She could tear Nico's hair out. Every curly strand.

"I can't believe you," she said, shaking her head.

"I don't understand. What did I do that's so terrible?"

What did he do? "You went behind my back, that's what."

"I was trying to help you."

"Funny, I don't recall asking for it. In fact, *I specifically asked you not to help*." Turning on her heel, she marched to the bench but was too aggravated to sit down.

Nico marched up behind her.

"What was I supposed to do?" he asked. "You were putting your plans on hold because of the man. Was I supposed to stand back and let your dreams fall apart even though I have the ability to stop it?"

"Yes!" she hissed as she spun around to face him. "That's exactly what you should have done."

"You're kidding."

"No, I'm not. It wasn't your dream to save. It was mine."

"But you weren't doing anything. To save it."

"And that's my decision to make, too. I don't need you coming in and taking over."

"Taking over?" He looked stunned, as though someone had told him pigs could fly. "What are you talking about?"

He was kidding, right? They were arguing about his influencing a banker on her behalf and he was asking her to explain herself?

Then again, maybe he didn't understand. Taking over was so ingrained in men like him, they didn't know how not to be in control.

Louisa shook her head. When she'd found out about that damn staff meeting, she should have realized then, but she'd let him sweep her concerns away. Same as she did whenever she talked about going back to the palazzo. He need only touch her and poof! Her arguments disappeared.

Because nothing felt as safe and perfect as being in his arms.

"All I wanted was to help," Nico continued. "I thought it would make you happy."

"Well, it didn't," she said, sitting down. Kind of ironic they would be arguing about this in the same spot where they'd kissed a few days earlier. The harvest festival had been one of the most magical days of her life.

How much of those memories were real? "What else have you influenced without my knowing?" she asked. "Oh my God, the baptism. Did you ask your sister to make me Rosabella's godmother?"

"No. Of course not. No one tells Marianna what to do. You know that."

"Maybe. I don't know what to believe anymore." Other than knowing she'd created some of the problem herself, that is. Leaning on Nico came too easily. His strength made her feel too safe. What was it she'd said the day of the festival? *You'd rescue me.* From the moment the news about Luscious Louisa broke, she'd come to rely on him to catch her when she fell.

"I'll tell you what you can believe," Nico said. He was kneeling in front of her, holding her hands, his eyes imploring her to let him catch her one more time. "You can believe that I would never try to hurt you. I love you."

"I know." If only he realized, his saying he loved her only made things worse.

Suddenly, she understood why she'd been so frightened when he'd said those words earlier. Deep inside she knew that if she accepted his love, then she would have to acknowledge the feelings in her own heart. Nico was already her greatest weakness. Once she admitted her feelings, she'd lose what little power she had left. Before she knew it, she would be swallowed alive again. "I promised myself that would never happen again."

"What would never happen again?" he asked.

She hadn't realized she'd spoken aloud. Since she had, however, she might as well see her thoughts through. "I swore I would never let anyone control my life again," she told him.

"Control? What the…?" Nico sat back on his heels. "I'm not trying to control you."

"Maybe not on purpose," she replied. No, definitely not on purpose. "You just can't help yourself."

Same way she wouldn't be able to help herself from letting him.

"Goodbye, Nico." She pulled her hands free. "I'll pick up my things later on."

"I'm not Steven."

She was ten feet away when he spoke. The comment was soft, barely loud enough for her to hear. Turning, she saw Nico on his feet, hands balled into fists by his side. "I'm not Steven," he repeated, this time a little louder.

"I never said you were."

"Then stop running from me like I am!"

Didn't he get it? She wasn't running from just him. She was running from herself, too.

CHAPTER TWELVE

NICO STARED AT the vine-covered wall. Once upon a time, climbing to the other side meant escaping the turmoil that engulfed his house and finding tranquility. Too bad that wasn't possible anymore. Only thing crossing the wall would do today was make the pain in his chest more acute. Either because he didn't see Louisa or because he did, and she pushed him away again.

He was still trying to comprehend what had happened the other night. One moment he was declaring his love, the next... How had everything gone so horribly wrong?

"Signor?"

He forgot that Mario was waiting for an answer. They were scheduled to harvest the fields at the palazzo today. The final field of the season, Nico always saved it for last because the grapes took the longest to ripen. Mario wanted to know if he planned to check on the workers' progress. Thus the quandary over crossing the wall.

"You go ahead," he decided. "You can supervise on your own."

The young man straightened. "If you think so."

"I do." No need for the student to know that Nico was a coward, and that was why he didn't want to visit.

Besides, there was someone else he needed to speak with.

Marianna answered the door in a long floral dress, looking uncharacteristically tousled and unmade-up. Holding Rosabella on her right shoulder, she looked him up and down. "You look worse than I do," she remarked, "and I haven't had a good night's sleep in days. What's the matter?"

"I think I might have messed up," he replied.

"Messed up how?"

"With Louisa." As briefly as he could, he explained what had happened a few nights earlier, including what happened with Dominic.

"Tell me you didn't," she said when he finished.

"I was trying to help," he said. Why did everyone have a problem with him talking to the banker? "I gave my recommendation, same as I would for Rafe, or Ryan, for that matter."

"But we aren't talking about Rafe or Ryan—although it's nice to know you would speak on my husband's behalf—we're talking about Louisa. A woman who found out her husband had been lying to her about everything. And you went behind her back. Twice!"

"To help," Nico reminded her. "Steven Clark was a thief."

"Yes, I know, but surely you can see how keeping a secret, even a well-meaning one, would feel like a betrayal to her?"

Yes, he could.

"You owe her a very large apology," Marianna told him.

"If only the solution was that simple."

"You mean there's more?" The baby started to squirm, and she switched shoulders. "What else did you do?"

"Not me—her ex-husband."

"What did he do? Besides steal from all those people?"

Nico ran a hand through his curls. He'd already said too much. Having already broken Louisa's faith, he didn't dare break it further. "Let's just say he believed in holding the people he loved as close as possible."

"Oh. I think I understand."

"You do?"

"I think so. And if I'm right, then yes, you've messed up very badly."

"She accused me of trying to take over her life. I wasn't," he added when Marianna arched a brow.

"Not intentionally anyway," she murmured.

"Louisa said the same thing."

That his sister laughed hurt. "Poor Nico," she said, using her free hand to pat his knee. "It's not your fault. It's your nature to want to rush in and take over. You tried to with Ryan and me when I was pregnant."

"Great. So now you're saying I tried to control your life, as well."

"Don't be silly. I'm used to you. I learned a long time ago to ignore you when you start giving orders I don't feel like obeying. But I'm not someone like Louisa who is struggling to rebuild her life. I can imagine your interference would make her feel very powerless. Especially since you kept your actions secret. Why didn't you tell her?"

"Because I…" Because he knew she would tell him no. "I was trying to help," he finished, as if his intentions excused his actions. "I wouldn't have talked to Dominic if I didn't have faith in her."

"I know you wouldn't, but can you see how someone in Louisa's position might see things differently?"

Yes, he could. Especially someone who'd spent so many years trapped in a controlling relationship. Nico washed a hand over his face. So focused had he been on making Louisa happy, he'd let his desires blind him to what she truly needed. "I'm no better than her ex-husband, am I?"

"Your heart was in the right place."

Small comfort when life blows up in your face. He'd trade his good intentions for having Louisa back in a second.

At that moment, Rosabella started to squirm again, wriggling her tiny torso against Marianna's body. "I

SAVED BY THE CEO

swear," his sister said, as she tried to make the baby comfortable, "this little one is part eel. Spends half her day squirming. Don't you, Rosabella?" She nuzzled the baby's curls. "You know what, why don't you hold her for a few minutes? Maybe Uncle Nico is what she needs to settle down."

Doubtful. He could barely keep *himself* calm at the moment. "Marianna, I don't think—" Too late. She deposited his niece in his waiting arms and he found himself looking into Rosa's big brown eyes. For the second time in his life, Nico's heart lurched.

"She's so little," he said, risking a finger stroke against Rosa's cheek. The baby responded with a sleepy blink.

"She likes you," Marianna murmured.

"Louisa said I'd fall in love," he whispered.

"Excuse me?"

"When we were talking about being godparents. She told me I would fall in love with Rosa."

He remembered every detail of their conversation, from the advice she gave to the way the sun crowned her head as he said goodbye. "She was right in more ways than one."

His heart threatened to crack open, the way it had every hour since Louisa had said goodbye. Struggling to keep the pieces together, he looked to his sister. "I love her," he said in a quiet voice.

"I know."

Neither of them had to say what they were both thinking. That finally after years without it, Nico had found love, only to chase it away.

"I tried to explain myself the other night but she wouldn't listen, and now she won't take my phone calls," he said. "I'd go to the palazzo, but I'm afraid she'll refuse to come out." Or send him away. Either outcome frightened him into inertia. "Tell me, Marianna. What do I do?"

"I don't think you're going to like my answer."

"If you're going to tell me there's nothing I can do, you're right. There has to be something I can do." Surely she didn't expect him to sit around and do nothing while the love of his life slipped through his fingers. "If I could only get her to talk with me."

"Why? So you can explain and try to charm her into forgiving you?"

Nico held his sleeping niece a little closer. "Is that such a bad plan?"

"I don't know. How well did charm work for her ex-husband?"

"I'm not him."

"Then prove it to her."

"How? How do I make her see that I don't want to control her?"

"You let her be her own person. And that includes letting her come to you for help when she's ready.

"What if she never comes to me again?"

He didn't realize his knee was bouncing in agitation until Marianna put her hand on his leg. "Poor Nico. So used to being in charge of the situation. Haven't you figured out by now that love isn't something that makes sense? If it did, our parents would never have gotten together."

Their parents. Despite his sadness, he had to smile at her comment. "Never were two people less suited for one another," he said.

"Or more meant to be," Marianna replied, squeezing his knee. "I think you and Louisa are meant to be, as well, but you have to be patient."

"I don't know if I can." Each day that passed without speaking to her made the hole in his chest a little wider.

"Of course you can, Mr. Viticulture. Think of it like a harvest. You wouldn't pick a grape with a poor Brix level, would you?"

"No," he replied. "But waiting on a grape is a lot less painful, too."

"You can do it."

He smiled at the woman beside him. His beautiful baby sister all grown-up and glowing with motherhood. "When did you get so wise?"

"Oh, I've always been wise. You just never bothered to ask me for advice. Might as well face it, dear brother," she said, "when it comes to love, you've got a lot to learn."

Yes, he did. He only hoped he'd be able to learn with Louisa by his side.

If space was what she needed to find her way back to him, then space was what he would give her.

His resolve lasted five minutes. Then the phone rang.

"After weeks of speculation, the Halencian royal family confirmed today that Prince Antonio and Princess Christina are expecting their first child. The royal heir is due to arrive early next spring. No other details have been released..."

The television screen showed a photo of Antonio and Christina dancing at their wedding. The same photo that had reignited the Luscious Louisa scandal. Nice to know news outlets recycled resources.

Clicking off the news, Louisa tossed the remote onto the cushions. She was happy for the royal couple. Really she was. They may have had some bumpy times at the beginning of their marriage, but the pair were very much in love.

Funny how that had happened to a lot of the people she knew in Monte Calanetti. The whole "love conquering all" thing, that is. Too bad it missed her. Then again, maybe it was her fault. After all, she'd loved Steven and love hadn't come in to conquer anything. What made her think the situation would be any different simply because she loved—

Oh God, was she really ready to admit she loved Nico?

She checked her phone for messages. What was a little salt in the wound when you were already miserable, right? Nothing. After six impassioned voice mails, Nico had stopped calling. Guess he'd finally gotten the message. Or lost interest.

Make up your mind, Louisa. What do you want?

Nico, a voice whispered. She shut the voice off. What she wanted was to stop feeling as if she'd been kicked in the chest. Nothing she did seemed to curb the ache. Every day she immersed herself in cleaning and home renovations, working herself to the point of exhaustion. There wasn't a piece of wood she hadn't polished or a weed she hadn't removed from the back garden. But despite collapsing in a deep sleep every night, she woke in the morning feeling the same emptiness inside.

The doorbell rang. "Go away," she called to whoever was on the other side.

"Louisa!" Nico bellowed from the other side of the door. "Open up. I need to talk to you."

Careful what you wish for. The anger in his voice could mean only one thing. He'd found out about the Realtor.

He pounded on the door again. "Louisa! You let me in this minute or so help me I will kick the door in."

Nothing like a threat to kill her self-pity. Anger took over and she reached for the doorknob. "If you damage so much as a speck of dust, I'll…"

Dear Lord, he looked awful. One of the qualities she'd noticed from the beginning was Nico's robust appearance. The man on her doorstep looked tired, his healthy color turned pale and sallow. His eyes, while flashing with anger, were flat and lifeless beneath the spark. He looked, to be blunt, as bad as she felt.

"Is it true?" Without waiting for an invitation or answer, he stomped inside, toward the main staircase. There he stood at the foot, arms folded across his body, waiting.

"Tell me you're not seriously thinking of selling your home."

"You got the call, didn't you?"

"But why?" he asked.

"Seriously, you have to ask?" He and Monte Calanetti were irrevocably entwined. How was she supposed to stay in the village and live her life when every corner she turned would present some reminder of him?

"I thought it would make things easier," she told him, walking into the living room. Maybe if she dismissed him…

Of course he followed. "For who?" he asked. "You?"

"Yes." And for him. He wouldn't be forced to share his hometown with an ex-lover as his neighbor.

Nico didn't say a word. Instead he crossed the room, to the cabinet where she stored the fernet. At first she thought he might pour himself a glass, but he put the bottle back on the shelf.

"Amazing," he said, shaking his head. "You do like to run away from your problems, don't you?"

"Excuse me?"

"Well, you ran away from Boston to Monte Calanetti. You wanted to run away when the paparazzi came and now you are running away from me."

Louisa couldn't believe him. "I'm not running from you," she said.

"Oh really? Then what are you doing?"

"I'm…" She was…

Starting fresh again. In a new place. Away from Monte Calanetti.

All right, maybe she was running away. Maybe she needed to run away in order to save her independence.

"What I do or don't do is none of your business," she snapped. "If I want to sell the palazzo, I will."

"Is that so? And here I thought I exercised such control over your actions."

Damn him. Who did he think he was, twisting her words? "If I am leaving Monte Calanetti, it's because you tried to take over my life, and you know it."

"I did no such thing."

"Oh yeah? Then what was calling Dominic?"

"A mistake."

A damn big one, too. She was tired of having this argument. As far as she was concerned, they'd already had it one too many times.

Unfortunately, Nico thought differently. "It was wrong of me to call Dominic without telling you. I was excited to be able to help you, and I didn't think about how my help might make you feel."

Louisa had liked the conversation better before. Anger was so much easier to oppose than this softer, conciliatory tone.

She stared out the window. The Tuscan hills were starting to turn. Shades of brown mixed with the green. In another few months, it would be a year since her arrival. Seemed like only yesterday she and Dani had met on the bus from Florence. And she remembered the first time she'd met Nico. He'd sauntered through the front door without knocking and demanded proof she owned the palazzo. *Here's a man who insists on being in charge*, she remembered thinking. Her insides had practically melted at the thought, and that had scared the hell out of her. Because she didn't want to be attracted to a strong man.

"Scared," she said, her breath marking the glass.

"I don't understand." He replied.

"Your going to Dominic. It frightened me."

"I made you feel powerless."

She shook her head. "No. You made me feel like I'd met another Prince Charming. Actually, that's not true," she said, looking over her shoulder. "I already knew you were Prince Charming. Calling Dominic made it obvious."

"I still don't…"

No surprise. She probably wasn't making much sense. "I liked that you came to my rescue," she told him.

"And that scares you."

It terrified her. With a small shrug, she turned back to the hills. "I need to be my own person. When I'm with you, it's too easy to give in and let you run the show."

"Could have fooled me. In fact, I seem to recall more than one argument over my trying to run the show."

His shadow appeared in the window. Louisa could tell from the warmth buffeting her back, or rather the lack of it, that he was making a point of keeping his distance. "Do you know why Floriana and I didn't work?" he asked.

The odd shift in conversation confused her, but Louisa went along with it. "No. Why?"

"Because she was too perfect. I realized that just now."

"If this is supposed to make me feel better…"

"Wait, hear me out," he said. "Floriana… She and I never argued. She was always logical, always agreeable, always in tune with my thinking."

"She was perfect." While Louisa was the imperfect American who ran away from her problems. Both descriptions sickened her. "I get it."

"I don't think you do" was Nico's reply. The warmth from his body moved a step closer. Not too much, but enough so Louisa could better feel its presence. "Floriana might have been perfect, but she wasn't perfect for me. That was why I couldn't truly love her. Do you understand?"

She was afraid to.

"I need a woman who challenges me every single day,"

he said. "Someone who is smart and beautiful, and who is not afraid to put me in my place when I overstep."

"You make it sound simple."

"On the contrary, I think it might be very hard. I don't know for sure. I've never been in love until you."

Until her. The declaration washed over her, powerful in its simplicity. Nico Amatucci loved her. And she… Panic clamped down on the thought like a vise.

"I know you are afraid," he said when she let out a choked sob. The anguish in his voice told her how much he was struggling between wanting to close the distance and respecting her need for space.

"I know that Steven left you with some very deep scars and that you are afraid of making the same mistakes. I am not Steven, though. Please know that no matter what happens between us, I will always want you to be your own person.

"So," she heard him say, "if you want to run away, that's your choice. All I ask is that you don't use me as your excuse." There were a lot of things Louisa wanted to say in response, but when she opened her mouth to speak, the words died on her tongue. In the end, she stayed where she was, afraid to turn to look lest she break down when she saw Nico's face. She heard his footsteps on the tile, the click of the front door, and then she was alone.

She'd said she wanted to stand on her own two feet. She also wanted Nico's arms around her. Desperately. What did that say about her?

That you love him. The words she'd been fighting to keep buried broke free and echoed loud in her heart. No amount of running away or lying to herself would make them disappear. She loved Nico Amatucci. She was *in* love with Nico Amatucci.

Now what? With a sob, she sank to the floor. Did she

continue with her plans? Move again and spend her life being haunted by two past mistakes?

Or did she stay in the village she'd come to think of as home and somehow find the courage to let her love for Nico grow?

Wiping her eyes, she looked out once more at the Tuscan hillside and the vineyards that stretched out before her. How much she'd come to love this view. And this palazzo.

She looked around at her surroundings. A lot had changed around here in nine months. If her ancestors could see this place now, they wouldn't recognize their old home. It wasn't the same crumbling building she'd found when she'd arrived.

Maybe she wasn't the same woman either. She certainly wasn't the impressionable young girl who'd fallen in love with Steven Clark. She'd loved, lost, withstood public scorn and found a new home. *You're a lot stronger than you give yourself credit for*, Nico had once said. Maybe it was time to start giving herself credit. Time to believe she *was* strong.

Maybe even strong enough to fall in love with a strong man.

"I asked Lindsay Sullivan if she would stop by the meeting, as well. It might be useful to get a professional event planner's input, even if she does specialize in weddings. Is that all right with you, Nico?"

"A wedding planner is fine," Nico replied. "Whatever you want to do."

"Whatever I...? All right," Rafe said, plopping down on the other side of the table. "What have you done with the real Nico Amatucci? Usually by now you would have rearranged the agenda items and brainstormed three or four new ones. Instead, you've hardly said a word. What gives?" Folding his arms, the chef tipped back in his chair and waited.

No doubt he found Nico's shrug an unsatisfactory response. "It's your committee."

"That I started with the full knowledge that you would take over. Honestly, I wouldn't have gone to all this trouble if I didn't think you would do the bulk of the heavy lifting."

"Sorry to disappoint you," he replied.

"Leave him alone, Rafe. He's nursing a broken heart." Walking past, Dani gave her husband a playful smack on the back of the head. "Remember how depressed you were when I left Monte Calanetti?"

"Depressed is a little strong. Ow!" He rubbed the back of his head. "I was joking. I was also trying to distract him from his problems."

"News flash. The playful banter isn't helping." Each quip was like salt in his already raw wounds.

"We're sorry," Dani said, taking a seat.

"No, I'm sorry," he quickly replied. "You shouldn't have to censor your happiness for my sake." Then, because he was clearly a glutton for punishment, he added, "I don't suppose you've heard anything?"

She shook her head. "Nothing. I called a couple of times, but she isn't picking up her phone. She's still in town, though."

"I know." He saw the lights on in the palazzo. Yesterday, while in the vines, he thought he caught a glimpse of her on the balcony, and he almost climbed up to join her. But since he was practicing patience, like his sister suggested, he stayed away.

"Do you think she'll go through with selling the palazzo?" Rafe asked.

God, but Nico hoped not. "It's up to her." He personally hadn't returned the Realtor's call. Probably should or else risk losing the property altogether. The idea of someone—anyone—other than Louisa living next door... Grabbing a fork, he stabbed at a *cornetto*. Far preferable to stabbing anything else. "It's her decision to make," he repeated, as much to remind himself as anything.

"Whose decision to make what?" a beautifully familiar voice asked. Nico looked up in time to see Louisa walking into the main dining room. She was dressed in a navy blue suit, the kind a banker might wear. The dark material made her hair appear more white than ever. Perhaps that was why she was wearing it pulled back in a clip. This, he realized with a jolt, was a different Louisa than the woman he'd left the other day. The woman before him carried herself with confidence and grace.

"Sorry I'm late," she said, setting a leather portfolio on the table. "Oh, please tell me that carafe is American coffee."

"Espresso," Rafe replied. He sounded as astounded as Nico felt. A quick look at Dani said she shared the feeling, as well.

Fortunately for all of them, Dani didn't have a problem saying something aloud.

"We didn't think you were coming," she said.

Pink appeared in her cheeks. "I wasn't sure I was going to attend either. I didn't make up my mind until last night."

"And the suit?"

"Confidence booster," she said, reaching for the plate of pastries that was in the center of the table. "I have a business meeting after this one."

"You do?" Nico sat up straighter. This was what he feared. She'd come to say goodbye. "You found someone to buy the palazzo?"

"No, someone to help me turn it into a hotel." Her blue eyes found his. "It appears I'm not leaving Monte Calanetti after all."

"You're not?" For a second, he was afraid he'd heard her wrong. There was a smile in her eyes, though. Would she be smiling if she was about to break his heart?

The rest of the restaurant faded into the background. Nico was vaguely aware of Rafe and Dani excusing themselves from the room, not that it mattered. He only had eyes for the woman in front of him. Everything else was background noise.

"What made you change your mind?" he asked.

Of course, her staying didn't mean she wanted him back in her life. He tried to remind himself not to get his hopes up. She'd never even said she loved him.

But she was smiling. They both were.

"For starters? A good long look at where I was." Her lip trembled, breaking the spell between them. She looked down at her pastry. "I realized I'd been stuck in the past. Not so much regarding what happened—although I was stuck about those things, too—but more like frozen in time. In my head, I saw myself as that same impressionable twenty-one-year-old girl. I forgot how much time had passed.'

Afraid she was about to beat herself up, he cut in. "Not so much time."

"Enough that I should know better," she told him.

She wasn't making sense. Confused, he waited as she got up from the table. Her high heels tapped out her paces on the terra-cotta.

"I should have known that the person I am today isn't the same as the person I was back then. At least I shouldn't be, if I let myself grow up.

"I'm not making much sense, am I?" she said, looking at him.

"No."

"I was afraid of that." Her small smile quickly faded away. "What I'm trying to say is that you were right. I was afraid of repeating the past. For so long I thought I was trapped in my marriage. Then the trial happened, and suddenly I had a second chance. Throughout the entire trial, I swore to myself I would never let myself become trapped again."

And along came Nico charging in to make everything better. Exactly what she didn't need. He'd heard enough. "It's all right, Louisa. I understand."

"No, you don't," she said, walking to him. "I should have realized that I can't make the same mistake, because I'm not the same person. I can make new mistakes, but I can't make the same ones."

Through her speech, Nico had been fighting the kernel of hope that wanted to take root in his chest. All of her rambling sounded suspiciously like it was leading to a declaration. Until he heard the words, however, he was too afraid to believe. "Are you saying…?"

"I'm saying I've fallen in love with you, Nico Amatucci. I started falling the day I arrived in Monte Calanetti, and I haven't stopped."

She loved him. "You know that I'm still going to want to rush in and fix things."

"And I'll probably get mad and accuse you of trying to take over."

"I'd expect no less."

The eyes that found his this time were shining with moisture. "Because no one said love had to be perfect."

"Just perfect for us." After days of separation, Nico couldn't hold himself back a moment longer. Jumping to his feet, he rushed to take her in his arms. Immediately, he felt a hand against his chest.

"I still have scars," she said. "You're going to have to be patient with me."

"I'll wait for as long as it takes," he promised. "There's no rushing the harvest. A long story," he added when she frowned. "I'll tell you about it later. Right now, I'd much rather kiss you."

Her arms were around his neck before he finished the sentence. *"Bella mia,"* he whispered against her lips. *Thank you*, he prayed to himself. All his dreams, everything he'd ever wanted, he was holding in his arms right now. Nothing else mattered.

As his lips touched hers, one last thought flashed across his mind.

No sweeter wine...

EPILOGUE

February 14, Valentine's Day

IF YOU ASKED LOUISA, the palazzo had never looked lovelier, not even when the place had hosted the royal wedding party. Standing in the ballroom doorway, she couldn't stop smiling at the crowd of people who were there to celebrate the opening of her hotel.

This weekend, the palazzo would only host a handful of overnight guests, mostly friends who had agreed to be guinea pigs and test the service. They would open to the general public on a limited basis next weekend, and she hoped to be fully operational by summer.

The crowd was here for the first annual St. Valentine's Ball. Billed as an opportunity to experience medieval romance and pageantry, the idea was the tourist development committee's first official success.

A flash of red sequins caught her eye. "Lindsay's outdone herself this time, hasn't she?" Marianna said, appearing by her side. "No wonder she does so many A-list weddings."

"No kidding." The room was a gorgeous display of roses and red tapestry. "We were lucky she offered to help, what with her schedule." But then, the woman had a soft spot for the village since it was where she'd met her husband. He was here with her tonight. A quick look across the dance floor found the two of them stealing a kiss in the corner. They were caught by Connor and Isabella, who'd apparently had a similar idea. Yet another couple who had found love here.

Monte Calanetti seemed to have a romantic effect on people.

"I overheard a couple talking in the lobby about booking a room for next year's ball," Marianna was saying. "I hope you're planning to take advanced reservations."

"Of course," Louisa replied. Talk about a foolish question. "My business partner would kill me if I didn't," Louisa replied. "Speaking of, where is your husband anyway?"

"He went upstairs to check on the baby and her nanny."

"Didn't you just check on them five minutes ago?"

"I did, but Ryan has to see for himself. Daddy's little girl, you know."

Louisa laughed. Sometimes she thought her two friends were competing to see who could dote on their daughter the most.

The idea of asking Marianna's husband, Ryan, to invest in her project had happened completely by accident. Literally. Louisa had almost knocked him over the day she had taken the palazzo off the market. As luck would have it, he'd been looking for a new start-up project. Neither Nico nor Marianna had any idea until the partnership was official.

Naturally, when he found out, Nico had teased her about going behind his back. In reality, he was excited for her. It was a sign of how good things were going between them that they could joke about that terrible night last fall.

A tap on her shoulder pulled her from her thoughts. "Nico told me to have you join him in the other room," Marianna said.

It never failed. As soon as she heard Nico's name, a shiver ran down Louisa's spine. The man would forever have that effect on her. "Did he say what he wanted?"

The brunette waved her hand. "You know my brother tells me nothing. I think he and Angelo are up to something. I saw them and Rafe with their heads together. Their poor, poor wives."

"You might want to include yourself in that category," Louisa reminded her. "Whatever they're up to, I'm sure it's only a matter of time before Ryan's involved, too."

"He'd better not be."

The two of them walked toward what was now the hotel lobby. Of all the changes that the palazzo was undergoing, this was the most drastic. What had been the plain entranceway was now a richly appointed lobby. Louisa had done her best to keep the structural changes to a minimum, although she did concede to installing a small built-in counter that served as both the front desk and concierge location.

The staircase remained the same, however. Richly polished, the stairs made a welcoming statement to everyone who walked in. It was in a group gathered around the bottom banister post that Louisa found her man. He was talking with his brother, Angelo, and Angelo's wife, Kayla, who had flown in from New York City. Rafe and Dani were also chatting.

Nico stepped to the side slightly, drawing her attention, and her heart stuttered. He sure could wear a tuxedo. Wasn't fair. Tomorrow he would be back in his T-shirt and jeans and would look just as sexy. Worse, she'd bet he would look just as good fifty years from now, while she'd probably end up with gray hair and a thickening waist.

So you think the two of you will be together in fifty years, do you? Nico caught her eye and winked.

Yeah, she decided. She did.

At her arrival, Nico leaned in and whispered something in Angelo's ear. His brother nodded. "There you are, *bella mia*!" he greeted. Wrapping his arms around her waist, he pulled her into a lingering kiss. Same as she did whenever Nico touched her, Louisa melted into his embrace.

Such an overt public display of affection surprised her. She chalked it up to the champagne and the atmosphere.

"I missed you," Nico whispered before releasing her.

"Down, boy. This dress isn't made for manhandling." She smoothed the wrinkles from the pink chiffon skirt before whispering in return, "I missed you, too.

"Is that why you wanted to see me?" she asked. Not that she would ever turn down a kiss, but again, even for Nico, the behavior seemed extreme.

"The kiss was merely a bonus. I was looking for you because I have a surprise."

"For me?"

"No, for my brother, Angelo. Cover your eyes."

Louisa did what she was told and seconds later, she felt Nico's breath tickling her ear. "I wanted to do something to congratulate you for everything you've done with the palazzo. Carlos, he would be proud. I know I am."

Warmth filled her from head to toe. She didn't need a surprise. Nico's respect meant everything. "Okay," he whispered. "Open them."

"Nico, I don't need— Mom?"

The silver-haired woman standing at the foot of the stairs offered her a watery smile. "Hello, Louisa."

"I—" She couldn't believe her mother was standing the lobby. "How—"

"Signor Amatucci flew me here. He wanted me to see what you've done. It's wonderful, sweetheart."

"Mom..." She couldn't finish the sentence. Instead, she ran and threw her arms around the woman, holding on to her as tightly as she could. "I missed you so much," she managed to choke out. Until this moment, she hadn't realized just how much. "I'm so sorry."

"No, sweetheart, I am. I let us grow apart, but I promise I won't let that happen again." Pulling away, her mother cupped her face like she used to do when Louisa was a little girl and had a bad dream. "Okay?"

Louisa nodded. This was the best surprise she could imagine. "Thank you," she said when Nico joined them.

"My pleasure," he replied before looking serious "You're not angry I went behind your back?"

"Are you kidding? No way." If anything, his kindness only made her love him more. A pretty amazing feat, since she already loved him more than seemed possible.

She saw the same love in Nico's eyes. "Good. Because a woman should always be able to share her engagement with her mother."

Her engagement? A warm frisson passed through her at the words. She'd be lying if the idea of spending the rest of her life with Nico hadn't crossed her mind during these past few months. Trying to imagine life without him was... Well, it was like staring at a blank wall.

Still, she wasn't about to let him know that. The man needed to be kept on his toes, after all. Arms folded, she lifted her chin and said in her most haughty voice, "There you go, taking charge again. What makes you think we're getting married?"

"A man can hope, can't he?" Nico said, reaching into his pocket. Louisa gasped when she saw the small velvet box.

Bending on one knee, he held it out to her with a shaking hand. "Louisa Harrison, my beautiful, haughty American princess, you are the only woman I will ever love. Will you marry me?"

There was only one answer she could give. Same as there could only be one man she would ever want to be with forever. "Yes," she breathed. "Yes, I will marry you, Nico Amatucci."

He pulled her into another kiss, and this time Louisa didn't care how wrinkled her dress got. As his lips slanted

over hers and the crowd burst into applause, she felt the
last ghosts of her life with Steven disappear forever. She'd
found a new life, a new home, a new love, here, in the
vineyards of Monte Calanetti.

And they were better than she'd ever dreamed possible.

* * * * *

SHEIKH'S
FORBIDDEN
CONQUEST

CHANTELLE SHAW

For my sister Helen, with love.

CHAPTER ONE

'WHAT LUNATIC DECIDED to go sailing in this atrocious weather?' Lexi muttered into her headset as she piloted the coastguard rescue helicopter over the south coast of England and out across the Solent.

The narrow strait which separated the mainland from the Isle of Wight was a popular area for water sports and on a summer's day, when the sea was calm and blue, it was an idyllic sight to watch the yachts skim across the water with their sails tugging in the breeze. But October had blown in on a series of ferocious storms that had swept away the last remnants of summer and whipped the sea into mountainous waves which crashed against the chalk cliffs, spewing foam high into the air. The white horses reared up in the glare of the helicopter's searchlight but Lexi knew that an even greater threat lay beneath the sea's surface, where dangerous currents eddied and swirled, ready to drag the unwary and unwise down into the depths.

She heard the co-pilot, Gavin's response through her headphones. 'The yacht which has made an emergency call for assistance was competing in a race. Apparently the skipper thought they would be able to run ahead of the storm, but they've hit a sandbank and the boat is taking in water.'

Lexi swore beneath her breath. 'The skipper took a dangerous gamble to win a race. Jeez, I love the male ego!'

'To be fair, the storm is stronger than the Met Office predicted,' Gavin said. 'The complex tidal patterns of the Solent have caught out many experienced sailors.'

'The problem is that too many sailors *don't* have enough experience and fail to appreciate how unpredictable and dangerous the sea can be, like the man on holiday with his son who we were called to assist two days ago. The boy was only ten years old. He didn't stand a chance when their boat started to sink in rough seas.'

'We did all we could,' Gavin reminded her.

'Yeah, but we couldn't save the boy. He was just a kid with his whole life in front of him. What a bloody waste.'

Lexi struggled to bring her emotions under control and concentrated on flying the helicopter in the strong wind and driving rain. She prided herself on her professionalism. The first rule of working for the rescue service was not to allow your mind to linger on past events—even something as traumatic as the death of a child—but to move on and deal with the next incident.

'The Mayday call confirmed that the three males on the yacht are all wearing life jackets,' Gavin said. 'But they're unlikely to survive for long in these rough seas. The skipper reported that he has received a head injury, but he insisted that he wants his crewmen to be rescued first.'

'It's a bit late for him to be concerned for his crew now. It's a pity he didn't take their safety into account earlier and abort the race.'

Lexi constantly moved her gaze between the flight instrument panel and the window to scan the wild waves below. Three massive chalk stacks known as the Needles rose out of the sea like jagged teeth. The famous landmark was iconic but the strong currents around the rocks could be treacherous.

An orange glow suddenly flashed in the sky.

'Did you see the flare?' Gavin peered through the windscreen as Lexi took the chopper lower. A few moments later he gave another shout. 'I've got a visual—on your right-hand side.'

Lexi spotted the yacht. It had been tipped onto its side by the strong sea swell, and she could make out three figures clinging onto the rigging. She kept the helicopter hovering in position as Gavin went to the rear of the aircraft and prepared to lower the winchman, who was a paramedic, onto the stricken vessel. The buffeting wind made Lexi's job almost impossible, but she was a highly experienced pilot and had flown Chinook helicopters over the deserts of Afghanistan. A cool head and nerves of steel had been necessary when she had been a member of the RAF and those qualities were required for her job with the coastguard rescue agency.

She spoke to the paramedic over the radio. 'Chris, once you're aboard the vessel, remind the crew that the coastguard agency are in charge of the rescue and everyone is to follow your orders, including the skipper. If his head injury looks serious we'll winch him up first, whether he likes it or not. This is not the time for him to decide he wants to be a hero,' she said sardonically.

CHAPTER TWO

THE SEARING PAIN that felt as though Kadir's skull had been split open with an axe was the result of being hit on the head by the sail boom of the *White Hawk*—his brand-new racing yacht that was now residing at the bottom of the sea. However, his immediate concern was not for the loss of his boat but the welfare of his crew, who were being stretchered off the helicopter that had just landed at a hospital on the mainland.

The rescue had been dramatic—and just in time. Once Kadir had realised the yacht was sinking, everything had happened so quickly. He hadn't had time to feel fear, but for a few seconds he had pictured himself galloping across a golden desert on his black stallion Baha', and his heart had ached for what would become of the kingdom his father had entrusted to him.

But, like a miracle, out of the dark sky had appeared a shining light, and he had heard the distinctive *whump-whump* of helicopter rotor blades. Kadir had flown in a helicopter many times, and as he'd clung to the rigging of his wrecked yacht being battered by forty-foot waves he had recognised the skill and bravery of the pilot flying the coastguard rescue chopper in the worsening gale.

He knew that he and his crew had been lucky to sur-

vive. But the two young sailors who had crewed for him
since the start of the race in the Canary Islands were suffering from hypothermia and were in a bad way. As Kadir
watched them being wheeled across the helipad, frustration surged through him. His clothes were wet and stiff
with sea salt and the wind whipping across the helipad
chilled him to his bones. He lifted a hand to his throbbing
head and felt a swelling the size of an egg on his temple.

The coastguard paramedic gave him a worried look.
'Sir, please lie down on the stretcher and one of the medical staff will take you down to the A&E department so
that your injuries can be treated.'

'I'm fine; I can walk,' Kadir said impatiently. 'It's
my crew who I'm concerned about. I wish you had followed my instructions and rescued them first. They got
too cold because they were in the sea for so long. You
should have winched them up onto the helicopter before
you rescued me.'

'I was under instructions to rescue injured casualties
first and it was obvious that you had sustained a possibly
serious head injury,' the paramedic explained.

'My crew were my responsibility,' Kadir argued. He
was interrupted by another voice.

'I hardly think you are in a position to question the
professional judgement of a member of the coastguard
team when it was *your* poor judgement in deciding to
sail in atrocious weather that put your crew in danger.'

Frowning, Kadir turned towards the person who had
jumped down from the helicopter cockpit. Like the other
members of the rescue team, the figure was wearing a
bulky jumpsuit, but as they removed their flight helmet
Kadir's confusion grew.

'Who are you?' he demanded.

'Flight Captain Lexi Howard. I was in charge of the rescue operation. The helicopter crew acted under my instructions, which were to winch up injured casualties first.'

'You're...*a woman*!'

The instant the words left his lips Kadir realised he had made a crass fool of himself. There was a crowd of people standing on the helipad—medical staff and a team of firemen, who were required to be present whenever a helicopter landed at the hospital, and everyone fell silent and stared at him.

He could blame his shocked reaction to the female helicopter pilot on his recent trauma of nearly drowning, and also on the fact that—despite the new laws and policy changes he was gradually trying to introduce—gender equality was still a relatively new concept in his country, the isolated desert kingdom of Zenhab. But it was obvious from the pilot's icy expression that any excuse Kadir might offer for his tactless comment would not be well received.

'Full marks for observation,' the Flight Captain said drily. 'If the fact that I'm a woman bothers you so much I could always drop you back in the sea where I found you and your crew.'

The reminder of the two injured sailors reignited Kadir's sense of frustration that he was not in charge of the situation. He was used to making decisions and having them obeyed without question, and he was struggling to accept that in this instance the female Flight Captain was in control. It didn't help matters that his head felt as if it was going to explode. He gritted his teeth, fighting the nausea that threatened to overwhelm him and destroy what was left of his dignity.

'As the yacht's skipper, it was my duty to ensure the

safety of my crew,' he insisted. 'I was in a better position to judge their physical condition than you were and I could see that they were both exhausted.'

'It was my duty to ensure the safety of *all* the casualties in need of rescue, as well as the safety of my flight crew,' the Flight Captain said coldly. 'How dare you question my authority?'

How dare he? No one had ever dared to address Kadir with such insolence, least of all a woman, and certainly not in public. The knowledge that he was indebted to this self-assured young woman for saving his life made him feel emasculated. The fact that she was the most beautiful woman he had ever seen only made him feel worse.

In the nightclubs and casinos—the playgrounds across Europe of the rich and bored—Kadir had met countless beautiful women, and in his youth he had bedded more of them than he cared to remember. For the past decade he had lived his life in the fast lane and played hard, but at thirty-two he felt jaded. It was a long time since his curiosity had been aroused by a woman, but Flight Captain Lexi Howard intrigued him.

Beneath the floodlights on the helipad, her complexion was flawless and so fair that the skin stretched over her high, slanting cheekbones was almost translucent. Her long braid of ash-blonde hair suggested possible Nordic ancestry and the impression was further enhanced by her light blue eyes that reminded Kadir of the cool, clear skies above the Swiss Alps where he skied every winter.

He found he could not look away from her and he felt a sudden tightness in his chest as if a fist had gripped his heart. Heat surged through his veins. He tried to convince himself that the fire inside him was a natural response after his recent brush with death, but deep in his core something hot and hungry stirred.

'Surely you checked the Met Office shipping forecast and realised that a storm was approaching?' Lexi glared at the yacht's skipper, infuriated that he'd had the cheek to criticise how the rescue operation had been carried out. She guessed he was an inexperienced sailor, and his failure to respond to the worsening weather conditions had compromised the safety of his crew.

Her mind flew back to the incident the coastguard helicopter had attended two days ago and the young boy they had been unable to save. 'Not every rescue can be successful,' the coastguard station commander had reminded Lexi at the debriefing afterwards. 'Part of the job is to accept that you can't save everyone.'

Lexi's RAF commanding officer of the Medical Emergency Rescue Team in Afghanistan had said the same thing. Many of the things she had seen, the terrible injuries received by soldiers caught in landmine explosions and sniper fire, had been harrowing, but if she had gone to pieces she wouldn't have been able to do her job. The same was true working for the coastguard rescue. Her common sense told her she must not allow one tragedy to haunt her, but in her heart she had taken the failure to save the boy hard.

The tragedy two days ago and the incident today could have been avoided if the yacht's skipper in each case had acted more responsibly, she thought grimly. She was tempted to tell the man standing in front of her what she thought of him, but something about him made her swallow her angry words. Despite his dishevelled appearance and the large purple swelling above his right eye, he had an aura of power about him that set him apart from other men.

He was looking at Lexi in a way that no man had looked at her for a long time. *Too long*—the treacherous thought slid into her head. She tried to push it away but a picture flashed into her mind of the man's strong, tanned hands on her body, dark against pale, hard muscle pressed against soft yielding flesh.

Shocked by her wayward imagination, she narrowed her eyes to hide her thoughts as she studied him. He was sinfully attractive, with exotic olive-gold skin and over-long, thick black hair that curled at his nape and fell forward onto his brow so that he raked it back with an impatient flick of his hand. Lexi's gaze was drawn to his dark brown eyes—liquid pools of chocolate fringed by ridiculously long, silky lashes and set beneath heavy black brows. The gleam in his eyes unsettled her, and the blatantly sensual curve of his lips made her wonder how it would feel if he pressed his mouth against hers.

She shook her head, trying to break free from the disturbing effect he had on her, praying he hadn't noticed that she had been staring at him. She did not understand her reaction to him. It had been a long time since she had looked at a man and felt a quiver in her belly. Too long, she acknowledged ruefully.

'You should have waited for the weather to improve, instead of putting your life and the lives of your crew at risk.' She spoke sharply, desperate to hide her confusing awareness of the yacht's skipper. 'Your behaviour was irresponsible. Offshore sailing is not for inexperienced sailors.'

The man arrogantly threw back his head, drawing

Lexi's attention to his broad shoulders. She assessed him to be several inches over six feet tall.

'I'm not a fool,' he said curtly. 'Of course I checked the marine forecast and I was aware of the storm. The *White Hawk* could easily have run ahead of the bad weather, but we must have hit something in the water that ripped the keel from the hull and resulted in the yacht capsizing.'

He broke off abruptly. Following the direction of his gaze, Lexi saw two men hurrying towards them. The helipad was strictly out of bounds to the public but, as she stepped forward to ask the men to leave, they halted in front of the *White Hawk*'s skipper and, to Lexi's astonishment, bowed to him. She had learned enough Arabic during her tours of duty in the Middle East to recognise the language they spoke. After a brief conversation with the men, the skipper swung away from Lexi without giving her another glance and strode across the helipad, followed by his two companions.

'A word of thanks for saving his life would have been nice,' she said disgustedly, not caring if her words carried across the helipad to him. She glanced at the coastguard paramedic. 'Did you see how those men bowed to him as if they were his servants? He actually clicked his fingers for them to follow him! Who the hell does he think he is?'

Chris gave her an amused look. 'I take it from the way you ripped into him that you didn't recognise him? That was His Royal Highness, Sultan Kadir Al Sulaimar of Zenhab, and I'm guessing that the men who came to collect him *are* his servants. Not only is he a Sultan, he was the skipper of the Zenhab Team Valiant who won the America's Cup in the summer.' He grinned at Lexi's startled expression. 'I got the feeling that he didn't take kindly to you calling him an inexperienced sailor.'

'I still think he was irresponsible to have sailed when he knew that a storm was coming,' Lexi argued. 'But I guess he couldn't have known his yacht's keel would fail,' she conceded reluctantly. She knew enough about sailing to be aware that catastrophic keel failure was uncommon but not unheard of, and it was the main cause of yachts capsizing quickly, giving the crew little warning or time to radio for assistance.

She winced as she remembered how she had accused the man of being an inexperienced sailor. Now that she thought about it, he *had* seemed vaguely familiar, she mused as she climbed into the helicopter cockpit and prepared to take off from the helipad. During the summer there had been extensive news coverage of the famous America's Cup yacht race held in San Francisco, when the Zenhabian Team Valiant had beaten Team USA to win the prestigious trophy. Sultan Kadir Al Sulaimar had been interviewed on live television by an overexcited female presenter who had clearly been overwhelmed by his exotic looks and undeniable charm.

Lexi told herself that it wasn't surprising that she had failed to recognise the Sultan when he had been battered, bruised and dripping wet after being rescued from his sinking yacht. To her annoyance, she could not stop thinking about him. At the end of her shift she went back to the old coastguard cottage that had been her home for the past year but, instead of finishing packing up her belongings ready to move out, she wasted an hour looking up Sultan Kadir Al Sulaimar on her laptop.

She had no trouble finding pictures of him, mostly taken at social events in Europe. He was invariably accompanied by a beautiful woman. Blonde, brunette or redhead, it seemed that the Sultan had no particular preference but, from the dizzying number of different women he was photographed with, it appeared that he liked variety. According to the press reports, he was a playboy with a personal fortune estimated to be in the billions. He owned a luxury chalet in St Moritz, penthouses in New York and London's Mayfair and an English country estate where he kept racehorses.

There was some information about the country he ruled. Zenhab was an independent Arab kingdom in the Arabian Sea. Kadir had succeeded his father, Sultan Khalif Al Sulaimar, who was credited with establishing peace in Zenhab after years of fighting between rival tribal groups. But while the previous Sultan had rarely travelled abroad or courted the attention of the world's media, his son was frequently spotted by the paparazzi at nightclubs in Paris, or at Ascot, where he owned a private box and entertained celebrities and members of the British royal family, or driving his attention-grabbing scarlet sports car around Belgravia.

In short, the spoiled Sultan was the absolute antithesis of the kind of man Lexi admired. When she had served in Afghanistan, she had met men who were brave and loyal and utterly dedicated to carrying out the missions they had been assigned even though their lives were often at risk.

The memory of how the Sultan had looked at her with a predatory gleam in his eyes slid into her mind and her stomach muscles clenched. Sexual attraction followed its own rules and ignored common sense, she thought ruefully. Or maybe it was just her body reminding her that it was perfectly normal for a twenty-nine-year-old woman to feel sexual desire.

It was over a year since she had broken up with Steven—

or, to be more precise, since he'd informed her in a text message hours before their engagement party that he couldn't marry her because he had a girlfriend and a baby daughter who he had failed to mention when he and Lexi had grown close while they had been stationed together at Camp Bastion. Rejection hurt as much at twenty-eight as it had when she had been eighteen or eight, Lexi had discovered. She had dealt with Steven's betrayal the same way she had dealt with all the disappointments in her life, by pretending that she did not give a damn and hiding her feelings from a world that had proved too often that people were unreliable.

Perhaps the women in the newspaper photographs, clinging like limpets to the Sultan of Zenhab, had the right idea, she brooded. At least if you were a playboy's mistress you would have no expectations that he might commit to the relationship or fall in love with you. And no doubt the sex was amazing!

As Lexi visualised Sultan Kadir Al Sulaimar's arrogantly handsome face, heat unfurled in the pit of her stomach. She would never be tempted to sacrifice her hard-won pride and self-respect for five minutes in the sexy Sultan's bed, she assured herself. An hour on the treadmill followed by a brisk shower left her physically spent, but when she flopped into bed she was kept awake by the memory of the sensual promise in his molten chocolate eyes.

Two days later, Lexi donned her coastguard agency uniform for the last time, checked the gold buttons on her jacket were gleaming and adjusted her cap, before she walked into the station commander's office.

'I'm sorry to lose you,' Roger Norris told her. 'You've done a fantastic job over the past year.'

'I'm sorry to go,' Lexi said honestly. 'I'm going to miss everyone on the team, but I knew when I came here that the contract for a second helicopter pilot was only for one year.'

'The number of rescues you have carried out has proved the need for a second rescue helicopter, but unfortunately the funding for the coastguard agency has been cut.' Roger's frown cleared. 'However, I have received a piece of good news. A private donor has offered to pay for a permanent second helicopter and crew. The details will still have to be ironed out over the next few months but, if the offer goes ahead, would you be interested in resuming your role of Flight Captain?'

Lexi's eyebrows rose. 'I'd certainly consider it. Whoever the private donor is must be very wealthy.'

'He's a billionaire, by all accounts. You met him two nights ago—' Roger chuckled '—although I heard from Gavin and Chris that you didn't recognise him. In fact you're the reason that Sultan Kadir of Zenhab has made his incredibly generous offer after you rescued him and his crewmen from his capsized yacht. He has asked to see you so that he can thank you personally. He's staying in the Queen Mary suite at the Admiralty Hotel and requested for you to meet him there at six o'clock this evening.'

Lexi's heart collided painfully with her ribs at the mention of the Sultan. She flushed as she recalled the shockingly erotic dreams she'd had about him for the past two nights. She was behaving like a schoolgirl with a crush on a member of a boy band, she thought disgustedly.

'I'm afraid it won't be possible for me to meet him,' she told Roger. 'I'm going to my sister's engagement party this evening and it's a couple of hours' drive to Henley, where Athena's fiancé's parents live. Can't Chris or Gavin go instead of me?'

Roger shook his head. 'Chris is on duty. Gavin is at the hospital with Kate, and it looks as though her labour pains aren't a false alarm this time. Anyway, the Sultan particularly asked to see you.

'I'll be honest, Lexi. It is vital that the coastguard agency secures his donation. This part of the south coast is a busy area for shipping, and the rescue service needs a second helicopter. Perhaps you could phone the hotel and arrange to meet His Highness this afternoon instead of this evening?' Roger gave her a level look. 'It might also be a good idea to apologise to him. I understand that you had a heated exchange of words with him the other night.'

Lexi frowned at the reminder that she had behaved less than professionally when she had argued with the skipper of the capsized yacht, unaware that he was the Sultan of Zenhab and an experienced sailor. But the coastguard commander's words tugged on her conscience. The Sultan's offer to make permanent funds available for a second helicopter was astonishingly generous and could mean the difference between life and death for accident victims on the south coast who needed to be urgently transferred to hospital.

She stood up. 'I suppose I could stop off at the Admiralty Hotel and meet him before I drive to the party,' she said reluctantly.

'Good. And Lexi, be nice to him.'

She turned in the doorway and gave Roger a puzzled look. 'I'm always nice, aren't I?'

'Certainly—' the commander smiled '—but you can be intimidating. You have an outstanding war record and demonstrated your exceptional bravery, both in the RAF and as a civilian rescue pilot. Sometimes people, men especially, are in awe of you.'

Lexi visualised the Sultan of Zenhab's haughty features and gave a snort. She couldn't imagine His High and Mightiness had ever felt intimidated.

Driving back to the cottage, Roger's comment played on her mind. Did people really find her intimidating? She had always been a popular member of her RAF squadron and, since coming to work for the coastguard agency, she had quickly established her place in the team. The guys treated her as one of them, yet she sensed a faint reservation in their attitude. She had thought it was because she was the only female rescue pilot. But it had been the same when she had been at boarding school. She'd got on well with the other girls but she had never made close friendships.

She telephoned the Admiralty Hotel, and when a vague-sounding receptionist told her that the Sultan was unavailable to take her call she left a message explaining that she could meet him at five o'clock rather than six.

The rest of the day was spent packing up her car with bags and boxes. Closing the door of the cottage for the last time, she felt an unexpected pang. After ten years in the RAF, constantly moving to wherever in the world her squadron was deployed, she had enjoyed making the cottage into a home—even though it had not been the home she had imagined she would share with Steven.

He had talked about them buying a house together. They had even visited an estate agent to discuss the kind of property they wanted, Lexi remembered. Just for a while she had bought into the daydream of a happy marriage, children—a family that was truly her own and a sense of belonging, after a lifetime of feeling that she did not belong anywhere. She should have guessed it was too good to be true. Steven's betrayal had reminded her of the sense of rejection she had felt when her parents had made it obvious that they preferred their own daughter, Athena, who had been born to them a year after they had adopted Lexi.

At five minutes to five, Lexi walked across the foyer of the Admiralty Hotel, praying that she would not slip in her stiletto heels on the polished marble floor. Usually she lived in jeans and running trainers, but because she was on a tight schedule she had changed into a black silk jersey dress that was suitable for a cocktail party and wouldn't crease while she was sitting in the car.

The hotel receptionist looked flustered as she dealt with a coach party of tourists who had just arrived. Lexi checked in the lounge and bar, but there was no sign of the Sultan. She glanced at her watch and decided she would have to take charge of the situation. Abandoning the idea of trying to catch the receptionist's attention, she walked over to the lift and asked a porter for directions to the Queen Mary suite.

CHAPTER THREE

KADIR WALKED INTO his hotel suite and took a moment to appreciate the rare luxury of being completely alone. At the royal palace in Zenhab he was always surrounded by courtiers and government ministers, and a retinue of staff and security personnel accompanied him when he visited his various homes in Europe. Even while he had been staying here in a tiny village on the south coast of England he'd given in to pressure from his chief adviser and brought two security guards with him, as well as his private secretary and his manservant Walif, who, despite his seventy-one years, insisted on serving the Sultan as he had served Kadir's father.

Since his yachting accident two days ago, his staff had driven him mad with their concern for his well-being and, fond as he was of Walif, he had struggled to control his irritation when the manservant had flapped around him like a mother hen. Earlier today, Kadir's patience had finally snapped and he had sent everyone to his house in Windsor to wait for him.

The sense of freedom reminded him of how he felt when he raced his stallion Baha' across the desert with the cool wind whipping his face and a million stars studding the purple sky. Free from Walif's anxious concern for his health, he had spent two hours working out in the hotel gym.

The swelling above his eyebrow had almost disappeared, he noted, glancing in the bathroom mirror before he stepped into the shower cubicle. He had been lucky that the blow to his head from the sail boom had not knocked him unconscious, and even luckier that he had escaped from the capsized yacht with his life. Although it had not been luck, but the skill and bravery of the coastguard rescue crew, and especially the Flight Captain who had flown the helicopter in atrocious weather conditions.

Kadir pictured Lexi Howard's face. Her delicate features—the finely arched brows, defined cheekbones and perfect Cupid's bow lips—reminded him of the exquisite porcelain figurines in his grandmother's collection, which were displayed in a glass cabinet at Montgomery Manor. But the Flight Captain's fragile appearance was deceptive. He frowned, remembering her sharp voice and the dismissive way she had flicked her frosty blue eyes over him.

Immediately after he had been rescued from his doomed yacht, Kadir's pride had stung worse than his cracked skull. But now, with his equilibrium restored, he found Ms Howard's attitude refreshing. It had been a novelty to meet a woman who did not fawn on him or flirt with him. Too often he had found it too easy to persuade women into his bed. When he had been younger he had enjoyed being spoiled for choice, but a life without challenge was boring.

Lexi Howard was definitely a challenge. Desire kicked in Kadir's groin as he thought of the cool blonde beauty. He imagined teasing her mouth open with his tongue and tasting her. How long would it take to break through her reserve until she responded to him? he wondered, picturing her creamy complexion suffused with the rosy flush of sexual arousal.

Closing his eyes, he leaned back against the shower wall and visualised the icy, uptight Flight Captain melting beneath his hands. Slowly, he slid his hand down his body and stretched his fingers around his erection. He pictured Lexi Howard's capable hands on him, caressing him, stroking him lightly and then not so lightly... gripping him hard...

With a groan, he gave in to temptation and the urgent demands of his arousal. The cords in his neck stood out as he tipped his head back and the fire inside him became a furnace. His release came swiftly, awarding him momentary satisfaction that felt somehow incomplete.

But pleasuring himself was his only option, after the decision he had taken six months ago when his future bride had turned twenty-one and under Zenhabian law had become of marriageable age. Out of respect for Haleema, Kadir had ended his affairs with his European mistresses.

In the ten years that he had been Sultan of Zenhab he had been careful to avoid personal scandal in his desert kingdom, and had earned the support and respect of the population. It had been suggested to him by some of his advisers that monogamy was not a requirement of his arranged marriage as long as he was discreet, but he had every intention of fulfilling his role of husband to the best of his ability, to honour the promise he had made to his father.

Kadir had only been sixteen when Sultan Khalif had suffered a stroke that had left him a prisoner in his body—unable to walk, and with limited speech. Under Zenhabian law, the Sultan's brother had been made an interim ruler until the rightful heir came of age. But when Kadir had turned twenty-one, Jamal had been reluctant to hand over the Crown to his nephew, and he'd had support from tribal leaders in the mountain territories.

In order to claim the Crown from his uncle, Kadir had been forced to agree to marry the daughter of Jamal's strongest ally, Sheikh Rashid bin Al-Hassan. At the time he had signed the agreement, Haleema had been a child of eleven. But now she was twenty-one and, since the death of Sheikh Rashid two months ago, Kadir had come under increasing pressure from his uncle to set a date for his wedding. He knew he could not put if off for much longer. Haleema's family would consider a lengthy delay to be an insult to the princess of the mountain tribes, and Jamal—the most poisonous snake in Zenhab—would waste no time stirring up trouble that could threaten the stability of the country.

For the sake of Zenhab and for the love he felt for his father, Kadir would honour his duty. But there was a part of him that rebelled against the old ways of his kingdom. He had been educated in England and at university he had felt envious of his peers, who were free to live their lives without the burden of responsibility that had always been his destiny.

He had never even seen his future bride, but that would soon change. On his return to Zenhab he would travel to the mountains to meet Haleema's brother Omar, the new leader of the northern tribes, and begin formal proceedings for his marriage. He might even be permitted to meet Haleema, but according to the old customs he would not have an opportunity to be alone with her until she became his wife.

Kadir's thoughts turned once again to Flight Captain Lexi Howard. She had proved when she had rescued him and his crew that she was a highly skilled pilot, hence his decision to offer her a job as his private pilot in Zenhab. He knew it might be viewed as controversial to appoint a woman in what was considered by traditionalists to be a male role, but he fervently believed that his kingdom needed to modernise and accept that women were equal to men. The helicopter he had recently purchased would allow him to travel to Haleema's home in the mountainous northern territories more easily. And with that last thought of Haleema, his future had been decided for him ten years ago, he felt a sense that prison bars were closing around him.

Abruptly he switched off the shower, dried himself and pulled on a pair of trousers. Midway through shaving, he heard a knock on the door of the suite, which he ignored, forgetting that he had sent his staff away. Three impatient raps followed, and he cursed as the razor slipped in his hand and the blade nicked his chin. Grabbing a towel, he strode out of the bathroom and across the sitting room to fling open the door.

'Ms Howard! This is a surprise!'

Lexi frowned. 'Is it? I left a message with reception saying that I would be here at five.'

Kadir recalled that the phone had rung as he'd been on his way out of the door to go to the gym, but he hadn't bothered to answer it. 'I'm afraid I didn't receive any message,' he murmured.

How could his smile be so wickedly sexy? Lexi jerked her eyes from the sensual curve of his mouth and tried to ignore the fact that Sultan Kadir Al Sulaimar was half naked and had obviously just taken a shower. Droplets of water clung to the whorls of black hairs that grew thickly on his chest.

When she had rescued him, his body had been hidden beneath a bulky waterproof sailing suit. But now Lexi was faced with rippling muscles, gleaming olive-gold skin, broad, satin-smooth shoulders and his tight-as-a-drum abdomen.

Her eyes were drawn to the fuzz of black hairs that arrowed down from his navel and disappeared beneath the waistband of his trousers, which sat low on his hips. Her mouth suddenly felt dry. She lifted her gaze back to his face and her stomach swooped when she discovered that he was even more gorgeous than she remembered from their first meeting.

The combination of his lean, chiselled features and deep-set dark eyes was mesmerising. His mouth was full-lipped, and curved into a sultry smile that sent a tingle through Lexi's body. Her breath seemed to be trapped somewhere between her lungs and her throat. She needed to say something, anything to break the prickling silence that became more intense with every passing second so that she was sure he must be able to hear the loud thud of her heart.

She said the first thing that came into her head. 'You're bleeding…on your chin. No, closer to your lip…' She pointed, trying to direct him as he lifted the towel he was holding and pressed it against his face.

'I started shaving when I was fourteen. You'd think I'd be better at it by now,' he said ruefully. He thrust the towel at her. 'Will you play nurse?'

His voice was as sexy as his smile—deep and rich, caressing her senses and conjuring up images in her mind that were shockingly inappropriate.

'I should go,' she muttered. 'This is obviously not a convenient time...' Not when her heart was beating painfully fast. Lexi did not understand why he affected her so strongly. For ten years she had worked in a predominantly male environment and had met her fair share of good-looking men. *But none like him*, whispered a voice inside her head. Even his title—Sultan of Zenhab—was exotic and made her think of a desert oasis beneath a starry sky, a tent draped with silks, and him, naked, his bronzed, muscular body sprawled on satin cushions and his dark eyes gleaming as he beckoned to her to come to him.

Lexi swallowed. What on *earth* was the matter with her? She felt as though her body was on fire.

'You're not bothered by the sight of blood, are you?'

The amusement in his voice pulled her back from her erotic fantasy. Thank goodness he couldn't possibly have known what she had been thinking. His question jolted her mind back to her experiences of a real desert— the dry, unforgiving landscape, clouds of choking sand stirred up by the downdraught of the Chinook's rotor blades, the screams of wounded men, the smell of blood and dust and vomit.

'No, blood doesn't worry me,' she told him calmly, in control once more. The cut near to his bottom lip was still bleeding. She pressed the corner of the towel against his face and somehow, without her being aware that either of them had moved, she found herself inside his suite and he shut the door.

She immediately became conscious of how close they were standing. His warm breath whispered across her cheek and the mingled scents of soap, his spicy cologne and something more subtle—the sensual musk of maleness—stirred her senses. Her breasts brushed against his bare chest and the contact with his body sent a ripple of awareness through her.

Panic was an unfamiliar emotion for Lexi, but she was shaken by her reaction to the Sultan. She lifted the towel to see if the cut had stopped bleeding and saw that her hand was trembling. In Afghanistan, when she had flown behind enemy lines to pick up casualties, her nerves had been as steady as her hands on the helicopter's control stick. Why did this pampered playboy prince who had probably never done a day's work in his life disturb her?

Thankfully, the cut on his chin had closed up. She handed him the towel and stepped back from him. 'You'll live. I'm sure legions of women will be relieved,' she said drily.

His smile remained fixed, but Lexi sensed a sudden stillness in him that made her think of a panther about to pounce on its hapless prey. She reminded herself that the playboy was also a powerful Sultan who had kept peace in Zenhab despite the often volatile situation in other parts of the Middle East.

'Your sailing accident was widely reported in the press, Your Highness,' she murmured. In fact the tabloids had only carried a paragraph or two about his capsized yacht and had been more interested in reporting stories of his affairs with supermodels and actresses.

It wasn't as if she was in the least bit interested in a promiscuous womaniser, Lexi thought. She had only agreed to meet the Sultan because Roger Norris had asked her to.

'I understand that your yacht has been retrieved from where it sank in the Solent and it was discovered that the keel had been ripped from the hull.' She hesitated. 'I'm afraid I was rather hasty the other night when I jumped to the conclusion that you had ignored the reports of an approaching storm. I…apologise if my attitude was less than professional.'

Kadir just managed to stop himself from laughing out loud at Lexi Howard's grudging apology. She had spoken politely, but he sensed her reluctance to be here. It was obvious that she had been sent to see him, and it was easy to guess the real reason for her visit. Her next words confirmed his suspicion.

'Roger Norris explained that you have made a very generous offer to finance a second rescue helicopter.'

Kadir idly wondered if the coastguard commander had told Lexi to dress up for their meeting and perhaps try to persuade him to donate even more funds. Catching the cool expression in her eyes, he dismissed the idea. No one would dare tell Lexi Howard what to do—which made her choice of outfit interesting.

He ran his eyes over her, noting how the stretchy fabric of her dress moulded her toned figure and emphasised the shape of her firm breasts. The dress stopped at mid-thigh-level and below the hemline her slender legs, sheathed in sheer black hose, looked even longer with the addition of three-inch stiletto heels. Recalling his erotic fantasies about her while he'd been in the shower, Kadir felt the simmering heat in his gut burn hotter.

'The least I can do is to make a contribution to the rescue agency responsible for saving my life and the lives of my crew,' he said abruptly. 'I must also apologise, Captain Howard, for not thanking you for your skill and bravery after the rescue the other night. I am conscious that I owe you a huge debt of gratitude.'

'I was simply doing my job,' she muttered.

'I understand from Roger Norris that you no longer work for the coastguard agency.'

'My contract was only for a year. Although, if there is to be a second rescue helicopter, I might get my job back.'

'But you don't have another job to go to at the moment?' Kadir knew he was staring at Lexi but he could not help himself. She was so damned beautiful! He cleared his throat. 'I asked you to meet me because I have a proposition I want to discuss with you.'

'What kind of proposition?' The gleam of sexual interest in his eyes, and memories of the stories in the newspapers about his playboy lifestyle, sent Lexi's imagination into overdrive.

Kadir was irritated that Lexi obviously believed the garbage which had been written about him in the tabloids. But she was not nearly as composed as she would like him to think. Her breathing was shallow and the downwards sweep of her long eyelashes was too late to hide her dilated pupils. He roamed his eyes over her in a slow, deliberate appraisal, and was rewarded when the hard points of her nipples became clearly discernible beneath her clingy dress.

Suddenly he understood, and a feeling of satisfaction swept through him. He had seen her scornful expression when she'd referred to the reports of his alleged playboy lifestyle. Most of the stories about his private life, which had been printed alongside the news of his yachting accident, were either rehashed from years ago or greatly exaggerated. Kadir had felt no inclination to defend himself to Lexi, but he'd been annoyed by her readiness to judge him.

Now, as he watched her cross her arms defensively

over her breasts, he realised that the waves of antagonism she had been sending out were a frantic attempt to disguise the fact that she was attracted to him. Perhaps she hoped that her frosty attitude disguised her sexual awareness of him, but Kadir *knew*—just as he always knew when a woman was interested in him. He had played the game of chasing women who wanted to be caught too often, he thought cynically.

But this time the rules were different. When he returned to Zenhab he would honour the promise he had made to his father and marry the bride who had been chosen for him. Although he desired the Flight Captain, he had no intention of actually catching her. But Lexi did not know that!

'Why don't we sit down,' he murmured, 'and make ourselves comfortable?'

Lexi swallowed as she watched the Sultan lower himself onto the sofa. He stretched his arms along the back, drawing her attention to his bare torso. His broad shoulders gleamed like burnished copper in the golden autumn sunshine slanting through the window, and his chest and forearms were covered in a fine mat of silky black hairs that accentuated his raw masculinity.

Conscious that her heart was thudding uncomfortably fast, she made a show of checking her watch. 'I really must be going. I expect you want to finish getting dressed,' she said pointedly, 'and I have to be somewhere at seven-thirty, and I want to hit the motorway before the evening traffic builds up.'

'Do you have a date this evening? And there I was thinking you had worn that very sexy dress especially to meet me,' Kadir drawled.

Lexi flushed. 'It is not a sexy dress,' she said tightly.

'It's a cocktail dress suitable for a cocktail party to cel-ebrate my sister's engagement.' The idea that the Sultan assumed she'd dressed up for him was infuriating but, to her shame, she felt a frisson of awareness shoot through her when his dark eyes gleamed with a hard brilliance.

'Surely you don't have to leave just yet if the party doesn't start for another two hours?' To Lexi's conster-nation, he sprang up from the sofa and walked over to her, moving with the speed and grace of a jungle cat. He was too close and towered over her so that she had to tilt her head to meet his intent gaze. Heat radiated from his body, or maybe the heat came from her, making her feel flushed and flustered and acutely aware of her femininity.

Desperate to hide the effect he had on her, she launched into an explanation. 'The journey to Henley-on-Thames, which is where my sister's fiancé's parents live, will take over an hour, and I daren't risk being late and upsetting Lady Fairfax.'

Lexi frowned as she recalled how tense her sister had sounded on the phone. Athena had confided her worry that Charles's parents did not approve of their son's choice of bride because they had hoped he would marry some-one with a similar aristocratic pedigree to the Fairfaxes. 'The engagement party is my chance to prove that I can be a good wife to Charlie and a sophisticated hostess when he invites business clients to dinner,' Athena had said earnestly.

Lexi had struggled to picture her accident-prone sister as a sophisticated hostess, but she had kept her doubts that Charles Fairfax was the right man for Athena to herself.

Her thoughts scattered when Sultan Kadir spoke. His deep, dark voice curled around her like a lover's caress.

She caught her breath as he lifted his hand and brushed the back of his knuckles oh-so-lightly down her cheek. It was a blatant invasion of her personal space but her feet seemed to be rooted to the floor and she could not step away from him.

'I am disappointed that you must rush away before we've had a chance to discuss my proposal. Perhaps we can arrange to meet again at a more convenient time?'

She licked her dry lips and told herself she was imagining the predatory gleam in his eyes. 'Your Highness...' Her voice sounded strangely breathless.

'Please call me Kadir, Lexi.'

The way he said her name, with that soft huskiness in his voice, was too intimate, as if he had stroked each syllable with his tongue.

Lexi felt as though she was drowning in his molten gaze, but a tiny part of her sanity remained and asked why she was letting him get to her. He was a notorious womaniser, and in the past when other men like him had tried to come on to her she'd had no trouble shooting them down.

Of course she would not allow herself to be seduced by the Sultan, she assured herself. But she could not deny that his interest was flattering and a salve to her wounded pride after Steven's betrayal. Without conscious thought, she swayed towards Kadir, bringing her mouth even closer to his. Her heart pounded and her eyelashes swept down as she waited, tense with anticipation, for him to brush his lips over hers.

'You've been a long time in the shower. I've been getting bored waiting for you.'

Lexi froze and jerked her head towards the petulant female voice. Shock slithered like an ice cube down her spine when she saw a woman standing in the doorway that connected the sitting room and bedroom. Through the open door she could see a big bed with rumpled sheets. The woman—girl—was no more than seventeen. Lexi recognised she was Tania Stewart, daughter of the local yacht club president Derek Stewart, who also owned the Admiralty Hotel.

Tania frowned at Lexi. 'What are you doing here?' She turned her wide-eyed gaze to the Sultan and allowed the sheet that was draped around her body to slip down, revealing her bare breasts. 'Don't keep me waiting any longer, Kadir,' she murmured in a sex kitten voice that somehow emphasised how painfully young she was.

'Go and put some clothes on, Tania.' In contrast, Kadir spoke in a clipped tone that was as coldly regal as his expression, Lexi noted, when she looked at him.

She instantly grasped the situation—it didn't take a genius to work out what was going on—and she felt sick at her stupidity. How could she have almost been taken in by the playboy prince's charisma? It stung her pride to realise that she had no more sense than the silly girl who had just crawled out of his bed.

She glanced at Tania and back to Kadir. The reason he was half undressed in the afternoon was now abundantly clear and she supposed she should be thankful that he had pulled on a pair of trousers before he'd opened the door to her.

'Forgive me, Your Highness, for not staying around to discuss your proposition, but I'm not into threesomes,' she said, her voice as biting as a nuclear winter.

His only response was to lift his eyebrows as if he found her reaction amusing.

Lexi's temper simmered. She looked at Tania, who

had at least draped the sheet more strategically around her naked body, and back at Kadir. 'You bastard. She's just a kid. Is that how you get your kicks?'

His eyes glittered with anger, but Lexi did not give him a chance to speak. She despised him, and at that moment she despised herself for her weakness. Dear heaven, she had actually wanted him to kiss her! Even now, as she wheeled away from him and marched across the room, her legs trembled and she had to fight the urge to turn her head and look at him one last time, to imprint his outrageously gorgeous facial features on her mind. Pride prevailed and she walked out of the door, closing it with a decisive snap behind her.

CHAPTER FOUR

Kadir watched Lexi Howard across the ballroom and felt a slow burn of desire in the pit of his stomach. She was startlingly beautiful, and he noticed that many of the other party guests glanced at her more than once. There was something almost ethereal about her ash-blonde hair, swept up into a chignon tonight, and her peaches and cream complexion. Her fine bone structure, with those high cheekbones, was simply exquisite. She was an English rose, combining cool elegance with understated sensuality in her short black dress and her endlessly long legs and high-heeled black shoes.

If he was a betting man he would lay money that she was wearing stockings. Kadir's nostrils flared as he visualised her wrapping her legs around his back, wearing the stockings and stilettos—and nothing else!

He frowned and altered his position in an effort to ease the hard throb of his arousal. It was a long time since he'd felt so intensely turned on by a woman, especially by a woman who clearly disliked him. In fact it had never happened to him before. Since his youth, women had thrown themselves at him.

Perhaps it was simply the novelty of Lexi Howard's frosty attitude that intrigued him. His mind flew to those few moments in his hotel room when he had nearly kissed her. What had started out as an amusing game had quickly and unexpectedly turned into something darker and hotter when he'd seen the invitation in her eyes.

He wondered what would have happened if the teenager Tania Stewart, who had followed him around like a lovesick puppy while he had been staying at her father's hotel, had not made her spectacular appearance. Kadir knew he would have covered Lexi's mouth with his and tasted her—and she would have let him. Instead, she had treated him like a pariah. His jaw clenched. The scalding fury that had been responsible for him gunning his sports car up the motorway still simmered inside him like the smouldering embers of a fire.

'I see you're looking at my future sister-in-law.'

Kadir's bland expression gave away none of his thoughts as he turned his head towards the man standing beside him. Charles Fairfax's face had the ruddy hue of a man who was on his fifth gin punch, even though it was still early in the evening. 'I'd better warn you, old man. You won't get any joy there. A couple of my friends have tried and reported that Lexi Howard is a frigid bitch. It's no surprise her fiancé dumped her. The guy was lucky the ice queen didn't freeze his balls off.' Charles laughed, evidently finding his schoolboy attempt at humour funny.

Charles had always been a pain in the backside when they had been at school, Kadir mused, fixing a smile on his lips to disguise his temptation to rearrange Charles's nondescript features with his fist. In truth, he was puzzled by his violent reaction to the Englishman's crude comments, and his desire to defend Lexi Howard. At Eton College he had never considered Charles Fairfax to be a close friend but, thanks to social media, he had remained in touch with many of his fellow students from his school days. Networking was always useful, and when Lexi had mentioned her sister's engagement party Kadir had known that there was only one Lord and Lady Fairfax living in Henley-on-Thames.

His eyes strayed across the room to where Lexi was chatting to a petite woman with a mass of dark brown hair and wearing a dress in an unflattering shade of acid-yellow. It was curious that the Howard sisters were so unalike, he thought.

He saw Lexi glance around the room and stiffen when she noticed him. From across the ballroom he felt waves of hostility emanating from her, challenging him, exciting him. Kadir felt his heart jolt against his ribs. He held Lexi's gaze as he raised his glass to her, before he sipped his Virgin Mary, feeling the peppery warmth of the drink heat his blood.

'Do you think I look fat in this dress? I wish I could wear black like you but it makes my skin look sallow.'

Lexi forced her mind from the humiliating spectacle that had taken place in Sultan Kadir of Zenhab's hotel suite earlier and concentrated on her sister. 'You look lovely,' she said, in what she hoped was a convincing voice.

Athena's face brightened. 'Lady Fairfax helped me to choose my dress. She said the colour suits me.'

'Did she?' Lexi suspected that Charles Fairfax's mother had her reasons for persuading Athena to wear the ghastly yellow satin dress. Charles was her only son and would eventually become the next Lord Fairfax, and Lexi had overheard several party guests comment that

Charles's parents wished him to marry a woman with a title.

Athena fiddled with the large satin bow on her shoulder. 'I wish I looked elegant and sophisticated like you,' she blurted. 'You would be a much better wife for Charlie than me. You would know how to talk to people at dinner parties, and you'd never spill your wine or drop your spoon into the soup. I'm so clumsy. Sometimes I think Charlie finds me an embarrassment.'

Lexi frowned. 'You can't help being short-sighted. Charlie should be more supportive. Presumably he asked you to marry him because he loves you, not because he wants you to be his unpaid social hostess.' She gave her sister an exasperated look and was tempted to ask Athena why she had agreed to marry Charles, who was a wimp with a distinctly spiteful side to his nature. 'To be honest, I'm not convinced that he's the right man for you.'

'Maybe you're jealous that I'm getting married and you're not.' Athena bit her lip. 'I'm sorry, Lexi. That was a horrible thing to say. It's just that since you broke up with Steven you've pushed people away more than ever, including Mum and Dad...and me.'

'I was over Steven a long time ago,' Lexi said curtly. 'I don't push people away.' She remembered the coastguard commander Roger Norris's comment that she came across as intimidating. 'I admit I'm independent, but I had to be when I was growing up. I always knew I had been adopted, but you are Marcus and Veronica's own daughter and it was natural that they doted on you.'

Athena looked as though she was going to cry and Lexi silently cursed her runaway tongue. It wasn't her sister's fault that she had been the favourite child.

'Mum and Dad are really proud of you, and they're

always telling people that you were a pilot in the RAF and received an award for bravery for your work in Afghanistan. They wanted to catch up with you tonight, but they couldn't make the party because their cruise was booked ages ago.

'I'm sure Mum and Dad wish I was as clever as you,' Athena admitted. 'They are both doctors and I suppose they naturally assumed I would be academic like them. They even named me after the Greek goddess of wisdom, for heaven's sake! I know they were disappointed when I failed to get the grades to go to university. At least they're pleased that I'm going to marry Charlie and I'll be Lady Fairfax one day.'

'You can't marry him just to win parental approval.'

'I'm not… Of course I love him,' Athena insisted, too earnestly, in Lexi's opinion. But she did not voice her concerns. Her sister was an adult and perfectly able to decide who she wanted to marry. In truth, Lexi was surprised that Athena had confided in her. The close bond they had shared as children had faded when Lexi had been sent away to boarding school.

She looked around the room. 'Where is Charlie, anyway? This is your engagement party but I haven't seen him all evening.'

'Oh, he's with one of his old school friends from Eton. Charlie was so surprised when Earl Montgomery phoned out of the blue earlier this evening and said he would like to catch up on old times. Naturally, Charlie immediately invited him to the party. I think they must still be in the library.' Athena squinted around the room. 'Oh, look, they're over by the bar. The Earl is very good-looking, don't you think? But don't tell Charlie I said so, will you?' she said worriedly.

Lexi could not reply. She felt as though her breath had been squeezed out of her lungs as she stared across the room and saw Sultan Kadir Al Sulaimar's mouth curl into a mocking smile. What the hell was he doing here at her sister's engagement party, pretending to be a member of the British aristocracy? She frowned. He couldn't be an imposter because Athena had said he had been at Eton with Charlie. But it was too much of a coincidence that the Sultan, or Earl or whatever he was, had decided to call up his old school friend tonight of all nights.

It was impossible not to compare the two men as they approached. Charles, sandy-haired and weak-chinned, was at least five inches shorter than his companion. But it wasn't only Sultan Kadir's height that set him apart from every other man in the room. He was like an exotic bird of paradise among a flock of pigeons, Lexi thought. His olive-gold skin gleamed beneath the sparkling chandeliers, and his hot chocolate eyes were slumberous and sensual, promising wicked delights that turned Lexi's insides to liquid. The last time she'd seen him he had been half-undressed, but he was no less devastating wearing a black dinner suit that had been expertly tailored to sheath his muscular body.

She hid her fierce tension behind a cool smile as Charlie made introductions, but the glint in Sultan Kadir's eyes told her he was aware of her reluctance to shake his hand; he clasped her fingers for a fraction too long and watched with interest the jerky rise and fall of her breasts as she sucked in a breath.

Lexi could not bring herself to allude to their earlier meeting at his hotel. She shuddered at the memory of how she had swayed towards him and practically begged him to kiss her. She wanted to believe that even if Tania had not interrupted them she would have come to her senses before anything had happened, but her pounding heart mocked that idea.

She affected a puzzled expression. 'I'm sure I recognise you from the newspapers and have read of your many exploits, but your name is not familiar.'

Charlie was quick to explain. 'Earl Montgomery is His Royal Highness Sultan Kadir Al Sulaimar of Zenhab.'

Lexi ignored her future brother-in-law as her eyes locked with the Sultan's. 'Should I address you as Your Royal Highness or My Lord?' she asked, mockingly deferential. She saw amusement and something darker and more dangerous in his intent gaze. The air between them was charged with an electrical current that made every nerve ending on Lexi's body tingle.

'I insist that you call me Kadir, Lexi.' His sexy accent lingered on each syllable of her name. He smiled, showing his white teeth, and a quiver shot through Lexi as she imagined him nipping her throat and the soft flesh of her earlobe. 'I find it is unwise to believe everything printed in the newspapers,' he murmured. 'So often, stories are reported incorrectly or are blatantly untrue.'

'That's a little unfair to journalists. I'm sure most press reports are properly researched and presented.' She thought of all those women who had revealed intimate details of their affairs with His Royal Hotness. Some of the stories must be true.

The sound of a gong rang through the ballroom, shattering the tense atmosphere.

'Charlie and I are supposed to lead everyone into the dining room for the buffet,' Athena explained. She slipped her arm through her fiancé's and promptly tripped on the hem of her long skirt, earning an impatient tut from Charles Fairfax.

Kadir offered his arm to Lexi. 'May I escort you to dinner?'

It was impossible to refuse without causing a scene, but she glared at him as she placed her hand stiffly on his arm and he drew her closer so that her thigh brushed against his as they walked into the dining room.

'How dare you...*infiltrate* my sister's engagement party,' she hissed.

His wide shoulders shook with laughter. 'It would have been bad manners to refuse an invitation from an old school friend.'

'You didn't worry about manners when you came on to me while your girlfriend—with emphasis on the word *girl*—was in the next room.' That wiped the smug smile from his face, she noted with satisfaction.

He dipped his head close to hers. 'Let's get something straight.' His voice was suddenly harsh. The charismatic playboy prince had disappeared and Lexi had a sense that Sultan Kadir Al Sulaimar was a powerful man and a dangerous threat to her peace of mind. 'I did not invite Tania Stewart to my suite and definitely not into my bed. I was as surprised as you were when she walked out of the bedroom.'

Lexi wondered why she believed him. 'Not that I care how you conduct your private life, or with whom, but, out of curiosity, how was Tania in your room if you didn't invite her in?'

'She admitted she'd taken the pass key from the cleaner's office. Her father owns the hotel and she knows where things are kept. When you saw her you immediately leapt to the conclusion that she and I were lovers.'

'She *was* naked under that sheet,' Lexi defended herself. She found she was unable to tear her eyes from Kadir's smouldering gaze.

'Forget Tania. This is about you and me.'

'There is no *you and me*!' She wished she could control her racing pulse. 'I'm not the slightest bit interested in you, Earl Montgomery, or Sultan of Zenhab, or whatever other fancy title I'm supposed to call you.'

'Kadir,' he said softly. 'Why are you uptight about saying my name?'

'I'm *not* uptight.' Glancing around her, Lexi flushed when she realised that her raised voice had attracted curious glances from the other guests.

The amused gleam in his eyes told her he was aware that she felt churned up inside and quite unlike her usual self. 'Perhaps later tonight we will have a chance to discuss my proposition.'

'I've told you I'm not interested in your proposition.'

'How do you know, when you don't know what it is?'

'Knowing of your reputation as a playboy, I have no qualms about turning down your proposition without hearing any of the sordid details,' Lexi said tartly.

Satisfied that she'd had the last word, she turned her back on him and began to select food from the buffet even though her appetite had disappeared. To her relief, Charlie returned to monopolise Kadir's attention and she was able to slip away to a quiet corner and forced down a couple of vol-au-vents filled with a cream cheese mixture that tasted overpoweringly of chopped herbs.

She brooded on her conversation with her sister. Athena—like the coastguard commander, Roger Norris—had accused her of putting up barriers to prevent people getting too close to her. It wasn't deliberate, but subconsciously, perhaps, her wariness of being rejected *did* make her appear remote and self-contained, Lexi acknowledged. She had learned from a young age that the only person she could rely on, the only person she could trust, was herself. When she had served with the RAF she'd learned to trust the professionalism of the people she worked with. But when she *had* lowered her guard with Steven Cromer and followed her heart instead of her head, his rejection had been hurtful and humiliating; she was in no hurry to experience either of those emotions again.

Waiters were circling the room offering glasses of champagne to toast the newly engaged couple. Lexi opted for iced water, hoping she would soon be able to slip away from the party and drive to West London, where she had arranged to stay at a friend's flat while she looked for another job. She sipped the water, but her throat still felt dry and scratchy and the headache that had started five minutes ago was rapidly becoming worse.

Lord Fairfax called for silence and proceeded to give a lengthy speech about how delighted he and his wife were to announce their son's engagement. Lady Fairfax's delight was not apparent on her haughty features, Lexi noted. Charlie looked bored and Athena was tense and had spilled something down the front of her dress.

'What does your sister see in an oaf like Charles Fairfax, apart from his money and title?' The husky drawl close to her ear brought a flush of heat to Lexi's face. She shot Kadir a glowering look and winced as the sudden movement sent a shooting pain through her skull.

'Athena isn't like that,' she said curtly, not about to admit to a stranger her own doubts about her sister's choice of husband. 'She loves Charlie.' She frowned. 'I thought he was your friend. Why else would you accept an invitation to his engagement party?'

'I knew you would be here.'

He was serious, Lexi realised. The smouldering sensuality in Kadir's eyes made her catch her breath. She looked away from him and tried to control her frantic heartbeat. But her chest felt constricted and her shortness of breath was not entirely down to her acute awareness of him. In the last few minutes she had begun to feel nauseous and strangely light-headed, as if she was drunk, except that she hadn't had a drop of alcohol all evening. She swayed on legs that suddenly seemed unable to support her.

'Are you all right? You've gone a strange colour.' Kadir's voice sounded from a long way off. Lexi closed her eyes to stop the room from spinning. She could feel beads of sweat on her brow, and she suddenly knew what was wrong with her. To her horror, she realised that she was going to be sick in front of a room full of onlookers.

She blinked and Kadir's handsome face swam before her eyes. He was the last person she would turn to for help, but she was feeling worse by the second and she had no choice but to abandon her pride. 'Please,' she muttered. 'Please...get me out of here.'

He gave her a sharp look and growled something beneath his breath, then the room spun, Lexi's head spun, as he scooped her up into his arms. She sensed everyone was watching them as Kadir strode past the curious guests and she heard Charlie Fairfax say loudly, 'She's obviously had too much to drink.' Kadir tightened his arms around her and Lexi, who had never been carried by a man in her entire adult life, rested her head on his chest and listened to the steady thud of his heart.

Athena dashed into the hall after them, looking anxious. 'Lexi… Lady Fairfax has just told me that the vol-au-vent filling contained prawns. You didn't eat any, did you?'

'Unfortunately, your warning is too late,' Lexi muttered drily. Noticing Kadir's puzzled expression, she explained, 'I have a shellfish allergy.' Her voice became urgent. 'I need to get to a bathroom—*quickly.*'

At first, when Lexi opened her eyes and did not recognise her surroundings, she wondered if she was in a bedroom at the Fairfax home, Woodley Lodge. Vague snatches of memory floated into her mind of sitting in a car and travelling very fast. She remembered that the car had stopped at least once and she had been ill by the side of the road. There were other memories of strong arms around her, supporting her while she had been sick, a cool hand stroking her hair back from her hot brow.

Where the hell was she? Ignoring the fact that she felt like a limp rag, Lexi sat up and froze as she pushed back the sheets and discovered that someone had removed her dress, leaving her in her sheer lace black bra and matching thong.

Kadir had rescued her from the ignominy of being ill in front of the guests at her sister's engagement party. Had he driven her to wherever this place was—a hotel, perhaps—and undressed her? She glanced around the bedroom, noting the floral wallpaper and an oil painting of a horse hanging above the antique dressing table. The décor of slightly old-fashioned elegance did not feel like she was in a hotel.

Her legs felt weak when she made the short journey into the en suite bathroom and a glance in the mirror revealed that she looked as washed out as she felt. There was a toothbrush among the toiletries on the vanity unit and she felt marginally better once she'd brushed her teeth and pulled a comb through her hair. Walking back into the bedroom, she stopped dead and stared wordlessly at Kadir.

'I knocked but you didn't answer, so I thought I'd better check on you.' His dark eyes drifted over her, bringing a tinge of colour to Lexi's wan face. 'How are you feeling?'

Vulnerable, but no way would she admit it to him. 'Better.' She instinctively crossed her arms over her breasts, wishing she had pulled on the towelling robe that she'd noticed hanging on the bathroom door. 'At the risk of sounding like a corny line from a film, where am I?'

'My English home, Montgomery Manor. Windsor is less than half an hour's drive from Henley-on-Thames, although it took longer to get here last night because you needed me to pull over a couple of times.'

Lexi felt mortified that he had seen her at her most undignified, throwing up in a gutter.

'Did you undress me?' she asked curtly. She had a hazy recollection of being carried up a flight of stairs and placed on a bed, and she remembered feeling her zip being drawn down her spine and the sensation of cool air on her body as her dress was removed.

'There you go, jumping to conclusions again, like you did about Tania,' Kadir said mockingly, but Lexi heard anger in his tone. 'You were so ill you couldn't even walk. Do you think I took advantage of your defenceless state to strip you…and do what—look at you, touch you?'

She bit her lip. 'I had a particularly bad reaction to shellfish last night. I don't remember much after you car-

ried me out of the Fairfaxes' house. All I know is that
someone took my dress off. I recall that someone stayed
with me and gave me some water.' Someone had slipped
an arm around her and held a glass of water to her lips.
She remembered gentle hands wiping a cool flannel over
her feverish brow.

'My housekeeper put you into bed and took your dress
away to be cleaned.' He shrugged. 'I called my doctor
and explained your symptoms, and he advised me to stay
with you until you'd stopped being sick.' His jaw hardened. 'Believe me, helping you to the bathroom a dozen
times did not send me into a frenzy of sexual excitement.'

Kadir watched a stain of colour run along her high
cheekbones and some of his anger abated. There were
dark circles beneath her eyes and she looked fragile, but
he sensed she would hate showing any sign of weakness.
He had never met a woman who infuriated and intrigued
him as much as Lexi Howard did.

It was a long time since he had been so turned on by
a woman, he acknowledged. He was even beginning to
question his plans to employ the Flight Captain as his
private pilot. But the truth was that she was exactly what
he needed and he would have to ignore his inconvenient
throb of desire and try to forget that the uptight Ms Howard had a penchant for skimpy, sexy underwear.

Last night, when she had been sick for hour after hour,
he had been more concerned about persuading her to take
sips of water to prevent her from becoming dehydrated,
as the doctor had instructed, and he'd barely noticed that
she was almost naked.

But he noticed now.

When she had emerged from the bathroom, his eyes
had been drawn to her nipples, clearly visible through her

bra, and the shadow of blonde hair beneath the tiny triangle of semi-transparent material between her legs. He had been right about her wearing stockings. They were held up by wide bands of black lace around the tops of her thighs. Kadir's pulse quickened and he dragged his eyes from her, feeling like a voyeur, or an excited teenage boy seeing a naked woman for the first time.

In a bid to ease the throb of his arousal he walked over to the window and pretended to be fascinated by the view of Windsor Great Park. 'Your dress isn't ready yet,' he said abruptly, 'so I brought one of my shirts for you to wear. It's on the bed.'

'Thank you.' Lexi hurried across the room and snatched up the shirt. It was much too big, and as she did up the buttons she felt marginally less exposed now that her underwear was hidden. She had only worn a seamless bra and thong so that they wouldn't show under her clingy dress. Kadir would have completely the wrong idea about her. She wasn't a flighty, flirty type of woman who dressed to impress men. She was sensible, serious—*boring*, taunted a little voice inside her head.

'As a matter of fact, all my clothes are in the boot of my car. After the party, I'd planned to drive to London to stay at a friend's flat.'

'I sent a couple of my staff over to Woodley Lodge to pick up your car.'

'Thank you,' Lexi repeated stiffly. 'I'm sorry to be such a nuisance.'

She looked across the room to where he was standing, half turned away from her so that she could see his proud profile. A weakness invaded her limbs that had nothing to do with her being ill the previous night. Dressed in faded jeans that moulded his firm thighs and buttocks and a cream cashmere sweater that accentuated his exotic olive-gold skin, he was the epitome of masculine perfection. Any woman would find him attractive, she consoled herself. Nevertheless, it was irritating to realise that she was no different to those women in the tabloids who had proudly described every intimate detail of their affairs with the playboy prince of the desert.

She thought about how he had stayed with her during the previous night and taken care of her when she had been ill. Perhaps there was more to him than his reputation as a jet-setting philanderer gave him credit for.

'Thanks for rescuing me from the party last night,' she said awkwardly. 'I guess that makes us even.'

'It's hardly the same thing. You saved my life.' Kadir swung round and gave her a brooding look. 'In fact, events have worked in my favour because now you are trapped here in my home, which gives us an opportunity to discuss my proposition.'

Needing a distraction from the realisation that without her car or clothes she could not leave Montgomery Manor, Lexi asked curiously, 'How are you an English Earl *and* the Sultan of Zenhab?'

'My mother is English. She met my father when he came to England to buy a racehorse from the Montgomery stud farm, and after a whirlwind courtship she married him and went to Zenhab as his Sultana. Unfortunately, my mother wasn't cut out for life in a remote desert kingdom far away from Bond Street,' Kadir said drily. 'My parents split up when I was seven and I continued to live with my father, but I visited my mother and grandparents regularly and went to school in England. When my grandfather, the tenth Earl, died, the title and estate passed to me. However, I do not spend as much time here as perhaps I should. It was my destiny to rule Zenhab.'

But there was a price to his destiny, Kadir thought heavily. To claim the Crown from his uncle, he had been forced to agree to an arranged marriage. His jaw clenched. It was time for him to honour his promise. This trip to Europe would be his last as a single man, and on his return to Zenhab he would set a date for his wedding.

The prospect felt like a lead weight inside him. He tried telling himself that most men faced with imminent marriage, even to a woman they loved, would feel a sense of panic. He did not love his future bride; he had never met her. But until three days ago he had been resigned to fulfilling his duty.

Why was it that since he had met Lexi Howard he had felt a sense that prison bars were closing around him, sealing his fate? Perhaps it was because she was off-limits. He had never denied himself a woman before, he thought derisively. Maybe the knowledge that he could not allow the simmering sexual chemistry that existed between them to ignite was the reason for the raw feeling inside him, the curious longing for something he could not define or explain.

He stared unseeingly out of the window while he struggled to bring his emotions under control. His desire for Lexi was irrelevant. It had occurred to him that it would be a good idea to employ a female helicopter pilot to fly his future bride around Zenhab. He knew that Haleema would only be permitted to travel to the palace accompanied by a chaperone, meaning that he would have no chance to meet privately the woman with whom he must spend the rest of his life.

Employing a female helicopter pilot would negate the

necessity for Haleema to have a chaperone, and perhaps there might be an opportunity for him to establish a rapport with the princess of the mountain tribes who would rule Zenhab with him and bear his children.

He swung round, and his eyes were as hard as his heart as he stared at Lexi. 'The proposition that I want to discuss with you is this. I want you to come to Zenhab and work for me as my private helicopter pilot.'

CHAPTER FIVE

HE WANTED HER to be his pilot! Lexi's face grew warm as she recalled how she had put a very different interpretation on Kadir's proposition. In her wild imagination she had even thought that he might suggest that they become lovers. Desperate to hide her embarrassment, she said crisply, 'Why me? You must have pilots in Zenhab.'

'Of course, but none of the military pilots who belong to the royal household are trained to fly the model of helicopter that I have bought. What I'm proposing is a six-month contract, during which time you will be my personal pilot and driver, and you will also instruct pilots from the Zenhabian air force on how to fly the AgustaWestland.

'You are ideal for the job,' Kadir insisted. 'Initially, when you joined the RAF, you were a chauffeur for the Commanding Officer of an air force base before you went on to train as a pilot. You flew an AW169 for the coastguard agency and know the helicopter inside out. In Afghanistan you were awarded a Distinguished Flying Cross for rescuing injured soldiers under fire.'

'You've certainly done your homework,' she said drily.

More than she knew, Kadir mused. Apart from her impressive military record, his security team had dug up a few other interesting facts about her, including the fact that she owed a significant amount of money to various credit card companies. The first time he had met her, he had formed the opinion that Lexi Howard liked to be in control. The news that she had money problems had surprised him, but it worked in his favour.

'Naturally, the salary I am prepared to pay will reflect your flying experience and expertise.'

The figure Kadir named made Lexi blink. Her job with the coastguard agency had been well paid, but she hadn't earned in a year what Kadir was offering for six months' work. The money was tempting, she acknowledged, because it would allow her to pay off the debts that her birth mother had accrued.

Lexi thought of the woman who had given her away when she had been a few days old. Ten years ago, with the help of the adoption agency, she had found her birth mother. But her dream of an emotional reunion had been disappointing. Cathy Barnes had bluntly admitted that she had been a teenager when she had given birth to Lexi, but she hadn't wanted a baby. *I don't know your father's name. I didn't ask names. I just met clients in hotel rooms and they paid me for what they wanted. They were mostly businessmen with fat expense accounts to blow.*

Lexi still remembered how shocked she had felt when Cathy had revealed that she had been working as a prostitute when she had fallen pregnant.

A few years after she had given Lexi up for adoption Cathy had married, but to this day she had never told her husband that she had a daughter.

It was painful for Lexi to know that she was her birth mother's shameful secret. She met Cathy sporadically and their relationship was friendly rather than close. But six months ago Cathy had revealed that she had terminal cancer and had broken down as she'd explained that her husband was unaware that she owed a fortune on credit cards. Seeing her mother's distress had tugged on Lexi's heart, especially as Cathy did not have long to live. To spare her mother further worry, she had arranged for the debts to be transferred onto her own credit card.

'What is your answer? I don't believe you will find a better job offer than mine.' Kadir's voice tugged Lexi's mind back to the present.

She couldn't disagree with him—it was a darned good job offer, and she needed a job. So why was she hesitating?

She had a sudden flashback to those moments in his hotel suite when he had almost kissed her. The spicy scent of his aftershave had intoxicated her senses, just as it was doing now, she thought. Her nerves jangled as she watched him walk towards her, and her heart thudded erratically as her eyes were drawn to his mouth and she remembered the taste of his warm breath on her lips.

A quiver of sexual desire shot through her body, so intense that it took her breath away. She did not want to want him, and she certainly did not want him to finish what he had started at his hotel, she assured herself.

'My new helicopter was manufactured here in England and is ready for collection,' Kadir explained. 'I plan to be in Europe for another week to attend a number of business meetings before I return to Zenhab.'

'The AW doesn't have the range to fly long-haul.'

'A plane from my Royal Fleet will transport the chopper to Zenhab. I assume you are able to start work immediately?'

'I haven't actually agreed to take the job,' Lexi reminded him.

He assumed way too much, she thought as she watched his heavy brows snap together in a frown. It seemed safe to assume that the Sultan was used to having his own way. 'What about accommodation in Zenhab?' she asked abruptly. 'Where would I live?'

'At the royal palace. I will need you to be available at all times.'

Lexi was annoyed when she felt herself blush, and she wondered if Kadir was deliberately playing with words to make her feel flustered.

'You will be allocated a suite of rooms at the palace with access to a private garden and pool, and my staff will do their utmost to fulfil all your needs. All you will have to do is fly my helicopter, and spend a lot of time relaxing in the Zenhabian sunshine. You know, I can't help thinking that maybe we got off to a bad start,' Kadir murmured.

Lexi's brows lifted. 'Whatever gave you that idea?' she said drily.

His mouth crooked into a sensual smile that caused the heat inside Lexi to burn hotter.

'Can we start again—as friends? I've seen that you are an excellent pilot, and I would very much like you to work for me, Lexi.'

She would be a fool to turn this job and high salary down. All she had to do was spend six months in his desert kingdom—at a royal palace. How hard could it be compared to a dusty military camp in Afghanistan? Lexi asked herself. A traitorous thought slid into her head that the palace staff could not fulfil *all* her needs—followed by the even more treacherous thought that undoubtedly the playboy Sultan *could*!

But she would never be any man's plaything. She would never be a rich man's whore like her birth mother had been.

Whatever had happened in the past, Cathy needed her now, Lexi reminded herself. Had she offered to help her birth mother because she subconsciously hoped that Cathy would love her enough so that she would publicly recognise the daughter she had kept secret for nearly thirty years? Deep inside Lexi there was still the little girl who had studied a family photograph and wondered why she looked so different to her parents and baby sister. That had been the day she had learned she was adopted, and even at the age of five she had understood that she was on her own.

She lifted her head and met Kadir's deep brown gaze, determined not to melt beneath his charismatic smile.

'I'm confident that we can have a mutually respectful relationship, Your Highness,' she said coolly. 'I accept your offer.'

A week later, as Lexi lowered herself into the turquoise pool on the rooftop of Kadir's luxury penthouse apartment in Monaco, she reflected that there were certainly benefits to working for a billionaire. The view of the Mediterranean sparkling in the early morning sunshine was breathtaking, and at this time of the day she had the pool to herself. Not that any of the other members of Kadir's entourage were likely to use the pool, she mused. His two bodyguards kept themselves to themselves, and the elderly manservant Walif, when he was not attending to his master's needs, or viewing Lexi with deep suspicion, was often to be found dozing in an armchair.

She wondered what time Kadir had returned to the

penthouse, or whether the party he had attended aboard a Russian oligarch's yacht had gone on all night. Lexi frowned, remembering the gorgeous bikini-clad women who had been gathered on Boris Denisov's super-yacht moored in Monaco's harbour. Like the other 'business meetings' Kadir had attended at the Folies Bergère in Paris and the prestigious Caves du Roy nightclub in St Tropez earlier in the week, she doubted he had spent much time discussing commercial deals when he'd been surrounded by all that naked, nubile flesh.

'There's no need for you to wait for me,' he had told her last night as he'd stepped out of the car onto the jetty and waved to the eager reception committee on the Russian's yacht. 'I'll make my own way back to the penthouse.'

'Are you sure you'll have the energy?' Lexi had murmured drily, earning her one of Kadir's outrageously sexy smiles that had a predictable effect on her heart-rate. Her gaze had been drawn to the girls on the yacht, with their golden tans and itsy-bitsy bikinis, and she had felt staid and inexplicably angry with herself, life and, top of the list, His Royal Rake—prince of the one-night stand!

It was partly her own fault she felt a frump, Lexi acknowledged. Before they had left England Kadir had chosen a pilot's uniform out of a catalogue for her to wear, which had consisted of an eye-wateringly short skirt and a tight-fitting jacket.

'I presume you're joking,' she'd said disgustedly. 'I'm a pilot, not a *Playboy* centrefold.' She had ordered a smart grey suit with a sensible mid-calf-length skirt, much to Kadir's amusement. He seemed to find her a joke and the more she treated him with icy politeness, the more he teased her and tried to draw a reaction from her. Over the past week a battle of wills had developed between them, and Kadir's weapons of choice were his laid-back charm and his sexy smile that Lexi suspected he was fully aware turned her insides to marshmallow.

She did not understand why she was letting him get to her, or why the wicked gleam in his eyes and his husky laughter when she gave him a withering look bothered her so much. She realised he was playing a game and she had no intention of taking his flirtatious behaviour seriously. But that did not stop her heart from thudding whenever he was near—and as he insisted on sitting next to her when she flew the helicopter, and he occupied the front passenger seat when she chauffeured him in the limousine, her nerves seemed to be permanently on edge.

Forcing her mind away from the man who disturbed her equilibrium, Lexi checked the strings of her halterneck bikini were securely tied. The silver bikini had been a crazy impulse buy after she had dropped Kadir at the marina. The three tiny triangles of material revealed more of her body than she was comfortable with, and the bikini was not as practical to swim in as the navy onepiece she usually wore. Cursing her stupidity, she struck out through the cool water and swam twenty lengths of the pool, hoping that strenuous exercise would ease the restless ache in her limbs.

She surfaced after completing the final length and shook her wet hair back from her face.

'You look like a water nymph.'

The husky drawl caused her heart to collide with her ribcage and she sucked in a swift breath as she looked up and saw Kadir sprawled on a sun lounger. His bow tie was undone, and so were several of his shirt buttons, affording Lexi a glimpse of his naked chest covered in whorls of black hairs. The night's growth of dark stubble shading his jaw accentuated his lethal sensuality. She had no idea how long he had been watching her. He moved with the silent stealth of a jungle cat, she thought irritably.

She arched her brows. 'Have you met many nymphs? I would have thought that you'd have your hands full with real women, without concerning yourself with mythological ones.'

He laughed softly and the sound sent a curl of heat through Lexi. 'What a delightful picture you paint. I can visualise myself with my hands full of women.'

One woman, if he was truthful, Kadir mused. He had been on his way to bed, and had stepped onto the rooftop patio for some much needed fresh air after the fug of cloying perfume and cigar smoke that had filled Boris Denisov's yacht. But the sight of Lexi wearing a sexy bikini, with her long blonde hair streaming down her back, had made him forget that he was tired after many hours of negotiations, during which he had persuaded the Russian oligarch to invest in a business venture worth billions of pounds to Zenhab's economy.

Kadir let his gaze drift over Lexi's slender body and her high, firm breasts, and the slow burn of desire that had simmered in his gut since he had first set eyes on her grew hotter and more intense. For the past week, she had driven him mad with her frosty attitude and sharp, often sarcastic, wit, her lack of deference for his royal status. Oh, she was polite, but he had a sense that she had judged him and found him wanting, and Kadir was finding it increasingly hard to resist the challenge in her cool blue gaze.

'I trust your business meeting was successful?' she murmured. 'By the way, you have lipstick on your collar.'

'The night was very satisfactory.' Kadir tucked his hands behind his head, thinking of the agreement he'd got from Boris to build a luxury hotel complex which would attract tourists to Zenhab.

Lexi pursed her lips. Had he had sex with the strumpet who had left a scarlet imprint of her lips on his white shirt? Maybe he'd had more than one woman last night. Probably—knowing his reputation. Acid burned in her stomach and she told herself she must have swallowed some of the chlorine in the pool. Kadir was lying back on the lounger, watching her through half-closed eyes. He looked indolent and beautiful and Lexi had never been more aware of a man in her life. *Why him—a man she did not even like, let alone respect?*

'I wonder what the Zenhabian people think of their Sultan who, as far as I can tell, spends more time partying and living up to his playboy reputation than trying to improve the lives of many of the population who live in poverty?' she said tartly. 'I've heard that your father devoted his life to establishing peace and security in the kingdom, but clearly you don't share his sense of duty.'

'What do you know about my country, and why do you care about my people?' Kadir demanded, stung by her comments. Duty and the desire to ensure long-term stability in Zenhab had made him agree to an arranged marriage with a girl who his weasel of an uncle had chosen for him, he thought bitterly. Lexi had overstepped the mark this time.

He was tempted to point out that many of the best business deals were made through networking and at social events. More deals were arranged over drinks at a bar than around a boardroom table. But he could imagine the response he would get if he told Miss Prim and Proper that he had been hard at work at last night's party.

'I've been reading about the history of Zenhab,' Lexi told him. 'After all, I am going to be living and working in the kingdom for a few months.'

'You would do well to remember that I am your employer,' Kadir said curtly, 'and I suggest you keep your opinions to yourself.'

'I'll try to remember that, Your Highness.' Lexi did not recognise the devil inside who seemed hell-bent on antagonising Kadir. She could tell she had angered him. His lazy smile had disappeared and the sensual gleam in his chocolate-brown eyes had been replaced with a hard stare that riled her, even though she acknowledged that she'd had no right to criticise him.

'While we are on the subject of your employment, I have a special assignment for you.' Kadir got to his feet and walked to the edge of the pool, meaning that Lexi had to tilt her head to look at his face. 'Later today you will fly us to Lake Como in Italy, to the home of a good friend of mine, Conte Luca De Rossi. Luca is hosting a business dinner and an American entrepreneur who I am hoping to do business with will be there.' Kadir hesitated for a nanosecond. 'I want you to be my companion for the evening.'

Lexi stared at him. 'I know nothing about business.'

'You don't have to know anything.' Again he paused and, to Lexi's surprise, he appeared almost awkward. 'I need you to be my date.'

'Your *date*?' Her eyebrows almost disappeared beneath her hairline.

'It's not difficult to understand,' Kadir said impatiently.

'Excuse me, but it is when I bet that any of the women you met last night would be gagging to be your date. Why is it important for you to take a partner to the dinner, anyway?'

He exhaled heavily. 'The American businessman, Chuck Weinberg, is bringing his nineteen-year-old daughter. I met Danielle a few months ago when I visited Chuck's home in Texas.' Kadir grimaced. 'Danielle is a very determined young woman who is used to getting what she wants…and she made it clear that she wants me. To be frank, I want to concentrate on discussing my business proposition with Chuck without having to fend off his daughter.'

'Yes, I can see how annoying that would be,' Lexi said in a cool tone that failed to disguise her boiling anger. She gave in to the childish impulse and splashed water over Kadir's designer suit, before she dived beneath the water and swam to the far end of the pool.

He had a nerve! She was so furious that she could feel her heart jumping up and down in her chest. *Why was she so stupid?* Lexi's anger was partly directed at herself. For a moment, when Kadir had asked her to be his date, she'd thought it was a serious invitation and he genuinely wanted her to accompany him to the dinner party.

Glancing over her shoulder, she saw him stride into the penthouse. She had conveniently forgotten that he'd said he wanted her to carry out an assignment. Now she knew that he wanted her to be his paid escort. She rested her arms on the side of the pool and stared over the rooftops at the sea in the distance. The bright sparkle of the sun on the waves made her eyes water—at least that was what she told herself. With an impatient gesture she dashed her hand over her damp eyelashes.

Her birth mother had been an escort. *It sounds classier than call girl,* Cathy had told Lexi when she had spoken about how she had been drawn into prostitution to fund her drug habit.

Lost in her thoughts, Lexi gave a startled cry when a muscular arm curled around her waist and she was half lifted out of the water as Kadir turned her round to face him.

'What's the matter with you?' he growled. 'I made a simple request…'

'You asked me to pretend to be your mistress. I don't call that a simple request; I call that a darned cheek!' With her face mere inches from his naked bronzed chest, Lexi numbly realised that while he had been inside the apartment he had changed into his swimming shorts.

Her heart kicked into life as she jerked her eyes back to his face to find him watching her intently. She licked her dry lips and his dark gaze focused on the tip of her tongue. The cool water lapped her hot breasts and she felt her nipples harden to taut peaks that chafed against her clingy bikini bra. She was standing with her back against the wall of the pool and Kadir placed his arms on either side of her body, caging her in.

'Nowhere in my contract does it state that one of my duties is to masquerade as your mistress to protect you from the clutches of women who want to climb into your bed,' she said fiercely. 'I don't want to pretend to be your dinner date and I doubt I could convince anyone that we have an intimate relationship.'

'Intimate,' Kadir murmured, his voice suddenly as sensual as molten syrup. 'I like the way that sounds. Don't underestimate yourself, Lexi. I'm sure you could be a very convincing mistress.'

Too late, Lexi recognised the danger she was in. 'Take your hands off me.' In a distant corner of her mind she knew she sounded like a Victorian maiden. What had happened to her military training? she asked herself impatiently. She brought her knee up swiftly between Kadir's legs, but he was quicker and trapped her leg between his thighs. Tension thrummed between them and the only sound was her own quickened breathing.

Deep down, Lexi acknowledged that she had been goading him since he'd arrived at the pool; since the moment she'd first met him, if she was honest. Now, as he lowered his head his eyes reflected the challenge in hers.

'It's not my hands you need to worry about,' he drawled. And then he brought his mouth down on hers and the world exploded.

He was merciless, taking advantage of her cry of protest to thrust his tongue between her lips and explore her with mind-blowing eroticism. Lexi had never been kissed like that in her life, hadn't known that a kiss could be so hot and dark and shockingly wicked. Any idea she'd had of trying to resist him was swept away by his shimmering sexual hunger. He crushed her mouth beneath his and demanded everything: her soul, her secret fantasies, her total capitulation to his mastery. She had dared to challenge him with her cool blue eyes and Kadir would show her that the desert king *never* refused a challenge.

Lexi's body burned with an intensity of need that made a mockery of her belief that she did not have a high sex drive. She had assumed that she was not a particularly sensual person and, although she was not a virgin, her previous sexual experiences had left her with a vague sense of disappointment and bemusement that sonnets had been written about something frankly so mundane.

Everything she thought she knew about herself was shattered by the white-hot desire that ripped through her. Kadir was not touching her body, only her mouth, as he crushed her lips beneath his and deepened the kiss, and Lexi sank into darkness and heat and danger. Compelled by an instinct as old as womankind, she pushed her hips forward, urgently seeking contact with his pelvis.

He should not have started this. The realisation drummed a warning in Kadir's brain. What had begun as a lesson designed to show Lexi that *he* was in command was rapidly becoming a test of his will power. She was so responsive, so hungry, meeting his demands with demands of her own and with a boldness that he should have expected from the strong woman he knew her to be. But he could not take what he so desperately wanted. He should not have made the ice maiden melt and he could not allow himself to burn in her fire. The temptation to sink into her yielding softness and rest his thighs on hers nearly broke his resolve.

Who would know if he enjoyed one last fling before he returned to Zenhab and the life of duty that awaited him?

He would know, Kadir thought grimly. He heard his father's voice inside his head. *To cheat others requires you to cheat yourself first, and who can respect a cheat?*

He wrenched his mouth from Lexi's, feeling ashamed of his weakness and his inability to resist her. She had responded to him, he reminded himself. He was not solely to blame. But the best way he could ensure that the situation never happened again was to fire up her hot temper.

'Remember, when we are sitting at the dinner table tonight with Luca and his guests, I'll be remembering how your tongue felt inside my mouth. Remember that I know your secret, Lexi.'

'What secret?' Lexi dragged oxygen into her lungs and forced her lips, stinging from Kadir's kiss, to form the question.

Kadir deliberately dropped his gaze to her pebble-hard nipples jutting provocatively through her bikini top and his satisfied smile made Lexi's skin prickle with shame. 'We both know I could have you. Did you buy your tiny bikini and imagine me untying the straps that hold it together? Perhaps I should take you here and now, and at the dinner party there will be no need for you to pretend that you are my mistress?'

Heat blazed on her cheeks. 'I don't have to listen to this. I certainly don't have to put up with being mauled by my employer. I resign,' Lexi told him furiously.

'You would walk away from the best-paid job you are likely to find because your pride has taken a knock? I didn't have you down as a coward, Lexi. I thought you had more guts.'

'I am *not* a coward.'

He shrugged. 'There is also the matter of a financial penalty if you break your contract.'

She had signed a contract which had made her a member of the royal staff, and she would owe him three months' salary if she left before completing six months' service. Lexi knew she could not afford to take on any more debt. 'A few thousand pounds is nothing to you,' she said bitterly.

She dragged her eyes from his exquisitely chiselled features and stared at his hands gripping the edge of the pool on either side of her. She had accused him of mauling her, but he had not actually touched her body. The knowledge that he had set her on fire simply with a kiss compounded her humiliation.

Kadir's knuckles were white, and Lexi had the strange sense that he was holding on to the edge of the pool as if his life depended on it. The muscles of his forearms and shoulders were bunched as if he was under intolerable tension and he was breathing hard, his big chest rising and falling jerkily, matching the frantic rhythm of her own heartbeat. She looked into his eyes, expecting to see mockery, but the hard brilliance in his gaze revealed a hunger that shocked her. The realisation that this was not a game to him scared her as much as it excited her.

'Release me from my contract. Let me go before this gets out of hand,' she pleaded in a low, shaken voice.

Logic told Kadir she was right. Taking Lexi to Zenhab would be madness now that he had tasted her. What had started out as a challenge—to melt her ice—had changed irrevocably now that he had discovered her heat and softness and incandescent sensuality.

But the fact remained that he wanted to employ a female helicopter pilot to fly his intended bride around Zenhab. His desire for Lexi was an inconvenience that he would have to deal with, Kadir told himself firmly. His life was mapped out and the path he must take had been plotted by his uncle Jamal. For stability in Zenhab, and for the promise he'd made to his father, he would marry the bride who had been chosen for him.

'We will leave for Italy at two o'clock,' he said abruptly, dropping his arms to his sides, his fists clenched as if he couldn't trust himself not to reach for Lexi's slender body and pull her into the heat of him, the need that burned bright and fierce in his gut.

In a dignified silence that somehow simmered with fury, she climbed the steps leading out of the pool, water streaming from her limbs and her long white-gold hair.

Kadir watched her walk into the penthouse and cursed savagely before he ducked beneath the surface of the pool and powered through the water.

Lexi did not look round, did not even stop to snatch up her towel as she ran inside and almost collided with Kadir's manservant. Walif—as she had come to expect— did not speak to her, but she sensed his disapproval and, when she hurried into her bedroom and glanced in the mirror, the sight of her swollen lips, reddened from Kadir's kiss, brought a flush to her face and strengthened her resolve to keep her relationship with the Sultan of Zenhab on strictly professional lines from now on.

CHAPTER SIX

HIS LAST NIGHT of freedom!

It was not quite as dramatic as that, Kadir acknowledged, the corners of his mouth lifting in a wry smile of self-derision. A royal wedding would take months to arrange, and technically he was free until he led his new bride into his private bedchamber and they were alone for the first time.

But this evening would be his last in Europe for many months, until after his wedding to Haleema had taken place. What better place to be than at Conte Luca De Rossi's breathtaking villa on the shores of Lake Como?

Kadir was grateful to his old school friend for arranging the dinner party and inviting Chuck Weinberg. The American businessman had seemed enthusiastic about investing in the developing telecommunications industry in Zenhab during initial discussions that had taken place in Texas. Tonight, Kadir planned to utilise all his persuasive skills to hopefully secure a deal that would bring his desert kingdom fully into the twenty-first century.

There was only one problem—and she was making a beeline for him across the magnificent entrance hall of the Villa De Rossi. Danielle Weinberg had big hair, a big smile and big breasts that Kadir, who had a certain amount of hands-on experience of the female anatomy, was certain owed more to a cosmetic surgeon's skill than to genetics.

'Kad*eer*, I've been looking all over for you.'

She reminded Kadir of an over-enthusiastic puppy. As he gently but firmly unlocked Danielle's hands from around his neck, he was struck by the thought that his future bride was a similar age to the young American. His jaw clenched. In Zenhab a life of duty awaited him, but tonight he was determined to enjoy his last few hours of freedom.

Despite what he had told Lexi, he knew he could handle Danielle with the same diplomacy that he dealt with her father. But when he had asked Lexi to partner him at the dinner party he had lost his nerve—something that had *never* happened to Kadir before. Citing Danielle as an excuse had seemed like a good idea, but it had backfired spectacularly, and had led to him kissing Lexi in what had started out as a punishment and ended in searing passion that he knew he should not have allowed to happen. His behaviour had been inappropriate, and Lexi had made him aware of that fact on the helicopter flight from Monaco to the Villa De Rossi, when she had been as cold as a Siberian winter.

Kadir glanced at his watch. She was late coming down for dinner. His mouth tightened with annoyance as he remembered her excuse that she had nothing suitable to wear to a grand dinner party. Would she wear the evening gown he had arranged to be delivered to her room? He would give her five more minutes before he went to find her, and if necessary he would put the damned dress on her!

His attention was drawn to the top of the sweeping staircase, and his frustration with his stubborn, insubordinate pilot changed to white-hot desire as he watched her walk gracefully down the stairs. The dress was a Luca De Rossi creation, an elegant floor-length sheath of silk the colour of a summer sky that matched exactly the blue of Lexi's eyes. Her pale gold hair had been left loose and fell past her shoulders like a silken curtain, framing a face as beautiful and serene as a Raphael virgin.

Kadir was aware of every painful beat of his heart as he strode across the hall.

'Am I late?' Lexi gave him a rueful look. 'I couldn't reach the zip on my dress.'

'Why didn't you call one of the maids to assist you?'

She shrugged. 'It didn't occur to me to ask for help. I made a hook out of a coat hanger and managed to pull the zip up with it. I served in the armed forces for ten years and I'm used to working out solutions to problems,' she reminded Kadir.

'Did you often wear evening gowns in Afghanistan?' He did not know whether to be exasperated or amused by her fierce independence.

'Of course not...' She hesitated. 'I've never worn a House of De Rossi dress before, or any other designer dress, for that matter. It's beautiful, and obviously I will pay for it.'

'Fortunately, we have been called in to dinner,' he murmured, offering her his arm, 'so we'll have to save the argument until later.'

'We don't need to argue. You simply have to accept that I won't allow you to pay for my clothes.'

His eyes glittered. 'You always have to have the last word. Stubbornness is not an attractive quality in a woman.'

Lexi flashed him a cool smile that made Kadir grind his teeth. 'I'm not hoping to attract you, Your Highness. Unlike just about every other woman here tonight,' she added drily.

When she had first caught sight of him, dressed in a white tuxedo that looked stunning against his olive-gold skin, she had been blown away by his good looks and smouldering sensuality, and a glance around the room revealed that she was not the only woman who could not take her eyes off him.

They had reached the dining room, and Kadir held out a chair for Lexi to sit down. He was aware of the subtle and, in some cases, not so subtle glances directed at him from the other female party guests. Lexi was the only woman he wanted, but he could not tell her and he could not allow their mutual attraction to ignite. However, as she sat down, he was compelled by a force beyond his control to lower his head so that he could inhale the evocative scent of her perfume.

Lexi was suddenly conscious that Kadir had leaned closer to her and his face was almost touching hers. She held her breath as the close-trimmed stubble on his jaw scraped against her cheek, and only released it when he lifted his head and moved to sit down on the chair beside her. She took a sip of water and waited for her racing pulse to slow before she dared to look at him. His lazy smile did peculiar things to her insides. She wished she had not come down to dinner. She felt so tense that the thought of putting food into her stomach made her shudder. It had only been the thought that he was very likely to come to her room and force her to obey him that had persuaded her to put on the dress that she had discovered wrapped in tissue on the bed.

Heat stained Lexi's cheeks as it occurred to her that she had never in her life allowed a man to force her to do anything she did not want to do. And why did the idea of being made to obey Kadir conjure shockingly erotic images in her mind? What was happening to her? she wondered grimly. Tomorrow she would be going to Zenhab. Pulling out was not an option; she could not afford to pay the penalty clause in her contract. But, more than that, it was a matter of pride that she learned to deal with His Royal Hotness and prove that she had not been fazed when he had kissed her in the pool in Monaco.

Kadir was charming and entertaining during dinner, but it was his unexpected gentleness when he spoke to the over-eager Danielle that surprised Lexi. His charisma and sexual magnetism she could handle, just, she thought ruefully. But the discovery that he could be kind and, dare she even think it, sensitive, was an element to him she had been unaware of until now. Heavens, if he carried on being Mr Nice Guy she might even grow to like him!

'I understand you are a helicopter pilot and flew rescue missions in Afghanistan.' Chuck Weinberg's strong Texan drawl dragged Lexi from her thoughts. 'Is your father a military man?'

'My father...' Lexi's hesitation fired Kadir's curiosity. "He's a doctor. Actually, both my parents are in the medical profession; my father is a heart surgeon and my mother is a neurologist.'

'They must be clever people! It's curious that you didn't inherit an interest in medicine from your parents,' Chuck commented.

God knew what genes she had inherited from her biological parents, Lexi thought bleakly. Her mother had provided sexual favours for a living, and her father had been one of Cathy's clients. The man whose blood ran through her veins was nameless, faceless, and the knowledge that she would never know his identity made her feel incomplete.

After dinner the party moved into the orangerie, where there was dancing to a five-piece jazz band. Lexi withdrew to an alcove and watched Kadir work his way around the room. No female between the ages of eighteen and eighty was safe from his magnetic charm, she thought as he finished dancing with Danielle Weinberg and swept a white-haired lady onto the dance floor.

'I should have expected Kadir would try to seduce my grandmother, and that Nonna Violetta would adore him.'

Lexi glanced at Luca De Rossi, who had come to stand beside her. 'He's certainly the life and soul of the party,' she said drily.

An amused smile crossed Luca's handsome face. Similar in height and build to Kadir, he possessed film star looks, with jet-black hair, classically sculpted features and an air of polished sophistication that marked him out as a European aristocrat.

'Don't be fooled by Kadir's playboy image,' Luca murmured. 'He plays hard but he works harder and he is prepared to devote his life to Zenhab.'

Lexi restrained herself from asking what kind of work the Prince of Pleasure had ever done. 'I understand you became friends with Kadir at Eton? Did you also know Charles Fairfax at school?'

'He was in the year below Kadir and I.' The Italian shrugged an elegant shoulder. 'I can't say Charlie was a close friend. Why do you ask?'

'He's going to marry my sister.'

Luca looked surprised. 'How curious,' he murmured.

Lexi wanted to ask him what he meant, but her thoughts scattered as Kadir appeared at her side. 'You have monopolised my pilot for long enough,' he told Luca lightly, but beneath his easy tone was a possessiveness that made Lexi bristle. 'Dance with me,' he commanded.

She shook her head. 'I can't dance, and you are hardly short of partners. Every woman in the room is hoping it'll be her turn next to be swept onto the dance floor by the Arabian version of Fred Astaire.'

Kadir laughed softly as he clamped his hands on her waist and whisked her around the room. 'There's no need for you to be jealous. I only have eyes for you, angel face.'

'I am *not* jealous!' She knew he was teasing her, playing a familiar game that he had played all the past week, so why was her heart thudding painfully fast beneath her ribs? She brought the tip of her stiletto heel down on his toe and gave him a look of wide-eyed innocence. 'Oops. I warned you I can't dance.'

His eyes glittered with an unspoken challenge that sent a frisson of excitement down Lexi's spine. 'Be careful, or I might be tempted to expose your secret right here while we are dancing in front of all these people.'

'What secret…?' She snatched a sharp breath, remembering how he had kissed her in the swimming pool and she had arched her body towards him in an unmistakable offer that had revealed her desire. The memory of that kiss made Lexi feel vulnerable and exposed—to him. The hunger in Kadir's eyes—no trace of teasing now—caused molten heat to flood through her veins.

Confused by her reaction to a man she knew to be a playboy, she stumbled and Kadir immediately tightened his arms around her, drawing her closer so that her hips came into searing contact with his. The hard ridge of his arousal pushed against her pelvis. She did not dare meet his gaze but she knew from the harsh sound of his breathing that he was in as much danger of bursting into flames as she was.

Why him? she asked herself bitterly. Why had she never felt this intensity of need, this overpowering desire for any other man, including the man she had planned to marry? She had never come close to losing control with Steven. Until she had met Kadir she hadn't known what it was like to ache in every part of her body, or for her breasts to feel heavy and her nipples hot and hard, so that she knew without glancing down that they were visibly outlined beneath her silk dress.

'Excuse me…' She did not care that the tremor in her voice betrayed her tension as she pulled out of his arms and walked swiftly across the dance floor. She was simply desperate to regain control of her wayward body and wanton thoughts.

Kadir watched Lexi's slender figure weave through the other dancers, and it took every bit of his will power not to go after her, sweep her up into his arms and carry her off to—where? he asked himself derisively. Taking her to bed was not an option. It had to end now, this madness, the longing for something he could not have—and quite possibly he wanted all the more because Lexi was off-limits.

He saw Chuck Weinberg beckoning to him from the library, where they had arranged to discuss the business deal that would be hugely beneficial to Zenhab. His last night of freedom ended here, Kadir told himself as he strode towards the library.

* * *

Lexi checked her watch and saw that it was past midnight. The party was winding down and the guests were leaving. She was due to fly the helicopter to Milan Airport in the morning so that it could be loaded onto a transporter plane for the journey to Zenhab. It would be an early start to what promised to be a long day and she knew she should go to bed, but she had never felt less like sleeping in her life.

She wondered where Kadir was. He had disappeared from the party a couple of hours ago and Lexi had not seen him, or the attractive redhead who was almost wearing a daringly low-cut dress, since. He was not her responsibility, she reminded herself. She was employed as his pilot and his personal life was none of her business.

Hadn't he made it his business when he had kissed her? whispered a voice inside her head. She frowned. The kiss had meant nothing to him. He had been playing with her like he had done all week, but tonight he had obviously grown bored of the game and turned his attention to the well-endowed redhead.

Feeling restless and refusing to admit that Kadir was the cause, she stepped outside onto the long terrace that ran along the back of the house. The Villa De Rossi's magnificent formal gardens were dappled in silver moonlight but, as Lexi slipped like a shadow along the path leading down to the lake, the moon was partially obscured by clouds racing across the sky. She drew her pashmina tighter around her shoulders. Autumn in northern Italy was much warmer than in England but, as she stood at the edge of the lake, raindrops began to bounce onto the surface, falling faster and faster until the water seemed to dance.

A wooden summer house further along the path was the only place to shelter from the rain shower, and luckily she found the door was unlocked. Inky darkness greeted her as she stepped inside and an even darker voice demanded, 'What do you want?'

'*Kadir?*' Lexi's yelp of fright turned to shock and her heart leapt into her throat as a faint yellow light filled the cabin and she saw that Kadir had lit a gas lamp on the wall. 'What are you doing here?' Her eyes flew to an old sofa piled with cushions and realisation dawned. She guessed the redhead was hiding somewhere. 'I'm sorry if I've interrupted something.'

His heavy brows drew together. 'What do you mean?'

'I assume you are here with someone.'

'By *someone* I suppose you mean a woman?' Kadir growled. 'Why do you always jump to the worst conclusion based on rubbish the paparazzi have written about me in the past?'

Lexi flushed as it became apparent that there was no one else in the summer house. 'What was I supposed to think? Why were you sitting here in the dark?'

He shrugged. 'I went for a stroll because I needed some air and ended up at the summer house. I used to come here with Luca when we were teenagers; I stayed with him sometimes during the school holidays. He taught me to sail on the lake.'

They had been halcyon days, Kadir brooded, before his father had suffered the stroke that had left him paralysed and unable to rule, before his uncle Jamal had seized power, and before he had been forced to agree to an arranged marriage in a bid to maintain peace and stability in Zenhab.

Lexi glanced out of the window. Through the dark-

ness, the twinkling lights of the villages strung around
the shores of Lake Como revealed the vast size of the
lake. 'I imagine sailing is popular on the lake.' She remembered that he had skippered the Zenhabian team
that had won the America's Cup. 'Why did you decide
to take up offshore sailing?'

'There are no lakes in Zenhab,' he said drily. 'Away
from the coast, most of the land is desert and rock. How
do you feel about returning to a desert environment?'

'I'm interested to see a new country and, unlike Afghanistan, there isn't a war in Zenhab so I might get a
chance to see the beauty of a desert landscape without
having to worry about avoiding landmines.'

Kadir exhaled heavily. His father had ended the civil
war in Zenhab and established peace between the tribes
two decades ago. With his last breath Sultan Khalif had
begged his son to maintain unity in the kingdom. Kadir
had vowed to carry out his father's wish, for it was his
wish too. He loved the kingdom that he had been destined
from birth to rule. It was a small sacrifice to give up his
right to fall in love and marry a woman of his choice.
Perhaps it was even a blessing. He had learned from his
parents that love was a precarious base for marriage. His
father had been broken-hearted when Kadir's mother had
returned to England for good.

Lust, on the other hand, was easy to understand. It was
nothing more than chemistry, and it was a bitter irony,
Kadir mused, that the chemical reaction between him
and Lexi was blistering.

In the semi-dark summer house he was so aware of
her that every skin cell on his body tingled, and he could
feel the thunderous drumbeat of his desire pounding in
his veins. He had never met anyone like her before, never

admired any woman as much as he admired Lexi. She was beautiful, brave, intensely annoying, utterly intriguing—his brain told him to move away from her, but his body wasn't listening. His eyes locked with hers and his heart flipped a somersault when he saw that fire had replaced the ice in her bright blue gaze.

Was it so wrong to want to taste her one last time? To capture a memory that must last him a lifetime. *One kiss...* He lowered his head and watched her pupils darken, heard the soft catch of her breath as he grazed his lips across hers and felt them tremble and open like the velvet-soft petals of an English rose.

One kiss, he assured himself.

She was sweetness and fire, his delight and quite possibly his destruction. When he had kissed her in the swimming pool he had not dared allow their bodies to come into contact, but now she melted into him, soft and pliant against his hard musculature. With a groan, he wrapped one arm around her waist and threaded his other hand into her long silky hair. Her perfume—a blend of crisp citrus and sweet jasmine—so appropriate for her, he thought—wrapped around him and he closed his eyes and sought her mouth blindly, his other senses, of touch and taste, heightened so that the feel of her lips beneath his was beyond pleasure.

The first time Kadir had kissed her in Monaco, Lexi knew that his intention had been to prove a point and show her that he was in control. She had understood that he had been angry because she had challenged him. But there was no anger now. They had not been having one of their verbal sparring matches and, rather than trying to show her who was boss, Kadir seemed to have seduction in his mind. His lips were firm on hers and he

kissed her with demanding hunger, yet there was an unexpected tenderness in his passion that answered a need
deep within her. The bold thrust of his tongue into her
mouth shattered her resistance and destroyed the mental
barriers she *always* kept in place.

She could not control the tremor that ran through her
as he trailed his lips over her cheek, her throat, and found
the pulse beating frantically at its base. Distracted by him
sliding the strap of her dress over her shoulder, she felt
something hard at the back of her knees and belatedly
realised it was the sofa.

He eased her down onto the cushions and knelt above
her. The fierce glitter in his eyes was a promise and a
warning of his intent. Lexi held her breath as he slipped
his hands beneath her and ran her zip far enough down
her spine to allow him to peel away the top of her dress.
The air felt cool on her breasts; his palms felt warm on
her bare flesh. Glancing down, the sight of his darkly
tanned hands on her creamy pale breasts was incredibly
erotic, and when he rubbed his thumb pads across her
tender nipples the sensation was so exquisite that she
could not restrain a soft moan.

'You are more beautiful even than I imagined.' His
voice, roughened with desire, broke the intense silence
of the dimly lit cabin.

Reality pushed, unwelcome, into Lexi's thoughts. She
wasn't a novice when it came to sex; she was an independent woman, free to do as she pleased. She could no
longer deny that she wanted to make love with Kadir,
but choice also meant taking responsibility for herself.
'I'm not on the Pill,' she murmured. 'Do you have anything with you?'

Lexi's words were as effective as a cold shower. Once

again Kadir acknowledged the irony of bad timing. If she had asked him the same question six months ago he would have been able to assure her that he always carried condoms with him. But he had made a commitment to himself to end the playboy lifestyle, in preparation for his marriage.

His desire for Lexi was blazing out of control, but in his heart burned the need to prove to himself that he was an honourable man like his father had been, a man fit to be Sultan of Zenhab and fulfil the destiny of a desert king.

Ignoring the painful throb of his arousal, he got up from the sofa and tugged Lexi's dress back over her breasts. She caught her breath as the silk grazed her nipples, and the evidence of how sensitive her breasts were almost shattered Kadir's resolve to end what he should never have begun.

'We must go back to the house,' he said abruptly as he thrust her pashmina into her hands, and felt relieved when she wrapped it around her so that he could no longer see the hard points of her nipples jutting beneath her dress.

'Shouldn't we wait until it stops raining?' Lexi hesitated when Kadir opened the cabin door and she saw the torrential downpour. But he had already stepped onto the porch. He slid out of his jacket and draped it around her shoulders before he grabbed her hand and practically dragged her along the path.

'We need to go back now.'

His urgency filled Lexi with anticipation. In the cabin she had been aware of his hunger, the need for sexual fulfilment that had almost overwhelmed both of them. But safe sex could not be ignored and Kadir was clearly impatient to take her to his bedroom, where presumably he had contraceptives and they could make love with peace of mind.

Was she out of her mind? demanded a voice inside her head. It defied common sense to sleep with a playboy. But she was tired of being sensible. Her job as a helicopter pilot in the RAF and then with the coastguard agency had required her to take risks, but on a personal level she had played it safe for far too long. Why shouldn't she enjoy everything the Prince of Pleasure had to offer?

Lexi's heart was thumping as Kadir ushered her into the villa through a side door and up a back staircase used by the servants to the third floor, where the guest bedrooms were.

Her smile faltered and she gave him a puzzled look when he stopped in the corridor outside her bedroom and said brusquely, 'Goodnight.'

Goodnight! 'I…I don't understand. I thought…'

The memory of his barely restrained passion ten minutes earlier made her abandon her usual diffidence. She ached for him and she had been certain that he wanted her with the same white-hot need. His chiselled features gave no clue to his thoughts and some of Lexi's certainty faded as she stared into his eyes that were the colour of dark umber, without the teasing glint she was used to seeing. 'I assumed we were going to spend the night together,' she said huskily.

In his wilder days Kadir had slept with more women than he could remember, but he had never felt as much of a bastard as he did now for not sleeping with Lexi. The irony would be laughable if he felt like laughing, but he doubted that he would ever laugh again. There was no good way to handle the situation and only one thing he could say.

'I'm sorry. I should not have let things get out of hand the way they did.'

Lexi's racing heart juddered to a standstill. Oh, no, not sorry, she thought bitterly. Let him be mocking, sarcastic—anything but pitying. She heard Steven's voice inside her head.

'I'm sorry, Lexi. I shouldn't have allowed our relationship to develop when I knew that my girlfriend and baby were waiting for me back in England. It felt like you and I were in another world in Afghanistan. But the truth is that I'm not free to marry you because I already have a family.'

Rejection was hurtful and humiliating. After Steven had dumped her she had vowed never to put herself in such a vulnerable position again.

So what was she doing hovering outside her bedroom in the vain hope that Kadir might change his mind and take her to bed? *How much more vulnerable could she feel?* Kadir had been playing games with her ever since they'd met, Lexi thought grimly.

'Good manners prevent me from telling you what you can do with your apology,' she said, her voice so tightly wound that it shook with the strain of retaining her last dregs of pride. She opened her bedroom door and gave a cynical laugh. 'I should thank you for stopping me from making the worst mistake of my life.' Something in his darkly beautiful face made her insides twist. 'Everything is a game to you, isn't it?'

'*Damn it*, Lexi. Of course I don't think this is a game.'

To Lexi's astonishment, Kadir drove his clenched fist against the door frame, and it was a testament to the solidness of the wood that it did not splinter beneath the powerful blow. 'The situation is complicated,' he said savagely. 'I want to spend the night with you and make love to you. But I am not free to do what I want.'

'But…you are a Sultan. You can do whatever you like.'

'I wish that were true.'

Lexi felt a curious sense of déjà vu. Steven had admitted that he wasn't free to be with her because he had a long-term partner and a child. She lifted her chin and stared into Kadir's eyes. 'Why are you not free?'

An indefinable emotion flickered in his dark gaze. 'I am betrothed to the princess of the mountain tribes in Zenhab.'

'You're engaged to be *married*?' Her shock rapidly turned to anger. 'Then what the hell were you doing coming on to me when presumably you are in love with your fiancée—you…cheating *louse*?'

A nerve jumped in Kadir's cheek. 'I am not a cheat. Nor am I in love with Princess Haleema. I've never even met her.' He saw the confusion in Lexi's eyes and his tone softened. 'We are not engaged as you would understand the word. A marriage arrangement was made by our families, and I had to agree to it to keep peace in Zenhab. After his stroke, my father was convinced that the marriage would forge stronger ties with the mountain tribes and ensure stability in the kingdom that had once been torn apart by civil war.'

Lexi stared at him. The story of an arranged marriage sounded convenient, but she sensed that Kadir was telling her the truth. 'I didn't realise that arranged marriages took place in Zenhab.'

'*Forced* marriages will not be allowed under the new law I have introduced. And in fact they are rare. Many families believe in arranged marriages where sons and daughters are introduced to a potential spouse, but marriage can only take place if it is the choice of the bride and groom.'

'Did you have a choice about becoming engaged to the princess?'

'No,' Kadir said heavily. Agreeing to marry Haleema had been the only way he could claim the Crown—his birthright—from his uncle. 'It was my father's dying wish that I should ensure the future stability and safety of our country. Haleema was only a child at that time, but I gave my father my word that I would honour my promise and take her as my bride when she was old enough to marry. When I return to Zenhab I intend to fulfil my duty.'

Lexi guessed it was a duty that weighed heavy on Kadir's shoulders. She remembered Luca De Rossi had said that Kadir was prepared to devote his life to his kingdom and she felt a grudging respect for his determination to honour the promise he had made as a young man. But he had not treated her honourably, she thought with a flash of anger.

'You should have been honest with me from the start. You had no right to...to flirt with me.' She felt sick when she remembered his sexy smile and the gleam of sensual promise in his eyes. The realisation that it had all been a game to him was humiliating. Just like Steven, Kadir had not considered her feelings, she thought painfully. He had kissed her and started to make love to her, knowing that he was promised to another woman. To both men, she had been unimportant, and the realisation opened up the raw feelings of rejection that had haunted her for years.

'I know it was wrong of me to kiss you,' Kadir growled. 'I cannot deny that I desire you. From the moment we met, we were drawn to each other.' He held her gaze and dared her to deny it. 'But I give you my word that I won't kiss you again, and when we are in Zenhab I will treat you with courtesy and respect.'

'I can't go to Zenhab with you now! How can we forget what nearly happened between us tonight?'

'We have to forget,' Kadir said harshly. 'I still need a helicopter pilot.'

'You could release me from my contract and employ another pilot.'

He shook his head. 'I chose you especially because one of your duties will be to fly Haleema between her home in the mountains and the palace. Her family are very traditional and she will only be permitted to travel with a female pilot.'

'You want me to chaperone your fiancée?' Lexi was tempted to tell him what he could do with his damned job, but hot on the heels of her temper was the realisation that she still had to repay her mother's debts and she could not afford the financial penalty if she broke her contract with Kadir. It was also a question of pride. Kadir had guessed that she found him attractive, but if he could forget their passion that had almost blazed out of control in the summer house then so could she.

She stepped into her bedroom and forced her lips into a dismissive smile. 'Fine, I'll come to Zenhab as per our agreement,' she told him coolly. 'I'm sure I'll have no problem forgetting the regrettable incident that took place tonight, and from now on I will expect our relationship to be purely professional, Your Highness.'

CHAPTER SEVEN

LEXI STARED OUT of the plane window at the seemingly unending expanse of saffron-coloured sand that had been wind-whipped into towering dunes and sinuous ridges which resembled a giant serpent writhing across the land. In the far distance she could see craggy grey mountains, beyond which, according to her guidebook, lay Zenhab's wild and barren northern lands where a few ancient Bedouin tribes lived.

Looking in the other direction, she saw the outlines of modern skyscrapers alongside elegant minarets and curving mosque roofs. Zenhab's position in the Arabian Sea made it an important trading route, and its rich cultural history and architecture reflected the periods in time when the country had been under Portuguese and, later, Persian rule.

As the plane flew over the capital city, Mezeira, Kadir's chief adviser, Yusuf bin Hilal, pointed out places of interest. 'There is the royal palace. You see how the pure white walls sparkle in the sunshine as though the stones are mixed with diamonds? They are not, of course,' Yusuf explained. 'The bricks contain a special kind of sand that gives the jewel effect.'

'It looks like a fairy tale palace from *Arabian Nights*

with all those towers and spires. It reminds me a little of the Taj Mahal in India.'

'The people of Zenhab believe that *our* Sultan's royal palace is the most beautiful building in the world,' Yusuf said proudly.

'I understand that in the past there was unrest in the mountain territories of Zenhab,' Lexi commented.

Yusuf nodded. 'There was a terrible civil war. But the present Sultan's father, Sultan Khalif, established peace in the kingdom and for the past decade his son has introduced a programme of liberalisation and modernisation that has resulted in economic growth for the country. Sultan Kadir works tirelessly to attract foreign business and investment to Zenhab and he is regarded by the majority of the population as an inspired leader.'

Yusuf pointed to another building. 'That is Zenhab's first university, opened by Sultan Kadir five years ago and partly funded by him personally. His advancement of education for rich and poor alike, and especially for women, has gained him much support, and sadly a few enemies. The Sultan has received death threats, but he still insists on walking among his people whenever he can. He is a truly great man,' Yusuf said reverently.

Every member of Kadir's staff that Lexi had spoken to seemed to share Yusuf's opinion. Her own opinion of him as a playboy prince was changing since she had discovered that he was willing to sacrifice his right to choose a wife and had agreed to an arranged marriage because he believed it was best for his kingdom. She respected his determination to put his duty to his country above his personal desires, and she knew she should be grateful to him for being honest with her in Italy instead of taking her to bed. But she had lied when she'd told him that she would easily forget the passionate moments they had shared in the summer house. He dominated her thoughts, day and night, but now that they had arrived in Zenhab he would soon marry his Princess, she thought dully.

She had not seen Kadir since they had boarded the plane and he had walked past his entourage of staff in the main cabin on his way to his private suite at the front. Once the plane had landed, she'd expected him to reappear, but there was no sign of him as she'd followed Yusuf down the steps and onto the tarmac. To her surprise, the members of Kadir's staff who had travelled abroad with him stood with the plane's crew, forming what appeared to be a reception committee, and Lexi had no option but to stand in line with them. 'What's happening?' she whispered to Yusuf.

'By tradition, when the Sultan returns home, glorious from his conquests and battles abroad, although, of course, he has business meetings now rather than battles,' the adviser hastily explained, 'he is escorted through the streets of the city to the palace by horsemen.'

Yusuf's voice was drowned out by the sound of thundering hooves and Lexi turned to see a great dust cloud, through which appeared thirty or so horsemen wearing traditional Zenhabian clothes—white robes with brightly coloured short-sleeved jackets on top and white headdresses which billowed behind them as the horsemen raced along the runway.

Glancing up at the plane, Lexi's heart lurched as Kadir appeared in the doorway and stood on the top step. Like the horsemen, he was dressed in a white robe, and his jacket was exquisitely embroidered in red and gold. At his waist he wore a wide leather belt and a terrifying-looking ceremonial knife in a jewelled holder. His white headdress, which Lexi knew was called a *keffiyeh*, was held in place by a circle of black and gold rope. He looked regal and remote, the powerful ruler of his desert kingdom, and far removed from his alter-ego of an English Earl.

Even from the distance that separated Lexi from him, she could see the dark brilliance of his eyes. She could not stop herself from staring at him, riveted by his handsome face, and she felt the same curious ache in her heart that she had felt in Italy when he had admitted that he was not free to make love to her.

He descended the steps and walked past the line of staff. Lexi found she was holding her breath as he came closer. She willed him to turn his head and notice her, but he strode straight past, leaving in his wake the spicy tang of his cologne that hung in the hot, still air and teased her senses.

She closed her eyes, assailed by memories of when he had kissed her in the summer house at Lake Como. She remembered the heat of his body through his silk shirt, the feel of his hands on her skin when he had pulled her dress down and caressed her breasts. Frantically, she tried to block out the erotic images in her mind as she reminded herself that Kadir should not have kissed her because he was engaged to another woman. She felt as if a knife had sliced through her heart, and she swayed on her feet.

'Miss Howard?' Yusuf sounded anxious. 'Are you going to faint? The heat of the desert can take some getting used to, especially for someone as fair-skinned and delicate-looking as yourself,' the adviser murmured sympathetically.

Lexi's eyes snapped open. 'I assure you I am not in the least delicate,' she told Yusuf tersely. She was furious with herself for reacting to Kadir the way she had. It could not happen again. She was not a silly lovestruck girl, wilting beneath the desert sun and a surfeit of hormones. She had come to Zenhab to do a job and she *must* forget those passionate moments she had spent in the Sultan's arms, as it appeared that he had forgotten her.

Kadir had reached the group of horsemen and a huge black horse was brought to him. He swung himself into the saddle and reached behind his shoulder to withdraw a long curved sword from a jewelled scabbard that Lexi saw hanging down his back. The horsemen did likewise, and held their swords aloft, the steel blades glinting in the fierce sun as their Sultan gave a loud victory cry.

The scene could have taken place centuries ago, when the great Islamic leader Saladin had fought the English King Richard in the Crusades, Lexi thought. This was the real Kadir Al Sulaimar, she realised. There was no sign of the charismatic playboy she had met when they had been in Europe. The Sultan of Zenhab looked stern and forbidding, yet she could not forget how his mouth had felt on hers when he had kissed her, his unexpected tenderness as he had teased her lips apart and explored her with his tongue.

Her breath caught in her throat as Kadir turned his head and stared directly at her. Lexi had the strange sense that he was remembering the moments when they had fallen into each other's arms in the summer house. But the gleam in his eyes must have been sunlight reflected off his sword. He turned away and gave a blood-curdling cry before he galloped his horse down the runway, pursued by the thirty horsemen, in a cloud of dust and flashing horses' hooves and white *keffiyeh's* streaming behind the cavalcade.

* * *

She could not ask for a better place to work, Lexi conceded a few days later. She had been given a luxurious apartment at the palace with her own private terrace and pool, and she had access to the beautiful royal gardens, where it was pleasant to sit by the ornamental fountains and feel the cool spray on her face.

Kadir had a busy schedule and attended meetings and functions most days, requiring Lexi to fly him by helicopter to towns across the kingdom. The previous day she had flown him along Zenhab's stunning coast so that he could inspect the site of a new hotel complex, which his adviser Yusuf had said was going to be built by the Russian businessman Boris Denisov.

Apart from bidding her good morning, Kadir had not spoken to her, and he'd sat in the rear of the helicopter. He obviously intended to keep their relationship strictly professional, but Lexi had been aware of his brooding gaze burning between her shoulder blades during the flight.

She was lonely at the palace, and missed the sense of camaraderie she'd had with her friends in the coastguard agency and the RAF. From one of the tallest towers she was able to look out over the desert, and remembering the dusty military base at Camp Bastion in Afghanistan and the other pilots she had flown missions with increased her sense of isolation.

As was her habit, she turned to physical exercise to relieve her frustration, and went running every morning before the sun rose high in the sky and the temperature soared. She'd also discovered an air-conditioned gym in the palace where Kadir's bodyguards worked out. Ashar and Nasim were reasonably fluent in English, and Lexi spoke some Arabic. Once they had got over their initial hesitancy at sharing the gym with a woman, the two young men were friendly and their company went some way to alleviating her loneliness.

'I'll grant you that men are physically stronger than women, but in a test of stamina and endurance women can equal, or even beat their male counterparts,' Lexi argued one afternoon.

Nasim stepped off the treadmill. 'Okay, prove it. Push-ups until one of us gives up.'

Determination gleamed in Lexi's eyes. 'You're on. Ashar, you can act as judge.'

Kadir frowned as he walked down the corridor to the gym and heard voices from behind the door. He had been busy with matters of state since he had returned to the palace, and this was his first chance for a workout. He had hoped to find the gym empty but, as he opened the door, he came to an abrupt halt at the sight of one of his bodyguards and his private pilot stretched out on gym mats, pumping their bodies up and down in a series of push-ups.

From where he was standing he had a perfect view of Lexi's pert bottom covered in bright pink satin shorts—lifting and lowering, lifting and lowering in a steady rhythm that had a predictable effect on his pulse rate. He visualised her slender body arched above him, the tips of her bare breasts brushing his chest as she slowly lowered herself onto him... His arousal was instant and so hard that he hastily held his towel in front of him and cursed beneath his breath.

'What is going on?' He knew it was a stupid question, but the sound of his voice had the desired effect of making Lexi and the bodyguard stop what they were doing and jump to their feet. The guilty expression on Nasim's face heightened Kadir's anger. Why did the bodyguard look guilty, unless the push-ups were a prelude to another form of exercise? he thought grimly.

'Do you not kneel before your Sultan?' he demanded to Nasim and Ashar.

'Your Majesty!' The men immediately dropped down onto one knee, but Lexi remained standing and met Kadir's hard stare with a challenge in her eyes as she placed her hands on her hips.

'Is there a problem, Your Highness?'

You're damned right there's a problem, Kadir thought to himself. But he was not going to admit that his body felt as if it was about to explode, or that he was unbearably tempted to dismiss the bodyguards and make love to his feisty helicopter pilot right there on the gym mat. He was shocked and, if he was honest, ashamed of his ferocious desire for Lexi. No other woman had ever made him feel so out of control. He was a powerful Sultan, but she reminded him that he was also just a man with an inexplicable hunger clawing in his gut.

'My bodyguards owe you an apology. They should have respected your privacy and departed from the gym while you were exercising.'

Lexi shrugged. 'They offered to leave, but I don't have a problem with them being here. I was used to training alongside men when I was in the RAF.'

Kadir's jaw tightened. 'You must understand that we have different ways here than in England.'

Lexi knew that although Zenhab was one of the more liberal countries in the Middle East, there were rules regarding men and women socialising together. 'I understand that I wouldn't be allowed to mix with men in a public gym, but this is a private facility and surely the same rules don't apply? After all, the palace is your home, and you make the rules.'

'That's right,' Kadir said in a dangerously soft voice intended to warn Lexi that she was close to overstepping the mark, 'and my rule is that from now on you will be allocated separate times to use the gym when the men are not allowed in.'

Lexi could see that further arguing would be pointless. The Sultan had spoken. She glanced at the bodyguards, who were still kneeling, their heads bowed. Usually Kadir had an easy-going relationship with his protection officers and she did not understand why he was so annoyed. She did not want to lose her friendship with the two bodyguards. They were her only companions at the palace and if she was banned from spending time with them she knew she would feel even more isolated.

'Please don't blame Nasim and Ashar. It was my fault if any rules were broken.'

Her defence of the two men further fuelled Kadir's temper. He held the door open for Lexi to leave. 'I will deal with them as I see fit, before I deal with you.'

'*Deal* with me?' The vague threat was like a red rag to a bull. 'What are you going to do, send me to bed with no tea? Put me across your knee?'

'Would you like me to spank you?' Kadir murmured dulcetly. He had followed Lexi out into the corridor so that the bodyguards could not hear their conversation.

A shockingly erotic image of him holding her face down over his thighs while he chastised her flashed into her mind and fiery colour flooded her cheeks. 'Of course not,' she said sharply.

His husky chuckle warned her that he had read her

thoughts, and Lexi's embarrassment became more acute. But she wondered why he was clutching his towel in front of his hips as if his life depended on it. Her senses, acutely attuned to him, detected the undefinable essence of male pheromones, the scent of sexual arousal.

'Why does it matter to you if I hang out with Nasim and Ashar in my free time?' she burst out. 'There is no one else I can socialise with and I realise that it is not possible for me to go out in the city in the evenings on my own. I feel like I'm trapped at the palace.'

'You have been provided with excellent accommodation and leisure facilities; I did not realise you expected to have a full social calendar. The palace is hardly a prison,' Kadir said drily.

Lexi gave up trying to make him understand that she craved the company of other people. When she had served in the RAF she'd had a wide group of friends and had felt a sense of belonging that had been missing with her adoptive parents. Being alone gave her too much time to think, and stirred up her old feelings of loneliness and inadequacy she had felt as a child.

But Kadir knew nothing about her troubled background, and she had no intention of telling him. A dignified retreat seemed her best option but, as usual, she was determined to have the last word.

'Perhaps hard physical exertion in the gym will relieve some of your tension,' she murmured, before she turned and marched down the corridor, leaving Kadir fighting the temptation to go after her and kiss her sassy mouth into submission. There was only one kind of physical exertion that he knew was guaranteed to relieve his sexual frustration, but he could not make love to Lexi, no matter how much he wanted to.

* * *

Lexi had hoped that a punishing fifteen-kilometre run through the palace grounds would expend her anger with Kadir for criticising her friendship with his bodyguards. But when she returned to her apartment her temper was still simmering, and to cool down she dived into the pool and swam twenty lengths. Breathless at last, she hauled herself onto the poolside and shook her wet hair back from her face.

She stiffened when she saw Kadir was standing watching her. 'I assume you have no objection to me swimming in my private pool?' She hoped her cool tone disguised the heat that surged through her as she drank in the sight of him in cream chinos and a black polo shirt. His eyes were hidden behind designer shades and he was so outrageously attractive that Lexi almost jumped back into the pool to hide her body's reaction to him. Her nipples were as hard as pebbles and she hastily dragged the towel around her shoulders to hide her traitorous body from view.

He gave her a lazy smile, no hint now of his earlier bad mood. 'None at all,' he assured her, 'although I am wondering why you aren't wearing your silver bikini.'

She shrugged. 'A one-piece is more comfortable for swimming. But another reason is that I *do* appreciate the cultural differences in the Middle East. Although the pool is for my private use, the palace staff are around and out of respect for them I chose to wear a swimming costume. It's more demure than a bikini.'

Demure! Kadir wondered if Lexi had any idea how sexy she looked in her sleek navy costume, which clung to every dip and curve of her superbly toned figure. He could not forget the image of her taut buttocks covered in tight pink shorts pumping up and down when she had been doing push-ups in the gym. Fire heated his blood and he altered his position to hide the evidence of his arousal beneath his trousers, which suddenly felt uncomfortably tight.

'Anyway, there is no point in me wearing my bikini when I'm not allowed to socialise with anyone at the palace, or get a chance to meet a guy who I would like to untie the strings,' Lexi said defiantly.

Kadir's eyes narrowed. 'Always you challenge me, Lexi. You want to be careful that I do not rise to your bait.'

Her gaze did not waver from his. 'You have already demonstrated that that isn't going to happen. I made a fool of myself in Italy,' she said bitterly. She hated herself for the way she had responded to him like a gauche teenager on a first date. He was the only man who had ever made her lose control and the level of her desire had shocked and shamed her.

She suddenly became conscious of how close they were standing. The air between them throbbed with tension and every nerve ending on her body tingled with sexual awareness that she knew he felt too.

'I was the fool, for kissing you when I knew I was not free to make love to you,' Kadir said harshly. He picked up her robe and handed it to her. 'Put this on, before I forget my good intentions.' He gave a wry smile that did not reach his eyes, and Lexi had a sudden sense of how lonely his role as Sultan must be. His father was dead, his mother lived abroad and he was destined to marry a woman he had never met who had been chosen for him.

If he had not been contracted to his arranged marriage, she knew that they would be lovers by now. His desire for her smouldered in his dark eyes, but the firm set of his jaw told her that he would put his duty to his kingdom before his personal desires.

She pulled on the robe and tied the belt tightly around her waist. 'Why did you want to see me?'

Because he could not keep away from her, Kadir thought grimly. She was like a drug in his veins and even the knowledge that his desire for her was forbidden did not stop him thinking about her constantly.

'I came to apologise for my behaviour earlier. I appreciate that you might feel cut off from your friends and family. I have come with an invitation to tea from someone who I believe you could become friends with.'

Lexi eyed him suspiciously. 'Who?'

His grin made him look suddenly younger. 'I'm taking you to meet the most important woman in my life.'

'I'm seventy-six,' Mabel Dawkins told Lexi as she poured tea into bone china cups and nodded towards a plate of scones. 'Help yourselves. I always make scones when Kadir comes to tea. When he was a boy he could eat a plateful all to himself.'

Lexi settled back on the chintz sofa in Mabel's pretty apartment at the palace and bit into a feather-light fruit scone. 'So you were Kadir's nanny when he was growing up?'

'Lady Judith hired me when her son was born. After she left the palace and returned to England, Sultan Khalif asked me to remain here to give Kadir stability because it was a difficult situation for a young boy to grow up in two very different cultures, here in Zenhab and at Montgomery Manor in England.'

Lexi glanced at Kadir. 'It must have been strange to move between Western culture and Middle Eastern traditions. Do you think of yourself more as an English Earl or an Arab prince?'

'I love my mother and I was close to my grandfather, the tenth Earl. But I am my father's son, from an ancient line of desert kings, and my heart and soul belong to Zenhab,' he said without hesitation.

Recalling how, when they had arrived in Zenhab, Kadir had wielded a fearsome-looking sword and given a battle cry to rouse his horsemen, Lexi was learning that beneath his playboy image reported in the European press there was a far more serious side to the Sultan of Zenhab that the paparazzi never saw.

She was agonisingly conscious of him sitting next to her. The two-seater sofa was made even smaller because it was stuffed with Mabel's many crocheted cushions and, however stiffly Lexi held herself, she could not prevent her thigh from touching Kadir's. She could feel his hard muscles through her thin skirt, and the spicy tang of his cologne wove a seductive spell around her.

'What made you decide to join the RAF?' Mabel's voice dragged Lexi's mind away from her wayward thoughts.

She shrugged. 'I wanted an exciting career, the opportunity to travel.' She did not explain that one reason why she had joined the air force had been because she had been looking for somewhere where she felt she belonged. Her adoptive parents had not really wanted her, and she had been hurt that her birth mother had insisted on keeping her a secret from her husband, as if Cathy was ashamed of her.

'It must have been an exciting life, but dangerous too,' Mabel said. 'I expect your parents must have worried about you when you were stationed in Afghanistan.'

'I don't think so,' Lexi said wryly. 'My parents are busy with their own lives.'

'Kadir told me that you will be staying in Zenhab and working as his helicopter pilot for six months. That's a long time to be away from home, although I suppose when you were in the RAF you got used to living away from loved ones. Do you have a sweetheart back in England?'

Lexi was amused by the elderly nanny's curiosity. 'No, I don't.'

'I'm surprised. You're such a pretty girl. Are you gay?' Mabel asked bluntly.

Lexi choked on a mouthful of scone and hastily washed it down with a sip of tea. 'No, I'm not.' Realising that Mabel had no qualms about prying into her personal life, she murmured, 'Actually, I was engaged but it didn't work out.'

'Mabel, it's unfair to interrogate Lexi,' Kadir interrupted. He had felt the sudden tension that gripped her and forced himself to ignore his own curiosity about her love life. He recalled Charles Fairfax had mentioned that she had been engaged but her fiancé had ended the relationship. Was she still in love with the guy she had hoped to marry? he mused, wondering why he disliked the idea.

His phone rang and he glanced at the name of the caller. 'I'll have to take this, I'm afraid,' he said apologetically. 'Lexi, please stay and finish your tea. If you think Mabel's scones are good, wait until you try her sponge cake.'

'He works so hard,' Mabel sighed when Kadir had left. 'He told me that his latest trip to Europe was very successful and he managed to secure several big deals with companies who will invest in new businesses in Zenhab.'

Lexi remembered that Kadir's adviser, Yusuf bin Hilal, had said that the Sultan worked hard to attract foreign investment to his kingdom. 'The European press seem more interested in Kadir's private life and his reputation as a playboy.'

'Oh, the press!' Mabel gave a snort. 'Most of what is written in the foreign newspapers is rubbish. The paparazzi don't know the man that I know Kadir to be. He vowed as his father lay dying that he would devote his life to Zenhab and continue Sultan Khalif's work to maintain peace and bring prosperity to the kingdom.'

'Was Kadir close to his father?'

'Very. Father and son adored one another.' Mabel's lined face softened. 'Kadir was heartbroken when Khalif died but at the same time he was relieved that his father was spared any more suffering.'

Lexi felt strangely unsettled at the thought of Kadir being heartbroken. She had been too ready to believe the stories in the tabloids about him leading a charmed life of hedonistic pleasure, she acknowledged guiltily. But she was discovering that he was a man of deep emotions who had grieved for his father and vowed to rule Zenhab with the same devotion to duty as Sultan Khalif had done. 'Why did Sultan Khalif suffer? Was he ill before he died?' she asked curiously.

'He suffered a stroke when Kadir was sixteen, which left him completely paralysed and barely able to speak. Obviously, Khalif could not continue to rule the country,' Mabel explained, 'and Kadir was too young to become Sultan, so Khalif's younger brother, Jamal, became the interim ruler until Kadir came of age.'

'And Jamal handed the Sultanate to Kadir when he was twenty-one?'

'Unfortunately, it wasn't quite as simple as that. Jamal wanted to remain as Sultan, and he had followers who believed that he should rule Zenhab and who were opposed to Kadir's plans to modernise the country. Before Jamal would agree to step aside and allow Kadir to take his rightful place as Sultan, he insisted that Kadir sign a contract to marry the daughter of Jamal's great ally, Sheikh Rashid bin Al-Hassan. Since Rashid died two months ago, Kadir has been under pressure to go ahead with his wedding to Princess Haleema to unite the country.

'Jamal and his followers are against change and want Zenhab to return to feudal isolation as it was in the past,' Mabel said grimly. 'There have been plots to overthrow Kadir, and two years ago he survived an assassination attempt. A gun was fired by someone in a crowd, but fortunately the bullet narrowly missed him.'

The conversation turned to other matters, but later, as Lexi walked in the palace gardens, she could not forget Mabel's revelation that an attempt had been made on Kadir's life by his enemies. Far from being the playboy prince she had believed him to be, he was a dutiful Sultan who had dedicated his life to his kingdom.

The sun was sliding below the horizon, staining the sky flamingo-pink, and the fiery hues were reflected in the ornamental pools and many fountains in the formal gardens. Lexi strolled along an avenue of palm trees, but a familiar voice drew her from her thoughts, and her heart gave an annoying flip when she watched Kadir get up from a bench and walk towards her.

He had changed into a traditional white robe which skimmed his powerful body. As he came closer, Lexi could see the shadow of his black chest hairs beneath the fine cotton. He halted in front of her and smiled, revealing his perfect teeth, as white as his *keffiyeh* which framed his darkly tanned face.

'The gardens are so beautiful,' she said, looking around her because she dared not look at him, searching for something to say while she frantically tried to control her racing pulse.

'My father had them landscaped as a gift for my mother. She fell in love with the gardens at Versailles on their honeymoon and *Baba* wanted to re-create them at the palace. Unfortunately, the project took longer to complete than my parents' marriage lasted,' Kadir said drily.

He indicated a carving on the trunk of a palm tree, and Lexi saw the shape of a heart inscribed with the words *Judith will love Khalif for ever.* 'My mother made the carving. After she left, my father used to come and sit beneath this tree every day. He loved my mother until the day he died. When I look at the inscription I am reminded that people often do not mean what they say.'

'How true,' she said flatly, thinking of the many times people had let her down.

The emptiness in her voice stirred Kadir's curiosity. 'Why did your engagement end?'

For a moment Lexi did not answer. She rarely opened up about her private life. She did not understand the connection she felt with Kadir, but for some reason she felt drawn to confide in him.

'I met Steven when we were serving with the RAF in Afghanistan. Living in a war zone is a strange experience,' she explained ruefully. 'Your emotions are heightened by the constant threat of danger. When Steven proposed, I accepted because I longed for a settled life, a home and a family. We planned to marry as soon as we finished our tour of duty, but he had failed to mention that he had a girlfriend and a baby in England. He told me by text message on the evening that we were supposed to be holding our engagement party that he wasn't free to marry me.'

Beneath Lexi's tough exterior was a vulnerable woman who had been badly hurt, Kadir realised. He felt guilty that while they had been in Europe he had succumbed to the sexual chemistry between them and kissed her, knowing that he wasn't free to have any kind of relationship with her.

'Mabel reminded me that six months is a long time to be away from home,' he said abruptly. 'You are welcome to invite your friends and family to the palace. I thought you might like to ask your parents to visit.'

'They wouldn't want to come. But thanks for the offer.'

He was puzzled by her offhand response. 'It sounds as though you don't have a close relationship with your parents.'

Lexi shrugged. 'It's true that we're not close. I'm adopted. My parents believed they couldn't have a child but, after they adopted me, my mother fell pregnant and gave birth to a daughter, which rather made me redundant.'

Once again Kadir heard a note of hurt in her voice and he felt an unexpected tug on his heart. 'I'm sure your parents did not think that.'

'As a matter of fact I overheard Marcus tell another relative that he and Veronica—my adoptive mother— would not have adopted a child if they had known they could have a child of their own,' Lexi said flatly. 'From the age of eight I knew I was an inconvenience when my parents packed me off to boarding school so that they could concentrate on Athena.'

'I wondered why you and your sister do not look alike.

Did you resent Athena because your parents gave her more attention?'

Lexi thought of her awkward, accident-prone sister and gave a rueful smile. 'It would be impossible to resent Athena. She has the sweetest nature, and actually I think she has struggled to meet Marcus and Veronica's expectations.' She frowned as she recalled her misgivings about Athena's intention to marry Charles Fairfax.

While she and Kadir had been talking, day had turned into night as quickly as Lexi remembered from the desert in Afghanistan, and a sliver of silver moon was climbing the sky accompanied by the first stars. She wondered what he was thinking. His hard-boned face was impossible to read, but she seemed to be acutely sensitive to his emotions and sensed that his mood had darkened.

'Tomorrow I will require you to fly me across the desert to the old city of Sanqirah in the mountains,' he said tersely. 'The northern territories are much hotter and drier than here, where we are closer to the coast. You will probably be more comfortable wearing appropriate clothing rather than your pilot's uniform.'

Lexi's stomach plummeted as if she was riding a big dipper at the funfair. She knew that Princess Haleema lived in the mountains. And Mabel had said that Kadir's uncle Jamal had been pushing for him to honour his marriage agreement. Pride demanded that she kept her voice unemotional. 'What time do you want to leave?'

'Early, and we won't return until late.' Kadir's jaw tightened. Since he had received a phone call from Haleema's brother, Omar, to confirm their meeting tomorrow he had sensed that his freedom was ending.

He felt no joy at the prospect of taking a girl he had never met as his bride, but it was necessary to prevent his detractors and Jamal's supporters from challenging his rule and creating civil unrest in the kingdom. The time had come for him to honour his promise to his father. But the future seemed bleaker since he had been plucked from the sea by a woman who challenged him at every opportunity and made his blood run faster through his veins.

'*Lexi...*' Kadir watched her walk away from him and could not prevent himself from uttering her name in a low, driven tone.

She turned to him, her face serenely beautiful. Her long blonde hair seemed to shimmer in the moonlight. 'Yes.'

Her voice was not quite steady, and Kadir knew then that the night air, thick with the scents of jasmine and orange blossom, was bewitching her senses as it beguiled his. He saw wariness in her eyes as well as a hunger that she could not hide, and he knew he should walk away from her.

She had been hurt by her ex-fiancé and by her adoptive parents. He had no right to play with her emotions when he knew that it could only lead to him hurting her too. But she was so lovely. He had never wanted any woman as fiercely as he wanted her and he could not stop himself from walking towards her.

'Was there something else you wanted?' she asked innocently.

'Just...this...'

'*No.*' Lexi's soft cry was crushed by Kadir's mouth as he pulled her into his arms and claimed her lips. Her protest was carried away on the breeze that stirred the fronds of the palm trees. She had not expected him to kiss her and she had no time to muster any resistance, or so she tried to kid herself. But she was already lost to his magic, swept into his sensual spell as he swept her hard against him so that she was conscious of every muscle and sinew in his body, every beat of his heart.

His lips sipped from hers as he kissed her with a hunger that matched her own. Desire blazed white-hot, but underlying their passion was something indefinable, a connection between two souls as their two hearts thundered in unison.

Lexi gasped as Kadir skimmed his lips down her throat. The stubble on his jaw grazed her sensitive skin and the exquisite pleasure-pain sent a shudder through her. She arched her neck as he threaded his fingers into her hair and almost purred with pleasure when he cradled her head, angling her face so that he could plunder her mouth again and again until she felt boneless.

She could feel the solid ridge of his arousal pushing against her pelvis, and the evidence of his need excited her. But it was *wrong*. He had promised to marry another woman.

'No!' She tore her mouth from his, noting that he made no attempt to stop her. 'No more games,' she said quietly, proud that her voice was steady, even if her legs were not. Somehow she forced her feet to move, although it felt as if she had severed a limb when she stepped away from him. 'What do you want from me, Kadir?'

'Everything.'

The single word detonated between them as his harsh voice resonated with a depth of emotion that shocked Lexi. His eyes were black in the darkness. Kadir clenched his hands into fists to prevent himself from reaching for her. She could never be his and the knowledge felt like a knife blade through his heart. 'But I cannot take your beauty and your fire. And I can offer you nothing. I should not have brought you to Zenhab.'

The tortured expression on his face made Lexi's insides twist with a shared pain, and she suddenly knew that if she stayed in Zenhab they would destroy each other.

'Then let me go,' she whispered. 'This situation is unbearable for both of us. And it will be unfair on your young bride. Haleema may have led a sheltered life but she will notice the way we look at each other.' She swallowed. 'Steven made me an unwitting accomplice when he cheated on his girlfriend who was waiting for him in England. Our desire for one another is wrong, and the only way we can end it is for me to leave Zenhab and we will never see each other again.' The thought was agonising, but Lexi knew it would be even more painful to remain at the palace and watch Kadir marry his Princess.

Lexi was right. He had to let her go, Kadir acknowledged heavily. His duty to his kingdom and his promise to his father must come before his personal desires. 'I still need you to fly me to Haleema's home in the mountains tomorrow. My meeting with her brother, Sheikh Omar, is arranged and it will be seen as a great insult if I fail to attend. But after that I will release you from your contract…and you will be free to leave Zenhab,' he said harshly.

It was for the best, Lexi told herself. The madness had to end. Without a word, she turned and fled from Kadir, her chest aching with the leaden weight of her heart. As she ran through the dark gardens she did not notice one of the palace staff watching her from the shadows.

CHAPTER EIGHT

THE SULTAN WAS dressed in his robes of state, although he was not carrying a sword or a ceremonial knife in his belt, Lexi noted. The embroidered jacket he wore over his white robe was encrusted with dark red rubies which reminded her of droplets of blood.

She gave herself a mental shake, impatient with her fanciful imagination. But she could not tear her gaze from Kadir as he walked across the palace courtyard to the helipad, and she was conscious of his gaze skimming over her desert boots, khaki combats and vest top. She had tied her hair into a ponytail and the peak of her baseball cap cast a shadow over her face which she hoped disguised the dark circles beneath her eyes, evidence of her sleepless night.

'You said I didn't need to wear my pilot's uniform,' she reminded him, taking his silence as censure.

'You should bring a jacket. The temperature in the mountains can drop twenty degrees once the sun sets in the evening.'

Silence stretched between them, tightening Lexi's nerves. She could still taste him on her lips from when he had kissed her the previous night. 'Is it safe for you to go to the mountains?' she burst out. 'Mabel said that the northern tribes are your enemies and there has already been one attempt made on your life.'

His brows rose 'Why, Lexi, would you care if someone took a pot shot at me?' he drawled.

In her mind, she was back in Helmand province in Afghanistan, watching her co-pilot Sam jump out of the helicopter and run to the aid of an injured soldier. The sniper's bullet seemed to come from nowhere. One second Sam was running, the next he was lying lifeless on the desert sand. Death had been delivered in the blink of an eye. Lexi would always remember Sam's cheerful grin and zest for life.

She stared at the blood-red rubies spattered over Kadir's jacket and pictured a faceless figure in a crowd, aiming a gun and pulling the trigger. 'Of course I'd care, damn you,' she said thickly.

'Lexi.' Kadir swore beneath his breath.

She turned away from him, afraid he would see the raw emotions he evoked in her. 'Why do you have a different bodyguard?' She glanced at the man sitting in the front passenger seat of the helicopter. 'Where are Nasim and Ashar?'

'Ashar is away visiting his family. Nasim called in sick this morning.'

Lexi frowned. 'What's wrong with him? He seemed fine in the gym yesterday.'

Kadir closed his eyes and tried to dismiss the vision of Lexi's bottom in tight pink shorts moving up and down as she performed push-ups in a competition with his bodyguard. 'Your concern for Nasim is touching,' he said curtly. 'But no doubt you will strike up a friendship with Fariq.'

'I'm not so sure.' Lexi couldn't explain why she had

not warmed to the replacement bodyguard, or why her nerves felt on edge. She looked around the empty courtyard. 'Where are Yusuf and your other advisers who usually accompany you?'

'I am going to the mountains alone, and I am not carrying my ceremonial weapons to show my host, Sheikh Omar, that I come in peace.' By the end of today he would be officially engaged to Haleema and Zenhab would be looking forward to a royal wedding, Kadir thought with grim resignation.

Lexi held open the door of the helicopter and was gripped by an inexplicable sense of dread. 'I've got a bad feeling about this trip.' She shrugged helplessly. 'I wish we weren't going today.'

For a split second, emotion flickered in Kadir's dark gaze, a look almost of pain, before his thick lashes swept down like curtains hiding the windows to his soul.

'I have to go,' he said harshly. 'This is my destiny.' He glanced at the gold watch on his wrist. 'It's time we were on our way.'

The AgustaWestland was a dream to fly, and once Lexi had taken off she turned the helicopter towards the desert and prepared to enjoy the spectacular view. Beside her, the new bodyguard seemed restless and ill at ease and although the cabin was air-conditioned he was sweating profusely.

Lexi glanced at him. 'Are you nervous about flying, Fariq?' she asked him, speaking into her headset.

'No. *I'm* not afraid, but you should be.'

Puzzled, she turned her head to look at him and her heart catapulted against her ribs when she saw a gleam of grey metal and recognised the barrel of a pistol partly concealed in the bodyguard's jacket. 'Don't make a fuss,'

Fariq said softly. 'Fly the helicopter to these new coordinates.'

Lexi glanced at the piece of paper he placed on her knee. On the video screen she could see Kadir in the rear of the helicopter, putting on his headphones, and she guessed he was unaware of the situation. Her eyes jerked to the pistol that Fariq was aiming at her ribs. Her mouth felt dry, but her military training kicked in and she suppressed her fear by forcing herself to think logically and remain calm.

Moments later, Kadir's voice came though her headphones. 'Why are you heading towards the coast? You're flying in the wrong direction.'

The bodyguard turned around and pointed the gun at Kadir. 'There has been a change of plan, Your Highness. Hand over your cellphones, both of you.'

Kadir froze, and his first thought was that he should have questioned, as Lexi had, the fact that Nasim had unexpectedly been taken ill. Clearly, someone had wanted his protection officer out of the way and he prayed that Nasim had not been killed.

'Whatever it is you want, there is no reason for you to involve my pilot.' He spoke calmly to Fariq. 'Let Lexi land the helicopter. You can keep me as a hostage, or kill me if that is your plan. But let her go.'

'No!' Lexi felt a rush of emotion at Kadir's attempt to protect her. 'You can't kill the Sultan,' she told the gunman. 'You'll never get away with it. If you allow him to go free, I'll fly you to wherever you want to go and no one will know about this incident.'

Fariq laughed. 'Your determination to protect each other is touching,' he sneered. He stared at Kadir. 'The rumour that the western woman is your mistress is obviously correct. Nobody will get killed as long as you do as I tell you. Continue flying to the coordinates I gave you,' the gunman ordered Lexi, 'and don't try anything clever because I swear I will pull the trigger and we'll all go down.'

She could tell he meant what he said, and she could also tell he was nervous, which made him volatile and likely to panic. There was nothing Lexi could do but fly to the new destination. After fifteen minutes, during which time the mounting tension seemed to suck the air out of the cabin, they flew over the coast.

The sea was sapphire-blue and sparkled in the early morning sunshine. Did the world seem more beautiful because she had a gun aimed at her? Lexi wondered. She was conscious of her heart beating hard and fast in her chest as adrenalin pumped through her veins. On the video screen she could see Kadir sitting behind her. What if the gunman did actually intend to kill him?

Fear stole her breath. *She could not bear to lose him!* She couldn't bear to kneel by his lifeless body as she had knelt beside her best friend, Sam, desperately searching for a pulse but knowing it was too late.

Kadir is not yours to lose, whispered a voice in her head. And in a heartbeat she discovered that she wished he was.

Below them, a small island came into view, white sand and green palm trees rising up out of the sapphire sea. 'Land the chopper down there on the beach,' the gunman instructed.

Would they be ambushed by more gunmen once they were on the ground? Supremely conscious of the pistol barrel inches away from her, Lexi took the helicopter down and landed it on the beach.

'Now get out, both of you, and put your hands above your heads.'

Lexi jumped down onto the sand and raised her arms, and seconds later she was joined by Kadir. The gunman seemed to be working alone. She scanned the line of trees at the top of the beach and saw no sign of anyone else.

'I reckon we could take him,' she muttered to Kadir. 'We're two against one.'

'But the one has a gun,' he hissed back. 'Don't be stupid.'

His words had the desired effect, Kadir noted with relief as Lexi's eyes flashed him a furious look. She was as courageous as a tigress, but no way would he allow her to risk her life. He was confused by their location. Nothing made sense, and the situation became even more bizarre when the gunman locked the helicopter and pocketed the key.

Fariq ran down the beach, and it was then that Lexi noticed a motorboat half hidden behind some rocks. She watched Fariq push the boat into the sea before he leapt aboard and started the engine.

'He's leaving us here!' Her brain finally clicked into gear. Events had happened so quickly, but now Lexi stared at the boat as it sped away. *'Hey...'*

She spun round to Kadir. 'Terrific, we're stranded. From the air, the island looked uninhabited. But why would the gunman leave us here? Surely when you fail to arrive for your meeting with Haleema's brother, an alert will be raised that you are missing and people will search for you? What can anyone hope to gain by kidnapping us and dumping us on a deserted island?'

Kadir racked his brain for an explanation. Someone did not want him to meet Omar bin Al-Hassan to discuss his marriage to Princess Haleema, but who, and why? The only reason he could think of was that the person behind the kidnap plot did not want him to make peace with the leader of the northern tribes. Someone wanted to stir up trouble in Zenhab, and the most obvious suspect was his uncle. He dragged his mind from his confused thoughts as Lexi started to stride along the beach. 'Where are you going?'

She glanced over her shoulder. 'To find somewhere for us to shelter; it's the first thing I learned to do in RAF survival training. From the air I saw some cliffs on the other side of the island, and there might be a cave. We'll also need to find food, and collect firewood.'

Kadir hid his irritation that his pilot was too bossy for her own good and sat down on a rock. 'It sounds exhausting,' he drawled.

Lexi put her hands on her hips, her slender body practically quivering with impatience. 'Are you just going to sit there? You might be a Sultan, but if you think I'm going to wait on you like your staff at the palace do, think again.'

She marched away from him, her temper fizzing. But she recognised that her anger was a release of her pent-up emotions. She felt sick with relief that the gunman had not hurt them. Fear had churned in her stomach when the gun had been pointed at her, and she'd been terrified when the gunman had aimed at Kadir. Now, for some reason, she felt stupidly tearful and she was fighting a strong urge to run back to Kadir and throw herself into his arms.

The island was bigger than it had looked from the air and it took Lexi almost two hours to follow the coastline round to the other side, where she found a few low cliffs and no caves. She continued walking for another hour before completing a circuit of the island and finally ended up back at the helicopter. There was no sign of Kadir and, after dumping the driftwood she had collected to make a fire, she walked up the beach and into the shade of the palm trees. The ground was littered with branches and palm fronds that could be used to construct a shelter, she decided.

Pushing through the trees, she found herself at the edge of a desert plain. Beyond a line of dunes she could see more palm trees and the glint of water—an oasis, and next to it…a tent!

What on earth? Ignoring the fact that she was hot and tired from hours of walking in the burning sun, Lexi scrambled over the dunes, her progress hampered by her feet sinking into the soft sand. She was breathless when she arrived at the huge tent and stared in disbelief at Kadir lying on a hammock strung between two palm trees.

'Where *are* we?' She was beginning to feel as if she had fallen into the pages of *Alice in Wonderland.*

Kadir propped himself up on one elbow and regarded her lazily. He had changed out of his royal robes into a pair of frayed denim shorts that sat low on his hips and displayed his muscle-packed abdomen. Beneath the glare of the desert sun, his bare chest was the colour of burnished bronze overlaid with whorls of silky black hairs.

Lexi licked her parched lips, conscious that her pounding heart was not the result of walking over the dunes.

'We're on Jinan, which means beautiful garden,' he told her. 'It is a private island belonging to me personally, rather than to the Sultanate of Zenhab.'

'Why did the kidnapper bring us to your private island?' Lexi frowned as the meaning of his words be-

came clear. 'You must have known where we were when
I landed the helicopter. Why did you let me traipse around
the island looking for a place to shelter when you knew
that this—' she waved towards the tent '—was here?'

He shrugged and his powerful shoulder muscles rip-
pled beneath his satiny skin. 'You were determined to
demonstrate your survival techniques and it seemed a
shame to spoil your fun.'

In truth, Kadir had felt relieved when she'd stormed
off along the beach. He had needed some time alone to
control his emotions in the aftermath of seeing a gun
being aimed at Lexi. When her life had been threatened
on the helicopter he had been consumed with rage, but
his desperation to protect her had been tempered by the
bitter realisation that the kidnapper was quite literally
calling the shots.

Lexi glared at him, her temper flaring as quickly as
tinder set alight with a match. 'Bastard!' Her blue eyes
blazed as she walked towards him and Kadir tensed as he
watched her pull a penknife from the pocket of her combats. Without uttering another word, she sliced through
the rope which tied one end of the hammock to the tree
trunk and watched him land in an ignominious heap on
the sand before she strode into the tent.

It was the size of a marquee, Lexi realised as she
looked around the interior of the tent. Camping on Dart-
moor on military exercises with the RAF had *never* been
like this! She pulled off her boots and walked barefoot
across the richly patterned rugs covering the floor. In
place of chairs and sofas there was a raised platform
covered with brightly coloured fabric and sumptuous
silk cushions. Drawing aside a curtain, she discovered a
bedroom with a huge, low bed draped with satin sheets in

vibrant jewel shades. Behind a partition was a bathroom with a walk-in shower and at the far end of the tent was a kitchen area complete with a working fridge.

'Solar panels provide electricity, and the oasis is a source of fresh water,' Kadir explained as he followed her into the kitchen and opened the fridge to take out a bottle of drink. 'I keep a satellite phone here, but the kidnappers have taken it so we can't call for help,' he said in answer to Lexi's questioning look.

He watched her gnaw her bottom lip with her teeth and the giveaway sign of her vulnerability touched him more than it had any right to. 'I don't believe that whoever is behind the kidnap plot intends to harm us, because they would have done so by now. For some reason, someone wants me out of the way for a while.' He frowned. 'I have an idea who is behind this.' Jamal's weasel features came into his mind. 'But at the moment I don't understand why.'

'What if we are left stranded here for weeks?'

'That won't happen. My staff come to the island regularly to check on the place, and there is always a supply of non-perishable food here, certainly enough to last us for a few days before we have to go hunting for our meals.'

The amusement in his voice was the last straw. 'I can't believe I was actually worried that the kidnapper might hurt you,' Lexi snapped. 'I walked around the island for three goddamned *hours* while you were lazing here in luxury.' As she spoke, she swept her arms around the tent. 'I could *kill* you!'

Her hand collided with the glass Kadir held out to her, showering him in pomegranate juice. 'Oh, I'm sorry.' She stared at the rivers of red liquid running down his face and chest. The dark red juice looked like blood.

If the kidnapper had fired the gun at Kadir... The thought made her feel ill. 'I...I didn't mean that.' Her voice shook. She tried to firm her trembling mouth, but her lips wouldn't stop wobbling. 'I was scared on the helicopter,' she admitted.

'You, scared?' Kadir's voice sounded strained. 'Never. You are the bravest, craziest woman I've ever met.'

Suddenly Lexi did not care if she was revealing too much of herself. 'I was scared the kidnapper would kill you.'

'I would have ripped the gunman apart with my bare hands if he had tried to harm you,' Kadir said roughly. The shimmer of tears in her eyes tore him apart. His self-control exploded and he muttered a savage imprecation as he hauled her into his arms, crushing the air from her lungs as he lifted her and held her so tightly to him that Lexi felt the urgent thud of his heart beating in time with her own.

The threat of death had brought home to Lexi the immeasurable value of life. She had been running from the truth and trying to hide her feelings for Kadir, but she could not run or hide any longer.

She felt detached from reality, cast adrift in a world where only the two of them existed. The feel of his warm skin beneath her hands heated her blood, and the feral hunger glittering in his eyes evoked an ache in the pit of her stomach. She curled her arms around his neck and buried her fingers in his silky dark hair as he lowered his head and captured her mouth, kissing her urgently as if he was slaking his thirst after being stranded in the desert without water for many days.

His lips tasted of pomegranate juice, and the sticky juice running down his chest transferred to her. But Lexi did not care; all she cared about was that he should not stop the sensual sorcery he was creating with his tongue inside her mouth. She was only vaguely aware of him striding across the tent into the bathroom, and she gasped as he turned on the shower and stepped beneath the spray with her in his arms.

'I've still got my clothes on,' she muttered against his lips.

'Not for much longer,' he promised.

He let her slide down him so that she was standing on her feet, and whipped her vest top over her head. 'No bra,' he growled in satisfaction, cupping her firm breasts that he had bared.

'It's too hot to wear one.' She caught her breath as he rolled her nipples between his fingers until they hardened to turgid points and starbursts of sensation arrowed from her breasts to the pit of her stomach. His tanned hands splayed over her creamy pale breasts, caressing their rounded shape before he lowered his head and closed his lips around one nipple, suckling her strongly until she gave a moan of pleasure. He judged the exact moment when she could withstand no more of the exquisite caress, and moved to her other nipple, lashing the taut peak with his tongue, back and forth, tormenting her so that she gripped his hair and held his head to her breast in a silent plea for him to ravish her eager flesh.

'You are so damned beautiful, you're driving me crazy,' Kadir said harshly. 'When I thought the kidnapper might kill me, all I could think was that I was going to die without ever knowing the sensual promise of your body.'

In those seconds when he had faced his mortality the only person in his mind had been Lexi, and she consumed his thoughts now, making Kadir forget his responsibilities as Sultan, his duty to his kingdom and the promise he had made to his father. Time had halted, the universe had stopped spinning, and nothing mattered but the woman who had haunted his thoughts and dreams since he had met her.

His hands shook as he fumbled with the zip of Lexi's combats and pushed them over her hips. While she was stepping out of her trousers he hooked his fingers in the waistband of her briefs and dragged them down her thighs, his impatient fingers skimming over the neat triangle of blonde hair to part her and probe her silken heat.

'You want me.' His dark eyes gleamed with triumph, but Lexi could not deny her need when the wetness of her arousal betrayed her. Kadir gave a soft laugh as he slid one finger deep inside her, stretched her a little and inserted a second finger, swirling them in an erotic dance that drew a husky moan from her.

He handed her a bar of soap and Lexi smoothed it over his chest to wash away the sticky pomegranate juice. Now it was her turn to feel triumphant as she dragged her knuckles down his stomach and felt his body shudder. With deft fingers she opened the fly of his shorts and tugged the wet denim down his thighs before repeating the action with his black silk boxers. The size of his erection caused her a moment's panic. He was beautiful, and *huge*, and her insides turned to liquid as she imagined taking him inside her.

Kadir gritted his teeth as Lexi stroked her fingers lightly up and down his shaft, teasing him with butterfly caresses that increased the blood flow to his swollen tip. In retribution he circled his thumb pad over the tight bud of her clitoris and simultaneously circled his tongue around a dusky pink nipple.

The effect was electric; she trembled and gave a keening cry which he caught in his mouth as he lifted her up and claimed her lips in a slow, sweet kiss that made his gut ache. Her unguarded response stirred his soul. Something about this strong woman coming apart so utterly in his arms humbled him and at the same time he felt like a king who had captured a thousand kingdoms.

She wrapped her legs around his waist as he carried her out of the shower. The drumbeat of desire pounded harder in his veins. 'I can't wait,' he groaned, feeling the storm inside him building to a crescendo.

Lexi smiled against his mouth. Nothing mattered but that they were alive and she wanted to celebrate life in the most fundamental way, by making love with the man who had captured her heart. 'I can't wait either,' she whispered. She could feel his arousal nudging her belly and she wanted him inside her now, *now*...

Kadir stood her on her feet and turned her around so that her back was against his chest. There was a chair in the bathroom. He placed it in front of her and gently pushed her forward so that her body formed an arch over the wooden backrest and her hands rested on the seat. She was still wearing her baseball cap, and he pulled it from her head so that her long blonde hair cascaded around her shoulders like a river of silk.

'Hold on,' he murmured and felt a quiver run through her as he smoothed his hands over her perfect peachy bottom. The memory of her doing push-ups in a pair of tight satin shorts shattered the last vestige of his restraint and with a harsh groan he eased her buttocks apart and thrust deep into her moist heat, where his fingers had aroused her moments earlier.

Sweet heaven… Lexi could not hold back a cry of pleasure as Kadir entered her. Nothing had prepared her for the incredible eroticism of stretching forwards over the chair while he stood behind her and drove his powerful erection into the heat of her femininity. Nor had she been prepared for the intensity of emotions she felt as their bodies joined and became one.

He leaned forward and kissed the tip of her ear. She turned her head and sought his mouth and he kissed her with passion and a heart-shaking tenderness that answered a deeper need inside her.

He began to move, slowly at first to allow her to accommodate his size. Lexi gripped the edge of the chair as he increased his rhythm, each measured stroke building her excitement and her anticipation that the best was yet to come.

She spread her legs wider, encouraging him to drive deeper and harder. He wrapped his arms around her waist, cocooning her with his big body, and drew gasps of delight from her when he played with her nipples, heightening her sensual pleasure until she trembled and shivered with each new sensation created by his skilful mastery.

It couldn't last. The fire of their mutual passion swiftly became a furnace that blazed out of control. Lexi was vaguely aware of panting breaths and realised it was the sound of her breath being torn from her lungs as she strove to reach the pinnacle. Kadir held her there for breathless seconds, making her wait for the rapture of release. And then he thrust into her the hardest yet and sent them both tumbling over the edge into ecstasy. She cried his name and he soothed her with soft words in Arabic, his voice deep as an ocean as emotions he had not expected to feel, knew he should not feel, rolled over him.

As Kadir withdrew from her, Lexi's legs gave way and he swept her up in his arms and carried her into the bedroom. The satin sheets felt cool against her burning skin as he laid her on the bed. She stared up at him and held her hand to his cheek, traced the shape of his beautiful mouth with her fingertips. His smile stole her breath and the sultry gleam in his eyes warned her that he had by no means finished.

'Already?' She could not hide her shock as he knelt above her and pushed her legs apart. 'You're insatiable.'

'Insatiable for you,' he whispered against her lips before he kissed her deeply and made love to her again with such exquisite care that Lexi felt a sense of belonging she had been searching for her whole life.

CHAPTER NINE

SOMETHING WAS BRUSHING softly across her face. Lexi opened her eyes and discovered the mosquito net draped around the bed was fluttering in the breeze wafting into the tent. She was alone in the semi-dark. The luminous dial on her watch revealed that it was early evening, which meant that she had slept all afternoon. It was not surprising after her energetic sex session with Kadir, she thought. Her face warmed as she recalled how he had made love to her bent over the chair in the bathroom, and twice again in a variety of erotic positions on the bed.

Where was he? Fear gripped her as she wondered if the kidnapper had returned and taken Kadir away at gunpoint. *Perhaps the gunman had killed him?* Heart hammering, she slid off the satin sheets. There was a shirt draped over the arm of the chair; she assumed it belonged to Kadir and slipped it on before she stepped cautiously out of the bedroom, wishing she had a weapon to defend herself with if the kidnapper had indeed returned.

She walked noiselessly into the living area and found it empty. The tent flap had been tied back and through the opening she saw Kadir standing next to the oasis, staring up at the sky that was rapidly darkening as the sun completely disappeared. The heavens were filling with silver stars, like pins on a velvet pincushion. The wondrous beauty of the cosmos was displayed in breathtaking magnificence and, standing in the vast desert beneath the vast sky, Lexi thought how insignificant the human race was.

'My father loved to watch the stars.' Kadir turned as Lexi approached, sensing her presence although she made no sound. 'Many nights when I was a boy we sat outside the tent and *Baba* taught me the constellations.'

'You came to Jinan with him?'

'Yes, it was a special place for both of us, away from the palace and the many duties of a Sultan. Here we were simply father and son, and we used to go fishing and cook what we caught. My father taught me to enjoy the simple things in life.'

'Everyone I've spoken to says that Sultan Khalif was a great ruler of Zenhab,' Lexi said softly.

'He was the salvation of the kingdom.' Kadir's voice was fierce with pride. 'Before my father became Sultan, Zenhab was riven by civil war. He worked hard to establish peace and he gave hope for the future, but only if the population were willing to embrace change and welcome ideologies from the outside world.' His jaw clenched. 'There are still some people in Zenhab who want to return to the old ways.' Always he came back to the thorn in his side—Jamal—he brooded.

'You loved your father.' Lexi's voice pulled Kadir from his dark thoughts about his uncle. 'It's sad that he died when you were a young man and you did not have more time with him.' She felt a tug on her heart, remembering how Kadir's old nanny, Mabel, had said his heart had been broken by Sultan Khalif's death. 'At least you had a loving father while you were growing up. Mabel said the Sultan adored you.'

Kadir heard the wistful note in her voice and pictured her as a little girl whose adoptive parents had sent her away to boarding school so that they could concentrate on their own daughter.

'How old were you when you were adopted?'

'Four.'

He frowned. 'So, did you spend the first years of your life with your real parents?'

'No, I was placed into social services' care soon after I was born. Apparently I was fostered by a couple who planned to adopt me, but some time during the adoption process they changed their mind and I went back into care until the Howards adopted me two years later. I was too young to remember any of those experiences, of course.'

As an adult, Lexi had read various articles about attachment issues which could affect adopted children and the psychological problems resulting from negative early life experiences which could last into adulthood. The first failed adoption, followed by her failure to bond with the Howards was likely to be the reason why she was fiercely independent, yet deep down she wished she'd had a close, loving relationship like Kadir had enjoyed with his father. She'd been accused of pushing people away. It was true that she was wary of allowing anyone too close, she acknowledged. And when she *had* lowered her barriers with Steven, he had betrayed her trust.

Caught up in her thoughts, Lexi had only been partly aware that Kadir had led her back inside the tent. 'I thought you must be hungry,' he said, indicating the trays of food set out on the raised platform. He dropped down

onto the piles of cushions and indicated that she should do
the same. 'It's only crackers and dried fruits, I'm afraid.'

Lexi scanned the picnic and realised she was starving. 'It looks wonderful,' she assured him, biting into a
plump dried fig. 'It reminds me of the midnight feasts
we used to have at boarding school, only we had to eat
in the dark because if we were caught by the housemis-
tress it meant a week of detentions.'

Kadir thought of his own generally happy years at
Eton College. The only downside had been that he had
hated being separated from his father. 'What did you
think of boarding school?'

'It was hard at first, but I got used to sleeping in a dor-
mitory and only going home for the school holidays. In
many ways it toughened me up.'

'Did you need to toughen up? You were eight years
old,' he said softly. With her pale blonde hair falling
around her beautiful face she looked fragile and ethereal, but he knew she had a backbone of steel.

She shrugged. 'It helped. After a while I stopped caring that my adoptive parents didn't love me.'

'What about your biological parents? Have you ever
tried to trace them?'

'No,' she said abruptly. She did not want to tell him
that her birth mother had been a prostitute when she had
conceived Lexi.

She wondered how the Sultan of Zenhab would react
if she told him he had spent the afternoon having sex
with the daughter of a whore. Keen to turn the subject
away from her private life, Lexi focused on the meal he
had prepared.

'This is *baklava*, isn't it?' she said, picking up a little
pastry. 'Layers of dough stuffed with pistachio nuts and

honey. I tried them once before when I was serving in the Middle East and I remember they were delicious.'

'They're even better if you dip them in honey,' Kadir told her, pushing a bowl of thick golden liquid towards her.

She dipped the pastry into the honey and popped it into her mouth. A rapturous expression crossed her face. 'Mmm, I admit I have a weakness for sweet things.'

Kadir watched the tip of her pink tongue dart out to capture a crumb of pastry. She reminded him of a contented kitten, and her sensual enjoyment of the cake aroused a barbaric need in him to push her back against the cushions and thrust his throbbing erection deep inside her welcoming heat. He knew she would be ready for him. Her blue eyes—no longer chips of ice, but smoky-soft—had been issuing an invitation since she had stood beside him at the oasis.

'You've got honey on your chin,' he murmured as he lowered his head towards her. 'And as there are no napkins I'll have to lick it off you.'

Her impish smile tugged on something deep inside him. For a few seconds he glimpsed the child who had grown too serious too soon.

'I would be grateful if you would,' she murmured, as demure as a Victorian maiden. But Kadir had a vivid memory of earlier, when she had pushed him down on the bed and positioned herself above him, deliberately tormenting him as she had slowly, oh-so slowly, lowered herself onto his erect shaft before riding him hard and fast.

His breath hissed between his teeth as he struggled to control his hunger. His hand was already untying the belt of his silk robe, revealing his swollen manhood, and her little gasp when she saw how aroused he was drove him beyond rational thought.

It was impossible to rationalise anything that had happened since they had flown away from the palace that morning, Kadir brooded. Those moments on the helicopter when he had looked at death down the barrel of a gun had evoked a feeling of urgency to reaffirm life. He was aware that this was one stolen night. For a few hours, the past and the future did not exist and there was only now, with this woman. He could not fight his need for Lexi.

He brushed his lips over hers and his heart kicked when he felt her instant response. 'You taste sweet,' he growled, sliding his tongue into her mouth to explore her with mind-blowing eroticism that left them both shaking.

Lexi tasted salt on his skin when she kissed his throat. In the glow from the oil lamp his broad shoulders gleamed like polished gold, and his dark chest hairs felt abrasive against her palms as she ran her hands down his body, over his flat stomach and lower to clasp the rigid length of his erection.

His hands were no less busy opening the buttons down the front of her shirt and sliding the material from her shoulders so that she was naked beneath his glittering gaze. She made a startled protest when he dipped his fingers into the bowl of honey and trickled the sticky syrup over her breasts. He laughed at her surprise before closing his lips around one honey-coated nipple and suckling her until she sobbed his name.

'Sticky and sweet,' he murmured, transferring his mouth to her other honey-anointed breast and curling his tongue around its taut peak. 'From now on I will always be addicted to the taste of honey.'

It was sensuality taken to another level and before long Lexi was squirming and arching her hips in mute supplication for him to assuage the ache between her legs.

'Patience, *habibi*,' he teased. 'Let me discover if you taste sweet here, too.'

She shivered with anticipation as he hooked her legs over his shoulders and slid his hands beneath her bottom, lifting her as he lowered his head and pressed his mouth against her to taste her molten heat with his tongue.

The intimate caress felt unbelievably good. Lexi was lost from the first lick of Kadir's tongue up and down her moist opening, as he delicately but determinedly probed and delved and finally thrust into her feminine heat. Her body arched like a bow under intolerable tension, quivering as the pleasure inside her built. She curled her fingers into the satin cushions beneath her as he curled his tongue around her clitoris and created a storm of sensations that were too exquisite for her to withstand.

She exploded in a frantic orgasm, her hips jerking towards his wicked mouth, her breath forced from her lungs so that her gasps of pleasure filled the tent. It was impossible that anything could be better than what he had just done to her, but then he lifted his head and stood between her spread thighs to drive his powerful erection deep inside her, and Lexi began the delicious journey to nirvana all over again.

Lexi turned her head on the pillow and studied Kadir while he slept. The chiselled angles of his face looked softer, and his thick black lashes made crescents on his cheeks. Last night he had called her *habibi*, which she knew was an Arabic term of endearment, and when he had made love to her she had sensed tenderness as well as passion in his caresses. Had they simply had sex, she mused, or was it possible that he cared for her a little?

Dear heaven! What had they done?

She jolted fully awake, and the dreamy smile on her lips disappeared. Last night had been no dream. Of course he could not care for her. She and Kadir had had sex, but their passion was forbidden and they should not have become lovers. She glanced around the tent, filled with warm golden sunlight, and a chill spread through her body as cold reality hit her.

She had been flying Kadir to meet his fiancée when they had been kidnapped and stranded on the island. It was true that Kadir's arranged marriage was no love match. He had never even met Haleema. But he was contracted to marry the Princess, and they should not have allowed themselves to be swept away by passion, Lexi thought bleakly.

Her heart was beating so hard that she was sure she could hear it. She frowned when she realised that the sound came from a long way off and she recognised the low throb of a motorboat's engine. *Perhaps the kidnapper had returned to the island.* Their lives could once again be in danger.

'Kadir.'

His lashes lifted, and his smooth chocolate eyes regarded her slumberously. 'I thought I was dreaming.' He cupped her breasts in his hands and gave her a sinful smile. 'But these feel real.'

Fear made Lexi momentarily forget her feelings of guilt. 'I can hear a boat engine,' she said urgently.

He dropped his hands from her body and leapt out of bed, frowning as he heard a faint thrumming sound. 'Stay here,' he ordered, dragging on his shorts. 'Find somewhere safe to hide while I go and see what's happening.'

'You must be joking!' It took seconds to pull on her combats, but longer to wriggle her feet into her boots and tie the laces. 'Wait for me!' She cursed as he strode out of the tent, but common sense warned her not to run across the desert in bare feet and risk being bitten by a highly venomous death stalker scorpion.

Adrenalin pumped through Kadir as he hid behind a palm tree and watched a motorboat land on the beach. No doubt the kidnapper was still armed with a gun. He glanced around for something he could use to defend himself with. A tree branch would not be much use against a pistol, he thought ruefully, but he had the element of surprise combined with an implacable determination to protect Lexi from the gunman.

Shielding his eyes against the bright sun, Kadir frowned as he recognised the man. 'Nasim!'

'Sir!' The bodyguard tore up the beach and dropped down onto one knee before his Sultan. 'Your Highness, I feared Jamal might have had you killed.'

'I guessed my uncle was behind this,' Kadir said grimly. 'Do you know what he is up to?'

'He intends to depose you and make himself Sultan, and he has a few followers, including Fariq, working for him. I was held at gunpoint but I managed to escape. I overheard that Jamal planned for you and Miss Howard to be kidnapped and brought to the island. Your uncle has gone to the mountains to inform Sheikh Omar that, instead of attending the meeting to discuss your marriage to Princess Haleema, you chose to come to Jinan with your mistress.

'Jamal has spies at the palace, and one of them reported that he had seen you kissing Lexi,' Nasim explained when Kadir frowned. 'Jamal hopes that Sheikh Omar will believe that you have snubbed his sister, and he will incite the mountain tribes to join forces with your uncle to overthrow you.'

Kadir's jaw clenched. 'I must act quickly. It is time I dealt with my uncle once and for all.' He looked round to see Lexi running across the sand. After giving instructions to his bodyguard, he walked up the beach towards her.

'What is Nasim doing here? He's not working for the kidnapper, is he?' she demanded.

'He came to rescue us. As I suspected, my uncle is behind the kidnap plot.' Kadir threw her the helicopter keys. 'I need you to take me to the mountains to visit Haleema, and there is no time to lose. Wait here while I go and shut up the tent.'

Lexi stared after him as he strode up the beach and bit her lip. She did not know what she had expected from him, but his absolute indifference to the fact that they had spent the night together made her feel used and humiliated. His urgency to visit Haleema emphasised how unimportant she was to him, Lexi thought bitterly, just as she had been unimportant to her adoptive parents.

What the hell had he done?

As Kadir ploughed over the soft sand dunes, the sated ache in his groin was a mocking reminder of exactly what he had done to Lexi last night, and what she had done to him. She had made him forget *everything* except the thunder in his blood, his urgent, uncontrollable need to make love to her. But he could not blame Lexi for the fact that he had broken his promise to himself. And, despite the fact that he had just enjoyed the most amazing night of his life with her, he could not break the promise he had made to his father.

He heard Sultan Khalif's voice inside his head.

'The marriage arrangement that Jamal has brokered between you and the daughter of the leader of the northern tribes will ensure stability in the kingdom. The people of Zenhab deserve peace and prosperity after years of war and bloodshed. It is my dying wish, my only son, that when the time comes you will honour your promise to take Princess Haleema as your bride.'

Stumbling into the tent, Kadir sank to his knees and dropped his head into his hands as if he could somehow hold back the tidal wave of emotions rolling over him. Shame tasted as bitter as poison in his mouth. By making love to Lexi he had betrayed his personal code of honour and he had betrayed his father. It was no comfort that he had not technically had sex with Lexi in Zenhab and they had been on his private island, Jinan.

Even worse than letting himself down was the realisation that Lexi hoped, perhaps even expected, that having sex with her had meant something to him. Her soft smile when she had run towards him on the beach just now had made his gut twist, and the look of disappointment on her face when she'd realised that they could leave the island had been more revealing than perhaps she knew.

He cursed savagely, anger and guilt mingling with his shame. *He did not want to hurt Lexi.* The discovery shocked him. His many previous affairs had been with sophisticated European socialites, women who had understood he wasn't looking for a relationship that would continue outside the bedroom. Perhaps he could have been forgiven for believing that a tough-talking ex-RAF pilot knew the score. But he had glimpsed Lexi's vulnerability and heard the hurt in her voice when she had explained how, as a child, she had overheard her adoptive parents say that they wished they had not adopted her.

He was jerked from his thoughts by the *whump-whump* of rotor blades. Dragging himself to his feet, he stepped outside the tent and stared up at the helicopter hovering in the blue sky. *What was Lexi playing at?* He watched her fly a circuit of the island before the chopper dipped below the tops of the palm trees.

The rotor blades had almost stopped spinning when Kadir reached the beach. Lexi jumped down from the chopper onto the sand and watched him walk towards her. He had changed back into his royal robes, and in the breeze his white *keffiyeh* fluttered around his tanned face. His dark eyes were no longer warm but hard and unreadable, and with every step he took closer to her she sensed a widening distance between them.

'Why did you take off without me?'

She shrugged. 'I wanted to make a test flight on my own. Although I'd checked underneath the chopper and didn't find an explosive device, I couldn't be certain that the kidnapper hadn't tampered with the controls before he left us stranded here yesterday.'

Kadir was aware of a curious sensation in his chest, as if a fist was gripping his heart. 'Are you saying you flew the helicopter to check it was safe? What if the kidnapper *had* done something to it that caused it to crash? It's very likely you would have been killed.' His jaw clenched. 'You are the craziest woman I've ever met. You should have waited for me instead of risking your life.'

'It is my duty as a pilot to ensure the safety of my aircraft.' Lexi looked at him steadily. 'Your life is more important than mine. You are the Sultan of Zenhab and your people need you to rule the kingdom and build hospitals and universities and continue the work your father started to maintain peace.'

'Of course your life is as valuable as mine, you little idiot,' Kadir said harshly. He was beginning to realise how much harm her adoptive parents had done by failing to make Lexi feel loved and valued. He frowned as the full implication of what she had just said sank in. The possibility that the kidnapper might have placed explosives on the helicopter hadn't occurred to him, but now he visualised the chopper exploding with Lexi on board and imagined her lying lifeless amid the tangled wreckage of the helicopter.

He stared at her. Wearing army-issue combat trousers, a baseball cap and an attitude, she was beautiful and sexy, brave as a lioness yet vulnerable as a day-old kitten.

She'd been vulnerable in his arms last night as they'd made love over and over and—

Was it possible that she was pregnant with his child?

She had told him in Italy that she wasn't on the Pill, but when he had made love to her last night he hadn't given contraception a thought. He had been too swept up with his selfish need for her to think logically, he acknowledged grimly.

Feeling as though he had been struck by a lightning bolt, Kadir realised that *everything* had changed and nothing could continue as he had planned. He was bound by his duty to his kingdom and the promise he had given his father. But if Lexi had conceived his heir, then his greatest duty was to his unborn child.

The grey mountains of Zenhab were rugged and forbidding, and the Bedouin tribes who lived in some of the most ancient settlements in the world were as hardy as their surroundings.

As Lexi landed the helicopter in the central square of the fortress town Sanqirah, a large crowd of curious on-lookers gathered in front of the market stalls, although most people kept their distance and only a few daring boys surged forward to stare at the chopper.

Kadir's keen eyes noted that there were a couple of armed security guards posted around the square, but he was relieved that Sheikh Omar did not appear to be mustering his forces, which perhaps meant that Jamal's plan to incite the tribes into civil unrest had not yet happened. However, Kadir was aware that the situation could become more volatile after he had discussed his marriage contract to Princess Haleema with her brother.

He jumped out of the helicopter after his bodyguard Nasim, and spoke to Lexi while she was sitting in the cockpit. 'I want you to fly straight back to the palace. I don't know how long my visit will last, but when I return we will need to talk.'

What was there to talk about? Lexi wondered bleakly. Kadir had made it obvious that he was not going to refer to the fact that they had slept together. Presumably he regarded their stolen night of passion as a shameful secret, just as her birth mother regarded Lexi as a shameful secret. Her old feelings of insecurity returned. She had not been good enough for her adoptive parents or Steven, and now she was not good enough for Kadir. How could she have thought that he might want her when he was about to meet the Princess he was going to marry?

She watched him walk across the courtyard towards Sheikh Omar's palace, his robes billowing behind him. He was a regal, remote Sultan, but she pictured him on

Jinan wearing a pair of frayed denim shorts, or wearing nothing but a wickedly sensual smile, and her heart ached.

Sheikh Omar was a young man, and the responsibility of leading the mountain tribes which had been thrust on him after the death of his father, Sheikh Rashid, two months ago showed on his tense face as he greeted the Sultan of Zenhab. Once the servants had poured cups of rich black coffee and placed a plate of sweetmeats on the low table, Omar dismissed his staff so that he and Kadir were alone.

'Welcome to my home, Your Highness.'

'I apologise that my arrival was delayed,' Kadir replied. 'I understand that my uncle Jamal visited you.'

Omar nodded. 'I will speak frankly. Your uncle wishes me to lead the mountain tribes into civil war against you.'

'I know Jamal wants to seize back the Crown and rule Zenhab. Ten years ago he brokered a marriage arrangement between me and your sister, Princess Haleema, because he believed that with the support of your father he would have more power over me and be able to influence my decisions.' Kadir hesitated. He knew what he must do. His duty lay with Lexi, who might be carrying his child, but as he pictured his father's beloved face his heart ached with remorse. *Forgive me, Baba*, he begged silently.

'My greatest wish is for there to continue to be peace in the kingdom,' he told Omar. 'But I must be honest and tell you that I am unable to honour my marriage contract with Haleema. I intend to outlaw forced marriages, and this is one of many changes which I hope will allow all of the population of Zenhab, men and women, to live their lives with greater freedom.'

In the silence that followed, Kadir was aware of each painful beat of his heart. Would his decision lead Zenhab towards civil disturbance? He knew he was taking a great risk. Ten years ago, when he had sought to claim his right to rule the kingdom, he had been forced by his uncle to sign the marriage agreement with a girl he had never met. But he was no longer prepared to be swayed by threats. He was convinced that forced marriages were wrong, not just in his case, but for the whole population. He was determined to stand up for his beliefs, but he had no idea what the new leader of the mountain tribes thought. The old Sheikh Rashid had been a warmonger, much like Jamal. Was his son any different?

Omar stood up and walked across the room to open a door. When he returned to Kadir he was accompanied by a young woman wearing traditional robes and a headscarf. Her expression was calm and intelligent, and her dark eyes observed Kadir with curiosity.

'This is my sister, Princess Haleema,' Omar introduced her.

'I am pleased to meet you after so many years of wondering about you, and I am even more pleased that you do not wish to marry me, Your Highness,' Haleema said with an unexpected frankness that brought a smile to Kadir's lips.

'Haleema and I share your wish that the peace and prosperity which Zenhab has enjoyed under your rule and, before you, your father, Sultan Khalif, will continue,' Omar said quietly. 'We also share your views on forced marriages. My father told my sister when she was just eleven years old that her marriage had been arranged and she would not be allowed to choose her husband. Haleema wishes to go to university and train to be a doctor,

and she has my support. It was not possible when my father was alive. He believed in the old ways and would
not have understood my sister's ambition to follow a career, a vocation, which will allow her to help the people
in our remote part of Zenhab. But my father is dead and
I am the new leader of the mountain tribes.' Omar smiled
ruefully. 'Your uncle Jamal was not pleased when I told
him that I fully support your rule, Your Highness. I ordered my staff to lock him in his rooms, but I am afraid
he managed to escape.'

'I'll issue a warrant for his arrest and have security
staff at the airports and ports watch out for him. Jamal
cannot be allowed to go free after what he has done.' Kadir's jaw clenched as he remembered those moments on
the helicopter when the kidnapper had threatened Lexi
with a gun.

In the aftermath of being kidnapped, when they had
feared for their lives, it was perhaps unsurprising that
their desire for one another, which they had tried so hard
to suppress, had finally exploded in fierce passion. With
his arranged marriage ended, he had resolved one problem only to face a new one, Kadir brooded, thinking of
the possibility that Lexi might be pregnant.

CHAPTER TEN

KADIR COULD NOT fail to notice Lexi's suitcase standing in the middle of the sitting room when he followed her into her apartment at the palace. She had refused to meet his gaze when she'd opened the door, and he could feel the tension emanating from her slender frame as she stood on the opposite side of the room from him.

'Are you going somewhere?' he murmured.

'I'm going back to England. You agreed to release me from my contract after I had flown you to the mountains to visit Haleema,' she reminded him.

'The situation has changed. I agreed to you leaving before we became lovers.'

'We are not lovers!' She whirled round to face him, her blue eyes flashing. 'We spent one night together but we shouldn't have done. We should both have been stronger and not given in to desire.'

Lexi turned away from Kadir and cursed her traitorous heart for leaping when she sensed him walk across the room towards her. The familiar scent of his aftershave stole around her and she dared not look at his handsome face. The moment she had opened the door and seen him, dressed in black jeans and a polo shirt, she had struggled to maintain her composure. She wished she had left the palace before he'd returned, as she had originally planned to do. But she could not leave Zenhab without saying goodbye.

'I think it was inevitable that we would make love.' His deep voice broke into her thoughts. 'We were attracted to each other from the moment we first met.'

How could he sound so matter-of-fact about the most incredible night of her life? Perhaps because for him it had just been sex, Lexi thought bleakly. And, having satisfied his inconvenient desire for her, he had hurried to meet his future bride.

'I take it that you met Haleema? So, when is the wedding?'

Kadir heard the hurt in her voice and guilt washed over him because he knew he was to blame. Lexi might be acting like a spitting wildcat, but he had discovered on Jinan that she was so vulnerable.

'I did meet her and her brother. I told them that I wished to break the marriage arrangement, and Haleema and Omar supported my decision.'

'You broke your marriage contract!' Lexi's heart gave another painful lurch. 'But I thought you had to marry Haleema in order to keep peace and avoid civil war.'

'That was true when Sheikh Rashid was alive. My uncle Jamal could count on Rashid's support. But Omar is not like his father. He wants peace in the kingdom and welcomes changes to some of the old traditions.'

'So Jamal's plan to cause trouble backfired.'

'Yes, thankfully. My uncle is now in custody after he was arrested trying to leave the country.'

Lexi shivered as she remembered those terrifying moments when she had feared that the kidnapper might kill them. On the island her emotions had been raw, and she had been unable to resist Kadir because facing death had forced her to face up to the truth—that she was halfway to falling in love with him.

But even though he had ended his marriage arrangement with Haleema, she had no expectation that he wanted a relationship with *her*.

She picked up an envelope from the table and thrust it at him. 'It's my letter of resignation. You agreed to forget the financial penalty if I end my contract early, but if you've changed your mind I'll send you the money I owe when I'm back in England.'

Kadir opened the letter and skimmed his eyes over the terse two lines Lexi had written. 'How will you repay me when you have other debts?'

She stiffened. 'How do you know about my private life?'

'You know I had a detailed security check run on you before I employed you as my helicopter pilot.'

'It's a pity you didn't run a more detailed check on Fariq. It would have saved a lot of trouble.' If they hadn't been kidnapped and stranded on Jinan, their heightened emotions wouldn't have exploded in frantic passion and they would not have made love.

Lexi grimaced. Love hadn't been involved. They'd had sex, and just because it had been amazing, mind-blowing sex she had stupidly hoped that she meant something to Kadir. But the truth was she meant nothing to him and now that he was free from his arranged marriage he could choose who he wanted to marry. No doubt he would want a beautiful socialite to be his bride, she thought dully. In England he was Earl Montgomery and one of the most eligible bachelors in Europe.

Kadir slipped the letter into his pocket. 'The finan-

cial penalty clause in your contract does not apply because it is not your fault that you have to resign.' Kadir
paused and took a deep breath before taking a step towards Lexi. 'Have you considered the possibility that
you could be pregnant?'

Lexi's eyes widened.

'The Civil Aviation Authority's advice to female pilots is that they should not fly in the early stages of pregnancy,' Kadir continued.

Lexi bit her lip, wondering how he could sound so
calm about something so potentially life-changing. But
if she *was* pregnant it was not his life that would change,
she thought grimly.

'It's unlikely I'm pregnant. It was the wrong time of
the month for me to have conceived.'

He gave her an impatient look. 'We both know that
can't be predicted. We will need to know for sure.'

'Well, since I'm boringly regular, I'll tell you in just
over a week.' She hated herself for blushing, thinking
how ridiculous it was to feel embarrassed about discussing such a personal issue when Kadir had seen, touched
and kissed every centimetre of her body. 'I'm certain
there's nothing to worry about, but if there are any re-
percussions from our irresponsible behaviour I'll let you
know,' she told him with a forced airiness.

The situation felt surreal. She *couldn't* be carrying
Kadir's baby, Lexi assured herself. But the stark fact
was that pregnancy *was* a possibility after she'd had unprotected sex. Actually, she felt a bit sick, but she was
probably imagining it, she told herself. What she definitely felt was a fool. She was a sensible, responsible
twenty-nine-year-old and she had no excuse for risking
an unplanned pregnancy. But when Kadir had stripped

her naked in the tent on Jinan her only thought been how desperately she wanted him to hold her, to feel safe in his arms and for him to make love to her.

She picked up her suitcase and opened the drawer in the bureau to retrieve her passport. 'I'll phone you from England once I have any news.'

'If you are pregnant you will marry me.'

Her head whipped round, and the fact that the drawer was empty did not register in her brain at first. 'Don't be ridiculous.'

'You have a better suggestion?'

He was serious? Lexi laughed shakily. '*If* I'm pregnant, which I am quite sure I'm not because I can't believe fate would play such a ghastly joke, then it will be my problem and I'll deal with it.'

He swore. 'If by *deal with it* you mean what I think you mean…'

Something in his voice, an indefinable emotion, made her pause, and she paled as *his* meaning sank into her dazed mind. 'I would never do that.' Shocked beyond words, her hand shot out before she had time to think and she struck his cheek, leaving a red imprint of her fingers on his olive skin.

His eyes glittered dangerously and he caught hold of her arm as if he thought she might slap him again. But Lexi was horrified by her loss of control and her mouth trembled, betraying her intense hurt.

'My biological mother admitted that she wanted to abort me,' she said thickly, 'but by the time she found out it was too late to get rid of me.' She swallowed. 'If it turns out that I have conceived your child I will take care of it and…and *love* it, because I know better than most what it's like for a child not to feel loved.'

'And I know what it feels like for a child to *be* loved.' Kadir's dark eyes burned into hers. 'My father showered me with love and affection, and I have every intention of doing the same with my child. The baby that is possibly already developing inside you will be my heir, and if you are carrying my son he will be the future Sultan of Zenhab. But, more important, our child has the right to be brought up by both its parents. Far from being ridiculous, marriage is the only option I will consider.'

Lexi felt as if an iron band was squeezing her lungs. Kadir's words and, even more, the fierce emotion in them, filled her with a strange sense of relief that if the unthinkable had happened and she was actually pregnant, he would accept responsibility for his child.

He would be a wonderful father, she thought. In her mind she pictured a baby with olive-gold skin and dark curls and thick black eyelashes. She imagined Kadir cradling his son in his arms and she felt a sudden acute longing to be part of the tableaux, for Kadir to look at her with the same love in his eyes that he felt for his child.

What was she thinking? 'There are other ways that we could both be parents to our child without a sham marriage that neither of us wants,' she said stiffly.

'Not in Zenhab there aren't. The kingdom is becoming more progressive, but the Zenhabian people will not tolerate their Sultan fathering an illegitimate child.'

Kadir suddenly smiled and the sexy curl of his lips evoked a purely physical longing in the pit of Lexi's stomach. 'If we have to marry, it won't be a sham, certainly not in the bedroom. I already have proof that we are sexually compatible.'

Lexi saw determination stamped on his hard-boned features and panic gripped her. He was deadly serious that if she was pregnant he would insist on them marrying for the sake of their child. He had been freed from his arranged marriage, only to be faced with a marriage of convenience and she would be his unwanted wife, just as she had been her adoptive parents' unwanted daughter once they'd had a daughter of their own.

'I doubt the Zenhabian people would support a marriage between us if they knew the circumstances of my birth,' she said tautly. She had never revealed to anyone the truth of her background, but once Kadir learned the facts she was sure he would drop the crazy marriage idea. 'And they *would* find out about me. Your press may not be as intrusive as the European paparazzi, but someone will dig up the dirt about me.'

His eyes narrowed. 'What do you mean?'

'A woman named Cathy Barnes is my biological mother. During the early years of her life she worked as a prostitute, selling sex to fund her drug habit. My father was…' she shrugged helplessly '…one of her clients, a stranger who went to a hotel room and paid for sex with a woman he would never see again, much less know that his sordid transaction had resulted in a child. Me.'

'You told me you knew nothing about your real parents.'

'My background is hardly something to be proud of,' she said drily. She sighed. 'Like many adopted children, I imagine, I was curious about who had brought me into the world and, without any facts to go on, I created a fantasy that my real parents had been forced by tragic circumstances to give me away, but they had always loved me and were desperate for us to be reunited.'

The unconsciously wistful note in her voice evoked a pang of sympathy in Kadir but he knew she would hate any suggestion of pity. He strolled across to the window overlooking the palace courtyard where the helicopter was parked on the pad.

He remembered the night his yacht had capsized off the south coast of England and his relief when he had looked up and seen the coastguard helicopter piloted by Lexi which had come to his rescue. It was due to her fearlessness that his life had been saved. And she had demonstrated her bravery again when she had calmly flown the helicopter while the kidnapper had stuck a gun in her ribs. But, beneath her tough exterior, Kadir knew she hid a vulnerability that touched something inside him.

'How did you learn the truth about your biological mother?'

'When I was eighteen the adoption agency helped me to trace her. But my hope that I would feel an instant bond with her was quickly shattered. Cathy agreed to meet me, but there was no emotional reunion,' Lexi said wryly. 'She told me that she hadn't wanted a baby and had handed me to a social worker immediately after I was born. When I finally met Cathy, she had sorted her life out and was married, but her husband had no idea of her past life or that she'd had a child and, because she is ashamed of her past, she has never told anyone about me.'

'Do you keep in contact with her?'

'We meet a few times a year, always in secret,' Lexi said bitterly. 'Six months ago Cathy learned that she has cancer which is untreatable. She broke down when she told me that she had built up huge debts on credit cards that her husband did not know about. She knew he would be worried about the money she owed and she was upset that their last few months together would be spoiled, so I offered to pay the debts for her.'

'It was good of you to help her when she doesn't seem to have been much of a mother to you.'

'She's my mother,' Lexi said flatly. 'She was in a desperate situation when she gave birth to me, and I think she tried to do her best for me by having me adopted. Surely you can understand now, why, even if I am pregnant, you can't marry me. The Zenhabian people were expecting you to marry a princess and I doubt they would accept a whore's daughter for their Sultana.'

Kadir caught hold of her chin when she looked away from him as if she was embarrassed to meet his gaze. 'Lexi, whatever your mother was and however she lived her life has no bearing on who you are. No one could fail to be impressed by your courage and your compassion. If you are pregnant I can't think of anyone who would be a better mother to my child, and as my wife you would be a great role model to young women in Zenhab.'

Lexi swallowed. He sounded as if he meant what he had said, but a voice of caution inside her head warned her that she would be a fool to trust him. The truth was that if she had conceived Kadir's baby he was prepared to marry her *only* because he wanted his child.

She dragged her eyes from the molten warmth in his and spun away from him. 'This conversation is premature and almost certainly pointless. I'm sure I'm not pregnant. There's a flight leaving Zenhab for Dubai, from there I can catch a direct flight back to London, and I intend to be on it.'

She stared at the empty drawer in the bureau. 'I know I put my passport in here.' She suddenly remembered that the maid who cleaned her apartment had opened the drawer and quickly shut it again when Lexi had entered the room earlier. 'One of the staff wouldn't have taken it, would they?'

'Yes, on my instruction,' Kadir said coolly. 'But don't worry. I have it safely locked away in my study and if you are not pregnant I'll return it to you.'

Her shock turned swiftly to fury. 'You *stole* my passport?'

'Borrowed,' he drawled.

'That's *outrageous*. How *dare* you? I *demand* you return it immediately.' Lexi could feel her blood pounding through her veins, but her anger was mixed with apprehension when she realised that she was effectively a prisoner in Zenhab and probably at the palace, she thought, remembering the guards who protected the perimeter walls and gates. Kadir could not force her to marry him, she reminded herself.

As if he could read her mind, he said inexorably, 'If the news is positive, we will marry without delay before word gets out that you are carrying the Sultan's child.'

Kadir's jaw hardened. Taking Lexi's passport had been a panic reaction to prevent her from leaving, and he acknowledged that she had every right to be angry. But if she left she might refuse to return to Zenhab. And if she was pregnant she might decide to bring up her child—*his* child—on her own in England. He knew she was fiercely independent, and it was possible that she wouldn't want to spend her life in a remote desert kingdom.

He remembered how his mother had hated Zenhab and the restrictions of being the wife of the Sultan. Judith Montgomery had abandoned her husband and seven-year-old son to live at the Montgomery estate in Windsor, but whenever Kadir had visited his mother she had put emotional pressure on him to live in England with her.

Kadir grimaced as he remembered his mother's tears when he'd said goodbye to her at the end of each visit. He had loved both his parents and had felt torn between them. His mother had made him feel guilty for choosing to live with his father and he had spent his childhood shuttling back and forth between his parents and the two very different cultures in Zenhab and England.

If Lexi was pregnant, he would not want his child to go through what he had as a child, to feel torn loyalties and guilt, as he had done. Somehow he must try to convince Lexi that their child, if there was a child, deserved to be brought up by both of them in a stable family unit. But he could not abandon his duty to his kingdom. He was a Sultan and his child would be heir to the throne. Marriage to Lexi was the only option.

But what if, after a few years of marriage, she left him like his mother had left his father? How would he feel if she decided that life in the desert kingdom was not for her? Sultan Khalif had been heartbroken by his wife's desertion, Kadir remembered. As a teenager, he had watched his father sitting alone in the gardens that had been created for Judith, and he had vowed that he would never lose his heart to a woman. Love had been his strong father's one weakness, but Kadir knew better than to risk his emotions on something as unreliable as love.

Lexi stared at Kadir's chiselled features and wondered what he was thinking. He had insisted that if she was pregnant he would marry her, and she supposed she should feel relieved that her child would have a father. But the harsh truth was that his child was all he was interested in. He had proved that he was not interested in her when he had virtually ignored her after the night they had spent together on Jinan.

She tried to hold on to her anger. She needed to be strong to stand up to him and not allow him to push her into a loveless marriage that would be convenient for him but heartbreaking for her. But her fire and her temper had deserted her and she felt empty and alone, just as she had been all her life. No one had really wanted her or loved her, she thought bleakly. Memories of her childhood, when she had been made to feel a nuisance by her adoptive parents, still hurt. How could she marry Kadir, knowing that he did not want her—apart from for sex? she thought, remembering how he had said that they were sexually compatible.

'I wish none of this had happened,' she said in a choked voice.

An odd expression flared in Kadir's eyes. 'Do you regret making love with me?'

How could she regret the most beautiful night of her life? 'Do you?' she countered.

'No.' The night they had spent together on the island had been magical—a stolen night of pleasure when he had been able to forget the responsibilities of being a Sultan.

The molten warmth in Kadir's eyes sent a warning shiver through Lexi. She dared not soften towards him. When had he moved closer to her? The heat of his body and the evocative masculine scent of him tugged on her senses. If he touched her she would be lost! Suddenly scared of what she might reveal, Lexi tried to twist away from him, but he settled his hands on her shoulders and pulled her to him.

His body was all hard muscle and sinew, and the feel of his erection nudging her thigh made her insides melt.

'I will never regret the pleasure and the passion we shared on Jinan,' he said softly.

'Don't...' she pleaded as she watched his head descend. She struggled against the strength of his arms holding her, but her real battle was with herself and her body betrayed her the moment he claimed her lips and kissed her with the ruthless mastery of a desert warrior.

It was sweet rapture to be in his arms, to lay her hand on his chest and feel the erratic thud of his heart, to know that his arousal was as swift and all-consuming as her own. She had thought he would never kiss her again, that their stolen night was all she would ever have of him. She had no protection against his sorcery, no defence against the bone-shaking tenderness of his kiss as he eased the pressure of his mouth on hers and traced the swollen contours of her lips with the tip of his tongue.

'Do you still doubt we could make our marriage work?'

Lexi swept her lashes down to blot out the satisfied gleam in Kadir's eyes. Of course he looked triumphant when she had capitulated so utterly and responded to him so shamelessly, she thought bleakly. Her mouth was stinging from his hungry passion, and she told herself she must have imagined an underlying tenderness in his kiss that had tugged on her frayed emotions.

'It's just sex,' she muttered. 'I don't deny the chemistry that ignites whenever we're within a few feet of each other, but it's not a basis for marriage.'

She assumed he would step away from her, and was unprepared when he framed her face in his hands and murmured, 'Was it *just sex* we had on Jinan? I have never experienced such intense pleasure as when we made love, and I can't help feeling that we shared something more than merely physical satiation.'

On the island Kadir had tried to dismiss the surpris-

ing feelings that had swept over him in the languorous
aftermath of making love to Lexi. He had been aware
that he could not allow himself to feel anything because
he was bound by duty to honour his arranged marriage.
But since he had ended his marriage arrangement with
Haleema he could not stop thinking about the sex with
Lexi, which had been amazing. But he also remembered
that when she had fallen asleep in his arms he had remained awake to protect her if the kidnapper returned;
he had held her close to him and studied how her long
eyelashes curled against her cheeks.

'You're just saying that because if it turns out that I
am pregnant you want me to stay in Zenhab so that you
can be a father to your child.'

Kadir saw the mistrust in her eyes and understood it
all the more now that she had told him how her biological mother had rejected her.

'I don't deny I would want custody of my child,' he
admitted, determined to be honest with her. 'I would be
prepared to seek a legal ruling if necessary.'

He wanted much more, he acknowledged. He had told
Lexi once that he wanted everything, and he knew with
sudden insight that it was true.

She paled. 'Do you mean you would fight for custody
if I have a baby?'

For the first time since the nightmare had begun, Lexi
considered the real possibility that she was pregnant. Sup-
posing she had a baby, a tiny, vulnerable scrap of life, utterly dependent on her, that she could love and who would
love her unconditionally? Unconsciously, she placed her
hand over her stomach, the instinct of maternal protectiveness kicking inside her.

'I would *never* give up my child. I've told you how

my birth mother gave me away. How could you think I would do the same?'

The glimmer of tears in her eyes got to Kadir. 'I know you wouldn't,' he said roughly. 'So I suggest we stop the talk of fighting and custody and spend the next week or so getting to know each other better because, if you are carrying our child, then, like it or not, we will be spending the foreseeable future together.'

His suggestion of calling a truce made sense, Lexi acknowledged reluctantly. Nothing would persuade her to give up her child. Even if she managed to leave the palace and return to England, Kadir would find out if she was pregnant and he would use his wealth and power to claim his heir. In a strange way she was glad of his determination to be a devoted father, unlike the faceless man who had accidentally fathered her.

He took her silence as agreement. 'We'll start by having dinner tonight. Unfortunately, we won't be alone because Yusuf reminded me that the French ambassador is coming to dinner at the palace this evening, but it will be good practice for you if you become Sultana of Zenhab.'

She did not return his smile. 'The idea is laughable, isn't it?' she said in a low voice full of self-doubt, 'considering my genes. I don't know how to talk to an ambassador.'

'Just be you,' Kadir advised. He glanced at his watch. 'I'm expecting a phone call. Dinner will be at eight.' On his way out of the door, he glanced back at her. 'I've taken the liberty of ordering some clothes for you. I will be hosting several social functions over the coming week and you'll need evening dresses,' he explained quickly when he saw the battle gleam in her eyes.

'I don't want you to pay for my clothes...' Lexi stared

at the door as Kadir closed it after him. The snick of the catch made her feel trapped; although he had not locked her in her apartment and presumably she could walk around the palace and gardens, she was not at liberty to leave the kingdom—at least, not until they knew if she was pregnant or not.

If she *hadn't* conceived his child then, no doubt, she would find herself on the next flight out of Zenhab, and Kadir would be free to marry a woman of his choice.

She bit her lip and pushed away the crazy idea that she secretly hoped she was pregnant. She had spent her whole life hoping to find love, but she knew with painful certainty that her heart's desire would not be granted here in the Sultan's palace.

The evening was less of an ordeal than she had expected. The French ambassador had been invited to the palace, ostensibly to discuss opportunities for business investment in Zenhab but, with typical Gallic charm, he flirted with Lexi throughout dinner so that she soon relaxed and chatted away to him, earning her several hard stares from Kadir. Until her possible pregnancy was confirmed he had no right to look at her with brooding possessiveness in his eyes that in the flickering candlelight were the colour of bitter chocolate, she thought indignantly.

But once again the devil inside her enjoyed goading him, and she could not deny a sense of satisfaction when she met his gaze across the table and watched streaks of colour flare along his cheekbones. He might not love her, but he desired her.

She was glad she had abandoned her pride and worn one of the dresses that had been delivered to her apartment. The full-length black velvet gown had a modest neckline, in respect for Zenhabian culture, but it was expertly designed to show off her slim waist, and the colour was a perfect foil for her pale blonde hair that she had left loose so that it fell smooth and sleek to halfway down her back.

Kadir walked beside her as the party moved from the dining room outside to the terrace, where coffee was to be served. 'I commend your efforts to encourage Zenhabian-French relations,' he said curtly, 'but I would prefer you not to flirt with Monsieur Aubrech.'

Lexi gave him an impatient look. 'I was simply being friendly, and I have to say it wouldn't have hurt you to have been a bit more amenable during dinner instead of scowling at Etienne. What's wrong with you tonight?'

Where did he start? He had never experienced jealousy before, but every time Lexi had laughed at one of the ambassador's jokes Kadir had felt corrosive acid fizzing in the pit of his stomach, and he had spent the entire dinner fighting the urge to ignore social niceties and carry her off to have hot, hard sex with her on the nearest available flat surface.

Aware that he was scowling as she had accused him of doing, he muttered something about her pushing his patience and strode onto the terrace, determined to keep the over-friendly French ambassador away from Lexi.

At the end of the evening, Lexi's temper was still simmering over Kadir's unfair accusation that she had been flirting with the French ambassador. She walked into her bedroom and smiled as she dismissed the maid who had turned down the sheets on her bed. Picking up her hairbrush from the dressing table, she heard a faint sound behind her and whirled around with a startled cry as the bathroom door opened and Kadir appeared.

'What are…?' She broke off when he put a finger to his lips, warning her to be quiet.

'Has the maid gone?' he murmured. 'Go and lock your bedroom door.'

She marched across the room and turned the key in the lock before she turned to face him, and immediately wished she hadn't when she realised he was naked apart from a towel knotted dangerously low on his hips. He was rubbing his damp hair with another towel. Lexi forced her eyes up from his naked, bronzed chest to his face and felt her stomach dip as she studied the sensual curve of his mouth and the sexy stubble that covered his jaw.

'Why didn't you want the maid to see you?'

He shrugged. 'It's better not to publicly advertise our relationship just yet, at least until we know if you are pregnant. It is against Zenhabian custom for men and women to share a bedroom before marriage.'

'So instead you are skulking around the palace and visiting me in secret.' She welcomed her temper to disguise her hurt that once again she was a shameful secret. 'I have no intention of sharing my bedroom with you,' Lexi told him furiously. 'You said we should spend time getting to know one another better, but you obviously thought I would provide ten nights of sex. I don't suppose I'll even see you in the daytime.'

'On the contrary; I've arranged for us to spend tomorrow at the coast. I thought you might like to learn to sail my yacht, and we could anchor in a secluded little bay I know of and swim or even snorkel. There are some beautiful fish and the water is crystal-clear.'

'Oh…well, I guess that does sound fun.' She bit her lip, unable to drag her eyes from the sensual gleam in his, and her heart suddenly began to hammer. 'But that doesn't explain why you are here.'

'Why do you think?' he said softly.

The dangerous glitter in his eyes as he walked towards her had her hurriedly backing up against the door.

'I don't want to sleep with you.' She was aware that now he was free from his marriage contract there was nothing to stop them being lovers, but she did not dare have sex with him again. Not now she had revealed intensely personal things about herself and her background that she had never told anyone else. She had made herself emotionally vulnerable to Kadir. Damn it, she had fallen in love with him. But he did not love her, and she did not trust herself to make love with him without giving away how she felt about him.

'That's okay because sleep is the last thing I had in mind, too.' Lexi's spine was jammed against the door and Kadir trapped her there by placing his hands on either side of her head so that his body was almost touching hers. 'Shall I tell you what *is* in my mind, *habibi*?'

'Don't…call me that.' She turned her head so that he wouldn't see the tears that stung her eyes. Her emotions were see-sawing all over the place. Perhaps it was a sign she was pregnant? Distracted by the mental picture of holding her baby in her arms, she had no time to defend her heart against the sweet seduction of Kadir's mouth as he claimed her lips in a kiss that stirred her soul.

'I want you to trust me. I don't want to hurt you, Lexi,' he said softly.

But he would, she thought with a flash of despair. If she was carrying his baby he would insist on marrying her, but she would be his unwanted wife, and if she wasn't pregnant, his desire for her would fade as quickly as it had with his other mistresses.

Her brain urged her to resist his sensual foreplay, but he had lowered her zip and tugged the top of her dress down, baring her to his hungry gaze. His hands were exquisitely gentle as he cupped her breasts in his palms and rubbed his thumb pads over her nipples until they hardened and tingled and the pleasure was too intense for her to bear.

'Let me love you,' he said in his deep, dark voice that wrapped around her like a velvet cloak. She knew he meant *make love to you*, and she knew she would be a fool to succumb to his sorcery. But for the next few days and nights he would be hers, whispered a voice inside her head. Her future was on hold until she found out if she was pregnant so why not enjoy what he was offering now?

Anticipation licked like scorching flames through her as he swept her up in his arms and carried her over to the bed. Entranced by the magic he was summoning with his mouth and hands, she had no recollection of him removing her dress and knickers, and she was unaware of the savage kick of desire Kadir felt in his gut as he stared at the erotic contrast of her ash-blonde hair and creamy pale limbs spread against the black silk sheets.

Spread for his pleasure, Kadir thought as he pushed her legs apart and knelt above her. He had never known any other woman to be as responsive and generous a lover as Lexi, and he had never felt such powerful thunder in his heart as he felt with her. He wanted everything, he acknowledged. And the desert king always took what he desired.

CHAPTER ELEVEN

'WELL—ANY NEWS?' Kadir demanded the moment Lexi emerged from the en suite bathroom.

'Nothing yet,' she murmured. She slid back into bed and Kadir curled his arm around her and drew her into the warmth of his body. His spicy cologne teased her senses and the whorls of black hairs on his chest tickled her cheek. These moments in the early morning when they lay together, half dozing, muscles aching pleasurably after long hours of lovemaking the previous night, were dangerously intoxicating, she thought ruefully as she snuggled up to him.

'You're late.'

'It's not an exact science,' she said drily. But actually her monthly cycle was as regular as clockwork. Lexi felt a heart-thumping mixture of dread and excitement. She had never been even one day late before. She might be imagining it, but she was sure her breasts looked a bit fuller when she'd glanced in the bathroom mirror.

She couldn't be pregnant, she assured herself. And of *course* she did not want to be. She could never forget that she had been an accidental pregnancy, unwanted by her mother. It shamed her that she had made one stupid mistake and it would be better for everyone if there were no consequences.

She bit her lip as Kadir placed his hand on her flat stomach. What if his baby was inside her? For years she had been absorbed in her career and had never really had any maternal feelings. But when she had left the RAF, and with her thirtieth birthday on the horizon, she'd begun to feel wistful whenever she held one of her friends' newborn infants. For the past eleven days she had found herself scrutinising every tiny symptom that might mean she was going to be a mother.

'You had better do a test. And if it confirms what we both suspect I'll start making arrangements for our wedding.' Kadir rolled onto his back, taking Lexi with him, and slid his hand into her hair, urging her mouth down onto his. The kiss was slow and sweet, drugging her senses and stealing her heart as she sensed tenderness in his passion.

The past week and a half had been wonderful, she thought dreamily. Kadir had spent every day with her, only popping into his office briefly to deal with any urgent matters that his chief adviser deemed to require his attention. He had given her sailing lessons on his yacht, and they had swum in a turquoise sea that was as warm as a bath. Lexi enjoyed their trips to different parts of Zenhab, including driving out to the desert in a four-by-four, but, for all Kadir's determination to spend a few carefree days, he was still the Sultan and they were always accompanied by bodyguards. Only within the palace walls were they able to be completely private, and several times he had instructed the staff not to disturb them before making love to her on a sun lounger by the pool.

'What would you like to do today?' His voice was indulgent as he stroked her hair back from her face. 'Perhaps you had better not do anything too energetic in case the pregnancy test is positive.'

Kadir was growing increasingly convinced that Lexi had conceived his baby. The very real possibility that he was going to be a father made him miss his own father, and he wished Sultan Khalif could have seen his grandchild. Thoughts of fatherhood had also brought back memories of his childhood, when he had felt torn between his parents, and he was more determined than ever to persuade Lexi that they should marry and stay together for the sake of their child.

He traced his hands over her slender figure and imagined her belly swollen with his baby. Skimming lower, he began to stroke her buttocks in rhythmic circles. 'We could spend the day in bed?'

'I thought you said I shouldn't do anything too energetic,' she said breathlessly, instantly turned on by the sensuous motion of Kadir's hand caressing her bottom.

He gave a wickedly sexy smile as he flipped her onto her back. 'You won't have to do anything. I'll do all the work and you can just lie back and enjoy me pleasuring you.'

Oh, God! She curled her fingers into the silk sheet as he kissed his way down her body from her breasts to the sweet spot between her thighs and flicked his tongue over her clitoris until she moaned and pressed her feminine heat against his mouth. He took her with his tongue and then drove his rock-hard arousal deep inside her and took her to the peak again so that her first orgasm had barely ended when the next one began.

His passion seemed wilder, more uncontrolled, and when he came the cords on his neck stood out and he groaned her name as if it had been torn from his soul. Overwhelmed by the feelings that overspilled her heart, Lexi wrapped her arms around him and hugged him tightly, uncaring at that moment that her tender smile betrayed her.

'You know I have to leave tomorrow, and I'll be away for a week?' he said later when they had showered together and were eating a very late breakfast on the balcony. 'Sheikh Omar has organised meetings with the mountain tribes; I am hoping I can persuade them to swear their allegiance to the Crown.'

Kadir looked across the table at Lexi and thought that she had never looked more beautiful, with her long blonde hair falling around her shoulders and her bright blue eyes sparkling like precious gems. She seemed softer somehow, and he had noticed a dreamy expression in her eyes that made him wonder if his patience was paying off and she was beginning to trust him.

The rest of the day and night passed too quickly, and Lexi sensed an urgency in Kadir's caresses when he made love to her in the cool grey light of dawn, before he slid out of bed and headed into his dressing room to prepare for his trip to the northern territories. He emerged dressed in his robes of state, his *keffiyeh* held in place on his head by a circle of gold.

'I've left a pregnancy test kit in the bathroom. Try to call me if you have any news, but communication in the mountains is limited—something I will be working with Omar to improve in the future.' He dropped a brief fierce kiss on her mouth. 'I wish I didn't have to go,' he groaned. 'Why don't you do the test now?'

Butterflies leapt in Lexi's stomach. What if the pregnancy test gave a positive result? *What if it didn't?* Either way, her relationship with Kadir would be affected. She suddenly wished the past eleven days could last for ever.

'It will be better to wait a few more days to make sure the test gives a correct result.'

'All right.' He kissed her again, softer this time, his lips clinging to hers as if he really did not want to leave her, almost making her believe that he cared for her a little.

She missed him the second he strode out of the bedroom and closed the door behind him. An inexplicable sadness filled her, a feeling that the days they had spent together had been a golden time that had slipped through her fingers like the desert sand and now had disappeared for ever.

The hours without Kadir dragged, and the huge bed was a lonely place without him lying next to her.

Next morning, a trip to the bathroom revealed that the niggling stomach ache she'd had during the night was not indigestion as she had thought—as she had hoped, she acknowledged dully.

There seemed no point doing the pregnancy test now she had evidence that she had not conceived Kadir's baby. She ordered herself to feel relieved but her heart disobeyed and an unexpected torrent of grief ripped through her. Faced with reality, she admitted the truth. She would have loved to be a mother, loved to have Kadir's child— loved him, she thought painfully.

She'd felt so close to him recently that she had even started to believe that, if they were going to be parents, perhaps they could have a successful marriage. A few times she had caught Kadir looking at her in a way that had made her heart leap. But now reality brought her crashing back down to earth. He did not love her, and when he learned that she was not expecting his baby he would send her away from Zenhab and search for a suitable bride to be the mother of his heir.

The strident ring of her phone made her jump. She stared at the handset, wondering if Kadir was calling her. If it was him, shouldn't she break the news that he wasn't going to be a father?

Athena greeted her cheerfully. 'How is everything in Zenhab? I was thinking about you, and I had a funny feeling that something's wrong.'

Lexi forced an airy tone. 'You and your funny feelings!' Actually, she recalled her sister had had a 'feeling' when she had phoned Lexi in Afghanistan the day that her co-pilot had been killed. 'Everything is fine; couldn't be better, in fact.'

Afterwards, she did not know what made her confide in Athena, but she felt more alone than she had felt in her life and her sister's gentle voice reached out to her. The whole story of being kidnapped with Kadir and stranded on his island came tumbling out, along with the fact that she'd had unprotected sex with him, and his insistence that if she was pregnant he would marry her.

'But you're not pregnant,' Athena repeated what Lexi had just told her. 'What a shame. You would be a wonderful mother, and a great wife for the Sultan.'

'Of course it's not a shame,' Lexi said sharply. 'You're such a daydreamer, Athena. The fact that I'm not pregnant is good news. It means I can carry on with my career. I couldn't be happier...' she choked, and suddenly she couldn't hold back her tears. It was as if a dam had burst and her grief for the baby she had imagined holding in her arms poured out, along with a lifetime of pain and hurt at feeling rejected and unloved. Her secret hope that she would spend the future with Kadir and their child was over, and now she had nothing.

'Why don't you tell Kadir you love him?' Athena asked softly. 'What have you got to lose?'

'Apart from my pride, dignity and self-respect, you mean?' Lexi's chest hurt from crying so hard. She had never lost control of her emotions so violently before and she felt scared that loving Kadir had changed her, weakened her, and she would never be tough-talking, no-nonsense Lexi Howard again.

'I wish I was with you in Zenhab to give you a hug,' her sister said. 'I wish I could help. You know I love you, Lexi.'

Lexi swallowed. She *did* know that Athena cared for her, but she had always struggled to show her own emotions. 'You're a great sister. I...I love you too,' she said huskily.

She sensed Athena's surprise. 'You've never said it before. I think you should tell Kadir how you feel about him and give him a chance to explain why he seems so determined to marry you.'

'It was only because he wanted his child. But there isn't going to be one. He's the Sultan of Zenhab and needs to marry a woman of royal blood, not someone whose genes come from a very murky pool.'

'What will you do?'

'Come home, look for a job.' She still needed to pay off Cathy's debts, Lexi thought wearily. She remembered that Kadir had taken her passport and she would have to stay on at the palace until he returned from his trip to the mountains. It was only fair to tell him her news in person rather than leave a message on his phone.

Memories of the past days they had spent exclusively

in each other's company pushed into her mind. Had she imagined that they had had fun together, shared laughter, *friendship*? Could she do what her sister had suggested and tell Kadir she had fallen in love with him?

Her stomach swooped at the idea of risking his rejection. Kadir had only wanted her when he had thought she could be carrying his baby, and the traditions of his kingdom meant he could not allow his child to be born illegitimate, she reminded herself. She was certain he would be relieved not to be forced into a marriage he did not want.

The helicopter buzzed above the palace before dropping down to land in the courtyard. Kadir had hired a new pilot, an Australian guy called Mitch, who Lexi assumed would continue to work for the Sultan after she had gone.

She had carried her suitcase down to the entrance hall and as she watched Kadir walk up the palace steps she pulled the peak of her cap lower over her eyes. The clothes he had bought her were hanging in the wardrobe in the apartment she had first occupied when she had arrived in Zenhab. She had applied for a job in the UK, flying workers out to oil rigs in the North Sea, and she doubted there would be many opportunities to wear designer evening gowns in the cold winter in Aberdeen.

Wearing her pilot's uniform made her feel more like herself. A grey skirt and jacket teamed with a crisp white blouse, and her hair swept up beneath her cap, gave the impression of cool professionalism and hid the truth that her heart was breaking. Through a window, she studied the Sultan in his traditional robes and tried to feel distanced from him, but memories of Kadir, naked, beautiful, lowering his body onto hers, threatened to shatter her composure.

She took a few steps forward as he swept through the great palace doors, halting when his dark eyes immediately shot to her suitcase.

His smile faded. 'Do you have news for me?'

'I'm sure you will be as relieved as I am to hear that I'm not pregnant.' Her jaw ached as she flashed him a brittle smile. 'Our worries were needless, but now we can both get on with our lives.'

Kadir's eyes narrowed and he fought the urge to whip Lexi's damn cap off her head so that he could see her face. She sounded so cool and in control, reminding him of the ice queen who had rescued him from his capsized yacht and ripped into him for risking the lives of his crew.

He absorbed her words. There was to be no child. No son to love, as his father had loved him. No daughter to adore, with silvery-blonde hair and eyes the colour of mountain skies. No requirement under Zenhabian tradition to marry Lexi. She had said she was relieved not to be pregnant. Maybe she was right, he brooded.

'It's probably for the best.' He glanced around the entrance hall, suddenly aware of the presence of several palace staff. Ignoring his chief adviser who was hurrying towards him, he caught hold of Lexi's elbow and steered her into his study, shutting the door and locking it to ensure their privacy.

'Was it necessary to manhandle me?' she complained, rubbing her arm. 'Why have you brought me in here?'

He countered her question with one of his own. 'Why are you leaving?'

'I've told you why. I'm not carrying your baby. You

have hired a new pilot so there's no reason for me to stay in Zenhab.' It took all Lexi's will power to keep her voice steady. Kadir had said it was for the best that she wasn't pregnant. Of course he was pleased, she told herself. Of course he did not want a whore's daughter to be the mother of his heir. Of course he did not love her because no one, apart from her sister, ever had.

'You can't think of any reason to stay?' Kadir's jaw hardened when she shook her head. 'I thought you had enjoyed the days we spent together, and I know I gave you pleasure every night, just as you captivated me with your sensuality. We're good together, Lexi.'

Pride forced her chin up to meet his gaze. 'I don't deny we had some fun. But it didn't mean anything, did it? Now we know there is no baby it's time to move on.'

She was leaving him. Kadir's heart gave a painful jolt. In his mind he was seven years old, running down the palace steps after his mother, tears running down his face. *'Why do you have to go back to England, Mama? Why don't you want to stay here with me and Baba?'*

'I'll still see you, darling, when you come to stay at Montgomery Manor. But I don't belong in Zenhab. I can't live with the restrictions of being the wife of the Sultan.' Judith had bent down and kissed his cheek. Kadir still remembered the scent of the perfume she had worn that day. *'The truth is that I want to be free to live my own life.'*

Was that why Lexi had decided to leave him? Did she care more about her freedom and her career than him? 'I suppose you want to continue flying helicopters,' he said tersely.

'Yes, I love being a pilot.' Lexi made a show of checking her watch. 'Look, I really need to go if I'm going to catch my flight. You still have my passport,' she reminded him.

He was silent for a few moments before he gave a shrug. 'I'll tell Yusuf to bring it to you. The helicopter will take you to the airport but you'll have to wait while it's being refuelled.'

He moved suddenly and Lexi gave a startled cry when he pulled her cap off, freeing her hair so that it tumbled around her shoulders. Kadir slid his hand beneath her chin and tilted her face up, subjecting her to an unsparing appraisal that took in the dark circles under her eyes and the tears sparkling on her lashes. A fierce emotion stirred inside him but he ruthlessly suppressed it.

'Goodbye, angel-face,' he murmured before he strode out of the room, leaving Lexi with the exotic scent of his cologne and a heart that felt as though it had splintered into a thousand shards.

Her plane was due to leave Zenhâb's main airport in less than an hour, Lexi fretted. She had been delayed at the palace because apparently there had been a problem with the fuel pump for the helicopter, and once that had been sorted out she'd still had to wait for Yusuf, who had eventually appeared with her passport and a rambling explanation about how it had not been where he had thought it was and he had spent ages looking for it.

In half an hour it would be dark. She was used to the way the sun set quickly over the desert. Right now, the sun was a huge ball of fire that was turning the sea orange.

The sea!

Frowning, she turned to the helicopter pilot and spoke into her headset. 'Mitch, you're going the wrong way. The airport is in the opposite direction.'

'This is the direction I was told to fly. I'm just follow-ing the Sultan's orders.'

Below them, Lexi saw the black silhouettes of palm trees rising up from a desert island, and her heart gave a jolt as the chopper swooped lower over an empty beach. *Jinan.* 'Why have you brought me here?' she asked Mitch fiercely.

The pilot landed the chopper on the sand. 'This is where the Sultan told me to bring you.' Reaching under his seat, he handed her a jar of honey. 'He said to give you this.'

Thankfully, the fading light hid her scarlet face from the pilot. Memories of Kadir's unconventional use of honey when they had been trapped on the island flooded Lexi's mind. Was he playing some sort of cruel mind game with her? She made a muffled sound in her throat and curled her hand around the jar. 'It'll make a useful missile to throw at him,' she muttered.

'The Sultan said you'd probably say that.' Mitch grinned. 'It seems like Sultan Kadir knows you pretty well.'

What the devil was Kadir playing at? Lexi's heart was pounding as she marched up the beach. She scrambled over the sand dunes and saw the oasis and next to it the tent, illuminated by glowing lamps that cast shadows onto the canvas.

Pushing through the flaps, she stopped dead and stared at Kadir, sprawled on a pile of silk cushions. He was wearing a black robe tied loosely at the waist and re-vealing his bare chest. In the lamplight his body gleamed like polished bronze, and as he propped himself up on one elbow Lexi's eyes were drawn to his hard abdominal muscles and the line of dark hairs that arrowed lower. She remembered that the very first time she'd met him she had imagined the Sultan lying on silk cushions, beckoning to her to join him.

'Good, you brought the honey,' he drawled.

She gripped the heavy glass jar. 'Have you any idea what I'd like to do with this?'

'Show me,' he invited softly.

'Don't tempt me.'

'Why not?' He sat up and stared at her intently. 'You tempt me constantly. I think about you all the time.'

'Don't say things that aren't true.' She stared at the patterned rug on the floor, willing herself not to cry.

'I never took you for a coward, Lexi.'

'I'm not a coward, damn you.'

'Then look at me.'

Something in his voice, a tremor of emotion that felt like an arrow through her heart, made her slowly raise her head. His eyes were darker than she had ever seen them—dark with pain, she realised with a jolt. His teasing smile had disappeared and he looked serious and tense, almost—*nervous*. But that was ridiculous. What did the powerful Sultan of Zenhab, the desert king, have to fear?

'You really would have gone back to England, wouldn't you?' he said harshly. 'After everything we shared, the most beautiful time of my life, I thought, hoped you were starting to trust me.'

He couldn't sound hurt, Lexi told herself. She must be imagining the raw expression in his eyes. 'You said it was for the best that I'm not pregnant.' Her voice shook. 'You said goodbye at the palace and let me go.' Only now did she acknowledge she had been testing him, hoping at the eleventh hour for a miracle.

'I was hurting,' he shocked her by saying, 'and I was angry with myself for failing to do enough to convince you that we have something special. I went into the gardens and sat on my father's favourite bench. Remembering how much he loved me, the confidence I gained from my happy childhood, made me understand why trust is such a difficult concept for you. I understand why you are scared of emotions because you were rejected by your birth mother and your adoptive parents failed to make you feel loved.'

He stood up and walked towards her, stealing Lexi's breath with his masculine beauty, his powerful body all satiny skin and strong muscles.

'I do think it is better that you didn't fall pregnant the last time we were on Jinan.' He tipped her face towards him when she tried to look away to hide her pain and confusion. 'I can't imagine you would be happy to have an accidental pregnancy after what you told me about your biological mother,' he said with an intuition that touched a chord inside Lexi. 'When you conceive my baby I hope it will be an event we have planned, and our child will be longed for and loved from the moment of conception.'

Her heart was thumping so hard she could barely breathe. 'I don't understand,' she whispered. 'Why did you bring me here?'

He brushed her hair back from her face with gentle fingers. 'Jinan is where it began, although that's not quite true because it started when you hauled me out of a stormy sea and promptly wiped the floor with me.' He smiled. 'No one had ever spoken to me like that before. I was furious but at the same time all I could think of was how badly I wanted to kiss you. But I knew I couldn't. I had to honour my arranged marriage, and my desire for you was forbidden.

'I thought I would have no trouble resisting you,' he said roughly. 'Ever since I was a young man, I had resigned myself to the prospect that I must marry for duty, not love. And in some strange way it was a relief to know I would not suffer the heartbreak my father felt when my mother left him. My emotions would never be at risk, or so I believed. But when the kidnapper threatened you with a gun the truth hit me like a bullet through my heart.'

Kadir closed his eyes for a few seconds, haunted by the memory of the fear that had churned in his stomach when he'd thought she might be killed.

'I realised that if I lost you, my life would not be worth living. I also knew that I could not keep the promise I had made my father and marry Haleema. I could not marry without love, even though my decision meant I might lose my kingdom and my role as Sultan of Zenhab.'

Lexi was stunned by his revelation. 'I know how much it would have hurt you to break your promise to your father. You loved him so much.' She did not know what to think, and she was afraid to trust the expression in Kadir's eyes. He had told her he'd realised he could not marry without love, but that didn't mean that he loved her.

For some reason she thought of her sister. Athena had always been patient and loving, never asking Lexi for anything in return. She felt ashamed that it had taken her so long to tell her sister she loved her.

She remembered the magical days she had spent with Kadir and knew she hadn't imagined their friendship that had grown stronger every day. He had been kind and caring, patient and *loving*, but she had listened to her inse-curities and been afraid to listen to her heart. She *had* been a coward, Lexi acknowledged.

But a lifetime of feeling rejected was not easy to over-come, and her voice caught in her throat when she spoke. 'The days and nights we spent together while we waited to find out if I was pregnant were the most beautiful of my life too. I didn't want them to end but I knew they couldn't last and I was sure you couldn't feel anything for me.'

'Why couldn't I?' he demanded.

'You are the Sultan of Zenhab,' she said as if it ex-plained everything, 'and my mother was a whore.'

'I don't give a damn if your mother is a Martian.' Kadir seized hold of her shoulders and stared down at her startled face. 'Will you marry me, Lexi Howard?'

She so desperately wanted to trust the fierce emotion blazing in his eyes. Her bravery had never been put to such a defining test, not even when she had risked her life flying rescue missions in war-torn Afghanistan.

'There's no reason for you to marry me,' she reminded him.

He moved his hands up to frame her face and captured the tears clinging to her eyelashes on his fingers. 'I love you, Lexi. That's the only reason why I want you to be my wife and the mother of my children that, fate will-ing, we will be blessed with in the future. I want you as my lover and my best friend, and I hope you will be my Queen and help me rule my kingdom.'

He could not catch all her tears as they slipped down her cheeks, and he tasted them on her lips when he cov-ered her mouth with his and kissed her with such beguil-ing tenderness that Lexi's heart felt as though it would burst.

'I love you,' she whispered, and suddenly the words weren't hard to say because they came from her heart. She said them over and over in a husky litany that moved Kadir unbearably because he knew the demons she had faced and beaten to give him her trust.

He lifted her into his arms and carried her over to the pile of silk cushions, where he removed her skirt and blouse with hands that visibly shook. 'I will tell you every day for the rest of our lives how much I love you,' he promised. 'You are my heart's desire, the love of my life, *habibi*.'

From somewhere he produced a small box, which he opened to reveal an exquisite oval blue diamond ring.

'I knew the colour would be a perfect match for your eyes. Blue diamonds are rare and precious, just as you are to me, my angel.' He looked intently into Lexi's eyes. 'You haven't given me an answer. Will you make me the happiest man in the world and marry me? Will you love me for eternity, as I will love you?'

Lexi wiped away her tears and met his gaze, her blue eyes sparkling as bright as the diamond he slid on her finger. 'Yes, my Sultan, my love. I never knew I could feel this happy,' she whispered, shivering with anticipation as he removed her underwear and knelt over her.

'Tomorrow we'll start planning our wedding,' he promised. 'Luca De Rossi guessed how I felt about you when we stayed at his villa in Italy, and he will be my best man. Who will you choose for your chief bridesmaid?'

'My sister,' Lexi said instantly. 'Athena suggested I should tell you I love you.'

'Why don't you show me?' Kadir murmured.

'With pleasure, my Sultan.' She took him by surprise, pushing him back against the cushions and straddling him at the same time as she unscrewed the lid of the jar of honey.

'*Habibi*...where are you going to pour that honey?' Kadir groaned when she showed him.

* * * * *

LET'S TALK
Romance

For exclusive extracts, competitions
and special offers, find us online:

 facebook.com/millsandboon

@MillsandBoon

@MillsandBoonUK

Get in touch on 01413 063232

For all the latest titles coming soon, visit
millsandboon.co.uk/nextmonth